D1195445

THE SEVENTH SECRET

BY IRVING WALLACE

FICTION

The Seventh Secret
The Miracle
The Almighty
The Second Lady
The Pigeon Project
The R Document
The Fan Club
The Word
The Seven Minutes
The Plot
The Man
The Three Sirens
The Prize
The Chapman Report
The Sins of Philip Fleming

NONFICTION

Significa (Coauthor)
The Intimate Sex Lives of Famous People (Coauthor)
The Book of Predictions (Coauthor)
The Book of Lists 1 and 2 and 3 (Coauthor)
The Two (Coauthor)
The People's Almanac 1 and 2 and 3 (Coauthor)
The Nympho and Other Maniacs
The Writing of One Novel
The Sunday Gentleman
The Twenty-seventh Wife
The Fabulous Showman
The Square Pegs
The Fabulous Originals

IRVING WALLACE

A NOVEL

THE SEVENTH SECRET

E. P. DUTTON · NEW YORK

Copyright © 1986 by Irving Wallace
All rights reserved. Printed in the U.S.A.

No part of this publication may be reproduced or transmitted in any form or by any means, electronic or mechanical, including photocopy, recording or any information storage and retrieval system now known or to be invented, without permission in writing from the publisher, except by a reviewer who wishes to quote brief passages in connection with a review written for inclusion in a magazine, newspaper or broadcast.

Published in the United States by
E. P. Dutton, a division of New American Library,
2 Park Avenue, New York, N.Y. 10016

Library of Congress Cataloging-in-Publication Data
Wallace, Irving.
The seventh secret.
1. Hitler, Adolf, 1889–1945—Fiction. I. Title.
PS3573.A426S45 1986 813'.54 85-16022

ISBN: 0-525-24382-8

Published simultaneously in Canada
by Fitzhenry & Whiteside Limited, Toronto

COBE

Designed by Nancy Etheredge

10 9 8 7 6 5 4 3 2 1

First Edition

For
Sylvia Wallace
my wife
and
Ed Victor
my friend

Though a good deal is too strange to be believed, nothing is too strange to have happened.

—THOMAS HARDY

When you have eliminated the impossible, whatever remains, however improbable, must be the truth.

—SIR ARTHUR CONAN DOYLE

THE SEVENTH SECRET

1

When he walked away from the small private room and the press conference, moved through the crowded Café Kranzler restaurant, and emerged onto the sun-drenched Kurfürstendamm, he felt highly elated.

Standing on the broad sidewalk of the lively Ku'damm this early afternoon in late July, Dr. Harrison Ashcroft—and now, since last year, Sir Harrison Ashcroft—considered delaying further work to enjoy a brief respite. On this, his tenth visit to West Berlin in five years, he knew that he had reached the climactic moments of his monumental work. He was on the verge of solving the great mystery and bringing his project to a successful—perhaps world-shaking—conclusion.

He had managed a leave of absence from his post teaching modern history at Christ Church College at Oxford University to undertake this awesome biography. In the forty years since Adolf Hitler's end, the Führer's remarkable story had begged to be written by him. At last, as his fourteenth book, and perhaps his most memorable one, Dr. Ashcroft had determined to write the definitive biography, *Herr Hitler.* But he had realized at the outset that at his age—then sixty-seven—he could not tackle all the research and writing alone. So he had invited his lively thirty-four-year-old daughter Emily, a brilliant lecturer in history at Oxford, to collaborate with him. From the start, he had known that he could not have made a better choice.

Emily Ashcroft had been uniquely qualified to assist her father on their mammoth effort. After his wife's death in a climbing accident more than twenty years ago, Dr. Ashcroft alone had raised his daughter. It now seemed inevitable that the little girl, brought up in an atmosphere of scholarly curiosity, amid thousands of books, and constant travel, should have become a historian like himself. She too had specialized in the modern history of France and Germany, and spoke the languages of both those countries fluently. Also, she had been fascinated by the now distantly romantic Second World War and the dominant role the strange and enigmatic Adolf Hitler had played in it. Twice, during the earlier research stages, Emily had accompanied her father to Berlin. This time, on what might be his last and most crucial visit to West Germany's first city, Dr. Ashcroft had again left Emily behind in Oxford to organize notes for their final push.

Their final push meant solving the last mystery of Adolf Hitler's death with Eva Braun, his wife of one day, in the depths of the underground Führerbunker beside the Old Reich Chancellery on April 30, 1945.

Two months ago, after considerable firsthand research—in West Berlin talking to surviving eyewitnesses, and in East Berlin examining the medical reports and photographs made available by the Soviet Union through his friend and colleague, Professor Otto Blaubach—Dr. Ashcroft, along with Emily, had been ready to accept the standard and authorized version put forth by biographers and historians of Hitler's demise.

Returning to Oxford from his previous visit to West Berlin, where his definitive biography of Hitler had been widely publicized, and about to undertake the final section of the long work, Dr. Ashcroft had received a surprising and disturbing letter from West Berlin, an unexpected letter that gave him pause.

The letter had been written by one Dr. Max Thiel, who identified himself as Hitler's last dentist. Dr. Thiel had read about Ashcroft's important biography. As one of the handful of survivors of those who had known Hitler personally, Dr. Thiel wanted the book to be more accurate than any that had preceded it.

And then, at the close of his letter, Dr. Thiel dropped his bombshell.

All histories to date on Hitler and Eva Braun may have been wrong. Hitler and Eva may not have committed suicide in the Führerbunker in 1945. Both may have fooled the world. Both may have survived. In fact, Dr. Thiel had evidence to prove it.

After the first shock, Ashcroft began to regain his objectivity. As his daughter Emily reminded him, the survival theories and clues about Hitler and Eva had never ceased since their deaths. Crackpots abounded and persisted, and Dr. Max Thiel sounded like another one of them. Surely, Emily pointed out, Dr. Thiel had brought his so-called evidence to the attention of previous biographers. Obviously they had seen fit to ignore him. Emily had urged her father to ignore him as well, throw away the silly letter and resume work with her to bring the biography to a final conclusion.

Yet the letter nagged at Ashcroft. He had always been a perfectionist. He had toiled too hard to disregard any challenge to his scholarship. Rereading Dr. Thiel's simple letter several times, Ashcroft became convinced of its sincerity. The thing to do was to learn whether this Dr. Thiel was really the person he purported to be.

Had he actually been Hitler's last dentist? A week's investigation gave Ashcroft his disconcerting answer. Dr. Thiel had indeed been Hitler's last dentist, a Berlin specialist, really an oral surgeon, and he had treated the Führer a number of times in the last six months of the German dictator's life. Furthermore, Dr. Thiel himself had written the disturbing letter and was still alive, at the age of eighty, in West Berlin.

Below his signature, on the fateful letter, Dr. Thiel had boldly printed out his telephone number.

Dr. Harrison Ashcroft had no choice but to call that number.

Dr. Thiel himself had answered the phone. His voice was deep, firm, and assured. What he had to say was lucid and certain. No senility there. Yes, he had the evidence he had written about. No, he did not wish to discuss details on the phone. However, he would be happy to receive Dr. Ashcroft at his home in Berlin and let Dr. Ashcroft see for himself and make up his own mind.

The invitation was irresistible, and Dr. Ashcroft's curiosity had mounted.

Three days ago, Ashcroft had arrived in West Berlin alone, checked into the Bristol Hotel Kempinski, whose entrance was just off the Kurfürstendamm, and promptly gone to see Dr. Max Thiel. The meeting had been friendly, intriguing, and persuasive, and his scholar's heart had leaped at the chance to get at the truth.

To do so, he had realized, he would have to dig in what had once been the garden beside the Führerbunker, the garden where history books recorded that Hitler and Eva Braun's remains had been buried in 1945. One problem. The Führerbunker area was on the East Berlin side of the wall that divided the city, actually inside a no-man's-land area surrounded by a cement wall and wire fencing and East Berlin soldiers. To get permission to enter the Security Zone and dig, Ashcroft would need a go-ahead from the Communist East Berlin government and therefore from the government of the Soviet Union, which had long considered the matter of Hitler's death closed. Fortunately, Ashcroft had a well-placed friend in East Berlin.

Years ago, shortly after the Second World War, at an international conclave of modern historians held at the Savoy in London, Ashcroft had served on a panel with Professor Otto Blaubach of East Germany. Ashcroft and Blaubach had found that they had much in common, including a shared interest in the rise and fall of the Third Reich and Adolf Hitler. Ashcroft had entertained Blaubach at his own home in Oxford, and thereafter had met with him several times in East Berlin. Mostly, their friendship had ripened through correspondence. As time passed, Professor Blaubach's stature had grown in the German Democratic Republic. Now he was one of East Germany's eleven deputy prime ministers on the Council of Ministers.

If one wanted to unearth something in a highly guarded and forbidden zone in East Berlin, Professor Blaubach was obviously an influential person to contact. So Ashcroft had got in touch with his old friend, who had greeted him warmly. Blaubach regarded the request as unusual but possible to fulfill, and promised to try to obtain approval from his colleagues on the council for the dig.

The night before last, Blaubach had responded. Permission granted. Ashcroft could proceed with his dig.

Thrilled, Ashcroft had telephoned his daughter Emily in Oxford to report on his progress. Equally excited by her father's news, Emily had wanted details of Dr. Thiel's evidence that Hitler had not died in the Führerbunker. Ashcroft had held back, preferring not to go into it on the phone. He had preferred to wait and spell it all out for her when he returned from Berlin with what might be a stunning new ending to their book.

"I'm going to start the dig the day after tomorrow. First I want to have the press conference—"

"The what?" Emily had interrupted.

"Press conference. Just a few of the top television, radio, and print media reporters in West Berlin."

"But why, for heaven's sake? That's not your sort of thing, Dad, going public prematurely."

"I'll tell you why," Ashcroft had replied patiently. "Now that Dr. Thiel's theory is to be tested, after so many years, it occurred to me that there might be other people like him around. Others who knew Hitler, knew of his last days, who might be encouraged to come forward with new information. Emily, I intend our book to be the last word, the absolute truth. That's why."

"Oh, Dad, I wish you wouldn't do it," she had objected.

"What do you mean?"

"Don't make this public. I'm not sure how to put it to you, except this way. You have a worldwide reputation for pure scholarship. Conservatism in what you write, accuracy in what you write, has been your trademark. Our Hitler book will be the high point of your career. Don't mar it with far-out speculations. I know you've seen this Dr. Thiel and seen or heard some sort of evidence. But it could be fake, could be wrong. It could make you—us—look foolish. Dr. Thiel's conjectures go against every solid piece of existing fact. Hitler did shoot himself and give Eva Braun cyanide in the Führerbunker in 1945. Their bodies were observed being carried out to be cremated. They were cremated. Those are the facts."

Ashcroft had hesitated. In their five years of collaboration, he had rarely been at odds with his daughter. But then he had said, "Maybe. Maybe, Emily. Let's be sure. I have to go ahead."

He had gone ahead, swiftly, with determination to lay the last ghost.

For the dig, he had telephoned the Oberstadt Construction Company, one highly recommended to him. Then he had made arrangements for the press conference today—limited to twelve reporters, four from television and radio, the rest from the leading newspapers and magazines.

From his *guten Tag* to his *auf Wiedersehen,* the press conference had gone well. For one hour, he had spoken without interruption from the press and at the end had accepted questions. Everyone had known about his Hitler book. But he was here, he had announced, to make one final investigation of the deaths of Adolf Hitler and Eva Braun. Some "new evidence" required that he dig at the old burial site, and sift through it once more. Despite the numerous questions, he had been guarded about the "new evidence" and how he had obtained his lead. He had not mentioned Dr. Max Thiel's name.

Now it was over, a success, and if there were any more old Nazi-era hands, eyewitnesses to dredge up, this publicity might bring them into the open.

He stood before the restaurant, enjoying the activity on the busy Kurfürstendamm. It was one of his favorite streets in the whole world. It made Piccadilly and Piccadilly Circus look tacky. It really had the grandeur of the Champs Élysées, only it was livelier. He scanned the wide sidewalks, the numerous glass display cases on the sidewalks, the leafy green trees standing like sentinels on either side of the street.

Briefly, he considered taking a leisurely stroll up toward Breitscheidplatz with its Kaiser Wilhelm Memorial Church, the low octagonal modern house of worship made of glass and steel, incongruously standing next to the unrepaired war-torn clock tower of the original church. Maybe make a visit to the Europa Center, with its three floors of shops, theaters, cafés, and its nineteen stories of offices surmounted by the giant circular emblem advertising Mercedes-Benz. He might linger in the new Romanisches Café, not half so good as the old one he had known in his youth, but still nostalgic and the *Kaffee* was not at all bad.

Or more sensibly he might turn away and take the few steps

back to his room at the Kempinski. And have another look at the architectural plan of Hitler's Führerbunker before digging for the truth tomorrow.

The truth and Hitler won. No time for relaxation.

Harrison Ashcroft inhaled the warm summer air and started down the Kurfürstendamm toward the Kempinski Corner Café, a restaurant fronted by an outdoor terrace of tables and chairs. From there he could turn into Fasanenstrasse, the side street that led to the Bristol Kempinski's marble-faced hotel entrance.

Walking briskly, in good health at seventy-two and full of purpose, Harrison Ashcroft headed for the corner. His mind was on Dr. Thiel's unusual evidence, on tomorrow's dig, on Hitler's last day.

He had reached the corner, crossed over to the Kempinski Café, and turned right toward the hotel entrance.

That moment, turning, ready to resume his walk, he heard his name called out loud, or thought he did, and instinctively looked over his shoulder to see who had called him.

But there was nothing to see but the large metal grille of the heavy truck swinging into the side street to block his view. Suddenly, the truck screeched, jumping the curb, rising high, smashing the flower planter on the corner, sending screaming diners into wild retreat.

Then the truck, momentarily out of control, swerved sharply away from the café and roared along the sidewalk toward him.

The mammoth grille and tires loomed up over him, and the suddenness and fright of it paralyzed him.

The grille of the truck struck him full on, like a thud of Samson's fist, drove him off his feet and into the air, catapulting him into the side street itself.

He landed hard on his face, half-blinded, half-conscious, broken and bleeding. He tried to raise his head from the pavement, to protest the indignity and the obscenity, when he saw the truck's grille and thick tires once more looming directly over him as it careened back into the street.

Feebly, he tried to lift a hand to deflect it, but the tires were upon him, the last thing he would ever see in this life.

The tires rolled over him, squashing and crunching.

The blackness was instantaneous. The blackness was forever.

After the burial, sitting desolate in the rear seat of the funeral home's black Daimler, Emily's first instinct and desire as she began the return ride from the cemetery to Oxford was to tell her father about the funeral. She wanted to tell her father about the ceremony, so well attended by prominent people from the faculty, countless friends, all his relatives, several civil servants down from London, and even their favorite clerk from Blackwell's bookstore. She wanted to share this with her father, tell him about it as she always told him everything. But then with a jolt she realized that she couldn't because he wasn't there. He was in the ground. He was gone. It was unbelievable. For the first time in her life, he wasn't there.

She realized then who *was* there. In the rear seat of the Daimler next to her was Pamela Taylor, their mousy redheaded secretary and typist, dabbing yet another Kleenex to her puffy eyes and swollen nose. On Emily's other side, sitting stiffly, staring ahead at the chauffeur and the countryside, was her Uncle Brian Ashcroft, at sixty-nine her father's younger brother, head of an accounting firm in Birmingham.

They were all tearless now, cried out, emptied of emotion, and saving what was left of themselves for the postfuneral reception at her father's house—her house—several blocks from the university, where her father had lived a lifetime.

The dreadful news had come in early evening by telephone

from the police in West Berlin. Miss Emily Ashcroft? There has been a serious accident. Your father, Sir Harrison Ashcroft, knocked down by a truck and killed. A hit-and-run driver. Your father died immediately. Sorry, so very sorry.

There had been more, but Emily had been unable to comprehend it. In complete shock, somehow disbelieving, she had managed to phone their old family physician, irrationally thinking he might save her father. But the physician had understood the reality, had come over at once, had given her a sedative, and had then summoned Pamela, who in turn had summoned some of Dr. Ashcroft's closest faculty friends.

It was a terrible time, the worst of her entire life.

And she could not turn to Jeremy. That had been another death—not comparable to this, her father's death—but in a way a prelude to misery. That one had been almost six months back, after Jeremy Robinson had been part of her life for a year. It had begun when Emily was summoned to London to write and host a new BBC documentary television film on the rise and fall of the Third Reich. The filming of her scenes had progressed smoothly, professionally, and when her job was done she had eagerly accepted Jeremy's invitation to a farewell dinner for two.

Jeremy had attracted her from the start. He was a most handsome and charming middle-aged man. True, a married man. With two young children. Jeremy had wanted an affair, but Emily had hesitated. She had been that route before and knew it was a dead end. When Jeremy assured her that he was in the process of divorcing his wife, and wanted to marry her as soon as it was possible, Emily had dropped her resistance and they had become lovers, although she had chosen not to move in with him.

Their affair at his pied-à-terre near the studio had been exciting and promising. From the beginning Emily had told her father about Jeremy. Sir Harrison had approved immediately. His own wish was for his daughter's happiness. Then, six months ago,

Jeremy had phoned to cancel their customary weekend together in the country. He had been assigned to produce a dramatization of *Moll Flanders* for the BBC, starring the rising young actress, Phoebe Ellsmore. A plum of an assignment, but preparatory work would tie him up on the weekend. After that, he had canceled three more weekends and finally ceased phoning altogether. Then had come the shocking announcement in the press: Jeremy Robinson, having obtained his divorce, was about to marry Phoebe Ellsmore.

It had been the crudest sort of personal humiliation. For several days, Emily had not been able to face her father, but when she had he had consoled her and said she was better off knowing now what she might have got into.

Her hurt had remained, yet was gradually diminishing. Realistically she knew her pain had not been caused by the loss of love, but by wounded pride. Soon, looking back, she had been able to see that what she had really wanted was not Jeremy himself but conformity in marriage, a home, children of her own, and, mostly, a change of scenery. The idea of breaking away from lecturing, from confining research and writing, had appealed to her more than Jeremy had. She had been fond of him, of course. But when the air cleared, she had been able to see that an alliance with Jeremy would have been a disaster. After hurt had coagulated into distaste, the memory of him had begun to evaporate into the happier euphoria of good riddance.

Thank God, she'd had a fallback position. With renewed energy, she'd thrown herself into the completion of the Hitler biography. Increasingly, the book and her father had once more become the most important things in her life.

And now this, the most devastating loss of all.

Following the telephone call with news of her father's death, the living had done what must be done for the dead. Emily had wanted to fly to Berlin to be with her father, to accompany him home, but wiser heads had prevailed. Someone had helped her telephone the main police station in Berlin, and when her identity had been made clear, she had been transferred to Chief of Police Wolfgang Schmidt, who had spoken to her in English. The chief's manner had been warm, caring. He had reiterated the facts of the accident, and then tried to go into more detail. The truck out of control, jumping the curb, hitting Dr. Ashcroft on the sidewalk, flinging him into the street, and then by chance running over him. Dr. Ashcroft had been killed on the spot. The drunken driver with the truck—certainly he must have been drunk—had fled. Descriptions of the vehicle were varied because of the confusion, but efforts were being made to locate it. Chief Schmidt had little hope of success. Was deeply grieved by the accident.

After that, her uncle had forced Emily to rest. Pamela had followed through by telephone to make the final arrangements, and the body had been flown back to Oxford from West Berlin.

Now it was over. Her father peacefully asleep in the ground. His great work unfinished. And she, alone.

Dry-eyed, weak, emptied of all energy, she sat rigidly in the rear of the soundless limousine, trying to look ahead. But she could not see beyond the wake that would take place during the next two hours.

Wanting to blow her nose, she sought her handkerchief inside the purse that lay at her feet. She brought the purse to her lap, unclasped it, and was surprised to find two envelopes lying on top of her billfold and cosmetics bag. Locating the handkerchief beneath, using it, returning it, she became curious about the two envelopes. Then she remembered. Leaving the house for the funeral this morning, she had noticed the day's mail left on her desk by Pamela. Without interest she had riffled through it, and determined that most of the small square envelopes carried condolence notes. Two longer envelopes were also there, each bearing German stamps, one postmarked from East Berlin, the other from

West Berlin. Odd. She wondered who could be writing her from Germany. But there had been no time to open the envelopes and read the contents, with Uncle Brian and Pamela already at the door to escort her to the funeral. She had stuffed both envelopes into her purse, and left hastily.

Now the two envelopes remained sealed in her purse, waiting to be opened. Tentatively, she took them out, put aside her purse, and tore open the first envelope, the one postmarked East Berlin.

The letter inside, handwritten on a single page, bore the embossed letterhead of Professor Otto Blaubach. She recalled Blaubach. Her father's good friend, the historian, an expert on the Third Reich and Hitler, and now a deputy prime minister of East Germany. Her father had spoken to Blaubach the day before his death, had obtained permission through him to excavate the area around Hitler's old Führerbunker. She recalled having met Blaubach once, a stiff, somewhat Thomas-Mannish German, but the soul of courtesy and kindness.

His letter was in English.

My dear Emily Ashcroft,

When I heard on the television, and saw confirmed in the daily press, the news of your father's untimely and accidental death, I was filled with disbelief. I had spoken to him only the evening before. He never seemed more vital, and doubly so when I was able to inform him that permission had been arranged for him to excavate at the Führerbunker.

My heart is heavy. For several days I could not bring myself to put pen to paper. But I want to do so now. I want to convey to you my deepest personal regrets and to offer you my condolences. We both have at least the close memory of a great and modest man.

I still cannot believe and accept the means by

which the end came to your father. It was so unlikely an accident. While hit-and-run incidents happen all the time, I might say that it was an accident that was in this particular case almost statistically impossible. Yet we know in life that the impossible does happen.

What adds to my own loss is that your father had told me that you were both on the threshold of completing the book of which he thought he would be most proud. I am not unmindful of the major role you have been playing, as your father's daughter and a respected historian in your own right, in producing the Hitler biography. I fondly recall the occasion when you accompanied your father to lunch with me at the Opern Café in East Berlin three years ago, and the stimulating discussion that ensued about the biography. I know Herr Hitler needs only the ending to be written to complete the project. It is my strong hope that, in due time, you will bring the Hitler work to a conclusion. The world deserves to see it. Your father deserves to have it in print as a monument to his genius and scholarship.

Should you need my assistance in any way, please feel free to call upon me.

Faithfully,
Otto Blaubach

Emily blinked at the letter, touched by it, moved, and brought back somewhat into the world of the living.

Blaubach wanted her to finish the book, believed that this should be done and that she could do it. The request, the hope, slightly rattled her. Since her father's sudden death, she had not thought of their biography at all, at least not consciously. Without him, she could not imagine the work's having existence.

Yet Blaubach was right. The work was not dead. She had been one of the arteries that had pumped life into it. And she was still here, very much alive.

Slowly she refolded Blaubach's letter. She could not give it further thought, and certainly not serious consideration, not now in her bereavement. She would read it again another day. Stuffing the letter back into her purse, she became aware of the second envelope. She ripped it open, and extracted a typewritten letter. It was typed on the stationery of the *Berliner Morgenpost,* the respected West Berlin daily newspaper. Emily's eyes sought the signature. It was signed with the name Peter Nitz, someone unknown to her.

Dear Miss Ashcroft,

Although you do not know me, I should like to take the liberty to convey to you my sorrow at Dr. Ashcroft's death.

I never had the good fortune to meet Dr. Ashcroft. However, I did see him and was able to hear his last public utterances not many minutes before his death. As a feature writer and reporter on a leading West Berlin daily, I was assigned to cover Dr. Ashcroft's final press conference.

After briefing the gathered media about Herr Hitler, *the important biography which the two of you had been writing, Dr. Ashcroft announced that he had held up the ending of the book, pending further investigation into Adolf Hitler's final hours in his bunker. Dr. Ashcroft remarked that although all standard biographies and histories of Adolf Hitler stated unequivocally that Hitler had committed suicide along with his bride Eva Braun in the Führerbunker in 1945, a piece of evidence had come to Dr. Ashcroft's attention that indicated some possibility that Hitler had not died at that time, and may have escaped from the bunker altogether. Dr. Ashcroft added that, to verify this possibility, he had obtained permission to excavate the bunker area in East Germany in search of a certain piece of evidence. It was Dr. Ashcroft's hope that anyone in Berlin who heard or read of his undertaking, and knew at firsthand any more facts about Hitler's last hours, would contact him at the Bristol Kempinski hotel during the week to follow.*

Right after his announcement to us, Dr. Ashcroft said he was open to questions from the floor. Naturally, we had numerous questions to ask. Mostly they concerned the identity of the person who had given him the new evidence, and what form this evidence had taken. Dr. Ashcroft, understandably, would not answer us precisely, nor would he give us the names of the officials in East Berlin who had granted him permission to excavate in the Führerbunker area.

When Dr. Ashcroft concluded the press conference, he departed from the restaurant saying that he had to get back to the Kempinski to resume his preparations. While the other reporters prepared to leave, I realized that there was something I had forgotten to ask Dr. Ashcroft, and I went out into the street to catch up with him. I don't recollect what the question was at this date—assuredly nothing important—and it is not for that reason that I write to you but rather to report to you on what transpired after I rushed out of the restaurant to find Dr. Ashcroft.

I hastened down the Kurfürstendamm, going very swiftly, although the boulevard was extremely crowded with shoppers. I thought I had a glimpse of Dr.

Ashcroft crossing the next side street, and then when I reached this street I saw him plainly on the opposite corner, ready to turn up Fasanenstrasse toward the Kempinski entrance. I called out to him, shouted to get his attention, and he may have heard me. I am not sure. Events after that came too quickly.

Just as I had finished trying to get Dr. Ashcroft's attention, I saw a rather big delivery truck with a heavy metal grille and bumpers—the body painted blue I think, with balloon radial tires—come rocking unsteadily into the side street, suddenly careening left and jumping the curb as if it might plow into the Kempinski's outdoor café. Its front grille caught your father on the side and lifted him into the air, throwing him into the street. Dr. Ashcroft was obviously badly injured, but was making an effort to rise, when the truck suddenly swerved again, veering away from the café, rumbling back into the street and directly to where your father lay. The truck rolled over his stretched-out body, rolled fully over him, then accelerated at great speed and sped up the side street. By the time that any of us who had witnessed this realized what had happened, the truck had vanished from sight.

I was possibly the first, among several witnesses, to rush to your father's body. It was clear to all of us that he had been killed when hit the second time. He was dead before the police and ambulance arrived.

This is a painful story for me to recount to you, but I feel that I must do so for a special reason.

Dr. Ashcroft's death has been seen as an accident, and even noted as such in my newspaper. But from what I observed with my own eyes, it appeared to be something other than an accident. To my eyes, it was as if Dr. Ashcroft had been run down and killed with careful deliberation.

When the truck rolled over the curb, it was going too slowly to be out of control. When it struck your father the first time, it seemed to be aimed at him and picking up speed. When it swung back off the sidewalk and into the street, the driver must have been able to see your father lying there and could have avoided hitting him again. Instead the driver went straight for Dr. Ashcroft, crushing him, and then drove on and away even faster, in full control of his vehicle.

Of course, I cannot swear that this was a deliberate act by the hit-and-run driver. I cannot prove it. Perhaps, after all, it was one of those crazy accidents that do happen infrequently. But I must tell you what I saw and felt and what is on my mind today.

I did not voice my suspicions to the police. There was no purpose. I have not a shred of evidence that this might have been murder. As a newspaperman, I would have been believed by the police to be inventing some kind of story for my paper. So I kept my silence.

Still, I find it necessary to report this to you, on the chance my suspicion may make some sense to you. I wonder. Did Dr. Ashcroft have any enemies?

Again, I am sorry to have aggravated your wound. If you are ever in Berlin, do contact me at the paper. I should enjoy having a talk with you.

Sincerely,
Peter Nitz

P.S. *I wrote the obituary for your father in the* Morgenpost. *I enclose a cutting of it.*

Shaken, Emily automatically felt in the envelope, found the three-inch press cutting on her father, and scanned the German text. Then she lowered it and the letter to her lap, and glanced out the car window at the first sight of the buildings of Oxford.

The man's suspicions had unnerved her completely.

Murder.

It was inconceivable. Her father was the mildest and sweetest of men. An introverted scholar. He had not a single enemy on earth that she had ever known.

Yet a professional newspaperman had witnessed his accidental death and thought it possibly deliberate.

Could that be? Was this a madman writing her? Still, the letter was direct and sincere, and seemed to have come from a decent man.

The dullness was leaving her mind. She was thinking clearly now.

What possible motive would anyone have for killing her father? He had no possessions. He had no feuds—but there her mind gave her pause. He did have one possession, a unique one, something he owned that others may have wanted to take from him. Harrison Ashcroft had possessed evidence, and a burning belief, that Adolf Hitler had not died on April 30, 1945.

Maybe someone out there did not want this proved.

The Daimler was nearing their house in Oxford when Emily made her resolution. Until now she had been her father's junior collaborator, depending upon him, deferring to him, leaving decisions up to him. Now she was alone, and all present or future decisions were hers to make. She would replace her father. She would carry on their work. She would bring it to a successful conclusion.

She was going to West Berlin. She would see Dr. Max Thiel, and Professor Otto Blaubach, as well as the reporter Peter Nitz.

She would seek out the truth. If Nitz was right, she might be a sitting duck. Someone might try to stop her as they had stopped her father.

Even try to murder her too. Yet, by inviting it, she might prevent it, and solve two mysteries.

Harrison Ashcroft's death.

Adolf Hitler's survival.

2

In the week after the funeral, Sir Harrison Ashcroft's death, and his daughter's resolve to finish the epic biography of Adolf Hitler, made news all over the world. Not big news. But a tidbit worthy of interest almost everywhere.

Behind his desk inside his office in the Hermitage, Leningrad's massive art museum, Nicholas Kirvov, the recently appointed curator, nibbled a warm *pirozhok,* scanned the pages of *Pravda,* and came upon the news:

> In West Berlin, another of the decadent city's hooligans precipitated a fatal accident. An unknown drunken truck

driver lost control of the vehicle and ran down a pedestrian. Sir H. Ashcroft of Oxford University, the prominent British expert on Adolf Hitler, was killed almost instantly as he walked on the Kurfürstendamm. The hooligan could not be found. Ashcroft was in the process of completing a lengthy biography of Hitler in collaboration with his daughter Miss E. Ashcroft, also a historian. Reuters reports that Miss Ashcroft will undertake to finish the book.

Nicholas Kirvov chewed the last of his meat-filled pie and suppressed a yawn. He had no particular interest in the news brief he had just read. He had not the faintest idea who this Ashcroft was, except that he had been researching and writing about Hitler. The coincidence of the mention of Hitler in *Pravda* on this particular day, of all days, was what had piqued Kirvov's attention sufficiently to read the news brief through.

Kirvov had always been fascinated by the Fascist monster, Hitler, from his earliest schooldays following the Second World War until the present. Because Kirvov was an art expert, it had always tantalized him that a creature as mad and gross as the Nazi leader had once been an artist, had painted many watercolors and oils, and had also possessed a love for architecture and music. This killer who had soaked Russia's soil with the blood of millions, an artist! An incredible contradiction. To make sense of Hitler's schizophrenia, Kirvov began to search for examples of his art.

As other men collect stamps, coins, rare books, Kirvov had taken up the hobby of collecting Hitler's drawings and paintings. Kirvov had located eight of Hitler's art pieces moldering away in storage in the Red Army's archives, traced three more to East Berlin, and four to Vienna, obtained photographs of them for study, and finally, when he had been appointed the head of the Hermitage six months ago, he had acquired every one of the forgotten canvases on loan. To what end he had them stacked in the cupboards of his private office, the one adjacent to his public office, he did not know. Possibly for some future article or pamphlet. Maybe even some kind of showing. His purpose was unclear yet. He knew only that he had coveted the fifteen, and, with a collector's greed, coveted even more.

For that reason, today was an exciting day. For today, by sheer chance, Nicholas Kirvov was going to have an opportunity to set eyes upon a sixteenth Hitler painting, one he had never seen before.

The letter had come to Kirvov from Copenhagen a week ago. This letter, written in perfect English, was signed by one Giorgio Ricci, who claimed to be an Italian-American with an apartment in San Francisco. Mr. Ricci had introduced himself as a steward on a luxury cruise ship, the *Royal Viking Sky*, a Norwegian vessel based in San Francisco that took a summer cruise that encompassed stops at Copenhagen, Leningrad, Helsinki, Stockholm, Oslo, and London. Mr. Ricci had stated that he possessed a modest art collection, and, while visiting West Berlin recently, he had obtained from a reputable gallery an unsigned oil painting attributed to Adolf Hitler. Mr. Ricci had been uncertain whether the painting was authentic. Shortly afterward, he had come upon a magazine article that spoke of Nazi art, and the feature had included a reference to the early paintings by Hitler. It had also mentioned the names of several persons who were known to be experts on Hitler's artistic efforts, and one of these experts was Mr. Nicholas Kirvov, formerly an assistant curator at the Pushkin Fine Arts Museum in Moscow, recently appointed curator of the Hermitage in Leningrad.

Since Mr. Ricci was on the cruise ship that would stop over in Leningrad for two days, he had seen this as a wonderful opportunity to bring his questionable Hitler oil ashore and show it to Nicholas Kirvov at the Hermitage. Mr. Ricci had given the date of the ship's arrival, and hoped that Mr. Kirvov would be in the city and have time to see him.

Disappointed that Ricci had not described the Hitler oil, but excited that another of those unknown to him still existed, Kirvov had cabled the steward care of the Royal Viking office in Copenhagen and said that he would be pleased to meet with Mr. Ricci. Then, Kirvov had alerted the Leningrad customs office to pass Ricci through with his painting.

The appointment was for this very day, and, coming to work in the morning, Kirvov had been able to visualize the arrival of the sleek white *Royal Viking Sky,* which he had once seen glide into the harbor of Leningrad. If nothing had gone wrong, then Giorgio Ricci should be in his office, with the Hitler canvas, in—he glanced at the wall clock—in fifteen minutes.

Discarding the paper wrapping from his *pirozhok,* brushing the crumbs off his desk, Kirvov tried to think if he had any pressing museum business before receiving his caller. He was extremely attentive to his job because his appointment as curator had been a surprise and a tremendous honor. He had been doing nicely in a secondary museum spot in Moscow, had been able to live comfortably with his wife and young son, when the magic had happened. Curator of the Hermitage at the age of forty. The minister of culture had overnight made Kirvov one of the Soviet Union's intellectual names.

Kirvov had loved the Hermitage from the day of his arrival. He had loved the five buildings that comprised the museum—the original Winter Palace, the Small Hermitage, the Big Hermitage, the Hermitage Theater, and the New Hermitage—the first four of these lining the left bank of the Neva River. He had wished there were more funds to spruce up the main building, the Winter Palace that housed his offices—money to provide some fresh paint, some plastering, better lighting—but whatever money was available had been earmarked for new acquisitions. Not that there wasn't the best of everything on hand already. Ever since 1764, when Catherine the Great had authorized the first major purchase —225 canvases from the German merchant Johann Gotzkowsky, including a Franz Hals—the acquisitions had never ceased arriving. In 1772 Italian art had begun to flow in, Titian, Raphael, Tintoretto, followed by the French masters Watteau and Chardin. Then in 1865 a Leonardo da Vinci. After 1931, the Postimpressionists, filling the Hermitage in its upper halls with thirty-seven Matisses, thirty-six Picassos, fifteen Gauguins, eleven Cézannes, four Van Goghs, and countless other treasures.

The first organizer of this flood of paint had been known as a "custodian" in 1797. By 1863, a curator was added, and soon after two expert assistants. Gradually there were catalogues to popularize the collection, and eventually sophisticated equipment like an X-ray machine to detect forgeries or authenticate masterpieces. In fact it was X rays that had proved that the Hermitage's *Adoration of the Magi* by Rembrandt, thought to be the copy of the original in Sweden, was the original itself.

Now Nicholas Kirvov was the new curator and in control. He had used his first six months to arrange better placement for the masterpieces, and to undertake preparation of a new catalogue that would highlight the best of over eight thousand works of art in the Hermitage. A catalogue would accompany his first exhibit, and he wished he could find some way, some unusual approach, to popularize the exhibit further. There were more than three million people who came to wander through the Hermitage each year, but Kirvov wanted more, many more.

His eye caught the wall clock, and he realized that his musings had taken up most of his spare time and that his caller should be here any minute. That instant there was a rap on the door, and his secretary opened it and said, "Mr. Giorgio Ricci is here, sir."

"Show him in," said Kirvov, springing to his feet.

His visitor came tentatively into the office, carrying an unwieldy package under one arm. He was a slight, unprepossessing young man, maybe in his thirties, with big Italian round eyes and an undershot jaw. He wore a pale blue sweater and faded blue jeans. Some gold showed in his teeth and he smiled. "Mr. Kirvov," he said. "I am Giorgio Ricci, of the *Royal Viking Sky.*"

Kirvov came forward quickly, his stocky five feet ten seeming to make him much bigger than his visitor, and warmly shook his hand. "I am delighted you could come to see me," said Kirvov, leading his guest to a chair beside the desk. "Do sit down. Be comfortable. Can I get you something to drink—Pepsi, vodka, coffee, anything?"

"No, thanks. I don't want to take up too much of your time. And I don't have much myself."

"Very well," said Kirvov, settling in his seat at the desk. "Then we shall get right down to business. Let me see your so-called Hitler painting."

Ricci lifted the package to his lap. "They assured me at the gallery in West Berlin that it had been done by Hitler. Because it was not signed, they made it a bargain price. I could have been taken. I don't know. I hope you can tell me."

"Maybe," said Kirvov. His curiosity was getting the better of him. "Perhaps you'd let me see for myself."

Ricci had undone the brown paper wrapping and pulled free the picture. "I took it out of the frame," he said. "It's reinforced with these thin wooden slats."

It was apparently light, because he needed only one hand to grasp it and pass it over the desk to Kirvov.

Kirvov had it before him under the glare of his overhead fluorescents. He judged it to be fifteen inches across and twelve inches high. It was a dark oil canvas, a rather somber painting of what appeared to be the front of a weather-beaten official building of some sort or other. It had been rendered by the artist from across a wide street, so that one could see the pillars before the entrance to the six-story stone building. The inset entrance and the decorated wall to its left were dim and lost in shadows. There was no signature.

"A government building, I'd guess," said Kirvov. "It could have been done by Hitler. He was partial toward painting buildings in Linz, Vienna, Munich. But I don't recognize this one from what I know of those cities or of Hitler's other art." He looked up. "Any idea where and what this is?"

"No idea. The gallery wasn't sure, either. But they guaranteed me, from the provenance, it was by Hitler."

"What was the provenance?"

"They said they couldn't reveal that. It was part of their deal in acquiring it. Anyway, they were positive it was by Hitler." He hesitated. "I guess someone did not want to admit owning an original Hitler from the old days. Is it real?"

"Umm, possibly real," murmured Kirvov, studying the painting closely. "Mostly, he did not paint canvases this large. He was supposed to have made three hundred pictures. Only a handful have survived. He did some drawing in his youth, in Linz where he went to *Realschule*, what Americans would call high school. Then in 1907 he went to Vienna to enter the Academy of Fine Arts. There was a two-part test. In the first half, Hitler was told to depict, among other subjects, Cain killing Abel. In the second half, he had to paint or draw the Good Samaritan and Noah's Flood. His test verdict read, 'Test drawing unsatisfactory.' Hitler returned a year later for another attempt to enter the Academy of Fine Arts. His new samples were regarded as poor, and he was not allowed to take the test again."

"So he became a politician."

"Not yet. He was bitter about the Academy of Fine Arts' rejection and blamed his failure on the Jewish bureaucrats he claimed dominated the academy. Still, he didn't go into politics right away. He went on with his painting to support himself meagerly. He did watercolors of postcard size, copies from real postcards, and he had a friend who peddled them in return for half the income. His friend sold them to art dealers who needed innocuous pictures to fill empty frames for display, and to furniture dealers who varnished the pictures on wooden chairs and love seats."

"Did he do any larger pictures?" asked Ricci.

"Yes, eventually. Some twice the size of postcards. A few oils the size of this one you've brought me. Even some posters. He signed all of them 'A. Hitler.' He usually earned thirty-six to fifty-four rubles—ten to fifteen dollars in your money—for each one sold."

"And you know that he favored buildings over portraits?"

"Definitely. He had no feel for people. Someone once said that when he drew human figures they looked like stuffed sacks. But he had an eye for architecture. When he moved to Munich he registered himself as an 'architectural painter.' " Kirvov paused to examine the canvas on his desk again. "Considering Hitler's taste, this could have been done by him." Kirvov stood up, the canvas in hand. "One second."

He went to the door of his secretary's office, and opened it. "Sonya," he called out. "Have Comrade Zorin take a look at this." He handed the painting to his secretary. "Tell him this unsigned oil supposedly was painted by Adolf Hitler. Tell him I'd like his opinion."

Returning to his desk, Kirvov said, "Comrade Zorin is one of our experts who shares my interest in Hitler's youthful artistic follies. Most definitely, buildings. In 1911, he drew the Minorite Church in Vienna. Earlier, he drew or painted the Vienna Burg Theatre, St. Stephen's Cathedral, Schönbrunn Palace, the Feldherrnhalle, a watercolor he called *Street in Vienna.* After he moved to Munich he painted the *Der Alter Hof*—as late as 1914, I believe—*The Old Court,* which showed a grand house with a courtyard before it. Later, when Hitler came to power, he rounded up and destroyed many of his early efforts. Still, Hitler was not always displeased with his work. He once gave Albert Speer, his architect, a canvas of a Gothic church he had painted in 1909. He gave a few other canvases he liked to Göring and to Mussolini."

Ricci leaned forward. "Then you think what I've shown you is an authentic Hitler?"

"It certainly has some of the characteristics of Hitler's brush. First off, an official building as the subject. Then the style. Hitler praised his own artistry for its 'photographic exactitude.' That is what your painting offers—a photographic quality, very real, but unimaginative and ordinary. It has what Hitler so admired in an artist he himself collected, one Adolf Ziegler, a Munich second-rater—it has a kind of stilted grandeur. Yes, what you have shown me could be a genuine Hitler."

"I hope so," said Ricci nervously. He kept glancing at the door, obviously conscious that the verdict would soon be in. Then, as if to fill the passage of time, he asked, "Do you know anything of Hitler's own tastes, not as a painter but as a collector?"

Kirvov wrinkled his fleshy nose. "Hitler was devoid of any true artistic taste. When he became chancellor of Germany, he tried to wipe out all modern and avant-garde painters and paintings. He called them degenerates. He despised Picasso and Kandinsky. He liked classical art, anything derived from Greek-Nordic art. He called modern eroticism in paintings 'pig art,' although he admired healthy and innocent classical nudes. A dull and mediocre man, our artistic Hitler. Still he is elusive and mysterious as a person and it amuses me to collect his art."

For ten minutes, Kirvov discussed German art under Hitler, and then there was a knock on the door. Kirvov jumped up, opened the door, took the oil back from his secretary along with a note.

Sitting, Kirvov laid down the painting and read the note. He nodded to himself and took in his guest once more. "As I expected," said Kirvov. "My expert out there believes this might be a Hitler. Of course, he can't be positive with such a brief examination. He would need more time to study it. At any rate, I think you can rest assured that my associate and I believe it is probably authentic."

Kirvov stood up to return the canvas to his visitor.

The cruise steward also rose. "I appreciate this. I want to thank you, and pay you whatever you—"

Kirvov smiled. "No charge. On the house. In fact, I appreciate the opportunity to have been able to see an unknown Hitler painting." He started to hand over the canvas to Ricci. "You will be pleased to add this to your Hitler collection."

Ricci did not take the painting. "I have no Hitler collection. To be honest, I have no interest in Hitler's art at all."

"But then why did you . . ." He stared at his guest. "You want to sell it? Is that it?"

"No, not really," said Ricci. "I bought it in order to trade it for something I'd rather have, something else I've been collecting for a few years now."

Kirvov raised a quizzical eyebrow. "What are you collecting?"

"Icons. Old Russian icons. I love them. Actually I've been in Russia before on cruises, and made some contacts, and I have three so far. I'd like more. But I find them rather expensive." He hesitated. "I—I'd let you have this Hitler painting in return for a genuine icon, if you have any to spare."

Kirvov thought about the offer. But not for very long. He coveted the Hitler painting on his desk. It might be a rarity and would certainly enhance his collection. He had little doubt about its authenticity. As to icons, he had dozens to spare in storage, several that could please Ricci and yet were too mediocre to display in the Hermitage. As curator, he had complete autonomy when it came to trading minor or duplicate items.

Kirvov grinned. "Agreed. I have your Hitler. You will have my Jesus Christ."

31

Five minutes later, Ricci had his icon—small, glittering, a silver-plated frame holding a miniature painted head of Jesus, his robe a golden metal finish—and the ship's steward was thrilled.

Showing the steward to the door, Kirvov stopped him for a moment. "Just one more thing. The name of the gallery in West Berlin where you purchased the painting?"

Ricci's face was briefly blank. "I don't remember now. Somewhere near downtown Berlin. Let me—" He tried to think, with no apparent success, and shrugged his shoulders. "Never mind. It's on the receipt I mailed home. I'll remember to send it on to you the minute I get back there."

"Please do remember."

After Giorgio Ricci had left for his ship, Kirvov was once more alone in his office. He started slowly back to his desk, picked up the Hitler oil, studied it, and beamed.

For an idea had struck him as he had been showing the ship's steward out, the perfect unusual means to publicize and popularize his first major exhibit at the Hermitage. It was clearly defined in his mind now. He would segregate one hall on the top floor and label it THE ART OF THE FASCIST MURDERER ADOLF HITLER. From the four walls he would hang blowups of photographs of the Nazi devastation of war-torn Leningrad, Stalingrad, and the fall of Berlin, as well as the naked corpses of innocent people that greeted the Allied liberators in Auschwitz, Dachau, and the Warsaw ghetto. Then, as ironic counterpoints to this savagery, Kirvov would hang the fifteen pieces of Hitler's early art he already had in his possession. Once more the Russian public would be reminded that the German dictator had been an animal and a violent schizophrenic.

Yes, this latest oil, along with the other Hitler art he had on loan, would be the springboard to his first great success as curator of the Hermitage.

But then, studying the ponderous oil of the dark building,

Kirvov had one concern. Millions would see it and accept it as Hitler's, yet there might be one among them who would question its authenticity. Kirvov knew that he must be certain that this oil was by Hitler, and if possible learn what kind of building it portrayed and its location as well.

How to authenticate it immediately? At once, Kirvov remembered a recent article he had read by Professor Otto Blaubach, the East German government minister who was an eminent historian of the Third Reich and the Führer's life. If anyone could tell him about this painting, it would be Blaubach. Kirvov riffled through his desk calendar and saw the notations he had made on it. Next week he was to go with his wife and son to Sochi on the Black Sea for their annual vacation. In a way, that made it easier. He would send them ahead while he spent a week in East Berlin to see Blaubach. After that he would join the family at their vacation resort.

Perfect.

Nicholas Kirvov had never been happier. Then he would be ready for his spectacular exhibit here in the Hermitage.

A great time ahead. But first he must go to East Berlin.

In West Los Angeles, Rex Foster parked his compact red Chevrolet sports coupe in his reserved slot at the rear of his small office building on San Vicente Boulevard. After going through the usual contortions to get his lanky six-foot frame out of the cramped driver's seat, he ambled up the narrow walk that ran along the side of his building to the front door.

On the door was a gray plaque with gold and black lettering that read: FOSTER ASSOCIATES—ARCHITECTS.

The door, as usual, was unlocked, meaning his staff of three was already there and probably at work. They were always in at nine-thirty in the morning, and Foster tried to arrive promptly at ten o'clock. The reception room was momentarily empty, which told Foster that his receptionist-bookkeeper-secretary, Irene Myers, was most likely in his office preparing his coffee in the small kitchen.

Down the unadorned corridor there were three offices, the first occupied by his draftsman, Frank Nishimura, the second by his production man, Don Graham. The last and largest, his own office, was an airy room that had a wooden drafting table at one end and his oversized waxed pine desk, with a cluster of chairs ringing it, at the other.

Sure enough, in his office, Foster found Irene Myers at his desk, setting down his mug of hot black coffee and spreading out the morning's *Los Angeles Times* for him.

"Good morning, Mr. Foster," Irene greeted him cheerfully. She was a short, shapely brunette, invariably ebullient.

"Hi, Irene," he said, rarely talkative in the morning until he'd had his first cup of coffee.

She hesitated. "I'd hoped to clean up your desk a little before that lady comes."

"Lady?" he said blankly.

"The *Los Angeles* magazine reporter, Joan Sawyer. At ten-fifteen. She's doing a story on Southern California's leading architects. She'll be here in ten or fifteen minutes."

"I forgot," Foster groaned. "Okay, skip the desk. It looks clean enough. Just let me have my coffee before she gets here."

He waited for Irene to pass him and leave the office, and then he went behind his desk and settled down with his steaming coffee and the morning paper.

Sipping contentedly, he reflected for a moment on the blonde he'd had dinner with at Matteo's in Westwood last night. A young actress, maybe twenty-four, Cindy Something-or-other whom he had met at a large cocktail party. Impressed by her breasts and buttocks, he had invited her to dinner. A mistake. Too dumb and uninformed, but better in bed later, where she had proved to be innovative, acrobatic, and a squealer. Actually, enjoyable enough for an encore at midnight. However, he had been relieved when he had finally driven her back to her apartment at two in the morning. He had promised himself no repeat. He had more important things on his mind.

Drinking the coffee, mellowing, he lit his first pipeful of the morning and began to leaf through the *Los Angeles Times*, as was his custom before beginning the day. Terrible world, he thought, scanning the headlines and leads, absolutely awful everywhere, and then on page five a smaller headline caught his eye and he began to read the story from Associated Press:

> Sir Harrison Ashcroft, the world-renowned author and a member of the Faculty of Modern History at Oxford University, England, was laid to rest in the family plot outside Oxford yesterday morning. Ashcroft had met with a fatal accident in West Berlin while doing the last researches on his definitive biography of Adolf Hitler. A hit-and-run driver . . .

The ICM button on Foster's telephone winked yellow, and Irene's voice came on. "Mr. Foster, are you free? Miss Sawyer of the *Los Angeles* magazine is here."

He picked up the phone. "Irene, did you know that Dr. Ashcroft was killed in Berlin last week? I just read about it—"

"Killed? No, I didn't know . . ."

"Unbelievable," Foster said. He paused. "That changes everything. I had an appointment with him a week from Friday in Oxford."

"Yes. I made your plane reservation."

"Now what'll I do?" he asked helplessly. "Well, we'll talk it over after I finish the interview. All right, give me a minute to get my head together, then you can send in Miss Sawyer."

He sat trying to work out his problem. He had been toiling for three years, in his spare time, preparing and laying out an oversized picture book, a coffee-table book entitled *Architecture of the 1000-Year Third Reich.* It was an idea that fascinated him, reproducing photographs of all the buildings constructed in Europe during Adolf Hitler's reign (many of them had been reduced to rubble but old photographs existed), as well as of models or designs of buildings that Hitler had planned and hoped to have built after he had won the war. Foster had flown to Germany and, through a onetime U.S. Army buddy stationed in Berlin, had obtained most of what he needed from the archives of Hitler's architect Albert Speer at the Bundesarchiv in Koblenz, and from Speer's wife in Heidelberg, and then he had returned to Los Angeles to lay out his book. He had a good contract with a prestigious publisher in New York, and a firm deadline for delivery. Foster had felt high about the book, not only because it intrigued him but because it would enhance his image in the international architectural community.

At his home in Beverly Hills, reviewing his notes, he had come across the information that Speer had assigned one trusted associate to construct seven special buildings for Hitler. Checking his layout again, Foster found he did not have photographs, let alone the designs, of those seven buildings. Without those graphics, his work would be incomplete, and the publisher was counting on selling the book as the first and only complete book on architecture in Nazi Germany under Hitler. Worst of all, the deadline for delivery of his art book loomed just three months away. His only chance to acquire the seven missing pieces was to learn who Speer's associate had been, but no matter where Foster had searched, he had been unable to learn the name of the associate architect.

Then, by chance, he had discovered that the one historian who knew everything about Hitler was Sir Harrison Ashcroft of Oxford. Foster had promptly written Ashcroft asking if he might see him in Oxford and seek help in a matter concerning Hitler. He hoped personally to go through Ashcroft's architectural files so that the historian would not be imposed upon. Ashcroft had replied with equal promptness that he would be delighted to receive Foster, giving him the day and hour for their meeting. Relieved, Foster had made reservations to fly to England next week. Once he had the name of the associate architect, he planned to fly to Germany and meet with the man if he was alive, or with his family, positive that the man or his heirs would have the seven missing designs.

It was open-and-shut, until this morning. Now it was shut. Ashcroft was dead. Once more, Foster was left in limbo.

That moment, the door to his office opened, and Irene Myers announced, "Mr. Foster. Joan Sawyer of *Los Angeles* magazine is here."

Foster mumbled his thanks, and tried to get his mind on the interviewer. She was a tall, flat-breasted young woman, with squinting brown eyes behind thick-lensed spectacles, a longish nose, thin lips; she wore a tan pants suit and carried a tape recorder.

"How do you do," she said, making straight for his desk and setting down the recorder. "I hope you don't mind if I tape you. It's the best way to get everything right. I'm a stickler for accuracy."

"So am I," said Foster pleasantly, waving her to a leather-covered chair across from him. "I'll let you tape if you let me smoke."

"Your funeral," she said unsmilingly. She fiddled with the tape recorder, started it, tested it, then she eased into the chair and fished a typed set of questions out of her purse. "I told your secretary, when I made the appointment, that I was doing a long piece on the leading architects in Southern California. I did a little research on you, and you seem to qualify."

"How kind of you," Foster said playfully.

"I know you're a busy man," said Joan Sawyer. "So why don't we get going?"

"Suits me fine."

"By the way, we shot pictures of some of your recent structures. The Cornell Theater on Sunset Boulevard. The International Condominium in Westwood. The House of Neptune seafood place in Malibu. All quite original and impressive."

"Thank you, Miss Sawyer."

"When did it begin, your becoming an architect? You weren't one when you went into the army."

"I became interested after I got out. That's when I went back to college."

"Why don't we start just before that, when you were in the army. You were in Vietnam two years?"

Foster did not hide his frown. "Yes."

"How old were you when you enlisted?"

"Twenty," said Foster. "I wasn't particularly patriotic. I didn't even know what Vietnam was about. I just knew I was without purpose or direction, a dumb kid trying to figure out what to do with myself. Vietnam sounded exotic, a filler in time. So I went in."

"Then what?"

"Then what—" Foster repeated, his frown deepening. "I was a helicopter pilot attached to an engineer group in the Twenty-fourth Corps under Lieutenant General James W. Sutherland. There was some fighting. Along with the artillery and an MP battalion, we saw action in Quang Tri province near the Laotian border. Took a fair number of casualties. I was grounded by antiaircraft, so I spent more time with my M16 rifle than flying. Eventually I caught some shrapnel in one leg, and after surgery I was discharged. That was late 1971."

"How's your leg now?"

"No problem. I jog five miles three times a week. I'm in good shape for thirty-six, well, just about thirty-seven. After the war, I rattled about a little and finally went back to school under the GI bill. The University of California in Berkeley. That's where I became interested in architecture."

"How come architecture?"

"Well, my father had been an engineer . . ." He hesitated, and reflected upon it. "No, it was something else. A feeling I had. In the war, I had devoted a couple of years to tearing things down. Now I had the urge to build things up."

He saw the lady reporter eyeing him closely. She said, "You mean that?"

"Of course, I mean that. It's what civilization is all about. After each orgy of destruction, it behooves humans to rebuild, to build, to move ahead in an orderly way. Somehow, the war turned me toward architecture. In Berkeley they had a School of Architecture—we called it the Ark. I enjoyed Berkeley and worked hard. After four years, I had my bachelor of architecture."

"Then you opened an office?"

"Not so fast. Every graduate must serve a two-year apprenticeship. I did mine with a large firm in Laguna Beach. After that an architectural candidate takes the State Board Examination. One week of exams involving design, drawing, a half-day oral. Rigorous, and in California a bit offbeat. Here we have some extras like the seismic problem, making buildings as earthquake-proof as possible. Anyway, I passed. I became an architect."

"What were some of your earliest projects?"

"Easy ones in the beginning. A community center and a neighborhood bank, for example. The designs involve a lot of engineering, but you also learn about practical necessities, important unglamorous ones, like lighting and putting in bathrooms. Eventually I met someone who let me do a beach house, something modest. Finally I was in business. I was on my own."

Joan Sawyer glanced around her. "And this is your business. How long have you been, as you put it, on your own?"

"Let me think. This makes six years."

He observed that the Sawyer woman was extracting something that resembled notes from her purse. She was studying them. "Incidentally—our files say that about four years after you set up your business, you got married."

Foster hesitated. "Yes. I see you've done your homework."

"Valerie Granich. Daughter of Charles Granich. Land developer. Billionaire. Bel Air. I have it right, haven't I?"

"You have it right," he said coldly.

"Last year you were divorced."

"Public record."

Joan Sawyer looked up. "Have you remarried?"

"No, thanks."

"Would you mind telling me a bit about your marriage? Your divorce. Human details. Something personal always helps a story. Anything you can tell me?"

Foster compressed his lips.

There was plenty he could tell her, but it was not for reader consumption. From the time of the divorce he had vowed never to speak of his short marriage, never, not even mention Valerie's name to anyone, or even think about her.

Nevertheless, he thought about her now. When he'd met Valerie, he'd found her dazzling. A beautiful, slim brunette, polished, clever, sophisticated—he had been flattered that she had chosen him from so many, himself a relative nobody.

But he should have seen it was wrong from the start. They were together for the wrong reasons. She had nothing honest to give, in bed or out of it. No warmth whatsoever. Just fun and games, surface stuff, no intimacy. Her interests scarcely extended beyond parties, staging or attending them. And pseudocultural occasions, a theater opening, a concert, an art museum displaying old masters. Life was an opening night. She was completely Daddy's girl, spoiled, inconsiderate, self-centered. A society-column morsel.

When her father offered to set his son-in-law up in larger quarters, to feed him new clients, make him an instant success (and dependent), Foster turned him down. He wanted to do it on his own, and he wanted Valerie to live on his income. Valerie had been irritated and impatient with that nonsense. She didn't want to live like a budget-keeping bride in the San Fernando Valley.

Then there was something else. Being married to a struggling architect seemed, for such a one as herself, a lowly enterprise and demeaning. If he had been a graduate of the Bauhaus, an instant Gropius or Le Corbusier, a real ornament in her world, that would have been different. But a beginner who insisted on making his sweaty way up, that was almost an embarrassment. Soon she had wanted Foster to give short shrift to bread-and-butter architecture and to devote himself to art, to painting. At least a struggling artist was more respectable, so many hadn't been appreciated until they were dead, anyway.

Finally, while he was working steadily to make it on his own, she had begun to drift away and to occupy herself with some arty group in Pasadena. When he learned she was occupying herself with a supercilious and pretentious young blond abstract painter ten years her junior, and that she had become the young man's patron and finally his bed partner, Foster said enough. In a rage, he kicked her out, and Valerie's father arranged the divorce.

Following that, Foster had had nothing to devote himself to except his work until his Hitler book project came along. After Valerie and her father, Hitler began to look good. In the last year, Foster had absorbed himself in the architectural book, and continued to be distrustful of his own judgment about women. To him, each freshly encountered woman represented no more than the possibility of a romp. He did not like himself for the feeling, but there it was.

To his surprise, Foster heard Joan Sawyer's voice once more. "You haven't answered me, Mr. Foster," she was saying. "Is there anything you want to say about that?"

"About what?"

"Your marriage, of course. It could be a colorful background."

Foster was no longer laid back. He sat up. He was becoming truly annoyed with this aggressive young reporter on the make for a byline story. "Lady," he said, "you were invited here to discuss my role as an architect, not as a husband. No more diversions. Stick to the ground rules, or good-bye."

She was flustered, afraid to lose her story, he could see. "I'm sorry," she said, contritely. "You're right. I sometimes let myself get carried away. I was just trying to round out—you know, personalize the story. No more sidetracking, I promise you. Am I forgiven? Can we go on now?"

He relaxed slightly. She was decent enough. "Go on," he said.

"We were talking about your business here the last six years. Do you do it all yourself?"

"Oh, no. Too much work. Fortunately. You met Irene, my secretary and bookkeeper. There are two more of us. I'm the one who meets with clients. I do the original creative design on a structure. Frank Nishimura gets into it next. He's a professional draftsman, not a designer but a draftsman. Don Graham is a general contractor. He follows through on the nuts and bolts, the actual production of a structure after it's designed and the blueprints are okayed."

"Production of a structure," Joan Sawyer wondered. "What does that mean?"

"Well," said Foster, "making a building might be likened to making a human being—the outside, the façade, is important—

but more important is what goes inside, the muscles and bones. So when I speak of the production of a building, I mean creating mechanical systems, waterproofing, wearability, that sort of thing."

"All right," the reporter nodded. "Now suppose I wanted you to do a house for me. How would you start?"

Foster considered the question. "For one thing," he said, "I prefer not to initiate an approach. As an architect, I'd prefer to respond to a program, to what you see for yourself in a house, your desires." He tried to make this clear to her. "Architecture should be in response to a request. I like to complement what my client has in mind."

"I thought there was more creativity to architecture," Joan Sawyer said briskly.

"Oh, there is, there is, no doubt about that," he assured her. "Once I have some notion of what you want, I wait for a creative spark. I like to take a space and in my head edit it into a composition. At the same time, I try to cut people free of what they have or think they want and land them in a better space. I ask myself —what more can I do with what they want? Once I have it, I go to work. I'd say that ninety-nine percent of my work is done out of sight of the client. After four weeks, usually, I have my ideas and Frank's plans down on paper. Those drawings are eighty percent of the work. I get eighty percent of my fee at that time. Does that give you an idea?"

"I think so," said Joan Sawyer. She leaned over to check the tape recorder once more, than sat back. "Very good. Besides seeing interviewers, do you ever promote yourself or your work? Do you lecture?"

Foster wrinkled his nose. "Not much. But I like to write when I can."

"Write? Like what? Have you published any books?"

Foster responded cheerfully. "I'm about to. My first book is almost ready."

"May I ask what it's about?"

"The title will tell you. It's called *Architecture of the 1000-Year Third Reich.*" He waited for her reaction.

She sat up. "That's a new one. You mean the building done under Hitler?"

"Exactly. What he built and what he planned to build if Germany won the war. Here, let me show you."

He got to his feet and started to cross the room. She snatched up her tape recorder and followed him.

On the drafting table lay a portfolio. Before opening it, he said, "I've always been intrigued by World War II. As an architect, I focused in on what Hitler had built and planned to build. I wanted to know more, and tried to find books on the subject. There were none. So I decided to do one myself."

"Not because you liked Nazi architecture?"

"No, because I hated it, but I felt that a visual record of this period should be preserved. Hitler's building program is what we call Fascist architecture. It's anonymous, and quite ugly. Fascist architecture is like a baked potato or a pound cake. All filled in. There's no lightness to it, no personality, no romance, no emotion, no passion. Let me show you."

He opened the portfolio.

"These are photographs of buildings that went up under Hitler, and models in miniature of drawings of buildings he wanted constructed after he won the war. Happily, most never saw the light of day. Here is a photograph of the New Chancellery that Hitler did have Albert Speer build for him in Berlin. These are Speer's comments in my caption." Foster began to read to her from the caption. " 'Strictly speaking, the element Hitler loved in classicism was the opportunity for monumentality. He was obsessed with giantism.' "

Foster went on. "When Hitler first set eyes on the Old Chancellery, he abhorred it. He thought it something 'fit for a soap company.' He wanted his New Chancellery nearby to be majestic. Speer saw that it was exactly that. A visiting diplomat entered the building on the Wilhelmsplatz through a court of honor. He went up an outside staircase into a medium-sized reception room, and then through double doors seventeen feet tall into a large hall decorated in mosaics. Then up more stairs into a mammoth gallery four hundred eighty feet long—twice as long as the Hall of Mirrors in Versailles—going on past seemingly endless office rooms adding up to seven hundred twenty-five feet more. Only then did he reach Hitler's own reception hall, and finally Hitler's huge personal study with its desk bearing an inlaid design of a sword half out of its sheath, a marble-topped table at the window—used for conferences, after 1944—and gilded panels over the room's four doors. These panels depicted four of the virtues, namely wisdom, prudence, fortitude, and justice. The floors were marble everywhere. Hitler would not permit carpeting. 'That's exactly right,' Hitler said. 'Diplomats should have practice in moving on a slippery surface.' "

Foster slowly turned the pages that showed photographs of the exterior and interior of the New Chancellery. "Anyway," Foster went on, "Hitler loved it. 'Good, good!' he told his architect. 'When diplomats see that, they will know *fear.*' Later, Speer wrote about his buildings for Hitler, 'They were the very expression of a tyranny.' "

Foster resumed flipping the pages.

"Next, let me show you an example of something grand that Hitler never had a chance to finish. This is his plan for the Prachtallee—the Avenue of Splendor—in the center of Germania, as he intended to rename Berlin. Hitler was an admirer of Georges Haussmann, who designed the great boulevards of Paris. Hitler wanted to outdo Haussmann. This Avenue of Splendor was intended to be seventy-three feet wider than the Champs Élysées and three times as long, leading to the Führer's palace. For the top of the palace, Speer suggested a German eagle in gold holding a swastika in its talons. Hitler liked that but a few years later suggested the golden eagle should hold a globe of the world in its talons instead."

The reporter was pointing to a model of a vast indoor room. "What's that?" she asked.

"The dining hall of his palace, large enough to seat two thousand guests at once."

"My God," murmured Joan Sawyer.

"And so it goes, page after page of plans never carried out. Speer wryly called it his 'drawing-board architecture.' Now look at this. It's the quote I want to use to end this section and, indeed, my book. It is a very effective quote from Albert Speer's secret diaries kept in the prison at Spandau."

Joan Sawyer bent closer and read the quote out loud. "Albert Speer wrote: 'For what was never built is also a part of the history of architecture. And probably the spirit of an era, its special architectural aims, can better be analyzed from such unrealized designs than from the structures that were actually built. For the latter were often distorted by scarcity of funds, obstinate or inflexible patrons, or prejudices. Hitler's period is also rich in unbuilt architecture. What a different image of it will emerge if someday I produce from my desk drawers all the plans and photos of models that were made during those years.' "

Joan Sawyer straightened up and regarded Foster with new respect. "And that's exactly what you've done."

"I hope so," said Foster. He considered his portfolio. "That palace of Hitler's was going to be immense, full of two-story-high colonnades with ornaments of gold and bronze. But don't be fooled by that. Although he liked his buildings to intimidate visitors, both by their size and ostentation, Hitler preferred—deep down inside—structures that were stark, simple, native German, and with few international touches. You may not believe that, seeing his models. But it was so. Still, with the world in his talons, I guess he got carried away."

Foster closed his portfolio. "Well, there you are."

Joan Sawyer's eyes were glowing. "You're right, it's a fascinating project."

Foster gave up a half smile. "Like looking at a lineup of snakes."

"When is it coming out, your book?"

"When it's completed. I have a few more pages to finish. That's why I'm hoping to go abroad this week. To wind it up. The book should be published next spring."

"I wish you luck." Joan Sawyer shut off her tape recorder. "Would you mind if I came back with a photographer next week and had him shoot a few pictures from your book? Of course, you won't be here . . ."

"I'll be taking this copy with me. But my secretary has a duplicate copy. You can see her."

The reporter had gone to retrieve her capacious purse, and was stuffing her recorder into it. "They'll make wonderful illustrations for my story." Then, as if worried he might change his mind, she added, "It'll make great publicity for your book."

Foster grinned. "Why do you think I gave you all this time?"

Thanking him, she shook his hand, and hurried out the door.

For a few minutes, Foster lingered at his drafting table, spreading his portfolio wide and turning the pages.

What he saw again pleased him. A solid job. But then there were several blank pages at the end. For the seven missing plans he knew existed but had not been able to find.

This reminded him that Dr. Harrison Ashcroft had promised to help him locate them. Then he remembered that Dr. Ashcroft was dead.

He went back to his desk to find the *Los Angeles Times* story he had been reading but had not read entirely because of the reporter's interruption. He found the piece about Dr. Ashcroft's funeral and resumed going through it. He was sorry for the man, and for his own missed opportunity to meet with him.

He came to the last line of the dispatch, and sat up, suddenly revived. "Miss Emily Ashcroft, the daughter of the deceased, had been collaborating with her father on the book, and she has announced that she will finish the biography of Hitler alone, according to her London publisher."

Rex Foster felt a surge of hope once more. Of course his problem could be solved. Emily Ashcroft would know all her father's sources. She would be able to tell Foster who, among Speer's ten architectural associates, might have the missing plans.

Foster's instinct was to reach for the phone immediately, call Miss Ashcroft in Oxford, arrange an appointment with her, learn whom to see in West Germany, and get over there to complete his own work. Before reaching for the phone, Foster's eye fell on his desk clock. Late morning here meant early evening in Oxford. An acceptable time to call. Momentarily he hesitated, thinking it might be too soon after her loss to bother her. Then he remembered the deadline for his book.

Ringing Irene Myers on the intercom, Foster asked his secretary to try the telephone number they had for Dr. Ashcroft's home in Oxford.

A few minutes later, Irene was on the ICM again.

"Mr. Foster, I have someone at the Ashcroft number in Oxford. But not Miss Emily Ashcroft. Apparently she's not in. I have a Miss Pamela Taylor—"

"Who?"

"She's the secretary and she's been staying in the house since Dr. Ashcroft's death. Do you want to speak to her?"

"I'd better."

Foster got on the line.

"Miss Taylor? This is Rex Foster calling from Los Angeles. I don't know if you'll recognize my name—"

The soft-spoken British voice was uncertain. "I—I'm not sure."

"I had a recent correspondence with Dr. Ashcroft. I'm the architect who needed some information from him on Adolf Hitler. He agreed to see me. Next week, in fact. I had an appointment. But now . . ." He faltered. "I just learned what happened to Dr. Ashcroft. I can't tell you how sorry I am."

"It's a terrible loss," said Pamela Taylor. "Mr. Foster, you say? I do recall your name—the appointment . . ."

"Well, I was just wondering. Miss Emily Ashcroft was working on the biography with her father—"

"Oh, yes."

"—so it occurred to me that perhaps she would have the same information that her father had, and would be able to help me as he had agreed to help." He was apologetic. "I know it's a little soon—"

"I'm sure she would be most cooperative."

"Can you tell me what time you expect her back this evening?"

Pamela Taylor was regretful. "I'm afraid she won't be back this evening. She left London this morning for West Berlin."

"West Berlin?"

"To finish the project she and her father were working on."

"How long will she be in Berlin?"

"I don't know. Her stay is indefinite. It would be safe to say she'll be there at least two weeks."

"Can you tell me, Miss Taylor, where she's staying in Berlin? Perhaps I can look her up."

There was a brief silence on the other end. Then Pamela Taylor spoke. "It's supposed to be hush-hush—"

"Miss Taylor," said Foster patiently, "I'm sure she wouldn't mind. After all, since her father gave me an appointment, I'm positive she would, too."

"Yes, you're right. Very well. She's at the Bristol Hotel Kempinski in Berlin. Should be all checked in by now."

"Thank you, Miss Taylor. I appreciate it. I'll get in touch with Miss Ashcroft. Again, I'm terribly sorry about the accident. Hope to meet you one of these days."

Hanging up, Foster came to his feet, and hurried into the reception room.

Irene looked up from her typewriter. "Any luck?"

"Yes, definitely. Emily Ashcroft is in West Berlin. The perfect place to see her and get what I need. So, Irene, let's start right in. Book me on the first flight available to Berlin tomorrow. If tomorrow is impossible, make it the next day. Then call the Bristol Hotel Kempinski in Berlin. Have them hold a room for me, single, double, whatever accommodation they have."

"The reservation—for how long?"

"Who knows? Tell them a week. But it'll be for as long as I need. Just pray that Emily Ashcroft stays safe and sound. She's my big hope."

Having settled into a small, modern, air-conditioned room on the eleventh floor of the Hotel Guarani in Asunción, Tovah Levine sat at the dressing table reading *La Tribuna* and sipping the last of her breakfast coffee.

Feeling refreshed after her shower, feeling relaxed about being in the capital once more after the four exhausting weeks in the back country of Paraguay, Tovah was trying to catch up on the world since she had disappeared from sight. On page three the name Hitler jumped out at her, arrested her attention, and she brought up the paper to read the brief item in Spanish. Anything that mentioned a Nazi was grist to her mill.

> Sir Harrison Ashcroft, the world-famous historian from Oxford University, was laid to rest yesterday in a Methodist cemetery outside Oxford. Ashcroft, co-author of a forthcoming biography on the life of Adolf Hitler, suffered fatal injuries in a hit-and-run auto accident in West Berlin last week, where he was visiting to complete research on his book, *Herr Hitler.*

Tovah thought that Ashcroft's name struck a small chord in her memory. She might have read one of his earlier books while at the university in Jerusalem. She wasn't sure. In any case, she wasn't terribly interested in yet another book on Hitler, and she moved on inquisitively through the rest of the newspaper.

Soon she was through with the newspaper and her coffee, and she sat back in the chair a minute to organize her thoughts before her two o'clock luncheon date with Ben Shertok, who was coming in from Buenos Aires to meet with her. She had seen Shertok once before, upon her arrival in South America over a month ago. She had been impressed by him, his sharpness, his importance. He was high up in Israel's intelligence service and was the Mossad chief for four countries in South America. It was a key post, she knew. Only Mossad agents in West Berlin, in their unending search for Nazis—and in Syria, in the persistent hunt for Palestinian terrorists—had more responsibility and larger staffs. Paraguay, Chile, Argentina, and Brazil were still prime targets, as the favorite hideouts for many prominent leaders of the Third Reich, but Tovah had the feeling that the entire area was being phased out as a hunting ground. All of the most wanted Nazis were now in their seventies and eighties, and one by one they were dying off. Soon there would be few left to pursue, catch, prosecute. Still, even though Walter Rauff, inventor of the mobile gas chambers, had escaped them through natural death, there was from time to time a Klaus Barbie to be found in this area and extradited to

France to stand judgment. Remembering this alleviated one's discouragement.

Tovah had taken a LATN flight from Concepción to Asunción, and a minibus from Presidente General Stroessner Airport the fifteen kilometers into Asunción. The arrangement had been that she would have a single room at the Guarani Hotel for the day, meeting Shertok in the lobby, and together they would go out to a restaurant for lunch where she could make her report. However, upon her arrival at the Guarani reception desk, where she had a reservation as Helga Ludwig (the name on her passport, a German name more appropriate for a Latin country hospitable to Germans but wary of Jews), she found a telex waiting for her. Ben Shertok requested that they lunch in her room and talk. This sounded more sensible to her, the desire for privacy, and she looked forward to room service.

Now she considered the time. It was still morning, ten after eleven. Shertok would not be here until two o'clock. This gave her at least a full two hours to spend on her own. She did not know Asunción well. She had been in the capital city twice before: once for a week, eight years ago when she was nineteen and trying to polish up her Spanish during a six-month tour of South America, and again just recently for two days before she had undertaken her travels through Paraguay as a Mossad agent. She had the urge now to walk about the center of the city for a closer and more leisurely look. And maybe pick up a few gifts, trinkets for her parents and brothers in Tel Aviv, with whom she would be reunited the day after tomorrow.

She reached into her suitcase for something to wear, something light, a sleeveless blouse, cotton skirt, sandals, for it was warm outdoors and becoming more humid. Once downstairs, she walked into the Parque Independencia. The palacha trees of the plaza were all pink on this day, and the avenues lined with Spanish Colonial buildings were lovely with their jacaranda and orange trees. There were gleaming high-rises everywhere, and small whitewashed stuccoed buildings, mostly shops, with red-tiled roofs. She studied some new restaurants, several refurbished government buildings, and stopped to look at the goods the lace vendors had for sale. She purchased some handkerchiefs for her mother and favorite aunt.

In a roundabout way she headed for the Plaza de la Constitución, dutifully studied the Congressional Palace, and sat down in a shady spot to cool off and watch the foot traffic, which had thinned out after the siesta period had begun at noon.

Dreamily sitting on the bench, Tovah was in a mood to reconstruct the last three years that had brought her to this steamy, remote city. In school, earlier, her languages had been English (everyone among the young in Israel spoke English), Spanish (because it was challenging), and German (because her grandparents on both sides had been born in Germany, and lived and died there—died in concentration camps or gas chambers—but their children had been sent to Palestine, grown, met, married, and become her parents).

To improve her Spanish she had taken that first vacation to South America, and had twice accompanied her father to West Berlin, on a matter of reparations. Her paternal grandfather had owned a prosperous department store, suffered its confiscation by Hitler, and met his own death in the Nazis' Final Solution. West Berlin had been an alien place to Tovah, and despite its liveliness and excitement she despised it, despised what it had been. Yet she had found the young people decent and friendly and much like herself and her Israeli friends. When she had mentioned this softness in her to her father, he had laughed and said, "Don't worry about the young. They are not your enemies. Worry about the old ones, those from sixty to eighty. They were most of them Nazis, you can be sure. They are the ones who say, 'Ah, that was a good time under the Führer. Now our Berlin is filled with strangers, our young who are stupid and drugged by the Americans and other foreigners. We need to be harder on them. We need to clean out the garbage.' Those are the ones, Tovah, who wish for a nation of blondes again."

Languages aside, Tovah's major at the university had been journalism. From early on she'd had a reporter's curiosity and a reporter's eye. She had done very well in her journalism classes, and after graduation and her stint in the army she had been readily taken on by the *Jerusalem Post* as a feature writer. Near the end of her first year she had been called into the office of the managing editor, a rare occurrence.

"Tovah," he had said, "I have an unusual assignment for you, very unusual."

"What does that mean?"

"It means that the director of Mossad wants to give you an interview. The Mossad has never done this, has never even permitted one of our reporters into their building outside Tel Aviv. But this morning the director initiated the invitation. He specifically requested you."

Tovah had been astounded. She had always known the secrecy that surrounded this arm of the Israeli government, the secret service branch founded in 1951.

"Why me?" she had wondered.

"They've probably read some of your byline pieces and liked them."

"What can they possibly tell me?"

"Find out. Your appointment is with the *memuneh*—the father—the director himself. Ten tomorrow morning. Yes, you'll find out then."

Five minutes after she was closeted alone with the director of Mossad, a forceful and straightforward man with no words to waste, she had found out quickly what he had to tell her. He didn't want to give her a story. He wanted to give her a job.

"Our business is keeping an eye on people," he had said. "We've kept an eye on you for the last half year. While we have nine hundred agents and other personnel—one hundred in the headquarters here, the rest elsewhere in the world—most of the agents are not women. Like our previous chief, Meir Amit, I am uncomfortable using women. Sooner or later a female may find it necessary to use sex to get what she wants. I don't like that, but . . ."

He had shrugged, letting it hang there, and Tovah had become conscious that he was taking in her appearance. She knew—had always known—that she was attractive in a perfectly goyish way. Long flaxen blond hair. Blue eyes. Aquiline nose. Small mouth. Full firm bosom. Shapely legs. Nothing obviously Jewish. Aryan Germans might have regarded her as one of their perfect specimens.

Now the director had been measuring her womanhood.

She had felt the necessity to speak up. "I don't mind. About the sex part, I mean. I'm not a child. One does what one has to do in life."

The director had grunted. "For the agent in the field, it can be a dangerous job. We do not encourage assassination. We do encourage self-defense. Every agent is trained to use a weapon, many weapons. Every agent is taught to lie and cheat, when it is necessary. We care only about results. Our agents are civil servants, on government salary. For three years, it is a million three hundred ten thousand shekels—not much when you think in American currency, eight hundred dollars a month. None will become rich. All will know they are helping Israel survive. If you are interested, we can arrange things with your editor. You'd still be working for the *Jerusalem Post* here and abroad. That would be your cover. But your main job would be working for Mossad."

"Doing what?"

"Plenty. You would receive assignments abroad. First you

have to be trained during a twelve-month leave from the paper. Learn to send communications by code, learn to shadow a suspect and to shake a pursuer, learn hand-to-hand combat, learn to use a .22 Beretta. Then you would be ready."

"Why me?" she had pressed.

"I told you we've had an eye on you. We liked your looks and your tenacity. We liked your observant reporting. We liked your knowledge of German, Spanish, English." He had paused. "Well, what do you say?" He had paused again. "Or do you want to think about it?"

Sitting there, listening, she had been thinking about it, meaning her life. The newspaper work was all right, but had become somewhat repetitious and tiresome. Her love life was nothing special, although there had been someone more interesting recently. Still, there would be time for that later. She yearned for an exciting involvement in something that would mean something. Also, she yearned for travel, to break out of this tight community of sufferers, to see new places, new people.

She had stared back at the director. "I have thought about it," she said. "When do I start?"

Tovah had already been in the Israeli army. The Mossad training was a little more of the same, perhaps more rugged, more exacting, more varied, but continually fascinating. Then she had worked the rest of the year in the Tel Aviv headquarters, deciphering coded messages, debriefing agents, interrogating possible contacts.

Her first assignment abroad as Helga Ludwig, had been to research and write a major travel article on Paraguay. Actually, Mossad had obtained a fresh lead on the supposedly deceased Dr. Josef Mengele, the SS physician at the Auschwitz-Birkenau death camp who had sent 380,000 innocent people to their deaths in Hitler's reign of terror. Mengele had escaped from the American Zone in Austria to Argentina in 1951, and, with the help of German colonists there and in Paraguay, had eluded all Nazi-hunters. Now Mossad had come upon a fresh lead. Dr. Mengele had been seen in Nueva Germania, a small town in central Paraguay. Tovah had been ordered to verify the sighting of Dr. Mengele, and learn what she could about five other wanted Nazis, several of whom might still be in hiding in Paraguay. She had learned much, but the big catch proved as elusive as ever. Now the assignment was almost over and she could leave this godforsaken country. Tovah glided back into the present, the plaza bench in Asunción.

Her watch told her it was one-thirty, just time enough for her to get back to the lunch in her room with Ben Shertok and her report.

When she emerged from the hotel elevator and made for her room, she found Ben Shertok already there, leaning contentedly against the wall outside her door, puffing on a cigar. He resembled a professorial type, rumpled hair, horn-rimmed spectacles on a hawkish nose. A quiet and dedicated intelligence chieftain.

He planted a chaste kiss on each of her cheeks, and apologized for coming early. "Because the plane wasn't on time. It was early. So I'll excuse you if you want to go to the bathroom."

She let them into her room. "I feel guilty, living in this fancy hotel even for a day. I assure you, Ben, it wasn't like this for the last four weeks."

"You bet I know," he said. "I took the liberty of ordering from room service when I was downstairs. I don't have much time, and yet didn't want to rush our lunch. I have to be in Chile this evening."

"I'll just wash my face and hands," she said. "It was hot out there. What am I having for lunch?"

"I thought I heard you say, when we dined in Buenos Aires, how much you were taken by those dumplings of ground maize and onion on your first visit here."

"*Sopa paraguaya,*" she said. "You couldn't have done better."

"Some red wine, too," he added.

"Great. See you in five minutes."

When she came out in twenty minutes, she found that the food had already been served from a rolling cart set between the window and the bed. She realized that Shertok was showing someone out, a dumpy man in overalls carrying a kit.

She looked at Shertok questioningly, as he seated himself before the lunch cart. "Just a colleague," he explained. "He debugged the room. It's clean." Shertok began sampling the wine between sucks on his cigar. Tovah sought her purse, extracted a notebook, opened it, and laid it on the table as she sat opposite Shertok.

"If you haven't much time, I should start right in," she said, cutting into her first dumpling, chewing it, washing it down with the dry wine.

"How was the trip?" he asked.

"By my standards, a bust I'd say. I never caught up with a solid lead to the whereabouts of Josef Mengele."

"Is he here in this country?"

"Everyone says so, but I'm not sure, Ben. It has become a sort of chic thing to say—I'm speaking of the locals—that they have seen or met the 'renowned' Mengele himself. A great conversation piece, and kind of prestigious, if you understand."

"I understand very well."

Tovah consulted her notebook as she ate. "The locals all know that after the Allies overran Germany and Austria, Mengele used one of the Nazi escape networks to make his way to Rome, hid out in a monastery in the Via Sicilia, obtained a false passport in Spain, then entered Argentina in 1951. It's no news to anyone here that when Mengele realized pursuers were closing in, he crossed over to Paraguay, somehow became a Paraguayan, and lived quite openly and safely in Asunción."

Shertok nodded. "We leaned on the American president Carter to do something about it," he said. "Carter put pressure on President Stroessner here, and Stroessner reluctantly revoked Mengele's citizenship. After that Mengele vanished, slipped out of the capital and has lived in the back country ever since."

Briefly, she reviewed her notes.

"Then the director got this new lead," Tovah resumed. "He felt—"

"There have been plenty of leads lately," Shertok interrupted, "now that we've been joined by the West German government and a group of Americans in offering almost four million dollars in rewards for Mengele's capture. There was the lead, in June, that Mengele had gone to Brazil, lived under the name of Wolfgang Gerhard, had drowned and been buried in 1979."

"Well, as you know, Mossad never accepted the idea that Mengele had died and been buried in Brazil. They considered that the forensic report was based on a contrived plant. All a perfect ploy to put off further investigation, and allow the living Mengele to remain safely alive in Paraguay. Anyway, the director felt that Mengele was still very much alive. In fact, according to the director, Mengele had recently been seen hale and hearty in a Paraguayan town called Nueva Germania, a ratty little colony of German settlers founded by a German teacher and Jew-hater back in the last century. Mengele went there to treat some ailing leftover Nazis. In appreciation he was given the protection of the town, and I was sent to find out if he was still there."

Shertok sipped his coffee. "Did you know it was dangerous, Tovah?"

"Oh, I knew it was dangerous."

"Did you know how dangerous? Two of your predecessors, not Mossad agents, got too close to Mengele and paid for their curiosity."

"No, I didn't know that," said Tovah slowly. "What do you mean?"

"In 1961 an attractive Jewish lady named Nora Eldoc, who

had been sterilized by Mengele at Auschwitz, traced him to a resort here. She became acquainted with him. Before she could act, Mengele learned who she was. They found her corpse a short time later in Brazil. Next, Herbert Cukur, a rehabilitated Nazi, located Mengele in an Argentine hideout. Cukur's body was found in a car trunk in Uruguay."

"Anyway, when I reached Nueva Germania, he was already gone. Had left a week before. I tried to find out where he had gone, and got a number of leads. So I just tramped around the back country pretending to be a travel writer. I went to Hernandarias, Mbaracayu, San Lorenzo, and so on, winding up in Concepción. No Mengele anywhere. I'll tell you, there were plenty of Paraguayan Germans in every town and city. Someone told me there are 70,000 of them, the biggest ethnic group here. A few of them claimed they had seen Mengele, but no one told me where."

"In other words, no luck."

"None whatsoever. I'm sorry, Ben."

"Well, you tried. That's the most we can ask." Shertok was thoughtful a moment. "I was just wondering—do you think anyone will ever find Mengele?"

"I would think so. Definitely. I don't believe he was buried in Brazil. None of those I met could ever be tempted by any reward. They were Nazi diehards. But one day someone more fallible will want that four million. That's the person who will inform. I'm sure Mengele will be found, sooner or later. In fact, I'm counting on it."

Shertok indicated Tovah's notebook. "What about the others?"

Draining her coffee cup, Tovah went on. "Let me see. I was told to keep my eyes and ears open for Heinrich Müller, one of Himmler's Gestapo heads. Couldn't find out whether he was in Paraguay. Someone said he may have gone over to the Soviet Union after World War II to work for the KGB. Just a rumor."

"What about Josef Schwammberger and Walter Kutschmann?"

She was studying her notebook again. "Schwammberger. SS commander at the Przemyśl concentration camp in Poland. Now seventy-three. He's not in Paraguay. Definitely in Argentina, but invisible. As for Kutschmann, the Nazi executioner in Poland, he was also in Argentina, but several people thought he was here now. No leads, not one."

They had finished the meal, and Shertok sat back, lighting a fresh cigar.

"Anyone else?"

"One more. Didn't see him either. But heard definitely that he was here."

"Who?"

"Not a war criminal. A Nazi scientist. Professor Dieter Falkenheim. We have him on some list or other as missing."

"Now you've found him?"

"Definitely," said Tovah. "Falkenheim is somewhere in northern Paraguay. Want to know how he got out of Germany? The American intelligence mission, *Alsos,* assigned to round up Nazi scientists and bring them to the United States, found out that this nuclear physicist who was trying to put together a nuclear bomb was in the town of Ilm. When *Alsos* reached his laboratory in Ilm, they found it empty, hastily abandoned. I now know what happened. Falkenheim was smuggled to Denmark, and from there Juan Perón had him flown to Argentina. He worked for Perón until Perón was exiled. Then Falkenheim slipped over to Paraguay. He's been here ever since. There is some speculation that he may have shipped one hundred tons of uranium ore out of Germany during the fall of Germany. Remember when the Americans found eleven hundred tons of uranium ore hidden in a salt mine outside Stassfurt? Well, there may have been twelve hundred tons of ore. Maybe Falkenheim got the rest."

"Unlikely. I suspect it is just faulty arithmetic on the part of the Americans. Anyway, Falkenheim is not our primary target."

"But still a Nazi. I just thought it was interesting."

"Could be. I don't know. Try it out on the director when you get back. Speaking of the director, did he ask you to keep an eye out for Martin Bormann while in Paraguay?"

"No, not a word about Bormann. I think Mossad is satisfied that he was killed in an explosion while trying to get out of Berlin. I think they've all written him off."

"Maybe so." From behind a cloud of smoke, Shertok casually posed another question. "What about Adolf Hitler?"

Tovah looked startled. "Adolf Hitler?"

"In Paraguay. Anyone speak to you of seeing him?"

"Come off it, Ben. You must be pulling my leg. Hitler shot himself in the Führerbunker in 1945. Everyone knows that."

"Not everyone, Tovah. Not quite everyone." Shertok straightened himself across from her. "Ever hear of Sir Harrison Ashcroft?"

"Ashcroft, Ashcroft." She tried to remember. "Didn't I read something about him in the paper today?"

"You did. His daughter, Emily Ashcroft, and friends, buried him outside Oxford."

"So?"

"So this—the Ashcrofts were finishing a biography on Adolf Hitler called *Herr Hitler*. Then Dr. Ashcroft got a lead of some kind from someone in Berlin that Hitler didn't shoot himself in the bunker as everyone believes. The informant said it wasn't Hitler's remains that the Russians dug up. There were no remains of Hitler. Dr. Ashcroft went to West Berlin to look into it. The day before he was to excavate around the bunker, he was killed by a hit-and-run driver in a freak accident."

"A real accident?"

"We don't know."

Tovah studied Shertok's serious scholarly face. "Thanks for the information. What's that got to do with me?"

"Maybe something." Shertok shifted uneasily. "This morning I got a coded message from Chaim Golding, who heads Mossad in West Berlin. He says that Emily Ashcroft has decided to finish the job on her own. She arrived in West Berlin today. Registered at the Bristol Hotel Kempinski."

"How do you know all that?"

"Chaim Golding knows everything that goes on in Berlin, both Berlins, especially when it has to do with Hitler." Shertok hesitated. "I realize you've had a rough assignment here and you're tired. You have a vacation due you. You're planning to go straight back to Tel Aviv and have a reunion with your parents and boyfriend. But—well . . ."

"You want me in Berlin."

"Golding wants it. So does the director. You know the city. You know German. You know how much we want the truth—whatever it be—about Hitler. Mossad would like you to postpone Tel Aviv. Stay in Berlin for a week at least."

"To do what?"

"To meet Emily Ashcroft. Find out what her father knew, or what she knows now, about Hitler's not having died when he was supposed to. You can be Tovah Levine again. Use your old cover, the *Jerusalem Post.* Maybe try to—to interview her."

"Ben, you know better than that. She's not going to want to talk to any reporters."

"Her father did."

"Yes, Ben, but look what happened to him."

"You may be right. Well, no matter how you do it, on some pretext or other meet her, ingratiate yourself. Find out what she knows. I don't think anything will come of it, but who can tell? We've got to be sure, Tovah, that the big one didn't get away."

"Whatever you say. When?"

"Tomorrow morning to Buenos Aires. From there straight to West Berlin."

"My hotel?"

"You're already booked into the Bristol Hotel Kempinski."

"Cozy."

"Yes, I told you, we want you as close to Emily Ashcroft as possible." He handed her the plane tickets. "Maybe this time you'll come up roses."

She smiled wanly. "In my hand, I hope. Not on my grave."

In West Berlin, at ten o'clock in the morning of an overcast day, Evelyn Hoffmann had emerged from the Café Wolf and stood briefly beside the bookstore on the corner of Stresemann Strasse and Anhalter Strasse to inhale the fresh morning air.

What she was doing now, and would do the remainder of the morning and part of the afternoon, was a routine that she had followed for twenty-two years, certainly almost without variation for the last ten years.

But this morning, before beginning her routine, Evelyn Hoffmann paused briefly to study her reflection in the window of the Café Wolf. What she saw did not displease her. At seventy-three, one could not expect to appear as one had at twenty-three. In the early days she had been a beauty, everyone had agreed. She had been taller than medium height, with ash blond hair, slender, sophisticated, reserved, with pride in her long shapely legs. She still cherished a description that dear Keitel—Field Marshal Wilhelm Keitel—had given of her after the war: "Very slender, elegant appearance, quite nice legs—one could see that. She seemed to be not shy, but reticent and retiring—a very, very nice person." In fact, she had modeled for the great sculptor, Otto Brecker, in the nude, and had hoped to be a film star in Hollywood after the trouble was over. That had been long ago. No matter. Now, at seventy-three, she decided, she still cut an imposing figure. She had bent very little to the passage of time, was still of erect bearing and trim, her hair dyed brown now, her face crisscrossed with tiny wrinkles now, but not too badly for an older woman. Her mind and memory were as sharp as ever. Only her walk had given in to the years. It had become slower, more tentative, her breath shorter.

So now the routine.

Evelyn Hoffmann moved away from the café window and went to the narrow shop next door bearing a sign over the entrance that read KONDITOREI. She waited her turn, and then had a box filled with fresh *Nusskuchen* and had it wrapped with a ribbon to resemble a gift.

Leaving the shop, she walked slowly across the street, purse in one hand and the box of cakes in the other, to Askanischer Platz, halting briefly on Schöneberger Strasse to buy today's copy of the *Berliner Morgenpost.* Seeing that it was sold out, she settled for the tabloid *BZ*—the *Berliner Zeitung*—which she rarely read, and took her place in the bus shelter to await the approaching number 29 bus that would bring her to the Ku'damm in twenty minutes.

On the bus, she began scanning her *BZ.* The lead photograph and story reported that the American cowboy president had dispatched more nuclear missiles to West Germany, their warheads to be aimed at the Soviet Union. This satisfied her, since she hated the Russians even more than the Americans. As the bus rumbled along, Evelyn absently leafed through her paper. A lesser headline caught her attention, and she noted that the first paragraph beneath it was datelined London:

> A British publishing house, Ryan and Maxwell, Ltd., announced yesterday that it was going ahead with plans to bring out the long-discussed biography of Adolf Hitler, *Herr*

Hitler, authored by Sir Harrison Ashcroft and his daughter Emily Ashcroft, of Oxford. There had been some question about the future of the unfinished book when Dr. Ashcroft, pursuing his research on Hitler's final days in Berlin, met an untimely death in an auto accident. However, yesterday the British publishing house announced that Emily Ashcroft had agreed to complete alone the biography that she and her father had been preparing for five years.

Involuntarily frowning, Evelyn read on, lost patience with the rest of the news, and folded the tabloid, stuffing it into her purse.

On the bustling Ku'damm, she dismounted from the bus and slowly traversed the few blocks on Knesebeckstrasse that brought her to the six-story apartment building where her closest relatives lived. On the third floor, in a large modern apartment, dwelt Evelyn's beloved Klara Fiebig, who worked part-time as an artist for advertising firms, and her husband, Franz Fiebig, a somewhat acidic but clever schoolteacher who taught modern history at the Schliesion Oberschule in the Charlottenburg district. Klara's mother, Liesl, invalided and often in a wheelchair, lived with the Fiebigs. Liesl had been Evelyn Hoffmann's maid in better days—the first of two maids with the same name—younger than Evelyn by three years and a distant cousin. Liesl had bought the expensive apartment for her daughter and son-in-law in return for their care.

Evelyn was usually cheerful, looking forward to her weekly visit and tea and gossip with the family—a remote family, to be sure, but the only family that she had left—but somehow the ride on the bus this morning had changed and dampened her mood, and upon arrival at the apartment she was lost in thought and somber.

Inside the apartment parlor there was an inexplicable atmosphere of joy. Franz was away teaching his classes at this hour, but attractive Klara, hugging Aunt Evelyn, and Liesl in the wheelchair, were both beaming with some secret wonderful news.

"Tell her, tell your Aunt Evelyn," Liesl croaked from the wheelchair.

Klara held her Aunt Evelyn off, her face wreathed in the broadest smile. "Auntie," Klara said, "I'm pregnant."

Evelyn, feeling faint, grabbed her niece and smothered her with kisses. "Pregnant, pregnant," she whispered. "Thank God, at last."

Evelyn had begun to give up hope. Klara had married late, at thirty, and after five years there had been no sign of a child. A few more years and it might be difficult to conceive, even impossible. But now at thirty-five, Klara was pregnant, finally, already in her sixth week, and everything was going smoothly.

As Klara prepared their tea, bubbling with optimism, Evelyn had given her the weekly token gift, the box of cakes, wishing that she had known so that she could have brought something more lasting and memorable. Then she remembered why she no longer brought Klara and Franz expensive presents. It was because of the reception accorded her last important gift to them on their first wedding anniversary. She had given them one of her prized possessions, a valuable heirloom, the magnificent realistic oil painting of a stately government building. Klara had appreciated it, but her husband Franz had not masked his distaste. "Handsome, of course," he had said politely, "but a little grim. Reminds me of all those brooding Third Reich pictures. Anyway, thanks Aunt Evelyn. Thoughtful of you."

Evelyn had noted later that the oil never hung in the living room or dining room, but had been consigned to Cousin Liesl's rear bedroom.

So Evelyn had ceased bringing valuable gifts. After that, and ever since, it had been chocolates or pastries or colognes.

This morning it was pastries, and Klara, humming joyously,

was passing the platter of cakes to her mother and her Aunt Evelyn. Klara was sitting now, and Evelyn feasted her eyes on the young woman and drew her own pleasure from Klara's pleasure. Klara prattled on about the new life inside her, and how happy it had made Franz, and discussed the names being considered if the infant was a he or a she.

Evelyn, an eye on the mantel clock (she never liked to keep Wolfgang Schmidt waiting for their weekly lunch, knowing how busy he was), listened and decided that next week she would shop for white baby booties, feeling secure that such a present would be accepted favorably by both the mother and the father.

Leaving at exactly a quarter to twelve, Evelyn walked back to the Ku'damm, and then turned down to Mampes Gute Stube, the restaurant where she and Schmidt had been meeting for these weekly lunches for so many years.

Approaching the restaurant, Evelyn could see that Wolfgang Schmidt was already there. The black Mercedes used by Berlin's chief of police, with the chauffeur dozing behind the wheel, was parked in a reserved place. Seeing the car made Evelyn realize, once more, her good fortune in having so dear and trustworthy a friend, and one so powerful, in what had become a new and bewildering metropolis.

Actually, Evelyn recalled, Schmidt had started in a lowly law enforcement position and through sheer effort and skill had worked his way to the top. Discharged from the defeated Schutzstaffel, seeking employment that was suitable, Schmidt had returned to his native Berlin and applied for police work. Applicants were being screened carefully by the new democratic government, but Schmidt's credentials both as an SS blackshirt and as a longtime secret anti-Nazi were the most impressive of all. Among the many officers under Count von Stauffenberg—who had tried to blow up Hitler, to assassinate him at Rastenburg in July of 1944—Schmidt had been the only major conspirator to escape punishment. Schmidt had eluded all Nazi traps set for the plotters and survived to become an anti-Nazi hero. Evidence of this was all the city of Berlin needed to give him a job on the Berlin police force. Ten years ago he had become chief of police, and was in that position still. Other than Klara and her cousin Liesl, this was the person Evelyn Hoffmann depended upon most in the outside world.

Entering Mampes Gute Stube through the glass-enclosed sidewalk café area, Evelyn went into the dark coolness of the restaurant. She walked past the buttonback brown upholstered chairs and tile-topped tables to the solitary table next to the decorative antique porcelain stove in the far corner of the room, the table that had been isolated by the management out of respect for a regular customer who was the chief of police.

Seeing Evelyn, Chief Wolfgang Schmidt clambered to his feet with the grace of a bull elephant. His countenance had the Prussian cast of Erich von Stroheim, Evelyn thought, only Schmidt was larger, much larger, bald head gleaming, muscles bulging, stomach protruding, and as ever he was not in uniform but in a businessman's blue suit.

Evelyn sat comfortably across from him at the table.

"You've ordered?" she inquired as always.

"Taken care of," he said.

That meant her *gemischter Salat, Rühreier mit Speck, Wecke,* and her second tea of the day, and his plate of *Rinderroulade* or *Leberwurst, Bratkartoffeln,* and stein of Weihenstephan beer would be here shortly.

"How are you, Wolfgang?" she asked.

"Never more fit," he replied. "And you, Effie, how are you?" He was the only one alive who dared call her by her old intimate nickname, and it warmed her that he did so.

"An eventful morning," she said. "I have some wonderful news to tell you. Klara is pregnant."

Schmidt responded with a broad smile, and reached for her

hand. "Congratulations, Effie, I know what this must mean to you."

"It means everything. I thank you for your good wishes."

Schmidt shook his massive head. "I wondered if it would ever happen. So now at last you are going to be a grandmother."

Evelyn furtively glanced about. "I am going to be a great aunt," she corrected her friend.

"If you insist."

"You know it is for the best, Wolfgang."

He nodded. "I suppose that it is."

Both fell silent as an aproned waiter served Schmidt his rolled beefsteak and fried potatoes, and Evelyn the mixed salad, scrambled eggs and bacon, and basket of buns.

Stuffing a piece of steak into his mouth, Schmidt said casually, "Have you read today's paper yet?"

"You want to know if I've read about the Hitler biography being done in London? I read about it. I also read that Dr. Ashcroft's daughter is going to complete the book for him. This is not surprising. I thought she or someone would."

Schmidt studied Evelyn from beneath his bushy eyebrows. "That is not the latest news, Effie."

"Oh, no?"

"The latest news is that Emily Ashcroft arrives in Berlin shortly. She'll check into the Kempinski." He paused. "You know this is not a social visit."

Evelyn waited.

"Of course she is here to discover whether the Führer survived the war, and if so when and where his life really ended."

Evelyn gave a short nod. "How foolish of her," she said softly.

They both finished their lunches in silence, neither alluding to the matter again until the meal was over and they were ready to take leave of one another.

Rising, standing, Evelyn spoke almost as an afterthought.

"Emily Ashcroft," she murmured. "I suppose it would be interesting to know what she uncovers."

Schmidt was on his feet smiling. "Have no concern, Effie. We will know everyone the young lady speaks to, and about what. Leave it in my hands. You've always been able to trust me. You can trust me now."

She squeezed his fingers. "My friend," she said, and she was gone.

A half hour later, descending from her bus at Askanischer Platz, she waited for the traffic light, then crossed the street, walked past the corner bookshop and entered the Café Wolf. The few scattered tables were empty, but at the bar to her left a secretary from an office in the block was paying for a ham sandwich to take back to her employer.

Evelyn went slowly to the far side of the café, then entered the kitchen through a swinging door. There were, as usual, two unobtrusive but strapping guards posted, both dressed as chefs. One, the older of the pair, was familiar to her. The other, the younger one, was not. She cast them a fleeting smile as she moved past them.

The younger of the two, his hand reaching out, made as if to intercept and block her way, but the older man grabbed him by the arm, pulled him back, and nodded respectfully at her as she passed by them. She opened a door on the far side of the kitchen, revealing a stairway, and disappeared from sight.

The younger guard protested to his colleague. "But she didn't show her identity card."

The older guard offered his partner a shake of the head. "You're new here, Hans. Did you come in with that last batch from South America?"

"Yes. I was warned that everyone entering must display an identity card."

"Except her. Not her," said the older guard.

"Why not? Who is she?"

The older guard smiled. "Well, behind her back her nickname was always the Merry Widow."

"The Merry Widow?"

"That's because in the old days her lover was rarely with her, and she was alone so much."

"But her real name?"

The older guard leaned closer to the younger one and said in an undertone, "You have just met Eva Braun. More precisely, Frau Eva Braun Hitler. Yes, my friend, welcome to the Third Reich."

3

After Emily Ashcroft had registered at the reception desk of the Bristol Hotel Kempinski, she had gone with the clerk to the lift, taken it to the third floor, and been shown into suite 229. It was an excellent suite, with a small sitting room that would be comfortable for her work, a large bedroom with a double bed, and a connecting tiled bathroom. There were fresh flowers in bowls on both the bedroom bureau and the sitting-room coffee table. Atop the television set rested three bottles—scotch, vodka, pink Tavel wine—as well as glasses, napkins, a bucket of ice, and on the writing desk beside it a platter of cheese and crackers, with a card reading, *Compliments of the Managing Director.*

A hospitable beginning.

Picking up the green booklet on which her suite number was printed, she saw that the first page was headed *Herzlich Willkommen im Bristol Hotel Kempinski Berlin.* The other pages contained photographs of, and information on, the amenities that the hotel offered. Then Emily realized that underneath the booklet there was a telephone message that had been left for her.

Reading it she saw that it was from Peter Nitz, the *Berliner Morgenpost* reporter, who had written to her last week to tell her he had witnessed her father's accident. She had answered to inform him that she was coming to Berlin to finish the research her father had begun, and that she hoped she could meet him soon after her arrival not only to thank him in person for his kindness but to get an overview of what she could expect in Berlin. The telephone message, taken at the reception desk this morning, told her that Peter Nitz would be pleased to call upon her at two o'clock. If he did not hear from her, he would come directly to her suite.

This gave her time to unpack and take a bath and get into some fresh clothes. After her three pieces of luggage had been deposited in the bedroom, Emily had opened the garment bag and hung it in a closet. Then she had unstrapped her two suitcases. One contained blouses, underthings, and shoes, as well as a small travel kit of toiletries. The other contained books and files that were part of the reference material needed for the final chapters of *Herr Hitler.*

Taking up her kit of toiletries, Emily moved into the bathroom. There were mirrors everywhere. As she undressed, Emily became conscious of her naked body. Not half bad for a schoolteacher—Jeremy Robinson notwithstanding, the bastard. Her auburn hair, green eyes, tilted freckled nose with delicate nostrils, and her full lips might not be found unappealing by someone decent, someday. The breasts, perhaps, might be a bit small for some tastes, but they were firm. The stomach was flat—the strenuous daily exercises paid off—the small waist supple, and the brown beauty mark below the deep navel not uninteresting. The hips were acceptably feminine, the thighs full yet the legs long and shapely. Still, this attractiveness had never found her the right man. After graduation from college, enamored with a literature professor fifteen years her senior, she had eloped. It had been an ill-fated union. He was immature, arrogant, a womanizer, and worst of all a lush. The marriage had lasted only six months. After that, there had been several mild attachments and affairs, but none with any depth or real commitment.

Gradually, she had found her main satisfaction in teaching and writing. Five years ago, when her father had invited her to join him in researching and writing alternate chapters of *Herr Hitler*, she had been thrilled. But sometimes, more frequently than before, she longed for the love, companionship, and bodily warmth of a wonderful mate. The meeting at the BBC with Jeremy Robinson had given her hope, but with hindsight she could see that it was her need for a mate and not her feelings for Jeremy himself that had propelled her into the relationship. Blindly, she had not permitted herself to see that Jeremy had been a hope misplaced. Following that disaster, her absorption in Adolf Hitler and his incredible court of Nazi clowns had become more fulfilling than ever.

Now, with a last glance at her nude figure, Emily immersed herself in the tepid bubble bath and pondered whether she alone would solve the riddle of Hitler's end. Peter Nitz was a fair enough start. As a newspaperman, he might offer her some leads. And there would be Dr. Max Thiel, who believed that Hitler had survived the war, as well as the East German, Professor Otto Blaubach, who might give her permission to excavate at the Führerbunker site.

Once she had finished her bath, and dried herself with the terrycloth robe provided by the hotel, Emily sought a softcup skintone bra and string nylon panties (she disliked panty hose), then dressed herself in a simple white blouse, cool pleated blue skirt, and low-heeled pumps. No stockings. She had just finished applying her makeup when she heard the buzzer and noted that Peter Nitz was exactly on time.

He proved to be a short, thickset man with thinning black hair and a receding hairline, small bright eyes, and a scraggly mustache, and he was holding a cigarette. There was a flick of a smile, but she could see he was a serious sort.

Nitz stood in the middle of the room watching her.

"I'm so pleased you could come, Mr. Nitz," she said. "Will you have lunch? I can ring room service."

"I've had lunch, thank you. But you go ahead and order for yourself."

"I had a snack on the plane. It should last me a while. Maybe you'll have something to drink?"

"Well—"

"There are some bottles on the TV, and ice."

Unceremoniously he stepped to the television set, uncapped the bottle of Scotch, dropped some ice into a glass, poured himself two fingers, and took a sip. Smacking his lips, he patted down his wet mustache and walked to the couch where Emily had seated herself. He lowered himself at the far side of the couch.

"Most of all," Emily began, "I wanted to see you to thank you in person for your kindness in sending me that letter."

"It was something I felt I had to do. I hope it didn't upset you?"

"On the contrary."

"I mean where I wrote you all I had witnessed of your father's death."

"I'm glad you were so forthcoming. I wanted to know what actually happened." She hesitated. "You suggested it might not have been an accident."

Nitz shrugged. "It could have been. It might not have been.

How does one know? I thought that the hit-and-run looked—well, deliberate. Still, I couldn't be sure. Did you speak to the Berlin police?"

"A man named Schmidt. The chief of police. He had little to offer except that they'd be watching for the truck. But he didn't even know what make of truck it was. I don't think the police will be able to do very much."

"They won't," Nitz agreed.

Emily showed her bewilderment. "But if the accident was deliberate, who would want to do it and why? My father knew few people here. As far as I know, he had no enemies."

Nitz tinkled the ice cubes in his glass and drank. "No enemies —that is, unless Adolf Hitler did survive when he was supposed to have died."

"Does anyone truly believe that?"

Nitz downed the remainder of his drink and set the glass on the coffee table. "Since the afternoon of April 30, 1945, when Hitler was supposed to have committed suicide with a bullet in his brain and his bride, Eva Braun, allegedly killed herself with potassium cyanide, the speculations have never ceased. Josef Stalin himself always believed Hitler had escaped in a submarine, possibly to Japan. General Eisenhower told reporters that there was reason to believe Hitler had slipped away unharmed. British intelligence often maintained that a Hitler double had been incinerated in the Chancellery garden. Russian identification of the charred bones, skull, and jawbone that they recovered beside the Führerbunker were always contradictory and uncertain. But you know all that, Miss Ashcroft."

"I know one thing," said Emily. "Since Hitler could not be tried at Nuremberg, he was tried in absentia by a Munich denazification court in the fall of 1947 to settle his estate. Forty-two witnesses testified as to Hitler's death. The Bavarian Ministry of Justice announced its conclusion in October of 1956. The court declared, 'There can no longer exist even the smallest doubt that Hitler took his own life on 30 April 1945 in the Führerbunker of the Reich Chancellery in Berlin by shooting himself in the right temple.' "

"Correct," Nitz said.

Emily stared at the German reporter. "In the light of that, Mr. Nitz, do you think it is possible that Hitler survived? Do you believe he got away?"

Without hesitation, Nitz replied, "No, I don't believe he got away." He paused. "But your father surely entertained that possibility. I heard him personally say so at a press conference before his death. Let me remind you, your father spoke of some evidence indicating that it was not Hitler's jawbone and teeth that had been found by the Russians. He felt that this could be verified, or dismissed, after he was able to excavate the Führerbunker area. Do you know what your father was looking for?"

"I don't, I'm sorry to say. We were about to undertake the conclusion of our biography, when my father received a letter from someone in Berlin who had been close to Hitler. This person stated that the accepted version of Hitler's death was false. My father learned that this informant was not a crank, and so he came to Berlin to see him. My father phoned me in Oxford the night before his death. He was in a jubilant mood. His informant had advised him to dig for something in the Chancellery garden area, and my father told me that he had received permission to dig. He intended to begin his excavation the day after his press conference."

"You know, of course, who his informant was—and is."

"I do. But I'd rather not mention any name until I have permission to do so."

"Do you know what he told your father to dig for?"

"No. My father didn't want to tell me on the phone. Now I hope to find out for myself." Her gaze held on Nitz. "But you think that's fruitless. You think there's no chance Hitler survived."

Nitz dug into his jacket for a package of cigarettes, plucked one out, and put a lighter to it. "Look, Miss Ashcroft, I don't want to discourage you. It would be wise to satisfy yourself. At the same time, as a journalist who has seen and heard so much nonsense, I am a cynic, and I remain a cynic in this matter. I think Hitler and his lady died as history tells us. Before you meet your dissenting informant, and maybe go off the deep end, you might speak to an actual witness who was in the Führerbunker when Hitler took his life. There are still some of them around, scattered about Germany, old people now, but many of them with vivid memories of the events of April 30, 1945. In fact, there was one of them right here in the neighborhood."

Emily sat forward. "Who?"

"Ernst E. Vogel. He was an SS bodyguard at the Führerbunker when both Hitler's corpse and that of Eva Braun were carried out and cremated. I interviewed him for a short feature about two years ago. He was very convincing as he related the facts that he remembered."

"This Herr Vogel, is he still alive?"

"I should think so. He seemed healthy enough then. You might start with seeing him before you go further. Then you can judge for yourself. I have Vogel's phone number and address in my desk at the office. I'll call it in to you as soon as I get back."

"I'd be most grateful, Mr. Nitz."

"Once you've seen Vogel, you can then see your dissenting informant, and weigh their opposing views."

Emily was silent for a few moments, watching Nitz smoke his cigarette. At last, she gave an embarrassed cough. "I have a confession to make to you, Mr. Nitz. I want to be truthful. I don't have an appointment to see the German informant my father saw, the one who was close to Hitler. So far, he's refused to see me."

Nitz's ears seemed to perk up. "He won't? Why not? He saw your father."

"Yes," said Emily. "Then, after my father's death, I wrote him that I was coming to Berlin to follow through, and I hoped he would see me and give me the same cooperation and information that he had given my father. He answered me with one line—he could not see me or anyone else about the matter." She paused. "I wonder why the change of heart?"

Nitz considered this. "He may have been scared into silence by your father's suspicious death. He may have become worried about neo-Nazi fanatics—oh, yes, some of them still exist." Noting the quick curiosity on Emily's face, Nitz decided to elaborate the point. "Miss Ashcroft, you are familiar with *Unternehmen Werwolf* created in the closing days of the war?"

Emily nodded. "Enterprise Werewolf, guerrilla groups of German soldiers established by Himmler, trained by the Waffen SS, after D day. They were dressed in civilian clothes, and were supposed to infiltrate the Allied lines and assassinate any important Germans who were collaborating with the enemy. You think there are some still around?"

"Not unlikely. They were secret fanatics determined to protect Hitler's image—and his life. Your informant might very well worry about these neo-Nazis, might fear one of them could search him out and kill him, too. I suspect your informant is simply afraid to see you."

"Well, I'm going to persuade him otherwise," Emily said with determination. "I'm going to use all the wiles I possess to make him see me."

Nitz stubbed out his cigarette and stood up. "I wish you good luck. Remember me if you get a story I might be able to use."

Emily was on her feet. "I won't forget. I owe you a good deal. Not only for your kindness, but for your suggestion about Vogel."

"Well, don't let Vogel discourage you with his firsthand stuff. Just listen to him. When you've heard him out, go after your reluctant informant even harder. Use the eyewitness stuff you learn from Vogel to bait the other man. That tactic often works. If you get lucky, go ahead with the bunker search." At the door, hand on the knob, Nitz halted, and appraised her. "Please heed one piece of advice I'm going to give you. If you *are* going ahead, if you do decide to dig, don't announce it publicly as your father did. Don't take any chances. Hit-and-run accidents in Berlin are not uncommon occurrences. Find the truth. But also stay alive."

Emily had waited restlessly in her suite for the telephone to ring.

Forty-five minutes later, true to his word, Peter Nitz had called her upon returning to his office at the *Berliner Morgenpost.* He had Ernst Vogel's telephone number and his apartment house address.

Emily had begun to thank him, when the reporter interrupted her. "Before speaking to Vogel, I think you should know something about the man," Nitz had said. "I pulled out my interview notes from two years ago, just to refresh my memory. Ernst Vogel was twenty-four on the day he claims Hitler died. That would make him sixty-four today. Vogel was an SS sergeant and honor guard on a twelve-hour shift. Very proud of the black sleeve band with 'Adolf Hitler' stitched in silver on it. On duty, he was armed with a machine gun and hand grenade. He was at the entrance to the Führerbunker during the last ten days Hitler was down there, the ten days between Hitler's fifty-sixth birthday and his announced suicide. Vogel must have been well trusted, because he got down into the bunker at several crucial moments toward the end. On the final day he was one of those who witnessed the cremation of Hitler and Braun. He'll tell you the whole story. He's a garrulous fellow with a good memory. Those ten days were the high spot in his life. If he's still around, you should find him at home. He's always worked out of his apartment."

"Doing what?"

"He runs a mail-order business. Rare books. German, of course. Oh, one more thing. You'll have to speak up when you're with him. He has a hearing defect. Both ears. From an injury suffered when he was at the Führerbunker due to the constant Russian bombardment of the Chancellery area. Anyway, try him. If he's there, I'm sure he'll see you. You can mention my name."

"I don't know how to thank you enough, Mr. Nitz."

"Never mind. Call Vogel for the standard version."

She had hung up, then dialed Ernst Vogel's number. After a few rings, a loud male voice had answered. With his impediment in mind, Emily had raised her own voice. Was this Ernst Vogel? It was. Emily had introduced herself and said that Peter Nitz, a reporter on the *Berliner Morgenpost,* had once interviewed him about Adolf Hitler's death and had thought he might be a reliable witness for her to contact. She hastily added that she had come to Berlin to wind up research on a definitive history of Hitler. She then had given Vogel her academic credentials.

"A book?" Vogel had shouted. "You are writing a book about Hitler's death?"

"Actually about his entire life, but it will include his death. I want it to be accurate. I hope you can help me."

There had been a pause. "Yes, I can help you. You've come to the right person." Another pause. "I suppose I owe it to posterity. Very well, I will see you. Do you have my address?"

Emily had read it to him.

"Exact," he had said. "Be here at four o'clock."

After that, with time to spare, she had considered also calling Dr. Max Thiel, the dentist whose doubts about Hitler's death had brought first her father and then Emily herself to Berlin. Eager to do so, she had hesitated, recalling Nitz's advice that she use whatever Vogel told her as bait to gain a meeting with Dr. Thiel.

Instead of calling, she had gone to the suitcase filled with her research files, taken out the files, sorted them. Finally, she had reviewed lists of Germans who had known Hitler or been in the Führerbunker during Hitler's final days, those people her father had already interviewed during his visits to Berlin. Ernst Vogel had not been among them. Curious, Emily had thought. Anyway, she would soon make up for the oversight.

She had taken a taxi for an eight-minute ride to what proved to be a five-story apartment building on Dahlmannstrasse, about a block and a half north off the Ku'damm. A mailbox in the small lobby had told her Ernst Vogel could be found on the floor above the street floor. Climbing the flight of stairs between scarred mahogany banisters and sickly green walls in need of fresh paint, she had arrived at Vogel's apartment.

To her surprise, the person who greeted her turned out to be a small man with sparse gray hair, a hearing aid set into one ear, an emaciated Goebbels-like face. She had imagined that all the Führerbunker SS guards had been giants.

Now, seated next to Ernst Vogel, she in an old fashioned armchair, he in a rocker, Emily intended to find out why her father had not interviewed this former SS guard.

"Another book on Hitler?" Vogel asked her once they were seated. "There have been so many. It has become an industry."

"True," said Emily calmly. "But most were written in the forties and early fifties when some of the members of Hitler's inner circle were not available to be interviewed. You may remember that they were taken to the Soviet Union for interrogation and confinement. The Soviets would not allow outsiders to see them. They were available only after they were gradually released and allowed to come back to Germany. My father thought it was time for a more complete and up-to-date biography of Hitler."

"I suppose so," said Vogel.

Emily brought her briefcase to her lap and took out one of her paperclipped lists. "These are the persons my father interviewed." She handed it to Vogel. "I could not find your name on it."

Vogel's eyes ran down the names. Handing the sheets back, he asked, "When did he interview these people?"

"He started ten years ago. He and I began writing the biography five years ago. But my father died recently, so I'm concluding the work alone."

Vogel had been leaning forward to hear her better. "Ten years ago, five years ago, I was not seeing interviewers. He probably wrote me and I did not reply. In those times, I thought I would write about my experience myself. So I would give my story to no one. Eventually I learned, despite all my notes, I am not a writer. I am a reader and a bookseller. But I wanted the story told, so I began to see interviewers. The young man on the *Morgenpost* . . ." He tried to recall the name.

"Peter Nitz."

"Yes, Nitz, he was one of the first I met with a few years ago. So you are writing a book on Hitler? I have never given an interview for a book. I suppose it will be printed in German also, and I will have copies?" He waved behind him toward the dining room area. The walls were lined with shelves of books, and the floor was littered with unopened crates. "Some are popular recently published books, but my main business is mail order of older books, rare ones. I inherited the business from my parents. They were killed in an American aerial bombing of Berlin, while I was in the army. Books are my life, but I also have a hobby. Hunting. I am a crack marksman. Have always been an expert shot since I was in kneepants. That's why I did well in the SS."

And that's how he came to be an SS guard at the Führerbunker, Emily thought. They wanted not only giants, but crack marksmen, too.

"Can we talk about Hitler?" Emily asked.

"About Hitler, I must say this. He was, in his way, a great man, no question. I had only two things against him. I did not agree with his anti-Semitism. Some of my parents' best customers were Jews. They were always decent and honest people. The other thing I held against Hitler was his trying to conquer Russia. Hitler and all his army and air force couldn't conquer Russia. That was the beginning of Hitler's downfall. But before that, he was a great man. So you want to know more about his death?"

"About the last day or two of his life. I have considerable material on what happened in the bunker. But material on his death is very contradictory."

"Everyone sees what he wants to see," said Vogel. "I can only tell you precisely what I saw and heard."

"That's exactly what I want you to do."

Vogel gently bobbed in the rocking chair as he adjusted his hearing aid. "I'm sorry, what did you say?" he asked.

"I said whatever you're prepared to tell me is exactly what I want to know," she said more slowly and distinctly. She pushed the lists back into her briefcase and withdrew a yellow pad and pen.

Vogel was fiddling with his hearing aid again. "This impairment—happened the last day—the Soviet bombardment of our Chancellery area was fierce—one explosion, the concussion from it, knocked me over—a rocket-firing Katyusha truck was nearby, I think. I had a ringing in my ears for months after that until I could get to a doctor." Satisfied with his adjustment of the hearing aid, he faced her directly. "Hitler knew it was the end five days before it happened. We knew that the Russians had encircled Berlin and were beginning to penetrate its perimeters. That's when he told Linge—Heinz Linge, the SS colonel who was his valet and head of his personal bodyguard—that he did not intend to be taken alive. 'I will shoot myself. When I do, carry my body into the Chancellery garden. After my death, no one must see me and recognize me. After I am cremated, go to my private rooms in the bunker, collect all my papers, and burn them also.' Hitler reaffirmed this decision to Otto Günsche, his SS adjutant and chauffeur. 'I want my body burned,' he said. 'After my death I don't want to be put on exhibition in a Russian zoo.' "

Emily was making her notes. Vogel waited. She looked up. "Those were his words?"

"So I heard. You know most of the events in the bunker, you say. What you want are details of the last day."

"Well, the last two days."

"All right. Let us begin with the evening of April 28, in 1945. Hitler announced that he was going to marry Eva Braun. To legitimize their long love affair and to repay her loyalty after she vowed she was going to die in the bunker with him. Anyway, Josef Goebbels found a justice of the peace, the very one who had married him and Magda. The justice was pulled out of a Volkssturm detachment fighting along the Friedrichstrasse. The marriage certificate was prepared, and signed by two witnesses, Goebbels and Martin Bormann. The wedding ceremony was held after midnight. About twelve-thirty in the morning on April 29. There were eight guests. They all celebrated with a small banquet after. Eva became slightly drunk on champagne. Hitler drank some, too, and tried to join the mood of gaiety. But once he was heard to mutter, 'It is all finished. Death will be a relief for me. I have been betrayed and deceived by everyone.' He meant Göring and Himmler, who—without authority—had tried to sue for peace and save their own necks, and some of his generals, who had lied to him."

Vogel watched Emily making her notes.

He resumed. From the smoothness of his telling, Emily realized that he had recounted the same story many times and was comfortable with it.

"In that underground bunker there was no day or night,"

said Vogel. "Hitler usually worked through the night and slept all morning. Before the wedding he called in his favorite secretary, Traudl Junge, and dictated two wills to her—a short testament in which he explained why he was marrying Eva Braun, and a longer political testament explaining the same nonsense about how the war had been forced on him by international Jewry. He waited up until Frau Junge had typed his three-page personal testament, and his ten-page political one, then he signed them and had his signatures witnessed, and then he was ready for sleep. But you know all that, don't you, Fräulein Ashcroft?"

"Most of it. What came next is what is most important to me. I hope you will omit nothing, Herr Vogel."

Vogel went back and forth in his rocking chair. "That morning, and between four-thirty and five-thirty A.M. on April 30, were the only times Hitler and Eva slept together as man and wife. At eleven in the morning on April 29, they were awake. By noon Hitler had held his last war conference, by rote, pointless. Next he sent off couriers with his testaments to get them out of Berlin. Then he began to get ready for death."

"Tell me how."

"He was worried about the efficiency of the potassium cyanide that Himmler had once given him. He wondered whether the capsules still had their potency and whether Himmler had given him the right ones. He wanted to be sure."

"That was when Hitler tried out a poison capsule on his dog."

"Ah, you know," said Vogel.

She could not tell if he was pleased with her knowledge or irked at being preempted. She decided not to show off her knowledge, but to let him tell as much as possible in his own words.

"His dog, yes," Vogel resumed. "Hitler summoned one of his four doctors in the bunker, Dr. Werner Haase. With considerable reluctance, Hitler said he wanted to learn whether the capsules were dependable and decided that a capsule should be tried out on his favorite Alsatian, Blondi. Dr. Haase forced a capsule into the dog's mouth. He reported to Hitler, 'Death was almost instantaneous.' This satisfied Hitler. That day Hitler also parted with his favorite possession. It was an oval painting of Frederick the Great that had hung over his bunker desk. Hitler had always worshipped Frederick because in 1762, near the end of the Seven Years' War and about to suffer defeat at the hands of the Russians, Saxons, and Austrians, Frederick had miraculously managed to survive when the alliance fell apart upon the czarina's death. Hitler took down this painting of Frederick and gave it to his favorite pilot Hans Bauer. He asked Bauer to keep it or preserve it in a museum. When Bauer tried to escape later, he took the painting out of its frame and slid it under his shirt. But the Russians caught and interned him—and presumably the painting as well."

Vogel went on to recall what of consequence had happened next. "By nine that evening—Sunday, the twenty-ninth—Hitler received a news flash, transmitted by Stockholm radio, that Mussolini had been caught in northern Italy by partisans and executed along with his mistress Clara Petacci. It is unlikely that Hitler knew the horrible aftermath. In any case, he didn't appear interested. At midnight, he learned that Berlin could not be defended any longer and that Russian soldiers would reach the Chancellery during the coming day. At two-thirty in the morning Hitler wanted to say good-bye to his immediate staff. Twenty of the staff lined up in the bunker corridor, and Hitler, with Bormann at his side, shuffled down the line briefly shaking hands with each. Near daybreak Hitler went to sleep with Eva."

"When did you say he awakened?"

"At five-thirty A.M. on April 30. His last day. He was told that the Russians were coming through the Tiergarten, had reached Potsdamer Platz, and one Soviet unit was no more than a block from the Chancellery and the bunker itself."

"Wasn't he scared?"

"Quite calm," said Vogel. "Perhaps catatonic. He knew the end had come. He ordered Günsche to round up two hundred liters of gasoline or petrol—"

"The same thing," said Emily, writing.

"Günsche phoned Kempka, the chauffeur who was in charge of transport supplies, and asked for the two hundred liters. Kempka couldn't imagine why so much was needed. He said there was not that much on hand and it would be risky to search for more. Günsche told him to find what he could, and bring the filled jerricans to the Führerbunker exit that opened into the garden. Kempka finally found one hundred eighty liters—there were about twenty liters in each jerrican—and got three strong SS guards to help him roll them up to the garden. While this was happening, about two-thirty in the afternoon, Hitler calmly decided to have his last lunch. He asked his two favorite secretaries, Frau Trudl Junge and Frau Gerda Christian, and his somewhat timid vegetarian cook, Fräulein Konstanze Manzialy, to join him. Eva Braun Hitler did not join them. They ate spaghetti and sauce, and a tossed salad. Meanwhile, the Russian artillery was sending barrage after barrage of shells into the area. One shell exploded near the bunker entrance, where I was standing guard, and the force of it knocked me over. I was terribly frightened. I crawled down the steps into the corridor to protect myself. That's when I saw, with my own eyes, Hitler's second and last farewell at the end of the corridor. He had just come out of his private rooms with Eva behind him. He was wearing his usual visored cap, field-gray jacket with the Iron Cross pinned on it, and black trousers and shoes. Frau Hitler was wearing a dark blue polka-dot dress and her imported Italian pumps. There were twelve men and five women in the corridor this time, as far as I could count. All lined up before the framed Italian paintings on the corridor wall. Hitler was limply shaking hands with everyone. Eva was hugging the women, and allowing the men to kiss her hand. Then Hitler and Eva went back to their rooms, as the others dispersed. At this point, Magda Goebbels burst out of her quarters and tried to speak to Hitler. Günsche blocked her way. Magda screamed something like, 'I must see him. He cannot commit suicide. There is still time to take off for Berchtesgaden.' So insistent was Magda that Günsche repeated Magda's message. Hitler mumbled, 'Too late, too late for anything.' Linge had joined Günsche, and Hitler said to Linge, 'Linge, old friend, I want you to join the breakout group and get away.' Linge asked, 'Why, my Führer?' Hitler replied, 'To serve the man who will come after me.' Then he added to Linge, 'Close the door. Wait in the anteroom. After ten minutes, open the door and come inside.' Then he and Eva killed themselves."

Emily interrupted. "But no one saw it?"

Vogel replied, testily, "How could they? His last instructions were to be left alone."

"How did they know he and Eva killed themselves?"

"Because after ten minutes they opened his door and found them both dead on the blue and white velvet sofa."

"They must have heard the shot?"

"They heard nothing. The steel double door to Hitler's private quarters was not only fireproof and gasproof, but also soundproof."

"Some historians wrote that a shot was heard."

Vogel shook his head vigorously. "No, no. That was a mistake. When Kempka rushed into the bunker later, to find out what was happening, Günsche told him Hitler was dead. Günsche used a familiar gesture, pointing a finger into his mouth as if it were a pistol, although he knew that Hitler had shot himself in the temple. Later, when Kempka was interrogated by American and British intelligence officers, they asked him whether he'd heard the suicide shot. Kempka knew what they wanted to hear, so he told them that everyone had heard the shot. Actually, no one had heard any shot."

"After ten minutes, when Hitler's aides entered his room, were you among them?"

"No," said Vogel regretfully. "I was ordered back to my post outside the bunker entrance. But I saw more afterward and I will tell you about that. Anyway, I heard what happened when the others went into Hitler's living room. Linge entered first, and he was nauseated by the smell of bitter almond and cordite in the room. He was followed by Bormann, Günsche, Goebbels, and Artur Axmann, head of the Hitler Youth, who had just arrived."

"They all saw Hitler dead?" said Emily.

"Saw both of them dead. Hitler was slumped in the left corner of the sofa. He had bitten a cyanide capsule and also, with his right hand, put the muzzle of the black Walther 7.65 pistol to his right temple at eyebrow level and pulled the trigger. The shot drilled a hole into his temple and blood was oozing from the wound. His pistol had slipped down to the carpet."

"And Eva Braun Hitler?"

"She was two feet away. She had kicked off her pumps, tucked her legs under her. She had bitten into the cyanide capsule and fallen against Hitler, her legs knocking over a white Dresden vase of tulips on the coffee table. She had apparently considered also using a pistol, a smaller Walther, but Linge found it unused on the table, its chambers still fully loaded. Dr. Ludwig Stumpfegger, an orthopedic surgeon, was summoned. He examined them, and pronounced them both dead."

"Both dead," repeated Emily. "Then the cremation?"

"I saw much of it myself," said Vogel quietly. "Horrifying." He was lost in thought a moment, then began speaking again. "Along with several other guards, I was one of the *Zaungäste*—what you would call peeping Toms. I was told the valet Linge threw a brown army blanket over the upper part of Hitler's body, covering his bloody face. Linge carried Hitler from his private room through the anteroom into the corridor toward the bottom of the stairwell leading up to the emergency exit into the garden. But Hitler weighed about one hundred eighty pounds and was too heavy for Linge alone. He handed the body over to the three young SS men, who carried it head first up the four flights of stairs. After that came Bormann, carrying Eva, partially covered with a blanket but her face clearly visible. Kempka told me Bormann was carrying her like 'a sack of potatoes.' Kempka knew how much Eva had disliked Bormann in life, so he snatched her body away from Bormann, and turned it over to Günsche who carried it up the stairs with the help of two more SS men. Briefly, between Russian shell bursts, I could hear or sense that something was happening alongside the Führerbunker. So I left my post and came around to see what was taking place."

"You saw them bury the two?"

"I saw it all," said Vogel. "The three SS men had come out hauling Hitler's body from the bunker."

"Could you see his face?"

"It was still covered. But I could plainly see his familiar black trousers and thick shoes sticking out from under the blanket. About ten meters from the exit there was a shallow trench. Hitler's body was lowered into it. Then they brought out Eva Braun. I could see her face. It looked peaceful. Also, I could see her feet in her Ferragamo shoes outside the blanket. They lowered her corpse into the trench beside Hitler. Immediately, nine of them came out of the bunker to watch in the windy afternoon. I recognized Linge, Goebbels, and Bormann, also Dr. Stumpfegger." Vogel winced at the memory of those moments. "Two of the SS men came forward with jerricans, and started dumping gasoline on the bodies—I would guess about fifty gallons. Linge tried to light something and set the bodies aflame, but a series of shell bursts drove them back into the bunker emergency exit. At last,

Linge managed to light an improvised torch, either some paper twisted into a cone or a rag, and he came forward and succeeded in throwing it on the doused bodies. Instantly, there was a blue flame and smoke. The nine witnesses who had retreated all lifted their arms in the old Nazi salute. The flames grew higher. The witnesses went back into the bunker and I crept back to my post."

"The cremation was over?"

"Not quite. It was not easy to burn two bodies in a shallow trench. Orders had been given to continue pouring gasoline on the bodies. So for three or four hours SS guards kept returning to the trench to pour more and more jerricans of gasoline on the cadavers. Then, before nightfall, while it was still light, I decided to have a look for myself."

"And you saw the remains of Hitler and Braun."

Vogel nodded. "No one was in sight, so I sneaked over to the trench. The flames were simmering down. I thought I could make out the contours of Hitler's face. It was terribly hot. Both bodies were steaming, the flesh on each boiled away. The lower part of Hitler had burned completely. I could only see his shinbones. As for Eva Braun's body, you couldn't recognize her, only that it was the charred body of a female. I turned aside and vomited. After that, I learned, the two bodies were buried."

"Did anyone tell you where?" Emily asked.

"I was told that SS Brigadeführer Johann Rattenhuber, chief of bunker security, ordered three other SS guards to remove the corpses from the shallow trench and bury them nearby. The SS guards got a piece of canvas tent, somehow placed what was left of the bodies, the bones and ashes, on the canvas and dragged it to a deeper shell crater not far away. They covered the crater with loose earth and rubble, and pounded the earth down with either a wooden rammer or shovel. I heard that Axmann had joined them and asked the guards to scoop up some of Hitler's ashes and put them in a box, which he carried away, God knows to where. Following that, the others in the bunker broke out, trying to save their lives. I was ordered to stay behind, along with three more SS guards, to dispose of any security leftovers inside the bunker. We all drank and slept a little, and then by morning the first Russians appeared in the bunker. They were from the NKVD. They wanted to know about Hitler. I told them what I've just told you. They wanted to see the burial site. One of our men led them to the dirt-filled crater. Shortly after, the Russians dug it up and from the pit came up with Hitler's jawbone. They managed to match the teeth to X rays of Hitler's teeth found in a dental file. They were satisfied that Hitler had died, and later been buried in the Führerbunker garden. There you have it, Fräulein Ashcroft."

Emily sat very still, resting her cramped writing hand. It sounded so real, so authentic, as if it were an event beyond all possible doubt.

Still, Emily had her job, her father's job, and she found herself blurting out, "The remains—the jawbone—could it have been that of anyone but Hitler?"

Momentarily, Vogel looked startled. "How could it have been anyone else?"

Emily reminded herself that Hitler's suicide had been the central point of Vogel's life, his entire life, this oft-told story, and that he would never suspect it or give it up.

And it sounded true. This she had to admit to herself. There had been so many witnesses, so many. Could all of them have agreed to lie? Impossible. Or been misled? Unlikely. Or had they wanted to believe because it had been, as it was for Vogel, a great historical moment in their lives, and they had wanted it to be true? Had it all really happened as just recited, and was it the full truth?

Emily wondered whether this was truer than the suspicions of one possibly crackpot dentist. Unless she saw the dentist and he was absolutely persuasive, she would have to buy Vogel's story, the accepted version, for the climax of the book. It was possible her father had been wrong, had been taken in. It was probable that what she had just heard was the whole truth, and that she did not need to pry further. She could safely finish the book with this account.

But the dissent still nagged at her. She had always respected her father, his diligence, his steadiness, his objectivity, and there had been *something* that disturbed him about the historical version. Besides, the reporter Nitz had warned her: *Don't let Vogel discourage you too much. . . . After you've heard him out, go after your reluctant informant even harder. Use the straight stuff you learn from Vogel to bait your dissenter.*

She realized that she must go on a step farther. One more step was demanded. If that was not the truth, then this was.

She was on her feet thanking Vogel, and promising to send him one of the first copies of the book.

Back in her suite at the Kempinski, Emily found herself wavering once more.

Ernst Vogel had been so convincing about the certainty of Hitler's death and burial in 1945 that any effort to refute it seemed utter foolishness. Perhaps her father's last quest in Berlin had been quixotic, a slippage from his normal stability, the sign of an inexplicable desire to produce a sensation in his waning years. Perhaps she, like most daughters, was automatically acting out the Freudian relationship that tied daughters to fathers. The father could do no wrong. In this civil war of uncertainty, she was almost prepared to retreat. Pack her bags, get out of Berlin, return to Oxford and finish the damn book.

But still the paternal ghost was watching her. She hesitated. It was difficult to disown her heritage so abruptly.

Although filled with doubt, she walked slowly into the bedroom, picked up the file of recent correspondence she had carried from Oxford, sat on the edge of the bed and leafed through it. She pulled out the letter to her father that had started all this—the letter from the dentist, Dr. Max Thiel of West Berlin. She began to reread it. "All histories to date on Adolf Hitler and Eva Braun may have been wrong in one major respect. It is quite possible that Hitler and Braun did not commit suicide in the Führerbunker in 1945. Both may very well have survived. I believe I have the evidence to prove it." She fingered the letter and recalled that her father had met with Dr. Thiel, and had been impressed enough to arrange to dig in the area of the Führerbunker for new evidence overlooked until now.

Emily continued through the file of correspondence. She found the copy of her letter in which she had written to Dr. Thiel that she intended to go on with her father's investigation, and that she needed Dr. Thiel's help. He was crucial to her research, she had written him, and it was imperative that she meet with him. Paperclipped to her letter was Dr. Thiel's curt one-sentence reply. "Dear Miss Ashcroft, I am sorry I cannot see you or anyone else about this matter."

Then something her father had said in their final conversation came back to her. He had said, "Emily, our book must be the last word, the absolute truth, the final word."

Quixotic? No. He had been onto something.

Emily put the file aside, resolutely marched into the sitting room, and placed herself before the telephone on the desk. Quickly, she dialed Dr. Max Thiel's number.

A ring. Two rings. A pickup.

An old woman's voice in German. "Yes?"

"Is this the residence of Dr. Max Thiel?"

A short silence. "Who is speaking?"

"I am the daughter of Dr. Harrison Ashcroft. I must speak to Dr. Thiel. I have come from England to speak to him."

"A moment, please."

Emily could hear muffled voices in the background. She waited tensely.

Her father had told her that when he talked to Dr. Thiel on the phone, the dentist's deep voice had been unfaltering and assured. After meeting with Dr. Thiel, her father had reported that the dentist had also been most friendly.

Yet the voice she heard now, a man's voice, was somewhat less than friendly, even gruff.

"Who is this?"

"Dr. Thiel? My name is Emily Ashcroft." Briefly, she told him about herself, and reminded him of her father and their book. "You invited Dr. Ashcroft to call on you. He did so, and found you most cooperative and gracious. I have come to Berlin to follow through on my father's work, Dr. Thiel–"

"Please do not use my name on the phone again," he said sharply.

"I'm sorry. I won't, if you don't wish me to."

"I don't wish you to. It is unwise."

She could sense a certain fear in his voice, and expected him to hang up. She spoke quickly. "I have come here to Berlin to talk with you."

"Impossible."

"But you saw my father. You were willing to help my father."

"Look what happened to him," Dr. Thiel responded, more gruffly than before.

"It was an accident."

Dr. Thiel's voice softened slightly. "Maybe. Maybe it was an accident. I am not sure." He hesitated. "I am sorry for your loss." Then he added stubbornly, "Anyway, I want to take no risks. Please do not bother me again. You go write what you wish."

"I wish to write the truth," she said emotionally. She remembered what Nitz had suggested. Use Vogel's account to bait the informant. "I suppose I can only use what Ernst Vogel told me–"

"Who?"

"Ernst Vogel. He was an SS sergeant and honor guard at the Führerbunker. He witnessed Hitler's last days. I saw him today. He confirmed what Linge, Günsche, and Kempka had given as sworn evidence. Vogel insists Hitler shot himself, and that he saw Hitler carried out to the bunker garden and cremated. He backed the standard story. He implied that any other version of Hitler's end could come only from cranks and crackpots."

Dr. Thiel took the bait. "Vogel is an absolute fool," he snapped with annoyance. "He believes what he was brainwashed to believe. I know of him. He is an idiot guard who never knew Hitler."

"But you knew Hitler?" she said innocently.

"Of course I did. Too well."

"And you knew something else that you had passed on to my father. It's a pity you won't tell me what you told him. Now I'll be forced to perpetuate the lie, not tell the truth, let history remain warped."

There was a short silence. "Does it really matter after forty years? Let sleeping dogs lie."

"But you hint that they may not be sleeping," she said passionately. "Yes, I think it does matter that everything about Hitler be known at last. So that such a man will not come among us again. If Hitler is still alive, he must be exposed and punished. He must not be allowed to go free. The truth matters very much, sir. My father thought so. I am his daughter and I think so. Do you believe the Vogels of the world should be allowed to perpetuate their false myths, if indeed they are myths? If there is more to the story, I wish you'd help me. For my father's sake. He was a good man who—"

"Yes, he was a good man," Dr. Thiel assented. "I found him

most charming. But he was a reckless man, and perhaps he paid for it." He hesitated. "Well, now, perhaps I am a reckless man, too. Maybe I can see you for just a little while. If we meet quietly, and no publicity this time."

"None. I shall be a mouse, I promise you."

"Very well. You have my address. I have an hour before dinner. Can you come over immediately?"

"Immediately."

Emily sat forward on what was the single chair in the small dental laboratory located in the business wing of Dr. Thiel's spacious two-story brick house set back from a wide boulevard called Heerstrasse, west of the river Havel and about twenty-five minutes by taxi from the Kempinski hotel. Dr. Max Thiel sat across from her, perched on a high white stool, one elbow on the formica counter behind him.

He was friendly and courteous from the moment of her entrance. He was a tall, stooped man, heronlike, with fine gray hair combed sideways, alert blue eyes behind gold-rimmed spectacles, a long horsy face. He wore a dark summer suit, white shirt, plain navy tie pressed against a starched collar. She judged him to be in his eighties.

After showing her into his laboratory, he had disappeared and returned bringing a tray holding two cups of tea and a plate of cookies sent by his wife, who had not appeared.

He had lifted himself onto the stool, noisily sipped at his cup of tea, and finally set the cup aside on the counter before speaking.

"So, Miss Ashcroft, we are here. Did your father tell you anything of our meeting a few weeks ago?"

"Nothing, except that whatever you told him excited him, and encouraged him to arrange for an excavation. He indicated that there was too much to go into on the phone, and that he would tell me about it when he returned to Oxford. So I know nothing of what happened between you. Only that it was of great importance."

"Now you shall know," said Dr. Thiel.

She leaned toward him with anticipation.

"You understand, of course, that the Soviets were the only ones to investigate Adolf Hitler's supposed death and burial."

"Yes, we have the records concerning his autopsy on file at Oxford. I have not reviewed them recently. I was going to study them when I reached the concluding chapter of the Hitler biography."

"To make the best use of our time, let me summarize for you the findings of the various Soviet investigators. To begin with, you must realize one vital omission in all the evidence. No one actually saw Hitler kill himself. No one saw Eva Braun kill herself. Not one person ever claimed that. We only know the scenario that the Soviets, as well as British, French, and American interrogators, heard from the Germans in and around the Führerbunker in April 1945. We heard the testimony that, with his cause hopeless and the Third Reich crumbling, Hitler planned to kill himself. After that we heard that he and his wife had committed suicide in privacy, had been seen lying dead, had been taken outdoors and put to the torch. But beyond the words of his staff and security guards, there never was any scientific proof that the couple that committed suicide was really Adolf and Eva. To prove a crime, self-inflicted or otherwise, it has generally been the rule of all courts to invoke the need for a *corpus delicti*—the material substance or body of the victim of violence. In this case there were no bodies—no corpses—to examine. The bodies had been hastily cremated, reduced to flaky ashes and charred bones. Without the bodies, how could any investigators be scientifically certain that Hitler and his wife had ended their lives?"

"But there was some material evidence," Emily interjected.

Dr. Thiel nodded. "Some. The Soviet investigators were convinced that Hitler and Eva were dead. But I was not convinced that they had actually died."

Emily's heart leaped at the last words. No wonder her father had been excited. She was becoming excited herself.

Still, she tried to contain her feelings, make one last feeble attempt at playing the devil's advocate. "Dr. Thiel, what you are saying is that Hitler may have survived and got away. If this happened, how could he have escaped? From transcripts I have seen, on this last day when the Soviets were ringing his bunker, he couldn't have got away on foot or by car. Possibly by airplane. But we were told by Hanna Reitsch, the woman pilot who visited him at the eleventh hour, that she herself flew the last available plane, an Arado-96, out of Berlin. Even Oberführer Hans Bauer, Hitler's own pilot, couldn't find a plane when he was ready to escape. He had to break out on foot and was captured and held in Russia until 1955. Besides, there were no German airfields left to take off from. SS Colonel Otto Skorzeny, the commando, testified that there wasn't a single airport left for the Nazis to use." Emily threw up her hands. "If Hitler survived, how could he have got away?"

Dr. Thiel's answer was simple. "I don't know, Fräulein Ashcroft. That's for you to find out. All I know, feel certain about, is that Hitler did survive his supposed suicide. He was not cremated that fateful day. The Soviets were wrong in their announcement, and I think I can prove it."

Once more, Emily felt a surge of hope and a rush of curiosity. In silence she waited for Dr. Thiel's evidence.

"Let me tell you what the Soviets found, and then I will tell you what I found," continued Dr. Thiel. "On the day before Hitler's supposed death, the Soviet command already inside Berlin organized a small special team of NKVD officers from the Russian Third Assault Army, assisted by a female interpreter named Yelena Rzhevskaya, to find Hitler's whereabouts, to locate Hitler dead or alive. Lieutenant Colonel Ivan Klimenko, a Soviet interrogator, officially led his own team to the Führerbunker. It was known by the Russians that this deep Führerbunker existed, and that Hitler already had spent one hundred five days inside it. Shortly before Klimenko began his search, other Russians had been directed to the Führerbunker, including twelve women doctors from the Red Army Medical Corps and around twenty Soviet officers. They had not been looking for Hitler, only for souvenirs. These booty-hunters confiscated everything from lamps to monogrammed silverware to Eva Braun's black satin French brassieres. On May 2, 1945, two days after Hitler's announced demise, Klimenko arrived at the Führerbunker and investigated it. By evening he had examined a male body that another team had found stuffed into an oak water tank. He ordered it laid out on the floor of a hall in the Old Chancellery next door and tentatively identified it as Hitler's corpse. Nevertheless, two days later, Klimenko returned to the Führerbunker. In a bomb crater in the Chancellery garden, Private Ivan Churakov had discovered the remains of a man and a woman. 'Of course,' said Klimenko, 'at first I didn't even think that these might be the corpses of Hitler and Eva Braun, since I believed that Hitler's corpse was already in the Chancellery and only needed to be identified. I therefore ordered the corpses to be wrapped in blankets and reburied.' Meanwhile, inside the Chancellery, German officers and diplomats who had known Hitler agreed that the first body, now lying on the hallway floor, was not Hitler. Possibly a double. But not the Führer. Then Klimenko remembered the two bodies he had ordered reburied in the bomb crater three meters from the Führerbunker's emergency exit. With a team, in a jeep, Klimenko rushed back to the site. Let me read to you what happened next."

Dr. Thiel opened a drawer beside him and pulled out a sheaf of papers and some photographic negatives.

"And they dug up the two corpses again," said Emily.

Dr. Thiel nodded, as he studied his notes. "Yes. The bodies were still wrapped in blankets. The Russians placed the bodies in wooden boxes, and sent them by truck to a field hospital in Berlin-Buch, a suburb of Berlin to the north. Here the extensive autopsies were begun by Soviet specialists."

"On the bodies?" asked Emily. "But there were no bodies."

"They weren't bodies in the strictest sense," replied Dr. Thiel. "These were actually remains of bodies. Let me read from the Soviet report. Concerning the male corpse, 'In view of the fact that the corpse is greatly damaged, it is difficult to gauge the age of the deceased. Presumably it lies between fifty and sixty years. The corpse is severely charred and smells of burned flesh. Part of the cranium is missing. Parts of the occipital bone, the left temporal bone, and the upper and lower jaws are preserved. The skin on the face and body is completely missing; only remnants of charred muscles are preserved.' " Dr. Thiel looked up. "No skin, therefore no fingerprints available." Dr. Thiel consulted the papers in his hand. "The next report. 'In view of the fact that the body parts are extensively charred, it is impossible to describe the features of the dead woman. The age of the dead woman lies between thirty and forty years.' Again, no fingerprints. However, the Soviet specialists had, they decided, an equally dependable means of identification. They possessed the upper and lower jawbones of both corpses, with teeth and dentures intact."

"Exactly what did they have to work from?"

"The male's upper and lower bridges. One had an old-fashioned window crown made of yellow metal, gold, that fitted on a molar. Then there was a gold bridge from Eva Braun's jawbone. The Soviet interpreter, Yelena Rzhevskaya, was able to run down Fräulein Käthe Heusemann, who had been assistant to Hitler's dentist, Dr. Hugo Blaschke, and Fritz Echtmann, the dental technician who had made the bridges. Fräulein Heusemann led the investigators to Dr. Blaschke's hospital office in the ruins of the Chancellery. There the last X rays of Hitler's and Braun's teeth were located, and these were compared to the bridges from the corpses that the Soviets kept in an old cigar box inside a satchel. The actual bridges matched the earlier X rays of Hitler's and Braun's teeth. While the Soviet Forensic Medical Commission required only ten matching points for positive identification, the commission claimed to have found twenty-six matching points. From this forensic autopsy, the Soviets announced on July 9, 1945, that they had finally found the remains of Adolf Hitler and Eva Braun."

"But you disagree," said Emily. "You do not believe they found Hitler and Braun. Why?"

"Because I, too, was one of Hitler's personal dentists. When Hitler no longer trusted Dr. Blaschke with certain specialized work, he brought me in. He wanted no problem with Dr. Blaschke, so my role was kept secret. As a consequence, since my dental work was unknown to others, I was not interrogated by the Soviets. I managed to obtain copies of the reports in which the Soviets explained their positive identification. I was able to compare their findings with my own work on Hitler. The bridges were the same with one minute difference. When I adjusted Hitler's bridges, I had added a tiny almost invisible clasp to Hitler's upper plate to make it fit snugly on the gold crown. This tiny clasp was not on the bridge that the Soviets had, according to their autopsy reports. This made me suspicious of what the Russians had found."

"But maybe your device on the bridge melted away," Emily speculated.

Dr. Thiel gestured impatiently. "No, no, impossible. The clasp device was gold. If it had burned, the entire bridge would have melted. No, I feel certain that the male corpse that the Russians identified as Hitler was a double, with dentures redone to match Hitler's own, but my added device was missing. However, if the body that was cremated was that of a Hitler double, I was left with a question. If that was a fake Hitler, what had happened to the real Hitler?"

"Is that why you suggested to my father that he dig in the garden of the Führerbunker again?"

"I suggested that he should search one last time for two pieces of evidence—another jawbone with another dental bridge, the very one I fixed for Hitler, the real one. If you, Fräulein Ashcroft, found that, you would know that Hitler had died and been cremated as so many claim."

"Dr. Thiel, that is only one thing to look for. You said there were two. What is the other?"

Dr. Thiel was shuffling through his papers. He held up one sheet. "See this?"

Emily moved closer. It was a crude pen sketch that resembled some kind of cameo bearing a man's face.

"What is that?" she asked.

"The second piece of evidence you must search for if you are allowed to dig in the garden. It is a cameo that Hitler wore on a chain around his neck, on his chest actually. Probably no one but Eva, who slept with him, knew that he wore it. I happened to see it quite by accident. The last time I did dental surgery on Hitler, I put him under a general anesthetic. First, to make him more comfortable, I opened the top button of his shirt. There, against his body, on his chest, lay this cameo, obviously a good-luck piece."

"What was it—whose face in the cameo?"

"You know the oil painting that Hitler kept with him wherever he traveled for six years, the one that hung above his desk in the Führerbunker right up to the end, the one he gave to his private pilot Bauer to carry away to safety before the Russians came? This cameo was a reproduction of the face in his favorite oil."

"The face of Frederick the Great."

Dr. Thiel's long countenance offered a complimentary smile. "One and the same. We are told that Hitler died and was cremated while fully clothed. If so, he would still have been wearing this cameo beneath his tunic and shirt when he was buried. No one had time to look. Yet the Soviets never found it, probably never even knew about it. So if that was actually Hitler's body the Soviets found, the cameo would still be there lost in the rubble and dirt. If you dig, and can find either the cameo or the gold bridge I worked on, you will have found the real Adolf Hitler and be able to confirm that the Soviets were correct in assuming Hitler was cremated and buried in the garden. But in digging, you must dig more thoroughly than anyone before. If you come away empty-handed, then it is very probable that Hitler did not die as the Soviets announced. You would have sound evidence that Hitler survived his supposed end and got away."

Emily had only one uncertainty. "What if Hitler took off his Frederick the Great cameo and draped its chain around the neck of his double?"

"I don't think he would have ever considered that. If he escaped, he escaped with the cameo still around his neck. It was his eternal good-luck charm. And if not the cameo, then there is still the gold bridge I prepared."

Emily's eyes held on Dr. Thiel. "So you think that I should dig?"

Dr. Thiel nodded his assent slowly. "Dig, Fräulein Ashcroft, dig deep if you want the truth. And should you come upon the truth, don't tell a soul—until you are far from Berlin and ready to tell the world. Yes, Fräulein, dig and be silent."

4

So here she was, at last, seated in the back of the air-conditioned Mercedes next to Peter Nitz and heading toward the wall that divided the two worlds of West Berlin and East Berlin.

Emily Ashcroft had awakened early, inspired by her meeting with Hitler's dentist and filled with determination to solve the mystery of Hitler's last days in hiding.

Her first move, after ordering breakfast, had been to contact a special operator and telephone Professor Otto Blaubach at his government offices in East Berlin. He had taken her call immediately, and had been the model of cordiality. Yes, he had received her letter, had been awaiting the call, and looked forward to a reunion with her. He would be delighted to see her again in East Berlin. Would two o'clock this afternoon do? Emily had told him that the time was perfect.

After breakfast, it had occurred to her that she had visited the East sector only once before, three years ago while accompanying her father. Her father had taken care of everything, and the crossover had seemed simple. This afternoon she would be alone, on her own. Her destination seemed more than ever alien, and she wanted an escort, someone familiar with East Berlin.

About to ring the concierge to ask for a private car with a knowledgeable driver, she had thought of someone else. She had phoned the *Berliner Morgenpost* and found Peter Nitz at his desk.

"I'm looking for a guide," she had finally said. "I'm going over to East Berlin, and it makes me a little nervous. I know this is nonsense, still—"

"You're quite right," Nitz had said. "I can help you. I have someone who is trustworthy. He is an independent chauffeur named Irwin Plamp."

"Plamp?"

"Perhaps a peculiar name for you. Like a mispronouncing of *plump.* He is plump. He goes to East Berlin almost daily. My newspaper uses him all the time. He drives a new Mercedes sedan. When do you want him?"

"This afternoon. I have an appointment at two o'clock with Professor Otto Blaubach, the deputy minister, in his government office."

"I'll see if Plamp is free. If he isn't I'll let you know. Otherwise he will be at your hotel. I think you should be ready at one o'clock."

"Perfect."

"I assume you are trying to get permission to make an excavation in the garden near the Führerbunker?"

"Exactly."

"Miss Aschcroft, have you seen the Führerbunker since 1961 when it was enclosed by the wall?"

"Yes, I have. I saw it briefly three years ago, and I'm fairly well informed about East Germany through my father's research."

"Perhaps I can fill you in a bit more before your meeting with Professor Blaubach. I should be only too glad to act as your guide into East Berlin."

"Would you? That would be wonderful, Mr. Nitz."

And now here they were in the rear of Plamp's cool Mercedes, Nitz agreeing to address her as Emily and she agreeing to call him Peter, and they were approaching a dirty gray concrete obstruction on their left. Nitz ordered the driver to stop.

"*Die Mauer,*" said Nitz. "The Wall."

"Appalling!" Emily exclaimed. She stared at the forbidding barrier of concrete.

"Hard to believe it went up overnight," said Nitz. "The Deutsche Demokratische Republik—the East German government—insisted they had built it to protect their population from Western invasion. You and I know better. In the dozen years before it was built, one-fifth of the East Berlin population left their homes and crossed over to West Germany. In fact, in the last month before the Wall went up, over one hundred forty thousand East Germans fled into West Germany. In the years since, seventy-two East Berliners have been killed trying to scale the Wall into West Germany.

"The entire wall between the two Germanys covers about one hundred twenty kilometers—for you, seventy-five miles—more than eighty-five percent of it originally solid concrete, the rest of it composed of wire fences. The actual Wall between West and East Berlin runs about forty-six kilometers or twenty-nine miles. Its average height is three point five meters, which translates to eleven and a half feet. Right here . . ."

Emily saw that they had turned and were driving parallel with the Wall. She saw again what she had seen on her previous visit. The Wall was a riot of graffiti—slogans and art—sprayed or painted on nearly every foot of it. It was topped, all the way, by some sort of concrete pipe.

"Beyond the Wall, as you have seen for yourself, over on the East German side," said Nitz, "there is still a squared-off military zone, with plenty of barbed wire and anti-tank crosses. These have deep underground supports. This so-called Frontier Security Zone has tall concrete watchtowers at intervals, each occupied by three East German soldiers, holding machine guns or using their binoculars. Inside the zone stands what is left of the Führerbunker. Not much to see, as you know."

Emily noted that they were slowing down as they approached a vacant lot overgrown with weeds that featured nearby a cluster of sightseeing buses, tourist cars, a flea market, a refreshment shop, a souvenir store with revolving stands of postcards, color transparencies, and maps for sale outside. Off to the right, only a dozen yards from the Wall, stood an observation structure with a platform on top, crowded with tourists peering across the Wall and into the area that was the East Berlin Security Zone.

"We will park here in the old Potsdamer Platz, if you like," said Nitz. "I thought you might want another look at the Führerbunker from the platform."

"Definitely," agreed Emily. "I told you my last look was only a short one. But now that the Führerbunker is my ultimate destination—well, let's go."

They were out of the Mercedes, and Emily was following Nitz to the foot of two wood-and-pipe outdoor staircases that ascended above the Wall. Together they climbed up short flights of steps to the viewing platform. They worked their way past a half dozen tourists to reach the railing at the edge of the platform. Once again Emily looked out over no-man's-land.

There was a manned watchtower at the far right, and a grayish brown motorcycle with a driver and occupied sidecar drawing up to it to discharge some replacement guards attired in dark green uniforms. There were abandoned streets made unusable by barriers formed of ugly jagged steel crosses, and in the distance a low fence and gate that admitted the soldiers from East Berlin.

Nitz was pointing ahead. "The Führerbunker," he announced.

Emily squinted off.

Nitz directed her gaze. "You remember? That mound of dirt, a sort of hump of earth about twenty feet high, to the left of the narrow road the guards use, back there about four hundred yards from where we stand."

"Yes, I can see it,"

"In 1947 the Russians bulldozed it, but not quite," said Nitz. "Apparently they just covered it over, because once an East German who was handy with a shovel tried to dig down into the bunker. He thought he could create a tunnel for East German refugees trying to escape. The German was stopped, but he found that some of Hitler's old chambers were then intact under that dirt mound. Anyway, the Chancellery garden, which you want to excavate, was this side of that dirt mound. How does it look to you?"

Emily gazed hypnotized at the mound. "Looks difficult, but it can be done. First I've got to get permission to go ahead."

"All right, then we should go ahead," said Nitz, taking her elbow.

After they had left the observation post, and were in the back seat of the Mercedes once more, their chauffeur Plamp twisted his pudgy body from behind the wheel and peered inquiringly at them through his maroon-tinted sunglasses. "Checkpoint Charlie next?"

"Checkpoint Charlie, definitely," said Emily.

It was not until they had arrived at Friedrichstrasse that Nitz spoke again. "Actually, there are six other entry points to get into East Berlin. But this one, Checkpoint Charlie, is the major one for non-Germans."

They drew near a sign that read: YOU ARE NOW LEAVING THE AMERICAN SECTOR. In the two tin sheds next to it were three soldiers. Nitz identified them as British, French, and American army Military Police. The MPs paid no attention to them, and Plamp drove past, braking before a barrier with a sign reading: STOP.

A rangy, dour uniformed East German guard came up to the driver's seat. Plamp showed him their passports. The guard raised the pole barrier and Plamp drove forward. From the glass enclosure atop a faded yellow concrete watchtower, two other East German guards were observing them. Emily noticed that there were three partially cobblestoned lanes into the checkpoint, and Plamp had taken the inside one. Plamp parked and then stepped out of the Mercedes and headed toward the first of three yellow sheds off the street on their right.

Nitz turned to Emily. "This will take about fifteen minutes," he said. "You know the routine. Plamp is showing them our passports, buying seventy-five German marks for the three of us, finally giving customs control the declarations we filled out. I'm sure you remember."

"I remember," said Emily.

In less than fifteen minutes, Plamp returned and settled behind the wheel. Instantly, two East German guards materialized, one at either side of the Mercedes. One opened a door to inspect the interior of the car, poking into the dashboard compartment, side pockets of the doors, under the seats. Emily watched as the second guard, who had remained outside, lifted the hood of the car, closed it, went around the Mercedes to raise the lid of the trunk, closed it, then picked up a broomstick with a rectangular mirror attached to the bottom and slid it beneath the car.

Emily shook her head sadly. "Why do they do this? They know people don't have to be smuggled in. Only out."

"They're searching for contraband. They know there's an eager black market in East Germany, as you'd expect."

The second barrier pole went up. Plamp inched the Mercedes forward to a third barrier pole. Another guard had taken the passports and was stonily comparing their photographs to their faces. Satisfied, he returned the passports to Plamp and the final barrier was raised.

The Mercedes moved ahead, and they were still on Friedrichstrasse but in East Berlin.

Emily exhaled her breath. "Peter, I wonder if Professor Blaubach is familiar with what goes on at the checkpoint?"

"He should be," said Nitz with a thin smile. "He is a leading East German functionary."

"But he seems so nice."

"I'm sure he is nice. It is his country that is paranoid."

As they came to a red light at Leipziger Strasse, Emily pushed forward from the depths of the rear seat to speak to the driver. "Take us to the Brandenburg Gate," she ordered. "After that, I want to go slowly down Unter den Linden so that I can have another look. Then you can take me to the address I gave you off Marx-Engels Platz where Professor Blaubach has his offices."

"But first," Nitz instructed the driver, "drop me at the Café am Palast. Then take Fräulein Ashcroft to her appointment, wait for her, and pick me up on the way back."

Plamp nodded and they were on their way.

In a few minutes, Emily saw and recognized the Brandenburg Gate through the car window. The three parts of the monument, the smaller ones and the huge central one, could be seen beyond the curve of a low wooden fence.

"Really impressive," said Emily. "It's ironic that the greenish sculpture on top is called the Goddess of Peace." As they turned right into a wide thoroughfare, Emily repeated breathlessly, "And Unter den Linden, so beautiful."

It *was* beautiful, one of the shadiest and most gracious avenues she had ever seen. There were sidewalks and gleaming shops on either side, and in the center a long, narrow pasture of a park lined on either side with green trees.

Emily half-turned to Nitz. "I keep forgetting that this was the very heart of Hitler's Berlin, as we have it in our book, before Berlin became a divided city and the East Berliners wound up with the main artery."

"But the West Berliners got the bigger share of the industry, parks, lakes, people."

"True," Emily admitted.

As their Mercedes proceeded up Unter den Linden, Emily could see that the boulevard ahead was clear.

"Hardly any cars here, no traffic," Emily said.

"Because cars are still too expensive, except for diplomats and DDR government officials," Nitz reminded her. He pointed to automobiles parked along the center strip dividing the avenue, fixing on a small compact. "That's the most popular, the Prabant. Did you know the body is actually made from pressed paper? It runs on a two-cylinder motorcycle engine. It costs five thousand four hundred pounds in your money, and the average East German earns maybe one thousand marks a month or three hundred sixty pounds. But he has little else to spend money on, so he often saves for such a car. It may take him six years of saving and waiting to get a Prabant. It would take him longer for the Eisenach over there, and the Wartburgh over there. Those have metal bodies, and are also made on this side of the Wall. As for the other sturdy numbers—that's a Czechoslovakian Skola, and next to it is a Landa produced by Fiat in Italy for the Soviet Union."

"I don't see any Russian soldiers around."

"You won't. Not in this city. They're all outside East Berlin, an enormous army."

As their Mercedes crept along Unter den Linden, Emily studied more carefully the buildings on either side. To the left, the Hungarian embassy, the Polish embassy. On their right the Soviet embassy with its white marble bust of Lenin in the forecourt. Then a Meissner Porzellan shopfront, an Aeroflot Agency, an Import Food store displaying edibles from Vietnam and China.

Gradually the structures grew in grandeur. Humboldt University, students coming and going. The Neue Wache—the Monument to the Victims of Fascism and Militarism—with its eternal flame inside and its goose-stepping changing of the guard outside.

"Plamp," Nitz called out. "If you don't mind, I'll get off on this corner."

"Why?" asked Emily, surprised. "Where are you going?"

"I'll be across the street at the Café am Palast. It's on the corner of the new six-hundred-room Palast Hotel built by the Swedes for the East Germans. Don't worry about me, Emily. I'll be reading the local newspapers and having some tea, and maybe a sweet. Irwin will take you to your good Professor Blaubach."

Nitz opened the car door, stepped out on the corner, but before shutting the door, he added, "Don't forget, Emily, you are now in the middle of the sector that was once Adolf Hitler's pride and joy. His Old Reich Chancellery was over here. Now it is a parking lot. And, of course, within the Frontier Zone, his Führerbunker. The ruins of the mighty Third Reich, Hitler's Reich meant to last a thousand years but which lasted only twelve years and three months." One more thin smile. "The Third Reich with its mysteries. Be sure you get the chance to solve them."

Settling into the chair facing Professor Otto Blaubach's polished oak desk, Emily realized that this was her opening bid to solve one of the major mysteries of the twentieth century, and it must succeed if she was to go further.

She watched Professor Blaubach making his way to the high-backed leather swivel chair behind his desk. He had not changed much since she had last seen him three years ago. He appeared somewhat older, slower, but his gray hair was neatly combed, the bow tie and dark gray suit and vest were immaculate. He was wearing his gold-framed glasses on the bridge of his narrow pointed nose. In greeting her, his countenance was as kindly as ever, creased with lines of sympathy, but his manner was still a trifle reserved.

He was sitting now, pulling himself in closer to the desk. "A drink, Miss Ashcroft? Soft or hard, as you wish."

"No, thank you. I don't want to take too much of your time." She smiled. "You called me Emily the previous times we met."

"Did I? Ah, that was because you were with your father and seemed more a young person to me. Now—now you are a grown lady, making a reputation on your own on television. But you are quite right. The use of Miss Ashcroft does seem inappropriate, all things considered. It shall be Emily." He picked a Spanish Toledo steel letter-opener, in the form of a miniature rapier, off his desk. Toying with it he said, "So you are resuming where your father left off?"

"That is what brought me to Berlin and to you," said Emily. "My father was so grateful that you obtained permission for him to excavate before his accident."

"Now you wish to do as he planned to do. You wish to dig up the garden next to the Führerbunker."

"Yes, the garden." On impulse she added, "Also, the bunker as well."

Professor Blaubach's eyebrows went up. "The Führerbunker too?"

She tried to understand her impulse to add the bunker itself.

She realized that it was more than impulse. She recalled Dr. Max Thiel's two pieces of evidence to search for. Hitler's real gold bridge with its tiny clasp. Hitler's cameo with the face of Frederick the Great. If they could not be found in the shallow ditch or bomb crater in the garden, there was still a possibility that Hitler had left both behind somewhere in the private quarters of his underground bunker. If the garden site produced no evidence, a search of the buried bunker might be helpful.

"Yes," she repeated, "it would be a good idea for me to try the bunker after excavating the garden."

"Umm. The bunker might give us a bit of a problem. We bulldozed it—actually the Soviets did so—plowed it over to remove it from public view. They were always afraid unrepentant Nazis might look upon it as the shrine of a martyr. Digging into it could make certain of my colleagues uneasy."

"Professor, I would leave a small area uncovered for a day or two, just for my search. I would then fill it in again. Restore it to what it is, a dirt mound. There would be no shrine."

Blaubach accepted her explanation. "I will inform my colleagues on the council of your intention. It should overcome any objections." He turned the letter opener slowly. "You are not searching once more for Hitler's and Eva Braun's bodies, I take it? I assume there is more, something else."

"Did my father tell you what he was after?"

"I must say, he did not. He was guarded about what he was after. He generalized to me. He said that some former occupants of the Führerbunker had lately revealed other means to determine the time of Hitler's death. I did not press your father. We were old friends. He had my complete trust. But yes, he was guarded."

She must be guarded, too, she told herself. Her father had not revealed the name of his informant, Dr. Thiel, and she must not reveal it, either. Of course, Blaubach could be depended upon.

Still, she had promised Dr. Thiel that she would not make known the source of her father's or her own suspicions about Hitler's death.

"Well," she said evasively, "I merely want to poke about for a few artifacts, exactly as my father planned to do. It is probably a longshot quest, but if I have any luck it might tell us either that Hitler and his Eva died precisely as history stated—or that they both misled us and survived."

Blaubach let the letter opener drop on the desk. "Of course, Emily, I shall cooperate with you as you desire. I simply hate to see you disappointed. Frankly, I think your undertaking—this dig—will be futile."

"Why?"

"After the Soviet Army overran Berlin, they sent at least five teams of their best soldiers to scour the area for Hitler's remains. They inspected the shallow trench, the bomb crater, the underground rooms of the Führerbunker itself. What they found of Hitler and Eva Braun—their bodies—and a few documents—they made public. I doubt that the Russians overlooked anything."

It was difficult, but Emily stood her ground. "If I may say so, Professor Blaubach, my father's research into the Soviet aftermath was intensive. I have studied his research. It is my impression that the Soviets did a hasty and haphazard job of investigation around the bunker and inside it. Really, it deserves another effort, one more postmortem."

"You may be right about our Russian friends," said Professor Blaubach agreeably. "They are not always as efficient as they make themselves out to be. Even so, I wonder whether you know that they were not the last to excavate at the Führerbunker site?"

"Yes, I know from our documentation there were others."

"Definitely others. Not many people are aware that after the Russians finished their search in May and June of 1945 the other Allies, mainly members of the American and British intelligence, asked on December 3, 1945, to go over the same ground again. On December 30, the Russians allowed them to dig for a day or two. Using eight German laborers, the Western Allies spaded up the area and came across no further corpses resembling Hitler and Braun. They turned up a few items of clothing monogrammed *E. B.*, obviously from Eva Braun's wardrobe. They unearthed some documents belonging to Josef Goebbels, who had also died a suicide with his wife and been buried nearby."

"But the Americans and British searched for only a day or two? Rather superficial, I'd say."

"Well, to be honest," Blaubach said uncomfortably, "they wanted to dig longer, but the Russians would not let them. The Soviets accused them of confiscating vital documents that rightfully belonged to the Soviet Union, and the Russians halted the dig and would not extend further permission."

"I see."

"But lest you consider the Russians totally ungenerous, I must tell you that a month or so later, I think it was in January of 1946, the Soviets invited a group from the French military in Berlin to come to the Führerbunker and resume digging in the garden area. The French did so, although they were not permitted to uncover the trench or bomb crater again, but they were allowed to dig around nearby. They found not a thing that was useful. There were more searches of the interior of the bunker by others, before a portion of it was blown up, and finally buried under dirt." Blaubach added hastily, "But, Emily, don't take it that I want to discourage you. You may find our East German officials more lenient than the Russians. You may get an opportunity to see for yourself. I will recommend, through proper channels, you be given permission to dig."

"I really appreciate that. Thank you, Professor Blaubach." Emily came to her feet. "Will it be long?"

"I should know quickly. You can expect to hear from me in two or three days at the most."

Emily extended her hand, and Blaubach bowed to kiss it, but after she turned to leave, Blaubach's voice caught her before she could reach the door. "Emily—"

She stopped and turned back to see him coming toward her.

"—there's one more thing," he was saying. "If you have a moment to spare, you can do me a favor."

Surprised that she might be able to help him in any way, she was instantly receptive. "Of course. Whatever you . . ."

He hesitated. "As an authority on Hitler, you can be of assistance in a matter that has come up."

"I'm flattered, Professor Blaubach, but I'm sure I'm far less an authority on Hitler than you are."

"No, no, that is not true," he persisted. "I have some expertise on the Third Reich and modern German history, and this does include a degree of knowledge about the late unlamented Führer, but yet I'm sure you have some knowledge that has evaded me."

"I'm less sure of that. Anyway, if I can be of use to you—"

"It is not me," said Blaubach. "It is for someone else. I have in the next office, going through some of my own files, a gentleman from the Soviet Union. He is a distinguished scholar in his own field, the fine arts. His name is Nicholas Kirvov, recently appointed curator of the Hermitage in Leningrad."

"Distinguished, indeed," said Emily, impressed.

"Kirvov's hobby is collecting paintings that Hitler did in his early years. I'm positive you are familiar with that phase of Hitler's life."

"Fairly familiar," Emily admitted.

"Well, Herr Kirvov has been planning to mount an exhibit of Hitler's paintings in the Hermitage, merely as a titillating sidelight. Recently, he acquired one more oil painting, unsigned. He believes it to have been executed by Hitler himself. Since it is something unknown, Herr Kirvov wishes to include it in his Hitler exhibit. Because his exhibit will receive considerable press and public attention, Herr Kirvov feels that he must go to great lengths to authenticate every item in his show. He brought this Hitler item to me for my opinion. I have analyzed it, and fortunately, from a study of the brush strokes and other small points, I am able to reassure Herr Kirvov that the oil is indeed a work done by Adolf Hitler. Nevertheless, there remains a minor problem. It is a problem you may be able to solve for him."

"I can't imagine, Professor, that I'd have any knowledge of a work of art, by Hitler or anyone else, that could possibly match Kirvov's own expertise. Still—" she shrugged— "who knows? My father and I built a modest file of research and graphics on Hitler's artistic phase." She touched Blaubach's arm. "Of course I'd be glad to meet Mr. Kirvov."

Blaubach's serious visage registered a look of pleasure. He quickly opened the door and led Emily into the corridor and then into an adjacent office. This proved to be furnished with only a set of brown file cabinets along one wall and a long conference table flanked by a dozen chairs in the center of the rectangular room. At the far end of the table, a sturdy middle-aged man sat concentrating on a pile of photographs. Upon the entrance of Blaubach and Emily, the man immediately pushed back his chair and leaped to his feet, puzzled.

Blaubach had Emily by the crook of an arm, and was bringing her forward. "Herr Nicholas Kirvov," said Blaubach, "I want to introduce you to Fräulein Emily Ashcroft, of Oxford, England."

Emily briskly stepped ahead and cordially shook Kirvov's outstretched hand.

"Fräulein Ashcroft is an eminent historian at Oxford University," Blaubach went on. "Her specialty, in recent years, has been the life of Adolf Hitler. Indeed, she is in the process of completing a biography of Hitler, and has just arrived in Berlin for some last-minute research."

"I am acquainted with your name," said Kirvov courteously. "I have seen it in print, even in the Soviet Union."

"Do sit down, Emily," said Blaubach, helping her to a chair. "You, too, Herr Kirvov." Blaubach lowered himself into a chair beside Emily, waiting for Kirvov to sit once more. "Herr Kirvov, I've already taken the liberty of briefing Fräulein Ashcroft about your quest, your Hitler painting. It is our good fortune to have Fräulein Ashcroft in Berlin at the same time as yourself."

Emily interrupted. "If there is anything I can do, Mr. Kirvov, I'll be only too pleased to cooperate."

"You are most, most kind, Miss Ashcroft."

She had liked him instantly. Despite a Slavic peasant quality in his physique—as a work of art he was all squares and cubes, brown hair cut squarely and short, square jaw, square broad shoulders—she liked him because of his eyes. She often judged men by their eyes. Kirvov's were dark, sensitive, almost mournful, and his mouth was a poet's mouth.

"Professor Blaubach just told me about your Adolf Hitler painting," said Emily. "I must say that is of interest to me, too. How on earth did you get your hands on it?"

Emily's question had loosened up Kirvov. His eagerness to discuss his find lit his face.

"I am happy to tell you," he said.

At once he began to tell Emily about his collection of Hitler paintings, about the letter from a ship's steward named Giorgio Ricci who wanted to authenticate a Hitler painting he had purchased, about Ricci's visit to the Hermitage, about his own acquisition of the Hitler oil in trade for a Russian icon.

"And now," said Emily, "you want to exhibit this new Hitler acquisition in a show at the Hermitage?"

"I do. It would be—how do you say?—a feather in my cap to include it. But first I had to confirm that it was authentic. I knew that Professor Blaubach here was a famous expert. So I traveled to East Berlin with the painting, with the X rays of it and of my other Hitler art, to put them before him."

"I understand Professor Blaubach authenticated your painting," said Emily. "Still you have a problem?"

"A problem," said Kirvov. "I will show you what it is, and then perhaps you can help."

As he spoke, Kirvov moved to the wall where the painting was leaning fully covered with a felt sack. Kirvov removed the cloth from the oil to reveal the picture of a large, unaesthetic stone building.

Kirvov held the painting before Emily. "Obviously, an official building of some sort," said Kirvov. "It does not resemble a residence, nor even one of the opera houses or museums Hitler favored depicting in his youth. The structure suggests a typical government building. Don't you think so?"

Emily nodded. "I'm inclined to agree with you."

"How does one authenticate a work?" Kirvov asked, more to himself than to Emily or Blaubach. "One does so through scientific analysis. This has been done. One seeks to trace its provenance. This we do not have. Finally, one requires identification of the subject of the work, when possible. Knowledge of it, its location, can turn away the challenge of doubtful critics." Kirvov slipped the painting into the felt sack once more, and placed it on the conference table. "That is my problem, Miss Ashcroft. I don't know what the subject of this painting is or where and when it was done. I can place the settings and subjects of all of Hitler's art pieces that I have previously acquired. Almost everything he drew or painted in his youth was done in his favorite town of Linz or in Vienna or in Munich. I have gone over early photographs or drawings of buildings in those cities. This government structure is in none of those places." His soft eyes met Emily's own. "You might know this. Did Hitler paint anything anywhere else?"

"He did and he didn't," said Emily, "but not really. When Hitler was an infantryman in the First World War, he undertook some drawings on the western front, mainly in Belgium, but none of these resemble the work you have. This painting you have, I'd like to look into it, for my own research purposes as well. Do you have any photographs of your painting?"

"Too many," said Kirvov shyly. "I made copies to pass around like Most Wanted posters of known criminals." He reached into the inner pocket of his jacket and pulled out an oblong envelope. From it he produced a five-by-seven-inch photograph of the painting and passed it over to Emily.

She examined the copy of the piece of art once more. "You know, it really looks like one of those dreary office buildings that the Nazis threw up in Berlin in the early 1930s. But, of course, it couldn't be. Hitler never painted them. I'd guess this is a government building in another large German city. Let me look into it. I'll call my secretary in Oxford and have her photocopy our Hitler art file and also the file of government buildings in major German cities during the Third Reich. Then we'll see. Where can I get hold of you, Mr. Kirvov?"

"I am presently staying in East Berlin. I intended to move over to West Berlin tomorrow for a few days. I planned to do some sightseeing—of government buildings. I assume you are in West Berlin, Miss Ashcroft?"

"At the Kempinski."

"I will stay at the Palace Hotel, not far away, where I have stayed briefly before."

Emily came to her feet, slipping the photograph into her purse. "Then I will contact you at the Palace, as soon as I have my photo files and have gone through them. Let's hope we have luck."

Kirvov had jumped up. "You don't know how grateful I am."

She smiled. "Be grateful only if I am helpful."

Professor Blaubach had preceded her to the door, opening it. He dropped his voice. "I thank you for this. As to your own request, I do not forget. We shall see what we shall see."

* * *

It was late afternoon when the hired Mercedes let her out before the glass entrance doors to the Kempinski.

After voicing her appreciation to Peter Nitz, who stepped out ahead of her, Emily told the driver Plamp, "If you are not tied up, I will need your services again in a few days."

Plamp touched the visor of his chauffeur's cap. "I am ready to serve you anytime, Fräulein."

Emily said good-bye to Nitz, then hastened into the hotel, crossing the lobby toward the concierge's desk. She was eager to get her key and reach her suite, where she could make telephone calls to the excavators her father had planned to employ in West Berlin, and to phone Pamela Taylor, her secretary in Oxford, on Kirvov's behalf. The building in the oil painting was one of those minor riddles that, for her, always made research more intriguing.

"Suite 229," she said to the concierge.

He turned to her with the key and a slip of paper. "Miss Ashcroft," he said, "there is someone waiting for you."

"Someone?" she said vaguely. She read the message on the slip of paper: "Miss Ashcroft, I hope you can spare a minute to see me. I have come all the way from Los Angeles to meet you. I am in the Bristol Bar." It was signed "Rex Foster," a name utterly unknown to her.

Puzzled, she turned to cross the length of the lobby toward the hotel's cocktail lounge.

Standing at the entrance to the lounge, she cast about to see who the occupants were. There was no lone man waiting for her. There were three couples, in different parts of the room, seated in black upholstered chairs with drinks on the tables before them. There were two women deep in conversation, an elderly man and woman who appeared to be a long-married couple, and two others, an attractive thirtyish man and a young and pretty blond woman, who sat at a small table near an antique Steinway grand piano. The attractive thirtyish man, glancing past his partner, noticed Emily. Mumbling something to the blonde, he came to his feet.

Emily watched as he swiftly approached her in long strides.

Could this be her unexpected visitor from California? she wondered. What an interesting-looking man, she thought.

He was upon her, a lopsided smile on his gaunt face.

"Are you, by chance, Emily Ashcroft?" he inquired.

"I am."

He indicated the message slip still in her hand. "If you're looking for Rex Foster from Los Angeles, I'm afraid you've found him. If it's a bad time, I hope we can make another appointment. In any case, I hope you don't mind the intrusion."

Her eyes fixed on him, she decided that she didn't mind anything at all. She hoped that her hair wasn't a mess and that her skirt wasn't wrinkled. Her original automatic reluctance to meet a stranger, possibly a pushy one, had been quickly dispelled by his person. His attraction for her, she realized, had been almost immediate. This time it wasn't only the earnest brown eyes. He was at least six feet tall, towering above her, with unruly black hair, craggy countenance, cleft chin, lean and athletic physique. She found that she had already done what men always say they do with sexy-appearing women—mentally undressed him. She had unwittingly done so—it had never happened before, not with Jeremy or anyone—and she marveled at her craziness.

To cover her thoughts and unease, she was unnaturally abrupt. "Well, what can I do for you, Mr. Foster?"

"Ideally, we could have a chat right here. But if you're pressed for time, we could make it any other day at your convenience."

Her instinctive feelings surfaced. She did not want to put him off. She wanted to be with him here and now and she wanted to know more about him and his interest in her. "I—I have a little time," she said cautiously.

"Wonderful," he said. "Perhaps you'd sit down and join us for a drink." He indicated his blond partner. "Then I can explain everything."

Emily took in his waiting partner, and momentarily her heart sank. The female with the blond mane was younger than herself, and certainly prettier. His wife? His lover? His girlfriend in Berlin?

Emily, patting down her auburn hair, said lamely, "I've been working," then erect as possible she trailed him across a small dance floor to his table.

Foster indicated the empty chair beside his own, and before Emily could take it, he introduced her to the breathtaking blonde. "Miss Ashcroft . . . Miss Tovah Levine from Israel. We've just met, and we're both waiting for you."

Relieved, Emily was able to acknowledge the introduction with a smile. Sitting again, Foster had summoned a waiter. "What can I get for you, Miss Ashcroft?"

She wanted to have whatever he was having, to show they were as one. But then she felt that she should show her independence and assert herself. After all, he had come all this distance to see her. "Whiskey and soda," she said, "no ice." She decided that she had better deal with her visitor. "You came here," she said to Foster, "to see me?" Then, she realized, she must acknowledge the blond young lady as well. "And, I gather, so did Miss Levine."

"You needn't mind me," said Tovah quickly. "I can wait my turn. Rex was here first."

Foster nodded appreciatively. "Thanks, Tovah." He faced Emily once more. "Yes, Miss Ashcroft, I came to Berlin primarily to see you."

"I can't imagine why."

"I'll explain," he said. "To begin with, I'm an architect."

"An architect?" She had never met one before. Somehow she had suspected from his appearance that he was a rich banker's indolent son. He seemed so relaxed and comfortable with himself, and confident. No, she corrected herself, not indolent. There was no indolence in the assurance and intensity of his manner. There was, she guessed, contained strength. "What—what do you do as an architect?" she blurted out foolishly, since she knew better but had been at a loss for something to say.

Foster replied seriously. "I try to make lovely things."

Fleetingly, Emily wondered if this was an intentional double entendre or an ingenuous remark on his part. She would love to have known. Anyway. "Buildings, presumably?"

"Buildings, of course. I work very hard at it because I enjoy creativity. I like to see things grow under my fingers."

His fingers, she noted for the first time, were slender and long. She wondered about their touch.

"And has that made you successful?"

"More or less," said Foster. "But even that's not enough. In America, it is not only the professors who must publish or perish. I am doing what I gather you've been doing, Miss Ashcroft, although I wouldn't dare compare the importance of my book project with your own. I'm preparing a book called *Architecture of the 1000-Year Third Reich.* About what Hitler had built in Germany—and what he planned to build had he won the war. So that's where our interests intersect. Adolf Hitler."

"I see."

"Frankly, like you, I've come to Berlin to finish my research and complete a book. I'm afraid I'll have some difficulty doing so without your help."

She adored his eyes, and was ready to do anything for him. "How can I help you, Mr. Foster?"

"All right. Here goes. My picture-and-caption book still has one incomplete section. There are some missing plans I had hoped to locate through the family of Hitler's chief architect, Albert Speer, but I have had to search elsewhere for the missing plans. I knew of your father's biography and I realized that if anyone knew about Speer's associates or assistants, it was your father. I had narrowed down my own hunt for the elusive plans to one of the ten associates to whom Speer may have assigned them, but I had no idea where to find this associate. It seemed to me that your father would likely know of this man. So I wrote to your father asking if I might come to Oxford and meet with him. He was kind enough to give me an appointment for the very next week. But then"— Foster paused—"I read about his accident." Foster looked steadily at Emily. "I can't tell you, Miss Ashcroft, how sorry I am. Not for me, of course. For you."

"Thank you. Please go on."

"Two days ago, in reading about your father in the press, I learned that you had been collaborating with him so I made up my mind to try to see you."

For an instant Emily was troubled. "How on earth did you find me here?"

"I telephoned your home in Oxford hoping to speak to you. I planned to fly to London and drive up to see you. Your secretary answered and, after we had talked for some time, she admitted you had gone to West Berlin and were staying at the Kempinski."

Emily frowned. "I made Pamela promise to tell no one I was here."

"I'm afraid I wheedled it out of her," Foster said apologetically. "I reminded her that I already had been given an appointment by Dr. Ashcroft, and I was sure his daughter would not object to seeing me. In light of this, your secretary felt it was all right to tell me where you were. I hope this doesn't upset you?"

"I take it you've had a lot of experience charming secretaries," she smiled. "At any rate, you got here."

"I came to the Kempinski hoping to catch you and make a

proper appointment. But you were out. So I decided to wait. Meanwhile"— Foster gestured toward Tovah Levine—"at the very moment I was asking the concierge about you, Miss Levine came up to the counter and overheard me. It turned out that she also had come to the Kempinski to see you. So we decided to wait for you together."

Puzzled, Emily directed her attention to the pretty blonde. "And you, Miss Levine, why did you want to see me?"

Tovah Levine, who had been listening and drinking, set down her glass. "To tell you the truth, Miss Ashcroft, I'm a working journalist. Recently, I was assigned to West Berlin to do a series of feature stories for the *Jerusalem Post.* When I learned you were coming here, I thought you'd make an excellent subject. Hitler still sells newspapers. Regrettable, but there it is."

Emily blinked at the journalist. "And how did you know I was at the Kempinski?"

"Easy," said Tovah Levine. "When I arrived, I checked into the Berlin foreign correspondents' press club. It keeps a record of the arrival of each and every celebrity in Berlin. It has connections with all the hotels in the city—with the concierges, assistant managers, receptionists—who pass on the names of foreign celebrities who've just registered. So I thought I'd come over and see if I could get a story."

"Well, I'm hardly a celebrity," said Emily, "and I certainly can't give you a story. Believe me, Miss Levine—you, too, Mr. Foster—I really meant to keep my business here a secret. If word gets out that I am working here, it could be dangerous for me at worst—or my project at the very least."

"Mum's the word, I promise you," said Foster, raising his right hand.

"Good enough," said Emily. "As to helping out on your architectural book, I hope I can give you what you want. When would you like to meet?"

"Tonight," said Foster. "Before you came into the lounge, I

invited Tovah to join me for dinner at a restaurant in the neighborhood. I'd be very happy if you'd also be my guest."

Emily feasted her eyes on him. He was so damn winning, irresistible in every way. Certainly she wanted to know him better, and soon. If Blaubach came through, she might be very busy. "Why not?" she said to Foster. "I was going to eat in my room. This is certainly a better offer. I thank you."

"Very good," said Foster enthusiastically.

Emily hesitated, gaze fixed on the blond journalist. "I can join you only if Miss Levine promises that whatever we discuss is strictly social and off the record."

"I'll promise anything," agreed Tovah Levine, holding up her own right hand in a solemn pledge, "because I am fascinated—and because I am hungry."

Emily laughed. "Ground rules set. Fine." She consulted her gold wristwatch. "It is almost seven. I need an hour to make several phone calls, and to bathe and change." She turned her full smile on Foster. "The lobby at eight o'clock?"

Foster unwound his lank form. "I'll be down at five minutes before eight watching the elevator, Miss Ashcroft."

"Emily," she said, rising.

"Me, Rex," he said with a grin. "I'll be waiting."

The Berliner Gasthaus was on Schlüterstrasse, a five-block walk from the Kempinski hotel, and the three of them had a table at the rear. Foster had made the reservation at this luxurious restaurant because, despite the fact that it advertised 1920s-style cabaret entertainment, including transvestite acts, he had found on his previous visit that he could dine quietly in the back room, well removed from the floor show.

Emily watched Foster past the flickering candles on their table as he selected dinner for all of them from the menu. She heard him ordering tomato soup, pepper steaks, tossed salads, and a red wine. Emily wished that she had him alone. Sipping slowly on her third whiskey of the evening, she told herself no more drinking before the meal. She wanted to keep her wits about her, and learn as much as she could about Foster.

After the hectic day in East Berlin, the chance meeting with Foster, she had felt wound up, on edge. In her suite, before dinner, she had been busy on the telephone. She had called Oxford first, and instructed Pamela Taylor to photocopy their file on Hitler's art career for Nicholas Kirvov, and their file on architecture during the Third Reich for both Kirvov and Rex Foster, and to try to get everything in the mail to Berlin by overnight courier.

After that, Emily had telephoned the excavator her father had planned to use at the Führerbunker site. She had found the name of the Oberstadt Construction Company among her father's papers. She talked to Andrew Oberstadt, who remembered the arrangement made with her father. "It would have been a fascinating excavation, and we looked forward to it," Andrew Oberstadt had said. "I was sorry about what happened to your father, and I was sorry not to have the opportunity to go ahead." Emily had told him that the opportunity might still exist. It would all depend on getting permission from the East Berlin government. "If I do get permission, it might be on short notice. Would you have a crew immediately available?" Andrew Oberstadt had reassured her that, for an undertaking like this, he would see that he had a trained crew readily available, and that he would supervise the excavation himself.

Feeling better, Emily had noted the brief time left before she must meet Rex Foster and Tovah Levine in the lobby, and she had bypassed a relaxing bubble bath for a quick shower. When she was ready to dress, she reached automatically for one of her tailored suits, then she hesitated. The one thing she had not wanted to look like was a stuffy academic. She had felt female and, for the first time since the funeral, had experienced a sense of pulsing life. She had reached instead into a drawer for a blouse, a fine white batiste blouse that buttoned up to the collar, then she had stepped into a short navy blue skirt and pulled on a pink Eton jacket. The outfit was better than a suit, gave her a feminine shapeliness, but still did not give her the look she wanted. She had opened the top button of her blouse, and then experimentally the second button, and finally, more daringly, she had opened the third button. Moving her arms, she could see that a bit of cleavage showed.

She had been satisfied. Demure and natural, yet sexy enough that Rex Foster, on seeing her, had permitted his eyes to linger on the open third button and the slight swell of her breasts and complimented her at once on her appearance. Stealing a glance at Tovah, Emily had seen that the young Israeli girl was rather smashing in a fuchsia silk-jersey dress that hid no curve of her well-endowed body. But Emily had not minded, since Foster seemed to have eyes only for her.

Now, beside him in the Berliner Gasthaus, Emily decided to become more businesslike and by so doing bring Foster closer.

"Rex," she began, "I'd like to know what you're really after. I'm only too willing to help, if I can. Exactly what is your problem with your book?"

"You don't mind talking shop? Very well. I mentioned that Albert Speer employed a number of associate architects. Ten, to be exact. I've pinpointed most of their buildings, and their plans for structures. They were in Speer's archives. But there is one architect missing, the one who devoted himself to constructing hideaways around Germany for use by Hitler when he did his traveling during the war."

"I think I know the hideaways you're referring to," said Emily. She cast a look at Tovah, to include her in the discussion.

"Hitler preferred to live deep underground as the war heightened above ground. Speer assigned one of his most competent associates, a young man by the name of Rudi Zeidler, to design and construct these private air-raid shelters and bunkers throughout Germany."

"Rudi Zeidler," Foster repeated. "He may be the architect whose plans I want."

"Zeidler was the one who designed an underground shelter in a hillside, beneath a forest, in Ziegenberg, near Bad Nauheim. There was a similar subterranean headquarters in Friedberg." She turned fully to Foster. "Do you have the information on them?"

"No, Emily. Those are new to me."

"Zeidler also designed the Führerbunker itself, where Hitler and Eva Braun spent the last days of the war," Emily went on. "The Führerbunker was far underground. There were two levels, and Hitler and Eva had a six-room private suite at the very bottom. The top of this Führerbunker was covered with eleven feet of concrete and six feet of earth. Considering the compactness, it was brilliantly designed."

"Yes, I have several crude sketches of it, but not the actual blueprint," Foster told her. "I didn't know that Rudi Zeidler was the architect. However, it's the actual plans for all those underground structures that I want from him. Do you suppose he's still alive?"

"He probably is. I know that he was a year and a half ago when my father interviewed him here in West Berlin."

"Would he be in the telephone directory?"

"No. Most of the old Nazis aren't listed anymore. I remember my father had some trouble locating him. When he did, Zeidler was most cooperative."

"Do you have any idea where I can find him?" Foster wanted to know.

"No problem. His address and phone number are in our files in Oxford."

"May I call your secretary for it?"

Emily smiled. "I've already sent for it. The entire architecture file, I mean. I didn't know what you'd specifically want from it. Zeidler is in it, and the file is on its way. I should have it tomorrow afternoon."

Impulsively, Foster leaned over and covered Emily's hand briefly with his own. "I'm truly grateful, Emily."

Embarrassed, excited, she pointed off. "Here comes the waiter with our food."

While the soup was being served, Foster continued to regard Emily with appreciation. "I wish there was something I could do for you to return the favor."

Emily wanted to tell him what he could do, but refrained. Instead, she said, "Never mind—" At once something practical did occur to her. "Actually, now that I think of it, you can do me a favor. Not for myself, but for a friend."

"Whatever I can do, I'll be happy to—"

"Today, for my own research, I went to East Berlin to see a government official, Professor Otto Blaubach, a long-standing colleague of my father's, and someone I already knew. He's trying to do something for me, so I'd like to do something for him. Professor Blaubach introduced me to a visitor he had been hoping to help and wondered if I could pitch in. The visitor, whom I met, was an extremely nice Russian, Nicholas Kirvov, the present curator of the Hermitage museum in Leningrad."

For the first time since their drinks were served Tovah spoke up. "What I'd give to see that museum!"

Emily addressed Tovah. "Well, maybe you can meet Kirvov and he'll invite you to Leningrad."

"I hope so," said Tovah, dipping a spoon into her soup. "Sorry I interrupted," she said. "You were telling about meeting Kirvov."

Emily had returned her attention to Foster. "Kirvov collects Hitler's drawings and paintings. He wants to exhibit them at the Hermitage."

"They're awful," said Foster. "Absolutely banal."

"Agreed," said Emily. "But that's not the point. They'd still make an interesting curiosity exhibit."

"I suppose so," said Foster.

"Anyway, Kirvov has just acquired an unsigned painting by Hitler of some kind of government building that no one can identify. Kirvov wants to know what the building is before he publicly shows the painting. I said I'd try to give him a hand. When I phoned Oxford I asked my secretary to send along our art file on Hitler—as well as our architecture file for both you and Mr. Kirvov. Rex, since you're an architect, and one who knows so much about Nazi architecture, you might know about the building in Kirvov's painting. Here, let me show you." Emily had opened her small purse and extracted Kirvov's photograph of the Hitler oil. She handed it to Foster.

As Tovah bent sideways to see it too, Foster studied the photo. "You're sure it's by Hitler?"

"That's what the experts say."

Foster shook his head slowly. "No building I can recall seeing in Munich or Frankfurt or Hamburg or anywhere, and I have a large collection of photographs of all the buildings that Hitler had thrown up during his time. Still, it does resemble so many of those dreary government office buildings that Hitler had constructed after he became chancellor. I may have seen something like this a dozen times—but where?" He squinted more closely at the photo. "It looks like one of a whole rash of buildings Hitler directed to be put up in Berlin in his first days as head of Germany."

"Berlin?" said Emily. "But this is a painting by Hitler, and as far as we know he painted exclusively in Linz, Vienna, Munich. Never in Berlin."

Foster's eyes remained fixed on the photograph. "No matter what, I'd still vote for Berlin."

"Maybe Kirvov can look around the city for it," Tovah suggested.

"That would be hopeless," Foster told Tovah. "The massive Allied bombings, toward the end of the war, and Marshal Zhukov's ground offensive leveled or ruined most of the government and industrial buildings in and around the city. There were two hundred fifty thousand buildings in Berlin at the close of the war. Of these, thirty thousand were totally demolished, twenty thousand badly damaged, one hundred fifty thousand partially damaged. Almost all the government buildings were among those totally destroyed. It's unlikely that this building exists any more." He held the photograph up to Emily. "Mind if I keep this print for a couple of days? I want to go through my portfolio and see if there are any old photos that resemble this painting."

"Of course, but let's check it against my own file when it arrives tomorrow."

Emily hastily took a few spoons of her soup, but signaled for the waiter to take it away when he was removing the other plates. Before they could revive their conversation, the hot steak entrees were being served, and they waited until everything was in place.

It was Tovah who spoke. "Emily, you've been generous in giving Rex information and trying to assist Kirvov, but you're the centerpiece. You've hardly told us a thing about yourself."

Emily was at once evasive. "You know why I'm here. To put the finishing touches on a biography my father and I had almost completed."

"What finishing touches?" Tovah persisted.

Foster offered Emily one of his incredible smiles, the one she found so melting. "*I* certainly would like to know more about what you're up to."

For Emily, that did it. She wanted to tell Rex anything on earth he wanted to know about her.

The smile still illuminated him. "What do you think?"

Emily looked directly at the Israeli journalist. "But can I trust you? This is confidential stuff. Tovah, you promised that everything we discussed this evening would be off the record."

"You had my word," said Tovah. "You have it again. I won't violate a confidence."

"All right," said Emily. She was pressured by the secrecy she had imposed upon herself. She was eager to gain Rex Foster's confidence. She wanted Tovah's friendship. "I'll tell you what brought me to Berlin."

She was ready to talk, and she talked. She spoke of the five years of work on *Herr Hitler* with her father. Toward the end of this recital, Foster interrupted sympathetically, "It must be difficult, writing so complex a biography."

"Actually, fascinating," Emily replied. "No, not difficult at all —except in one way." She contemplated something that had been on her mind a long time, and now she felt like giving voice to it. "Yes, I suppose in one way it *has* been difficult," she said, mainly addressing herself to Foster. "When one gets so involved in the minutiae of the life of another person, there's the danger of thinking of him as a human being like yourself. You know this man was an inhumane and terrible beast. You know what he really did to others in his lifetime. You try to reconcile the truth of his activities with the normal facts of a life you've uncovered. And you can't, because you're unable to reconcile the enormous contradictions in one being.

"You know for a fact that Hitler's *Vernichtungslager* existed. The extermination camps. Auschwitz, Buchenwald, Dachau, Mauthausen, Treblinka, thirty Nazi death camps in all. You know about Auschwitz, the most efficient, with its four great death chambers, two thousand helpless, naked victims suffocating and writhing in their death throes in each chamber every day, then being dragged away to have their rings taken off and dental gold fillings pulled out for deposit in the Reichsbank, and then the crematoria burning the bodies, with their ashes sold for fertilizer. The six million Jews and others gassed to death and fed to flames, the twenty million—real people—he caused to be killed during World War II, his utter cold disregard for the sufferings of his own followers, like the thousands he allowed to be drowned when he flooded the Berlin subways, and the million troops he allowed to be maimed or shot dead in the absolutely hopeless sixteen-day defense of Berlin. All of that was Adolf Hitler's doing, and no one else's."

Absently, she sliced off a piece of her steak, but then left the portion untouched to meet Foster's intent eyes once more.

"Yet, writing such a detailed, close-up biography of a man, you get caught up in his normally human behavior and frailties. You get confounded by this lover of Alsatian dogs and other people's small children, this vegetarian and nonsmoker, this man who would not wear pajamas but only nightshirts, this man who adored his mother, and who ran and reran and enjoyed films like *It Happened One Night.* You get confused because this human beast also had human vulnerability, his trembling left arm and hand, his loss of sight in the right eye, his swallowing all those medicines for Parkinson's disease."

Emily caught her breath, then went on.

"You have difficulty resolving another contradiction—his attention to the feminine details surrounding Eva Braun. He enjoyed sex with her and made love to her whenever he wasn't too exhausted or ill. His sweet Eva, whom he would not permit to ski lest she break a leg nor to sunbathe lest she get skin cancer. His sweet Eva who liked to listen to 'Tea for Two,' and wear the platinum watch set with diamonds he gave her, and wear pure silk garter belts and Worth's Air Bleu perfume he had confiscated from conquered Paris."

Emily shook her head, and went on again.

"All those microscopic human facts on the one hand. Yet on the other, all those six million men, women, children he condemned to be stripped naked and gassed—each of them a mother, a father, a daughter, a son, a grandchild, wanting to grow older and enjoy life, yet each of them helpless and each of them murdered, until finally, finally, the bloodletting was stopped by millions of better, more decent people than Hitler, people who sacrificed years, even their own lives, to blot him off the face of the earth."

Emily stared at Foster.

"I'm sorry, Rex—Tovah—for carrying on like this. But you asked and I had to answer. That's been the difficulty in writing this book. Getting trapped in all the human minutiae that make one of the greatest demons in history resemble a half-human being. Yet, he wasn't human, in no way was he human. He was a heartless savage inside, wallowing in his own ego, caring not a bit for anyone else on earth outside his close ones. And now—now I must wonder if he fooled the entire world, if he pretended suicide but actually slipped away to avoid the punishment he so justly deserved, and has survived. It—it's worth finding out about, not only for a mere book but for the chance to bring him to justice, if indeed he's still alive. I think what I truly feel was best stated by your American prosecutor, Supreme Court Justice Robert Jackson, at the Nuremberg Trials. As he put it, 'The wrongs which we seek to condemn and punish have been so calculated, so malignant, and so devastating, that civilization cannot tolerate their being ignored, because it cannot survive their being repeated.' "

Now Foster was staring at her. "Emily, are you telling us you think Hitler did not die in 1945? Do you think, in the end, he got away scot-free?"

Emily looked up. "Yes, it's possible. I don't know for sure. Let me explain." She resumed by relating the unexpected interruption of the *Herr Hitler* biography. That was Dr. Thiel's letter, although she did not mention Dr. Thiel by name. She went on from there. Her father's death. The suspicions about his death. Her decision to pursue the possibility that Hitler and Eva Braun had not died in the Führerbunker as previous history had it. Her own meeting with Dr. Thiel, but again no mention of his name. His encouragement that she dig for two clues. One, Hitler's real dental plates. The other, Hitler's cameo bearing a likeness of Frederick the Great. And finally about her application to Professor Otto Blaubach for permission to dig around and inside the Führerbunker.

"There you have it," Emily concluded, her voice reduced to a whisper. "That's why I am here."

She could see that Rex Foster was truly entranced. "What a fantastic story," he said.

Tovah was equally spellbound by Emily's account, but troubled by one point. "Hitler and Braun were seen dead on the sofa, and both were carried out and cremated before many witnesses. How can you explain that?"

"A double died for each of them," answered Emily simply. "Two look-alikes who killed themselves or were liquidated and cremated, while the real Hitler and Eva survived and got away."

"A double for Adolf Hitler," repeated Tovah, savoring it. "Wouldn't that be something to prove."

"Well, I intend to try to prove it might have happened by digging at the Führerbunker, if I get permission."

Tovah was half out of her seat. "And I want to dig, too—dig elsewhere—try to find out more about Hitler's doubles." As if afraid that Emily would object, Tovah quickly went on. "I'm a journalist, an investigative reporter. I'm used to burrowing for the truth."

Emily tightened her lips. "This is not a media story. Not yet. Remember what happened to my father."

"I wouldn't endanger you in any way," Tovah promised. "I'd just like to help you get the truth, but I want to help my own country, too. You know that half of Israel has been hunting for all those missing Nazis—not Martin Bormann but the rest. But to find Adolf Hitler, the biggest monster, the one we Israelis would like brought to the gallows . . ."

"If he survived," said Foster thoughtfully. "Emily—I'd like to help you, too."

"Thank you, Rex," said Emily. "I'll need all the help I can get." She paused. "But I remind you. My father also came here for the truth. Now he's dead. So"— she stared at Foster and Tovah—"let's be very careful. *Very.*"

5

The following morning, early, just as the alarm on her travel clock went off, the telephone began ringing. Half awake, she snatched the receiver off the hook, and immediately she was fully awake.

It was Professor Otto Blaubach on the other end.

"Emily," he was saying, "about your permission to dig at the Führerbunker—"

Her heart began to thump as she waited for the word.

"—there appears to be one more step necessary. The council members wish to know to what extent you intend to excavate. I must report back to them fully. Then we should have their decision."

Emily was bewildered. "How do I know how much I'll have to excavate until I can examine the site firsthand?"

"Exactly," said Blaubach. "That is what I have arranged for you to do. If you will join me after lunch, we will enter the Security Zone together. You can examine the site, show me just where you plan to excavate, and I will pass on your request to the council."

Sitting up in bed, she felt a flash of panic. She voiced her concern. "Of course, I'll be there at any time, but one thing worries me. I've never visited the site before. I recall photographs the Russians took of it when they first arrived in 1945. But today, I don't know what the dimensions of the bunker were underground nor exactly where the shallow trench and bomb crater were in the garden."

"Then bring along a map or diagram to guide you," said Blaubach patiently. "Surely you have something to go by. Or I have a better idea. Do you know anyone in Berlin who might be more familiar than I am with the site and can show you where you should dig?"

Immediately Rex Foster, with his knowledge of all Nazi architecture, came to mind.

"Yes, I do," she said confidently.

But Blaubach was already giving her instructions on where to join him in East Berlin, and she was jotting the directions on the pad beside her telephone.

"Three o'clock this afternoon, I will be there," Blaubach promised. "Meet me at three o'clock and we will proceed to the site together."

She tried to alleviate her excitement by moving forward in an orderly manner.

First she needed a shower to clear her head.

After that, dressing in her work clothes, a blue denim jumpsuit over her red cotton shirt with a red and white scarf tied at her neck, she considered her research. At once, she rummaged through the piles of folders for the diagram she had of the Führerbunker area. She found it, and studying it she realized that it might not be enough to locate the precise spots where she needed to dig. With Nitz, from the observation platform yesterday, she had seen the target site as it looked today. A mound of dirt surrounded by grass. She realized that the anonymity of the ground would offer her little guidance. Blaubach was right. She needed someone along who *knew* and could show her where everything had been in 1945 and where she must dig in 1985.

Ordering breakfast from room service, she tried to calm down before waking Rex. He would certainly know exact details of the Führerbunker. But the thought of having him near her was exciting in itself. She rang his room. The phone rang and rang. No answer. He had gone out early. He might be out all day.

Dammit. Was there anyone else? Whom to call?

Then someone else came to mind, and without losing another second she was on the phone to Ernst Vogel. The onetime SS guard had been there, had been so graphic in describing the events and setting of Hitler's supposed death that he might be more useful than Rex or Blaubach.

Luckily, Vogel was in and answering the phone.

She began to introduce herself to him again, but it was hardly necessary. He remembered their recent interview. She explained to him what she was scheduled to do this afternoon, although not giving him the real reason for her exploration. It was something, she told him, that she had to do for her book but that she could not do accurately alone. Her East Berlin contact had advised her to bring someone along, someone who had known the bunker site in the past.

"You mean me?" Vogel said. "You want me to come with you?"

"I was hoping. You seemed to remember where everything happened around there in 1945, and I thought you'd—"

"Remember it all still? You can depend on that. I will never forget. It will be a memorable moment to visit the old place after so long. Yes, I will be happy to accompany you."

"I have a diagram of the Führerbunker and the garden area. I can bring it."

"No need," said Vogel. "I will bring my own. I know my own is accurate."

"I'll have a car and driver. We'll pick you up no later than two-thirty."

"I shall be ready."

Finally, the car and driver. Again, no difficulty. Irwin Plamp and his Mercedes would be at the Kempinski at two o'clock.

Irwin Plamp had drawn his Mercedes to a halt near a high fence on Niederkirchnerstrasse in East Berlin, and Emily saw Professor Otto Blaubach standing before a jeep in front of a sentry box at the electronic entry gate waiting for them. Emily waved to Blaubach, who waved back.

Emily turned to Ernst Vogel. "Here's where we get out." She unlatched the rear door to let them out, but Plamp had hastened around the car to help her down.

"Thanks, Herr Plamp," said Emily. "You wait right here until we're through. We shouldn't be more than an hour . . . Herr Vogel, come along with me."

They walked toward the gate until they reached Professor Blaubach, who greeted Emily with warmth, then regarded Ernst Vogel questioningly. Emily quickly introduced them. As Blaubach led them to a jeep, where an East German uniformed soldier waited behind the wheel, Emily explained Vogel's credentials. "Herr Vogel was an SS honor guard both outside and inside the Führerbunker during the last ten days before the Russians came. He remembers the interior layout very well, and he witnessed Hitler's burial and cremation in the garden."

Blaubach assisted Emily into the rear seat of the jeep, cast

Vogel a cold look, and let him climb into the rear by himself. With surprising agility for a man of his age, Blaubach stepped up into the front of the jeep and sat beside the driver. "To the Führerbunker," he ordered in German.

They wheeled slowly through the gate, past the sentry box, from which two German soldiers saluted Professor Blaubach.

They drove inside the enclosed Security Zone, over a narrow dirt road running along a chain-link fence set in concrete posts and at intervals bearing ominous signs. GRENZGEBIET (Frontier Zone) was also spelled out in English, French, Russian. Below that, on the same sign, was PASSAGE IS FORBIDDEN printed in four languages.

As they wended their way along the dirt road, passing spiked paths, tank obstacles, a manned watchtower, Emily could see that they were moving closer and closer to the large dirt mound rising above the field not far from the inner wall. Unaccountably, she shivered. Soon they were parallel to the mound, and the jeep turned sharply left, leaving the road and bumping slowly across thirty feet of grassy, rock-strewn, weed-covered meadow toward the looming mound. Emily was too spellbound by the sight to speak. The oblong hump of earth, mixed with rubble and pieces of rock, rose fifteen to twenty feet above the jeep.

Abruptly, the jeep came to a halt. Blaubach beckoned for them to dismount, and they all stepped out and tramped in the sun to the base of the mound.

"Here it is," announced Blaubach, "the grave of the Führerbunker." To which he added disdainfully, "Hitler's catacomb." He faced Vogel. "So, you recognize it?" he asked somewhat mockingly.

Vogel stood uneasily, peering about the area as he adjusted his hearing aid.

Emily watched Vogel with a worried expression. "Does it make any sense, Herr Vogel? I must know exactly where the

Führerbunker is under the heap of dirt, and I must know the location of the trench where Hitler and Eva were buried and cremated, and the bomb crater where they were reburied and where their remains were found by the Soviet investigators."

Ernst Vogel had put on a pair of tinted glasses, and now he was tugging a folded sheet of paper out of his jacket pocket. He unfolded the sheet, which Emily could see was a meticulous diagram of the bunker and a map of the surrounding area. Vogel was studying it. He looked up, scrutinized the area once more, and stared fixedly straight ahead. Suddenly, his face brightened.

He pointed away from the mound, toward the south.

"I am sure that is where the New Reich Chancellery stretched for four-tenths of a kilometer—a fourth of a mile—along Voss Strasse," he said. He sought confirmation from Blaubach. "Am I not correct?"

Blaubach gave a short nod. "Yes, that is where it was situated."

"Then the rest is simple," said Vogel with growing confidence. "The Old Chancellery was right next door to us. Therefore—" He started around the dirt mound. "Come, follow me. I will show you exactly how the Führerbunker was situated underneath the mound. Please, follow."

Beyond the mound, Vogel stopped, waited for the other two to reach him.

For a moment, Vogel's good spirits vanished. He seemed transported in time. At last, he gestured. "You are now in the New Chancellery, in the ceremonial hall. You have an appointment to see Hitler, so you take a long tunnel to the Old Chancellery near us, walk into the Kannenberg Alley—the butler's pantry named after Hitler's fat butler Arthur Kannenberg—and you go down a circular staircase to the three steel-reinforced doors, the third one guarded by two SS soldiers. This leads into the top level of the Führerbunker—"

Vogel brought himself back into the present and started away from a portion of street curb, pacing the distance to a point just before the dirt mound.

"—right here," said Vogel, drawing a line in the grass with the toe of his shoe.

Emily moved beside Vogel. "When was the Führerbunker ready for use?" she wanted to know.

"The upper level or *Vorbunker* was excavated and built under the Old Reich Chancellery and its garden in 1936. At that time it was only thirty feet deep. After two years, Hitler decided that it was not large enough. In 1938, he ordered it made larger, which was done. Then in 1943, when things were starting to go badly in the war, Hitler had the bunker reinforced by the Hochtief Construction Company, and late in 1944 he ordered a much deeper second bunker built beneath the *Vorbunker*, the regular upper one. So, you see, there are two floors or levels to the Führerbunker. The lower level, used by Hitler and Eva Braun, was fifty-five feet below the ground."

"Where was the bunker entrance?" Emily wanted to know.

Vogel stepped over the line he had drawn with his shoe. "Right here down a short flight of concrete steps into the upper level of the bunker. There were thirteen small rooms on this top level, no decorations, unfinished plaster. Six rooms on one side, six on the other, and the general dining room in the rear. The rooms on this upper level were used for servants quarters, storage for lumber, storage space for food, a wine cellar, an office for the official Nazi news agency, *Deutsches Nachrichtenbüro*, a wireless that brought in BBC reports, a *Diätküche* or vegetarian kitchen, and the dining room or mess hall with an oak table for everyone to eat from. Once Hitler himself had moved into the Führerbunker, he lived below on the lower level, and rarely ever came up to the top floor."

"How did one get down to see Hitler?" asked Emily.

Vogel scrambled up the end of the dirt mound. "Here there was a concrete staircase with twelve steps that curved quite steeply down to the lower level. Then you were way down below ground where the main activity was."

Emily had climbed up the dirt mound to join Vogel, while Professor Blaubach remained on the field.

"Herr Vogel," Emily said, "can you explain to me the layout at the bottom level?"

Vogel opened the diagram in his hand once more. He bobbed his head. "I'll try. Follow me." He started going slowly along the right side of the dirt mound, describing what had been far below. "There were around eighteen cramped rooms on the bottom level, most of them painted gray, with a corridor forty-five feet in length and maybe nine feet wide dividing the rooms. The corridor had wooden paneling and some small Italian paintings hung on the walls. Hitler chose them himself. So as we walk here on the right side of the mound try to make-believe what you would see far below."

Progressing slowly, with Emily at his heels, Ernst Vogel said, "Here the boiler room. Next, Martin Bormann's office, and behind it the telephone exchange or switchboard. Next, Josef Goebbels's office, and behind this a cubicle for the duty officer. Next Goebbels's bedroom, and behind it the tiny surgery room and bedroom for Hitler's personal physicians. Now, the most important part, the left side of the corridor. I will show you."

Vogel retraced his steps on the mound and paced over to the left. Emily caught up with him, and together they began moving ahead once more.

"Beneath us are the general bathrooms and three toilets, and the dog-kennel room," said Vogel. "Next, Eva Braun's dressing room, bedroom, and a bathroom she shared with Hitler." A few more strides, and Vogel halted. "Also, far below, was Hitler's own private four-room suite. About here, his living room where he and

Eva died, and then an anteroom or waiting room between it and the corridor. Beside Hitler's living room was his private bedroom. Next, a small map room, and across the corridor his conference room where he met with his generals to direct the last defense of Berlin."

"What was in Hitler's living room?" Emily asked.

Vogel reflected on this, then rattled off a description of the furnishings. "In the narrow room, a sofa for two, a desk holding a framed photograph of his mother, and above the desk in a circular gilt frame the painting of Frederick the Great done by Anton Graff. Also, there were three valuable chairs from the Chancellery. The walls were paneled, and the floor carpeted, but still a cold room I was told."

"All right, Herr Vogel," said Emily, "you've stated that after Hitler and Eva committed suicide, the corpses were carried into the corridor and up some stairs to the garden. Do you want to point the stairwell out?"

"I can try to do so," Vogel told her. He walked to the front of the mound and veered off to one side. "Here, across from the conference room, were four flights of concrete steps that led from the bottom of the bunker to the very top inside the bunker, to a special emergency exit. You had to pass through a kind of outdoor rectangular blockhouse or vestibule leading into the Chancellery garden. After they carried Hitler out the exit—come, I'll show you . . ."

Vogel cautiously descended the dirt mound to a stretch of grassy field on one side. He waited for Emily to join him. Vogel consulted his diagram once more and carefully backed up a few steps.

"The emergency exit was close to this spot," he said. "Almost exactly between the exit and a round watchtower—about a meter from where you stand—there was a small moat, actually a shallow trench. That is where the two corpses were put down and buried."

"And when the bodies were reburied?"

"Turn a bit to your right—now count off three meters."

Emily pointed ahead. "There?" she asked.

"Yes, there was the crater with the bodies."

"Thank you, Herr Vogel." Emily realized that Professor Otto Blaubach was standing beside her. She met his eyes. "You heard all that? You'd know if it was reasonably accurate."

"To my knowledge, your friend is totally accurate," said Blaubach. "Apparently, his memory is unimpaired."

"It was an unforgettable experience for me," Vogel replied.

"And a happy time for the rest of the world," Blaubach added wryly. He drew Emily aside. "So now you know where you wish to excavate?"

Emily gave an assured nod. "Three exact spots. The trench and crater sites in this garden area. As for the Führerbunker, I don't need to uncover the whole thing, of course. Just one portion of the mound. I want to get down into Hitler's suite."

Blaubach was pleased. "Limiting your excavation of the mound enhances your chances for permission from the council. How much time will you need?"

"I have an experienced crew on call. I think three days should do it."

"Considering the time you'll want for searching, I imagine five or six days would be more realistic. I'll ask the council to allow you and your crew a week. How's that?"

"I'd be very grateful, Professor Blaubach."

"If you get permission, accept one piece of advice."

"Yes."

"Keep the purpose of your activity secret, absolutely secret. I think that is best for your success and well-being."

Werner Demke, the young pimpled junior reporter on *BZ*, the widely circulated Axel Springer tabloid, came routinely to his brief stopover at the Potsdamer Platz observation platform late every afternoon on his way back to the office. One of his assignments was to get a list of foreign celebrities who visited Berlin weekly. Usually the police department and a half dozen of the better hotels were his most productive sources. The observation platform at the Wall was a less productive source, but occasionally some politician or cinema star was brought here to clamber up to the platform and gaze over the Wall into the East German no-man's-land. As a cub reporter, Demke felt that he must ignore no possibility for an item or story.

Parking his Volkswagen, he strode over to the novelty shop and ducked into the doorway. He called to the proprietress, "Any high and mighty ones in the vicinity this afternoon?"

"None, Herr Demke. Sorry. Just a small British tour group from Manchester. They're probably up on the platform right now."

"Not exactly a hot story. Many thanks."

Demke turned away from the shop and started for his car dejectedly. It had been a barren day. Ascher, the city editor, wouldn't be too happy.

He heard a loud joyous squeal and glanced over his shoulder at the observation platform. There were two plump middle-aged women on top, at the platform railing, holding binoculars to their eyes angled down into the East German Security Zone. One of the women was squealing excitedly again. Then Demke saw the third member of the group, an older man, rush to the railing beside them, focus his camera on something in the Frontier Zone and begin shooting.

Werner Demke wondered what had drawn the attention of the tourists, and on a hunch he detoured from his car and strolled toward the platform steps.

By the time Demke reached the foot of the wooden staircase, the three tourists on the platform had finished and were coming jubilantly down the steps. They were chattering in English, and Demke was sure that these were the British tourists the proprietress had spoken about.

Demke stepped aside as the three completed their descent and now clustered within earshot.

"You're sure it was Emily Ashcroft?" said the older man. "I shot a whole roll of her and the two men, right up to their getting into the jeep."

The heavier woman spoke up. "James, I could recognize her the way I can recognize you. It was the woman on the telly, on the BBC, I'm positive."

"Right," said the older man, patting his camera. "At least we got one celebrity on this trip. Well, sort of a celebrity."

Listening, Werner Demke tried to recall the name of Emily Ashcroft. It rang a bell dimly. All at once, loudly. Of course, Ashcroft, the father, had been killed in a hit-and-run off the Ku'-damm some days ago, and his daughter was here to finish the Hitler biography.

Instantly, Demke saw the possibility of a story.

He eased up to the British trio and politely interrupted them. "Forgive me. I couldn't help but overhear you—that something was going on down in the East German Security Zone. Just out of curiosity, I'd like to know what I missed."

The heavier woman said proudly, "You missed one of our British television celebrities. There she was, down there in the middle of all those watchtowers and communist guards with two men."

"That's strange," said Demke. "No one has been allowed in there, except soldiers, in years."

The older man had elbowed closer, patting his camera once more. "I'll tell you what she and her friend were doing. I saw them around that heap of dirt that everyone says is where Hitler and his lady hid before they killed themselves. The Ashcroft woman and one of the men were marching on the heap and talking steadily. Then they came down off it and started looking around on one side—"

"The Chancellery garden," Demke murmured in an undertone.

"Whatever it was. They stood there talking, when another man joined them. After a while, they all walked to a jeep and were driven off." The older man brandished his camera. "I got it all. A nice souvenir."

Werner Demke's mind was in high gear. "You got pictures of the three of them?"

"A whole roll."

Demke swallowed. "How'd you like to sell that roll?"

The older man was startled. "Sell it?"

"Yes, I'd like to buy the roll."

The older man shook his head vigorously. "I'm taking pictures of our trip for my photo album, and I don't want to lose them."

"You wouldn't lose them," said Demke with haste. "You'd still get a set of the prints. I guarantee it. It's just that I want a set, too." He wondered how much he had in his wallet. Maybe a hundred marks. It was a gamble. Ascher might reject the whole thing. On the other hand, Ascher might be impressed. "I'll give you a hundred marks for the negatives and first set of prints."

The older man was shaking his head again. "No."

The heavier woman had pushed herself in front of the older man, obviously her husband. "Wait a minute, James, hold on." She confronted Demke. "What's this about? Who are you?"

"I'm a reporter on a German newspaper," Demke said. "You may have stumbled on an incident that could be a minor bit of news. It has been a long, long time, so far as I can remember, since anyone was let into that East German Security Zone to look over the remains of Hitler's bunker. The fact that Miss Ashcroft was there gives the photographs a certain amount of curiosity value. Maybe I'm wrong. Maybe my editor won't want to use any of the pictures. Nevertheless, it is worth all the money I have on me to at least let him see them. You'd gain a hundred marks and get a set of the pictures, besides."

The heavier woman was considering the proposition.

"How much is a hundred marks?" her husband was asking her.

She whispered to him. The older man's eyes blinked. "For just this roll?" he said.

The heavier woman grabbed the camera away. "All right, young man, you can have the roll. Let's see your money and a receipt first."

Late the next morning, Evelyn Hoffmann was in their familiar rendezvous place, the private table in the rear of Mampes Gute Stube, and she had already ordered *Bratwurst* and beer for Chief Wolfgang Schmidt and a *gemischter Salat* and tea for herself.

This meeting was unusual. For years they had met once a week, to enjoy each other's company, speak of the old times, exchange gossip. The routine was unvarying. Yet, early this morning, the message had come from Schmidt summoning her to a meeting an hour before noon, even though they had seen one another just a few days ago.

Strange.

Coming to the Ku'damm on the bus, she had speculated on the reason for the sudden meeting. Nothing of an urgent nature occurred to her. Yet, because it was unexpected, the message gave her some sense of urgency. As a result, she had found herself downtown almost an hour early. The choices were to go to the restaurant and wait, or to window-shop, or to drop in on Liesl and Klara to pass the extra time.

She had turned off at Knesebeckstrasse and walked over to the Fiebig apartment to look in on her close ones. Entering, she had realized a rare omission. In her confusion, Evelyn had forgotten to bring Klara a small gift of some kind. But then Klara was not there. Liesl was alone, and Evelyn was relieved. It was difficult to speak of the early days in front of Klara, and it was impossible to do so when Franz was present. He was a young radical who detested Germany's modern past, the Germany that had been Evelyn's glory. She and Liesl had learned quickly never to discuss those early days in front of Franz or even Klara.

"This is a surprise," Liesl had said. "What brings you here today?"

Waving off the Fiebigs' part-time housekeeper, Evelyn had rolled Liesl's wheelchair into the living room while telling her about Schmidt's message. Evelyn had been eager to talk to Liesl, and had barely begun to do so when she heard the scraping of a key in the front door.

"Klara," Liesl had explained. "She had an appointment with the obstetrician this morning."

Klara had come through the front door full of high spirits, but had also shown surprise at Evelyn's presence. "Aunt Evelyn! How good to see you." She had kissed Evelyn warmly. "What's the occasion?"

"I have to meet someone shortly," Evelyn had said vaguely. "More important, what did the doctor say?"

"Everything's perfect," she had said, her eyes glowing. Then she grimaced. "But I am to expect morning sickness." She had started out of the room. "I have to change, and go to the kitchen. Franz is coming home for lunch. He wants to hear the latest news. I hope you'll wait to see him, Aunt Evelyn."

Evelyn had already come to her feet. "Thank you, dear. I wish I could, but I can't. I must keep my appointment." Above all, she had wanted to get away before Franz Fiebig appeared.

She had succeeded in escaping.

Now she was at the restaurant table awaiting Police Chief Wolfgang Schmidt's arrival.

The salad and rolls and tea, which she had ordered for herself, and the beer for Schmidt, came first. She had finished sweetening her tea, and was about to reach for a roll, when she became aware that the burly Schmidt had arrived, was looming over her, taking her hand and kissing the back of it.

"How are you, Effie?" he asked, settling his big bulk at the table across from her.

"Fine, fine, Wolfgang," she replied. "Just wondering about your message."

"Didn't want to give you a fright," he said. "But there is something I felt I had to discuss." He tasted his beer, then gulped it down. "I'm a little pressed for time this morning, so I can't stay too long. Still, this is important."

"What is?" Evelyn wanted to know. "What's so important?"

"This," Schimdt said. He yanked a folded tabloid from his jacket pocket and began to unfold it. "This morning's *BZ*. I didn't think you'd see it."

"You know I rarely look at it."

"Today you should," he said, turning back the first and second page, and handing the paper to her so that she could see the third page. "That photograph covering the top half. Have a look."

Evelyn had the tabloid in hand, and she stared at the large photograph with curiosity.

It was a clear picture taken from the Potsdamer Platz observation platform in West Berlin and it was focused on the dirt mound that covered the old Führerbunker. Three persons could plainly be seen in this blowup, a young woman and two elderly men having a conversation beside the mound of the bunker.

The headline read: WILL THEY BE DIGGING FOR HITLER AGAIN?

She heard Schmidt speak. "Read the caption, Effie."

Her eyes went down to the caption. Swiftly, she read it. The three persons in the photograph were identified as Emily Ashcroft, the prominent British historian who was in Berlin to complete the definitive biography of Adolf Hitler; Herr Ernst Vogel, a onetime SS honor guard who had been a sentry at the Führerbunker in its final days; and Professor Otto Blaubach, an East Berlin authority on the Third Reich and a deputy prime minister in the East German government. The story went on to state that these were the first visitors to the site of the historic Führerbunker in at least a decade, and it speculated that there was every possibility that Miss Ashcroft was examining the site as a prelude to one more excavation of the area in search of a new clue to the Führer's end.

Evelyn raised her head, momentarily bewildered. "This is the young lady you told me about the other day?"

Schmidt crushed a cracker in his hand and downed the crumbs. "Emily Ashcroft, the British historian who checked into the Kempinski. I thought you should know she is going ahead."

Evelyn did not hide her concern. "Do you think she'll get permission to dig?"

"Her father did just before his fatal accident. So I'm guessing that she will. That fellow in the photograph, Blaubach, he's a big shot in the East German government. He could arrange it."

"But why dig now, so long after? Everyone in the world knows that the Führer and Eva Braun died in the bunker and were buried there."

"Evidently everyone doesn't believe it, Effie."

Evelyn was studying the photograph once more. Shaking her head, she said, "It's crazy. I wonder what she is looking for?"

"It does not matter," Schmidt said, retrieving the newspaper, folding it, shoving it into his pocket. "I just wanted to reassure you, Effie, in case you heard about this. I promise you there will not be an excavation at the bunker, no more digging into the past."

"You promise?"

Schmidt lifted his bulk out of the chair, his fat lips curled into a smile. "I promise. You need not be concerned about Miss Ashcroft again."

For Emily, it had been a busy morning in her suite at the Kempinski.

The courier package of files, sent by Pamela from Oxford, had finally arrived. The top folders contained information devoted to Hitler's career as an artist and the rest were photographic files of all the government buildings constructed in major German cities under Hitler. Emily wasted no time in telephoning the Palace Hotel to learn whether Nicholas Kirvov had checked in. He had, and Emily was soon speaking to him on the phone.

"I have the material from Oxford," she said. "Maybe it will tell you more about the building in your Hitler painting."

"How kind you are," Kirvov said. "Are you free for lunch? We can have it here in the Grillroom restaurant, if you like. Then we can go through the files together."

Emily made the date. No sooner had she hung up than the telephone sounded. She picked up the receiver.

It was Rex Foster, and Emily felt a girlish delight in hearing his voice.

"I suppose it is none of my business," he was saying, "but where were you last night? I must have called a half dozen times."

She was pleased. "I was out inspecting the excavation site until near dinnertime. After that, I had dinner with the man who is going to head the dig for me—presuming I get permission. I spent the evening with him and his wife, telling them what I'd seen at the bunker site." She paused. "Why were you calling me? Oh, I suppose it was to find out whether I could help you locate the architect Zeidler."

"No, Emily, that's not why I called you. I just wanted to know how you were—maybe see you if you were free—"

"If you want to know how I am, why don't you come along

with me to the Palace Hotel? I'm having lunch there with Nicholas Kirvov. Remember? Curator of the Hermitage in Leningrad. I'm going to try to help him with that Hitler painting of his. You could help, too. Bring along your portfolio of Third Reich architecture. Besides, you might enjoy meeting Kirvov. You have a lot in common."

"I'm more interested in what you and I have in common," said Foster. "So it's a date."

They agreed on a time to meet in the lobby.

And now, outside the Palace Grillroom at twelve-thirty, Kirvov was waiting for Emily, somewhat distressed. After welcoming Foster, he apologized to his guests. The Grillroom was crowded and they could not have their reservation for another half hour.

"Well, why don't we spend the time trying to solve the location of the building in your Hitler oil?" said Emily. She looked about her. "Maybe we could go to your room for more privacy, if you don't mind?"

"That would be perfect," said Kirvov eagerly. "Please come with me."

In a few minutes, Emily and Foster, with her photographic file and his architectural portfolio, were in Kirvov's room on the fourth floor. It was a pleasant room, Emily noted, pale velveteen drapes at the windows, the wallpaper a tan rice-paper fabric, a color television set with a vase of yellow rosebuds on top, a comforter on the double bed.

"Let's get straight to your oil," Emily suggested.

"Please, do be seated," said Kirvov, pulling two chairs up to a corner table, while Foster brought up a third chair. As they sat, Kirvov unwrapped his painting and set it down before his guests.

Constantly referring to the painting of the building in the Hitler oil, Emily peeled through her file of photographs of the government buildings of the Third Reich in Berlin. Meanwhile, also glancing at the painting, Foster was turning the pages of his architectural portfolio open on the floor beside the chair.

Emily gave a whoop. "I think I have it, Nicholas!" She pulled a photograph out of her file and held it up beside the painting. "Isn't this it?"

Foster, watching, jerked a leaf out of his portfolio and studied it alongside her photo. His was another shot of the massive building from a different angle.

Emily could see at once that they were one and the same. "That's it," she declared. "Of course, neither of us has an exact shot of the front entrance to match the painting. I'll phone Pamela to see whether we've got anything in the other files, just to make certain."

"Do that," Foster said. He turned to Kirvov. "But I still think we've found your building, Nicholas."

The Russian was grinning. "You have, I'm sure you have. Only—I'd like to know, what is it?"

"The *Reichsluftfahrtministerium*," Emily told Kirvov. "The Reich Air Ministry, also known as the Göring Air Ministry." She read from the caption in back. "Construction started in 1933, completed in 1935."

"A remarkable find!" said Kirvov with enthusiasm. "The only Hitler painting I know of done in Berlin."

"He must have done the building after 1935, but no later than the early 1940s," said Emily. "Because after that, he couldn't have painted it. Simply because it wasn't there. All of the Third Reich government buildings were destroyed, leveled flat, by the massive American and British air-raid bombings in the early 1940s."

Foster had brought his own portfolio piece closer and was rereading his caption. He lifted his head. "Not so fast, Emily. What you are saying is not quite true."

Emily was puzzled. "What do you mean?"

"All the big Third Reich government buildings were not totally destroyed and leveled by Allied bombings over Berlin in the 1940s. One building survived almost intact. One building only."

"Which one?" Emily wanted to know.

Foster indicated the photo attached to the leaf from his portfolio. "This very one. The Göring Air Ministry was the sole survivor of those bombings. It suffered thirty-five-percent damage, but the structure was never destroyed. The Air Ministry alone, of all this Hitler architecture, survived in Berlin. It stood in the 1930s and 1940s where it stands today in the 1980s."

"What are you saying?" Kirvov interjected.

"I'm saying," continued Foster, "that while Adolf Hitler may have painted your oil in the 1930s—he could just as well have done the painting anytime during or after the 1940s—he could have painted it in the 1960s or 1970s or 1980s. Because the building remains there to be painted. He could have painted it anytime after his suicide in 1945."

"If he lived," said Emily quietly.

"If he lived," agreed Foster.

Emily stared at the other two. "I think before we try to digest this, we should now have lunch."

"And a stiff drink," said Foster thoughtfully.

They had spent most of the afternoon with Nicholas Kirvov at the Palace Grillroom eating lunch and speculating on the possibility that identification of the Göring Air Ministry in the Hitler oil might tell them something of the Führer's actual fate. Emily had been forced to remind herself that they were still short of facts, and indulging themselves in a guessing game. Immediately, Kirvov had become more practical. He had thought that he would like to have a look at the building depicted in his Hitler oil, and Emily and Foster promised to lead him to it in East Berlin as soon as they were free. Meanwhile, Kirvov would keep himself busy trying to track down the art gallery that had sold the Hitler oil, since he had not yet received its name from the cruise steward.

Now, returning to the lobby of the Kempinski in the late afternoon, Foster said to Emily, "You mentioned Rudi Zeidler this morning. Did your secretary send anything on him?"

"Zeidler, the Nazi architect you wanted to find. The one with the missing plans. Of course. Forgive me, Rex, he slipped my mind. Yes, Pamela's package had some fat folders on Hitler's architects. I'm sure Zeidler's among them. I'll go through the folders right away and buzz you." She started for the concierge's counter. "Let me pick up my key and any messages."

"Go ahead," said Foster. "I have my key. I want to buy myself something to read. Meet you at the elevator."

Emily watched Foster veer off to the left, stopping at the stand that displayed numerous local and international newspapers and magazines. She went on to the concierge's counter and requested the key to her suite. When she turned away, she saw Foster walking slowly toward her. He had skimmed the front page of what appeared to be a German tabloid and was opening it to the second and third pages. Suddenly he halted in his tracks.

As Emily wondered what had gripped his attention, Foster resumed walking toward her.

He took her by the elbow, steered her away from the elevator in the direction of a table and three chairs in the lobby.

"There's something I want to show you," he said cryptically.

Puzzled, she sat down, eyes on him as he pulled up a chair next to her own.

'What is it, Rex?" she asked.

"You wanted to keep your visit here a secret, didn't you?"

"You know that."

"Who's in on your secret—I mean, here in Berlin?"

"Why just the people I have to work with like Professor

Blaubach, two or three others. And, of course, a few I felt I could trust like you, Tovah Levine, Nicholas Kirvov."

"But you told no newspaper people?"

"Of course not. Well, actually one man named Peter Nitz on the *Morgenpost*. But he's the one who first warned me to proceed secretly." She creased her brow. "Why are you asking me all this, Rex?"

He unfolded the tabloid in his hand. "Because now everyone in Berlin knows the reason you're here."

"I—I don't understand."

He had opened the tabloid to the third page, and placed it in her lap. "See for yourself."

She took up the morning edition of *BZ* and found herself staring at the photograph of herself with Blaubach and Vogel at the Führerbunker mound. For seconds, she was aghast. Her eyes riveted on the caption.

"They—they even have my name, and what I'm trying to do," she said half to herself. She raised her head. "Rex, how did they get this picture?"

"I don't know. Obviously taken by someone from an observation platform at the Wall. Maybe the press keeps a lookout for what goes on out there."

Emily lowered the paper. "This is terrible," she said. "But I'm not going to worry about it. I have too much to do. I'll simply do what I have to do and go home and finish my work."

"Admirable," said Foster, "except I think you should be on your guard. Look, let's face it, Emily. I don't want to scare you but I want you to be realistic. This kind of exposure can put you in danger. I mean it could incite some neo-Nazi fanatics who might want to stop you—see that you meet with an accident—like your father did."

Emily straightened her shoulders. "I don't think anything will happen," she said. "After all, my father may have died in a genuine accident. I can't believe there are many Nazis around after almost a half century."

"No?" said Foster. "Then why are you trying to dig up the Führerbunker? To prove that they all died when they were supposed to? Or to find out if any of them are still alive?"

"That's another matter," she said stubbornly. "That's merely historical research, double-checking the past. And frankly, I don't think anything new will come of it." She stood up. "I think we should both go on with our work. But first I'll go through those architecture files and find you what you need on Rudi Zeidler."

Foster was on his feet. "If you insist. There's no rush on Zeidler."

"You don't want to hang around here forever. I'll have something on him before dinner. If you'd like to, you can come to my suite for a drink before I have a bite to eat. I should have what you want by then."

"Do you have a date for dinner?"

"As a matter of fact, I don't. I was going to order up a sandwich."

"Do you mind company?" He was leading her to the elevator. "I'd enjoy having dinner with you. Not only tonight. Any night you're free."

At the elevator, she pushed the button and faced him. "An attractive offer. What's behind it? Are you trying to protect me?"

"That could be one reason," he acknowledged. "But the real reason is—I want to be with you."

At once, she relaxed and smiled up at him. "Better," she said. "In that case, drop by at eight."

It was a quarter to eight, and in his room Foster had become increasingly restless.

Emily Ashcroft occupied his mind entirely. The fact that she might be exposed to danger made him realize more keenly how much he had come to care for her. Actually, despite his wariness about emotional ties, Foster admitted to himself that what he felt was far more than merely caring. He had never quite felt this way about another woman, wanting to be with one every minute and wanting her to be his very own.

He finished knotting his tie, and slipped on his jacket. The mantel clock showed it was fourteen minutes before eight. He decided to be early. If she was not ready for him, he would make himself a drink while she finished dressing. At least he would be near her.

Leaving his room, he waited for the elevator. When it arrived he took it down to the second floor. As the elevator doors slid open, he saw that suite number 229 was up the corridor straight ahead.

Stepping out of the elevator, he saw a room-service waiter, a stocky young man carrying a tray of drinks, appear from another corridor, go to Emily's door, and without knocking use a passkey to let himself in.

Foster's first thought was that Emily had considerately ordered cocktails for them in her suite before dinner, and that the waiter was just delivering them. Pleased, Foster sauntered down the corridor, expecting the waiter to emerge and depart. But the waiter did not come out. Foster became aware that the door to the suite was partially open, so he decided to go inside.

Entering the living room, he was surprised to see it empty. The waiter was nowhere in sight, although he had set the tray of drinks on the desk. Curious, Foster peered into the bedroom, expecting to see the waiter hovering while Emily signed the bill. But no one was in the bedroom either. This was mystifying. Tentatively, Foster stepped inside the bedroom, moving toward the bathroom, intending to call out to Emily.

Then, to his surprise, he could see that the bathroom door was wide open and he went swiftly to it, wondering what was going on. Instantly, he saw what was happening, and the shock of it rooted him to where he stood by the open door.

For the bathroom was anything but empty.

Running water could be heard, and Emily was obviously still in the shower—and outside the glass shower door, his back to Foster, stood the burly waiter, very still.

For a moment, Foster thought he had come upon a voyeur, or possibly someone who was going to attempt a rape. That instant Emily turned off the shower, and as she did so the waiter pulled a knife from beneath his jacket and yanked back the shower door.

Foster could hear Emily's choked outcry of disbelief. The waiter, knife upraised, was about to enter the shower.

In that frozen second, Foster could feel all of his Vietnam-bred instincts to attack explode inside him, and he catapulted himself forward with a shout of rage.

Stunned, the waiter stopped and whirled about, knife still upraised, trying to make out what was happening. Foster was upon him like a madman, grabbing and twisting the waiter's raised wrist until the knife fell away to the floor. In a quick practiced judo motion, Foster crouched down, gripped the waiter, and flipped him high in the air over his head, sending the assailant crashing to the tiled bathroom floor behind him.

About to spin and grab the man, Foster's eyes held momentarily on Emily in the shower. He saw her naked and dripping wet, falling against a side of the shower, eyes closed, choking with fear, trying to keep her balance.

Assured that she was unhurt, Foster wheeled to deal once more with her attacker. But the burly waiter had managed to stagger to his feet, and without a backward glance he plunged into the bedroom. Breathing heavily, Foster started after him. By the time he reached the door into the living room, the waiter was gone. Foster rushed to the open door of the suite, and looked up the hotel corridor. He saw the waiter, on the run, disappearing around a corner.

He wanted to pursue the man, but he knew the murderous bastard would have carefully planned his own escape route. He would never catch him. He wondered whether he should phone down to the lobby, but he knew that interception was impossible, too. The killer would have found other means to enter the hotel and to leave it.

And all Foster really cared about at that moment was Emily and her safety.

He rushed back into the bathroom to help her. She was still in the shower. She had slid down the side of the tile shower and lay cringing beneath the dripping shower head in a state of collapse.

He ducked inside. Kneeling, he reached for her and tried to get hold of her wet, slippery body. As his arms went under her, trying to take a firm grip, Emily realized it was Foster who was holding her and that she was safe, and she laid her head against his shoulder with a moan of gratitude.

With little difficulty he lifted her off the tile floor, and, as she curled tightly against him, he backed out of the shower, snatched one of the hotel's terrycloth bathrobes, and dropped it over her. Carefully, he carried her across the bathroom and into the bedroom.

"How are you? How are you?" he kept whispering.

"Thank God for you, thank God."

"Here," he said, still holding her and awkwardly tearing back her bedspread and blanket at the same time. At last, he managed it, and gently he deposited her on the bed and pulled the blanket over her body, throwing the robe beside her.

Covered, she began to regain her composure, blinking up at him. "What happened, Rex? Who was it?"

"It was a room-service waiter bringing in your drink order, or so I thought when I followed him in here."

"But I never ordered from room service," she said. She pulled herself upright, holding the top of the blanket over her breasts. "I already had drinks here for us. There wasn't supposed to be any waiter."

"And there wasn't. Somebody came here to kill you. When I saw him in the bathroom, I went berserk." He peered at her. "You're sure you're all right?"

"I'm alive," she said. "I guess that's being all right." She paused. "Who could it have been?"

He gave her a lopsided smile. "Apparently a Constant Reader who saw a photograph in the morning paper, someone who didn't like your nosing about in the Nazi past."

She shook her tangled wet hair with disbelief. "But murder . . ." she said.

"You know a better way to discourage snoopy people?" He looked down at her again with concern. "Emily, how do you feel?"

"Still a little scared, but recovering. I'll be fine in a short while. I'm afraid I'm not up to dinner though. I seem to have lost my appetite. You know what? All I need is company, if you can stand being company on an empty stomach. Company and a long drink. Maybe Scotch. And you?"

"Company and a long drink," he affirmed, "and to hell with ordering dinner. This is cozier. I think we should both celebrate survival and togetherness by getting a little drunk. Let me pour a couple of Scotches for starters." He paused before going into the living room. "You know, Emily, I meant to tell you something tonight. I mean, at the first moment we were together."

"What?"

"That I think I love you, that's all. Now let's drink to that."

It was nearly midnight. In the bedroom of Emily's hotel suite, they had been sipping their drinks and talking for close to three hours. Emily had managed to pull on the unbelted robe, and pushed aside the bedcover. She was still sitting up in bed, the robe loosely hiding her breasts. Foster had soon moved from a chair to sit on the side of her bed. She'd had three drinks of Scotch, and he was finishing his fourth.

In the last hour, their talk had become more intimate. Sleepily, a trifle woozily, she had told him about her brief marriage, her juvenile mistake. And, feeling safe with him, she had related some details of her humiliating affair with Jeremy Robinson. In turn, he had discussed some of his encounters with other women, and his dissatisfaction with them. Finally, for the first time ever, he had volunteered to speak of his fiasco of a marriage with Valerie Granich. Emily had heard him out understandingly. "So we're both casualties," she murmured. "Casualties of—what?—the war between the sexes?" He had smiled. "I would put it more affirmatively. Survivors of bad judgment who've learned what we want."

Considering this, Emily had wondered aloud, "What do we want? What do *you* want from a woman, Rex?" Haltingly, he had tried to tell her and then she had begun to tell him what she hoped for from a man. The words closeness and empathy and tenderness were quietly reiterated.

Now they were silent, beyond the region of words.

He felt high, trembling inside with wanting her, desiring her, aroused by the natural perfumes of her breasts and skin, but unable somehow to make the transition from verbal to physical intimacy. He decided not to press it, to allow the relationship to mellow, to wait for another time.

He began to get up from the bed. "I think I'd better go now."

She stared up at him. "Why?"

Uncertainly, he answered. "To let you get some rest."

Her eyes held on him, and she seemed to be making some kind of decision. Deliberately, she set her empty glass on the side table. "I thought you said, long ago this evening, that you loved me. Did you?"

"I did."

"You said I shouldn't be alone any more. I hope you mean it. I don't want to be alone, Rex. I want to be with you." She pulled off the robe with which she had been partially covering her breasts. "You've seen me naked—"

"Well, hardly—" He found speech difficult, his gaze fixed on her small, firm, round breasts, the large brown circles accentuating the hardened and pointed nipples. "I didn't really see you . . ."

She pulled at the robe again and cast it entirely aside. "Now you can," she said. "I think turnabout is fair play. I want to see you naked, too. For Chrissakes, Rex, take off your damn clothes —that is, if you want to."

"I want to," he said, setting down his drink. "Are you sure you're up to it?"

"I'm up to it," she said. "The question is—are you?"

He had never undressed more quickly, flinging his clothes aside, until he stood before her naked.

Her eyes never left him, and they both knew that he was up to it.

She reached out to caress the hardness of his erection. "How lovely," she whispered.

He felt that his head would dissolve, and his rigid body, too, if he did not have her soon.

He lowered himself onto the bed beside her, and her slender fingers continued to flutter around his penis. She was staring at it with a half smile. "I like what I see," she said softly. "What I see looks very serious."

"It's as serious as can be, and it wants company."

She released him, still with her half smile, and fell back on the pillow. "You're invited," she whispered.

Rising to his knees, at last he saw her clearly nude. From below the protruding milky white and brown-tipped breasts, her abdomen was flat, her rib cage tautly outlined, her navel a slash, the auburn pubic hair down-thin, a marvelous stretch of triangle that revealed the bud of her clitoris and the pink narrow folds of her vulva and labia.

She spread her legs wide, and he bent between them to kiss her clitoris with his tongue.

"Oh, God, darling," she groaned.

Then he was over her, between her thighs, and sliding his penis deep inside her, feeling the fantastic sensation of the moist parting and the snug clinging and hotness of her vulva and his penis as they held together so deep inside her.

"Oh, God," she was repeating again and again.

He tried to find his voice. "I never—never—felt anything like this is my life. Emily, I love you."

And then he was moving steadily inside her, long, smooth strokes, and then faster ones, harder ones, unceasing ones.

He could see her gorgeous face, eyes shut, her head going from side to side on the pillow, her lips mouthing something he could not hear. He could see the rise and fall of her globular breasts, and feel the circular motions of her buttocks. She was lifting her hips higher, lifting her trembling thighs, and he drove deeper into her unremittingly. Her hands groped for and found his testicles, bunching them together. He sighed and came down on her fully, feeling the give of her breasts, seeking and finding her full lips, her tongue, hearing his heart and her own hammering in unison.

Her wetness below engulfed him, but he did not slow, driving, pulling, driving inside her slippery passage.

Abruptly her torso heaved, her buttocks rising, her thighs tightening around him in a vise of flesh in one great and prolonged convulsion. "Oh, darling," she gasped.

But he went on, and then she had another shuddering orgasm and, moments later, explosively, he came too.

They lay still in each other's embrace for what seemed countless minutes. After a while, he could see that her eyes were closed in sleep and he could hear her breathing in relaxed slumber.

Gently, he removed his body from her own, withdrawing his flaccid and sated penis.

After a while, sitting on the bed beside her, his legs crossed, he sat watching her in sleep. He had never felt more content, fulfilled, at peace with himself. Watching her with love, he could no longer quite remember this woman as she'd seemed when they had first met. He half remembered her as someone too composed, self-possessed, self-contained, forbidding in her scholarship and independence, desirable but seemingly unattainable.

And now she had bared herself to him totally, surrendered her passion to his own, fused herself to him, become a part of him as he had become a part of her.

The love he felt for her was almost unbearable. And so was his happiness.

Drawing the blanket back over her, he realized more than ever how precious she was to him. It gave him a jolt to remember what had happened not many hours before. Someone had tried to kill her. Someone might try again. He must not allow it. He didn't dare lose her.

Yet, he knew, she could be safe only if she abandoned the quest for Hitler and ignored the riddle of her father's death.

No matter how much she loved him, wanted to be with him, Foster realized with certainty that Emily would abandon neither hunt.

Slipping beneath the blanket beside her, he felt her stir slightly, then lay an arm across his chest. He searched her lovely face in repose, reached to put out the lamp, and tried to think what he could do to protect her, them, their future. In the darkness, it seemed insoluble. And soon he was lost in sleep.

6

When Foster awakened, at mid-morning, and focused his eyes on the ceiling, he knew that he was not in his own room, and for a lapsed moment was unsure of where he had been sleeping.

Instantly he remembered, and reached out for Emily in the bed, but felt nothing. Turning his head on the pillow, he saw that her place was empty.

He sat up immediately.

She was standing at the dressing table, fastening a manila envelope. Her hair was loose, uncombed, and she was wearing the terrycloth bathrobe that did not completely cover her breasts. Her legs and feet were bare.

He began to feel the swelling between his legs.

"Emily, what are you doing?"

She turned, smiling. "I found Rudi Zeidler's unlisted phone number and address. That's really what you came here for, isn't it?"

Rex smiled. "Who's Rudi Zeidler?"

"Well then you got what you came for, didn't you? Now you'd better go off and find those missing architectural plans, don't you think?"

"Emily," he said quietly, "I'm in love with you. I've never met anyone like you. I never want to meet any other woman again."

Her face had become serious. "Rex, do you mean that?"

"I want to be with you every second of my life from this moment on." His desire for her was all-consuming. "Emily, I want to be with you right now."

"Right now?"

"This minute," he said imperatively, making room for her on the bed.

"Why not?" she said.

Dropping the envelope, she pulled back her terrycloth robe, shook herself out of it, and let it drop behind her.

She posed nakedly beside him, her arms limply at her sides, but he could see the increased rise and fall of her breasts.

Between his legs, he could feel the rigidity grow.

He threw aside the blanket, and fell back, his arms outstretched to welcome her, and his erection pointed at her.

With a cry of pleasure, she bounded onto the bed, pinned his shoulders back, and straddled him. Easily, gracefully, she came down over him until the tip of his erection touched her vagina. She adjusted herself, so that her opening met the hardness of his erection. Then she eased herself lower and lower, as her vulva filled with his penetration.

Now she was riding him up and down, riding and rocking,

while they grasped each other, clutched each other, going on and on.

After many minutes, they gradually rolled to their sides, face to face, and he began to dominate the pelvic movements.

Soon he was above her, the rhythm of their intense coupling picking up.

At least a half hour later he let go, filling her with his orgasm, and as he finished she came, wildly, registering the release from fingertips to toes. After an interval he pushed himself off her and saw that her eyes were tightly shut and her hips swaying, so he reached down and began to caress her clitoris. She came quickly again. And then a third time, and a fourth.

Then they were done, and he took her in his arms, and she clung to him, head on his hairy chest.

When she wriggled free, she patted back her long hair, and propped herself on an elbow considering him.

"You know," she said, "we can go on doing this all day."

"And all night," he reminded her.

"But one of us has to be practical," she said. "As the man in the family, you'd better get to work. Go thou and see Zeidler."

He sat upright. "What are you going to do?"

"I'm going to have a big breakfast with the man I love. Then I'm going to pack him off to Herr Zeidler."

"And after I'm gone?"

"I'm going to have your key, and go to your room. I'm going to gather your things together, and move you into this suite. Two of us can stay here for about the price of one. It's never too early to economize. That is, if you agree."

"I insist," said Foster.

"And after I have your belongings down here with me, I'll start my pursuit of Herr Hitler again."

"But carefully."

"Very carefully."

He swung off the bed. "Let me shower and dress. Soon as we're done with breakfast, before trying to see Zeidler, I'm going to tell the management about the man with the knife. I'm taking no more chances with you, my pet."

She smiled up at him, and he bent down and kissed her and found it more difficult than ever to stop doing so.

In his fourth-floor single room, using the number that Emily had given him, Foster dialed and hoped that he would find Rudi Zeidler in.

The male voice answering the telephone on the other end sounded cheerful and young, and Foster wondered if it was Zeidler, since he figured that Speer's associate must be sixty-five years old by now.

The voice confirmed that he was, indeed, Rudi Zeidler. "Who is this?" he asked in German.

"My name is Rex Foster, and I've been trying to locate you for some time," Foster replied in German.

"You have an American accent," said Zeidler.

"Because I'm an architect from Los Angeles," explained Foster.

"Very good," said Zeidler, switching to English. "I am fascinated by the early California architecture, especially the Spanish Colonial or Mission style." He coughed. "Why have you been trying to locate me, and who gave you my number?"

"I obtained your phone number from a British friend of mine, Miss Ashcroft—she and her father, Dr. Harrison Ashcroft, were working on a biography about Adolf Hitler. Dr. Ashcroft interviewed you once."

There was a pause. "Yes, yes, now I recollect. A clever man. I spent an afternoon with him. So, now you are calling me. Why?"

"Also to spend a little time with you. I am completing a book on—" Foster hesitated, not wanting to use the word Nazi— "on German—on German architecture during the Third Reich. I understand that you played an important role."

"A minor one." Zeidler seemed to reconsider his self-assessment. "But, perhaps in its way, it was vital. Ah, it was crazy what I had to do for that lunatic man Hitler."

"I'd like to hear all about it, meet with you as soon as possible."

"As soon as possible is today. You are free today?"

"Anytime that is suitable to you."

They made a date for lunch.

Pleased with the arrangement, and grateful to Emily for having made it possible, Foster determined to use the better part of the next hour giving Emily a hand in moving his effects to her suite.

Humming happily as he thought of Emily and relived their lovemaking together, he emptied the bureau drawers of his few clothes and put them on the bed, took his jackets and slacks off hangers and transferred them to his garment bag, gathered together his toilet articles and placed them in a leather kit, and finally packed the clothes on the bed into his suitcase. Everything was orderly, and he would leave his luggage for Emily, who would have it moved to her suite and unpack.

Ready to depart, Foster called downstairs to the information desk and said that he would like to meet with the manager of the Kempinski as soon as possible. He added that it was to report an incident of grave importance. Since he refused to say anything more, he was advised to come down to the lobby where he would be met.

Putting on a freshly pressed plaid sport jacket, Foster took the portfolio of his architectural book under one arm, and headed for the elevator.

In the lobby, he found someone already waiting for him before the information desk.

The short, dapper gentleman, a Swiss as it turned out, proved to be not the manager but an assistant. The manager was in Baden Baden for a few days, but the assistant was temporarily in charge.

"You have some problem?" the assistant asked.

"Yes, and I think you do, too," said Foster.

Without wasting words, Foster recounted to the assistant manager what had happened in Emily Ashcroft's suite during the attempt on her life last night.

The assistant manager listened with growing horror. "A waiter from room service with a knife?" he mouthed. "You know it was a waiter for certain?"

Foster described the attacker's outfit.

"You could recognize the man if you saw him?"

"I had only a glimpse of him, it happened so fast. But I might recognize him."

"Very well, Mr. Foster. You wait. We have identity photographs for all our personnel, including those who handle room service. Let me bring them to you." About to start away, he said, "Do you mind repeating what you've told me to the head concierge over there. Perhaps he saw such a person, someone suspicious, leaving last night. What time did it happen?"

"Around eight o'clock. Just about."

"Please tell the concierge. I'll be back in a minute." The assistant hastened off past the information desk.

Foster crossed over to the counter behind which the uniformed concierge stood, and, in a low voice, repeated the story of the attack on Emily Ashcroft.

The concierge's ruddy face became ashen. "Terrible, terrible," he muttered. "Actually tried to stab her?"

"Actually tried."

"You should have notified us at once."

"I couldn't," said Foster. "Miss Ashcroft was badly frightened, and I wanted to comfort her." He paused. "The question is

—around eight last night—maybe a little after—did you see anyone hurrying through the lobby and leaving? A stocky, youngish man, dark-complexioned, muscular."

The concierge threw up his hands. "Mr. Foster, so many come and go at that hour—and I am so occupied here when I work early evening—it is difficult to notice anyone. I can't remember anyone last night in a particular hurry or suspicious in appearance, but—"

They were interrupted by the return of the assistant manager. He was carrying a rectangular, orange-covered photo album. "Our identity record of the personnel in room service," he said, opening the album as he handed it to Foster. There were passport-sized head shots of the various room waiters with their names and employment numbers imprinted below. "Go through it," insisted the assistant manager, "and see if you recognize the one who was in Miss Ashcroft's bathroom."

With care, Foster examined the photographs set in transparent plastic pockets in the album. He turned the pages, hoping for a flicker of familiarity. When he was finished, he knew that the assailant was not among these.

"No go," said Foster, handing back the album. "Obviously he came from the outside by some means and disguised himself as a waiter."

"I am trying to think of what precautions we can take," said the worried assistant manager.

The head concierge was leaning across the counter toward Foster. "May I make a suggestion, sir? Basically, I do not believe this is completely a hotel matter. It may require a greater capability."

"What do you mean?" asked Foster.

"That this matter must be reported at once to the West Berlin chief of police," said the concierge. "I happen to be personally acquainted with Chief Wolfgang Schmidt. I wish to phone him now, inform him that he must see you immediately. He's the best man to have on your side, a real crime-buster, as American television always says. As for politics, if this assault had political implications as you have hinted, you can be sure Chief Schmidt will become involved. He has an abiding hatred for neo-Nazis. He is always trying to root the last of them out of our society. You know, Chief Schmidt was a hero of the German anti-Nazi resistance—the only important conspirator to survive Hitler's purge after von Stauffenberg's plot to blow him up failed. I will phone him that you are on your way. Please report this without further delay."

Foster took a taxi directly to the *Polizeipräsident* of Berlin at Platz der Luftbrücke 6. He had plenty of time before his meeting with Rudi Zeidler, and his first priority was Emily's safety. If the police could not trace the assailant, at least they might find out what had motivated the attack and provide some protection.

After presenting himself to the security and information office before entering the large lobby of the four-story building, Foster was cleared and guided to a door lettered, DER POLIZEIPRÄSIDENT. Ushered into the chief of police's unostentatious office, Foster found Wolfgang Schmidt and his broad desk to be the only large objects in the room. On the wall behind the chief, between two shuttered windows, was a simply framed inscribed photograph of Konrad Adenauer.

Apparently Schmidt had been notified by the Kempinski concierge of what had happened last night and was ready for Foster.

Signaling Foster to a pull-up chair, he drew a yellow pad into the writing position and selected a ball-point pen out of a holder.

"I have a sketchy idea of what occurred yesterday evening in suite 229 of the Bristol Kempinski," said Schmidt. "At eight in the evening, wasn't it?"

"Give or take a minute or two."

"Very well," said the chief of police. "I think I'd better hear in your own words exactly what happened. Try to omit nothing, no matter how seemingly inconsequential."

As Foster spoke in a factual monotone, Schmidt industriously made notes on his yellow pad.

When Foster concluded his account, Schmidt looked up. "You're sure he brandished a knife?"

"I have the knife right here," said Foster. During the evening with Emily, he had gone into the bathroom to retrieve the knife from the floor, wrapped it in a hand towel, and stuffed it into his jacket pocket. This morning he had transferred the knife to his portfolio. Opening his portfolio, he brought out the wrapped weapon and placed it on the chief's desk.

Schmidt removed the towel, gingerly took the sharp blade by its tip and held it up. "An ordinary hunting knife, with a common brand name. There must be millions of these in circulation. I'm afraid the brand name won't tell us much. Still, there may be some fingerprints."

"I could have smudged them. I picked up the knife with my bare hand. I wasn't thinking."

"Then we'll have to fingerprint you, too, for comparison. Let us hope you left one clear print of the attacker," said Schmidt. "I'll turn this weapon over to be dusted." He replaced the knife in the towel, and pushed the towel aside. "The assailant? Can you describe him?"

"Not well, I'm afraid. Everything happened so fast. He was much shorter than I am. Perhaps five feet seven or eight. I threw him over my shoulder, and I can guarantee you he was heavy and muscular. I'd guess one hundred eighty pounds. He had black hair, dark eyes, wide flat nose. Somewhat swarthy."

Schmidt was writing. "A German, you think?"

"I have no idea."

Schmidt put down his pen, and sat back in his low swivel chair. "The intended victim, Emily Ashcroft," the chief said, "can you tell me more about her?"

"What would you like to know?"

"If, to your knowledge, she has any enemies in West Berlin?"

"Enemies?" repeated Foster. "She doesn't know anyone here, not really. She's a scholar from England, absolutely harmless. I can't imagine anyone having any reason whatsoever to harm her."

"So, she's here as a tourist then," Schmidt said offhandedly.

Foster considered his reply. If he wanted help, he had better be truthful. "No, not really as a tourist," he said. "She and her father were writing a definitive biography of Adolf Hitler together. Her father, Dr. Harrison Ashcroft, was killed in a traffic accident in Berlin—"

"I thought the name sounded familiar," Schmidt interrupted. "I spoke to his daughter on the phone. I remember investigating the unfortunate accident."

"—and then Emily Ashcroft came to Berlin alone to follow some leads she had on Hitler's last hours."

"What more could there be to find out?" Schmidt said with a shrug. "Everyone knows Hitler committed suicide in his bunker in 1945. The Soviets proved it."

"Well, Miss Ashcroft is a thorough historian. She wants to verify all the details. There is a possibility Hitler survived and got away."

Schmidt emitted a hoarse laugh. "Yes, I know all those wild rumors. The last one I heard was that Hitler was smuggled out of Germany and taken by U-boat to Japan." He laughed again. "Maybe Miss Ashcroft should go and research in Japan."

Foster found himself annoyed by the chief of police's mockery. Instinctively he began to dislike this bull of a police officer. "Someone did deliberately try to kill her here in Berlin," Foster said unsmilingly. "I'm told there are still old SS veteran groups around West Germany who worship Hitler and the good old days under him. As you must know, yesterday Miss Ashcroft's photograph appeared in one of your Berlin newspapers. She was seen in the East Zone visiting the site of the bunker. Maybe one of those SS veteran groups noticed her, didn't want any foreigner meddling around with Hitler's heroic finish, and decided to interfere with her search."

Schmidt's beefy countenance was solemn once more. "It is a possibility, but an unlikely one. True, there is a handful of Nazi dreamers around, neo-Nazis who remember the glory of the Third Reich. My department is always on the alert to find them. But the diehards are very few, very advanced in years, and totally ineffectual. Still, there might be one lunatic among them."

"And maybe such a lunatic hired someone to liquidate Miss Ashcroft."

Schmidt sat straight. "With that possibility also in mind, Mr. Foster, we will continue to infiltrate the neo-Nazi groups in this area and find out whether they are up to anything. But truly, this is not a source I would worry about."

"What *should* Miss Ashcroft worry about?" persisted Foster. "Someone *did* try to kill her last night."

"What happened sounds like an unmotivated attack by a deranged sadist. However, you are correct. An attack was made on a distinguished foreign visitor, and it is our duty to apprehend her attacker and bring him to trial. I myself will be in charge of the search." With effort, the chief of police heaved himself out of his seat. "You can assure Miss Ashcroft that she shall receive special protection from this day on. I am immediately going to arrange for the hotel to take better security measures for the length of her stay in Berlin. She will no longer have to fear the recurrence of a similar incident, that I promise." Schmidt stood up. "Meanwhile, I'll have someone meet you at the elevator to take fingerprints. Please inform Miss Ashcroft we will be vigilant."

"I will. Thank you, Chief."

But leaving the police station, Foster was still filled with a sense of distinct unease.

Foster followed Rudi Zeidler through his sprawling well-appointed one-story home located about a half mile west of Grunewald.

Zeidler, wearing a white sport shirt, white ducks, and tennis shoes, was as tall as Foster, but lankier, bonier, a sprightly man in his sixties. His English was excellent, and he used it to describe various pieces of sculpture and French expressionist painting as they passed through his ultramodern house filled with oiled teak Danish furniture.

At the rear, they came into an airy studio, awash with the sun that was pouring in through a skylight. Except for a flat-topped desk and several web-backed tubular chairs, the studio was furnished only with tables used for pinning down design plans.

Zeidler took in the room with a wave of his arm. "Part of my work suite," he said. He indicated the tables. "I still keep my hand in with some architectural commissions from time to time." He jerked a chair back for Foster to sit in, and himself went behind the metal desk. Foster noticed that the single piece of equipment on the desk was a green computer.

"So," said Zeidler, "your book is on German architecture. Do you want to tell me about it?"

"I'd prefer to show it to you," said Foster, lifting up his portfolio. He handed it over to Zeidler. "You can see it's called *Architecture of the 1000-Year Third Reich.* What was done and what was planned but never done. You don't have to bother going through the whole book. That's just to give you an idea of what I've got. Also, to give you an idea of what I haven't got."

Zeidler had started flipping the pages of photographs and

drawings in the portfolio. Without looking up, he said, "What haven't you got?"

"The buildings and designs you contributed to Albert Speer and Hitler, when you were Speer's associate. From what you told me on the phone it must have been a crazy time."

"Very crazy," Zeidler confirmed, as he remained absorbed in the portfolio. He finished it, closed it, and handed it back to Foster. "Yes, you seem to have everything except what I did."

"I want this book to be complete, Mr. Zeidler. I need to know what you did."

"Little enough. But still, of some importance."

"As far as I've been able to learn, you designed and constructed seven buildings for Hitler."

Zeidler moved his skeletal head in assent. "Seven exactly."

"I was not able to find photographs or even designs of any of them in Speer's papers."

Zeidler wrinkled his pointed nose. "Speer was not exactly proud of them. So he kept no copies. You would not find them anywhere else because they were meant to be secret."

"Secret? Why?"

"Because the structures were hidden underground headquarters for Hitler as he moved about Germany during the war," said Zeidler.

"They were actually kept secret?" Foster asked.

"Well as much as anything can be kept secret on construction jobs," said Zeidler. "After all, there are always a fair number of people involved in every construction. There are the laborers, although in most cases Hitler assigned each task to slave laborers —Jews, Poles, Czechs—and they were executed after the task was done. Once we were finished, Hitler moved a Wehrmacht general and staff members into each underground. The existence of these subterranean structures was not known to the Reich's enemies until the war was over."

"And those are the ones you designed and built?" prompted Foster.

"Every one of them," said Zeidler with a degree of pride.

"Do you have photographs of them?"

"Unfortunately, very few. When built and in use, I remind you, they *were* secret. As the war was being lost, and Germany overrun, Hitler ordered some of these bunkers evacuated and blown up. Others were discovered by the Russians, British, Americans, French, and destroyed. I may have a few pictures showing the ruins. But they hardly indicate the original architecture. I can send you what I do have. Where are you staying?"

"At the Kempinski."

"You shall receive them in a day or two." He had pulled open a drawer of his metal desk, taken out a piece of paper, and jotted a note. Then, feeling around inside the drawer, he removed a white-rimmed yellow Meerschaum pipe and a leather pouch. Filling the pipe, he asked, "You don't mind, do you?"

From a pocket of his sport jacket, Foster extracted his own worn briar pipe and a packet of tobacco. "I'll join you."

Zeidler pushed his pouch toward Foster. "Try some of my Dutch tobacco. Quite mellow."

Stuffing the tobacco into his pipe, Foster said, "If you don't have adequate photographs of your handiwork, perhaps you have the original designs of those seven underground structures?"

"I was about to mention the designs," said Zeidler with enthusiasm. "Those I do have, all seven of the original blueprints."

"Well, they would certainly do as well as any photos," said Foster. "That is, if you'll permit me to reproduce them in my book. They would complete my project."

Zeidler was having trouble keeping his Meerschaum lighted. At last, he managed. After a few puffs, he said, "No problem. You would like to see them now?"

"If you please."

Zeidler nodded. "I can retrieve them from my storage room. Let me see where they are. I have everything inventoried in my computer." He slid his chair along the desk to the computer. "There they are—Underground Bunkers. I'll be able to find them quickly. Give me no more than five minutes." He was already on his feet and heading into an adjacent room.

Foster sat back, pleased that his search had come to a successful conclusion. Those underground bunkers, properly captioned, would make a dramatic climax for his architectural survey. Briefly, he thought of the strange creature who had ordered this underground string of bunkers built. One could understand the ones that had been constructed in the latter days of the crumbling Reich as protection against Allied bombings. But the others indicated that Hitler had been an animal of the night, a creature of darkness, who wanted to burrow deep inside the earth far from the havoc and destruction he was creating above ground.

Contentedly, Foster blew smoke rings, awaiting the illustrations for his project.

In a few minutes, Zeidler returned, carrying tubes of blueprints under one arm. "Here we have them, all seven," he announced. He placed them on his desk. "Come closer. I'll show you what they are."

Foster jumped up, emptied his pipe into an ashtray, and went around the desk to stand beside Zeidler, as the German removed the first blueprint from a tube and began to spread it out.

"This is Bunker Doric, fashioned out of a cave in the Eifel Mountains," said Zeidler. "Actually, Speer started the design late in 1939. But Speer disliked it, because Hitler wanted it so plain and uninspired, and so he turned its completion over to me. I finished the design and supervised the construction in 1940." Zeidler's knobby forefinger ran over the blueprint. "Note the many rooms for electronic equipment. That one bunker cost what would have been about two million American dollars in those days."

Zeidler unwound another blueprint and stretched it over the first. "This is Bunker Felsennest, also in the Eifel Mountains inside Germany, but not far from Belgium. I used a cave again here. We had to clear the bats out before the construction began."

Zeidler was spreading a third blueprint before Foster. "Bunker Tannenberg," the German explained. "Beneath the Kniebis Mountain in the Black Forest."

Foster watched, fascinated, as the remaining blueprints were flattened out and shown to him. Zeidler's commentary continued. "The greatest and most intricate of them all. Bunker Redoubt inside the Obersalzberg Mountain at Berchtesgaden. You can see the many offshoot warrens, to house underground the other party bigwigs . . . Here is Bunker Pullach near Munich . . . And finally . . ."

Zeidler was spreading the last of the blueprints out with evident distaste, ". . . the one of which I am the least proud but which became the best-known of them all. This is the concrete Führerbunker, beside the Reich Chancellery and its garden, where Hitler holed up to the very end. Speer started it in 1936. I redesigned and enlarged it in 1938, using a dependable private firm, the Hochtief Construction Company, to make it foolproof. The Führerbunker was the most constricted and inconvenient of all the bunkers, and parts of it remained unfinished, because we never seriously believed it would be used, never believed Hitler would see Germany crumbling about him and would have to hide in it for his last months. Anyway, Mr. Foster, there you have it, the missing architecture."

"You said seven designs, Mr. Zeidler. I counted only six."

"There are seven," insisted Zeidler. "I will show you." He leafed through the blueprints, counting. "Four, five, six." He looked up, puzzled. "You are correct. There are only six here. But there were seven. I remember exactly, and the computer inventory confirms it. One seems to be missing."

"Maybe you left it in your storage room."

"Let me make sure." Zeidler quickly disappeared into the adjacent room, and almost as quickly reappeared. "No, it is not there." He stood at his desk, frowning. "I can't imagine what happened to it."

"Did you ever let these blueprints out of your hands?"

"I wouldn't have dared. I made one set for Hitler, which he kept, but I'm told he had it burned in the bunker before his death. The single other set that survived is this one, which I have kept with me."

"Could you have loaned the seven blueprints to someone?"

"No, I never did. There would have been no reason. I never—" He stopped abruptly, remembering something. "You are right. Yes, I did loan this set out once, I recall. I had word from Albert Speer, through his family, that he was considering doing an architectural book on the Reich similar to your own, more a technical memoir of his work, rather than a picture book such as you have done, and he wanted to review my work for him. Speer was only a year from finishing his twenty-year sentence. Anyway, I took the seven blueprints over to the prison, and left the set for him. When Speer was released from Spandau, he returned the entire set to me."

"The entire set minus one," Foster reminded the German.

"No question this is incomplete. The seventh bunker plan is missing. Speer may have returned six to me and misplaced the seventh, left it behind in Spandau. Conceivably with his friend Rudolf Hess, whom he sometimes consulted. That appears to be a possibility." He began rolling up and securing the blueprints on his desk. " I can have these six copied for your book. As for the seventh, I suggest you go to Spandau Prison and inquire—" He stopped and held up his desk calendar. "Wait for three days before you go there. Spandau continues to be supervised by the four victorious powers, which rotate control of the prison. The Russians are in charge now. But in three days they turn it over to the Americans. The Russians won't even see you. I can't speak for the French or British. I do know for certain that the Americans will be friendly and cooperative. You go and ask them whether they have that seventh print around. If they have it, and chances are it is somewhere in the prison, you can recover it and that will give you the complete set for your portfolio. Here, let me write you a note giving you permission to pick up the blueprint."

Zeidler dashed off a note, and handed it to Foster.

After thanking him, but before leaving him, Foster had one more question. "Do you remember anything about the missing seventh bunker?"

"Not too much, but I do remember this much. I had done one other underground fortress, Bunker Riese, next to the spa town of Charlottenborn. It was the most costly, at least sixty million in your money at the time. It was the biggest bunker of them all. Hitler did not like it and never used it. He had it destroyed, along with the blueprint. But then, I think it was in 1943, he had second thoughts and decided to duplicate it for location elsewhere. It was to be called Bunker Grosse Riese. But I was never ordered to build it, so only the plan exists, the design, not the bunker."

"It would still be valuable for my book."

"Then go to Spandau in three days, and see what you can find."

Tovah Levine had been so eager to be on time for the arranged appointment with her superior, that she had arrived at Im Café Carré fifteen minutes early. She hadn't minded being early because the outdoor cafe off Savignyplatz, somewhat removed from Berlin's business district, offered a peaceful retreat and a degree of privacy. The steel chair she had taken at the white table in the graveled courtyard was completely hidden from the street by a high green hedge. Tovah enjoyed the cloistered feeling and was somewhat startled when Chaim Golding suddenly sat down across from her.

He offered a brief good morning and ordered himself an ice cream soda. Since it was too late for breakfast and too early for lunch, Tovah, despite the fact that she disliked ice cream, ordered the same.

Golding occupied the next minutes with emptying out his jacket pockets and examining his notes.

Seated opposite him, Tovah was struck more forcibly than at their first meeting by the fact that Chaim Golding looked more like a perfect German Aryan than like an Israeli who was director of the Mossad operation in West Berlin.

As their ice cream sodas were being served, Tovah took in Golding, who had risen briefly to remove his seersucker jacket. The first time that she had met him, upon her arrival in Berlin, he had been busy behind his desk. Perfunctorily, he had clarified her assignment to become acquainted with a new arrival in Berlin, the historian Emily Aschcroft, and learn more about the clues she possessed that Hitler and his wife had survived the fall of the city.

Now, having requested this second meeting, Tovah was able to get a better impression of Chaim Golding. He appeared to be about five feet eleven, with a sinewy, hard, athletic physique; his facial features were deceptively Nordic, with their clear gray eyes and straight nose. As he seated himself once more, she could see that he was relaxed, more at ease than he had been in the Mossad office during their initial meeting.

"So," he said softly, skimming the heap of whipped cream off the top of his vanilla soda, "you have met Miss Ashcroft of Oxford at the Kempinski hotel."

Tovah was taken aback. "Oh, you know."

"My business is to know," he said without a smile. "Do you like her?"

"Very much."

"Does she like you?"

"I believe so. We've even had dinner together."

"Along with the Californian, the architect Foster."

"So, as usual, you know everything."

"Not enough." Golding met Tovah's eyes. "I want to know more. What is she after about Hitler?"

"You saw the picture of her at the mound of the bunker in *BZ*?"

"Of course," said Golding. "She wants to dig. But dig for what?"

Economically and precisely, as she had been taught to do during her Mossad training, Tovah related all that she had heard from Emily Ashcroft, and about the two clues that might prove that Hitler and Braun survived. Tovah went on. "She learned that one of the dental plates that the Russians identified as Hitler's was not the real thing. She learned, also, that Hitler always wore beneath his tunic a carved ivory cameo bearing a likeness of Frederick the Great. That's what she hopes to dig for. To find the real dental plates and cameo in the debris of the East German Security Zone. If they are not there—it would be some indication that Hitler and Braun got away."

"Who gave her these clues?"

"I don't know, Chaim. It was one detail Emily would not reveal. I'm surprised she revealed as much as she did, spelling out the two clues." Tovah leaned closer to the director. "Chaim, I'm breaking my promise to her. She trusts me implicitly."

"Well she may. Just as you can trust me." He sipped at the straws in his soda. "I will repeat none of this." He was silent momentarily. "So, Miss Ashcroft believes that Hitler and Braun used doubles, that the doubles were cremated, and that the Russians fell for it."

"Exactly. I offered her research assistance. I was intrigued by the whole idea of Hitler's employing a double. I told her I wanted to look into it. Do you think there is even a possibility that it could be true?"

With a neutral movement of his shoulders, Golding replied, "The suspicion of a double is one of the favorite fantasies of the conspiracy-minded."

"You don't believe in it then?"

"I could. Historically, the theory has plenty of support. The use of doubles by world leaders and lesser celebrities has not been uncommon. King Richard II of England was supposed to have had a double. President Franklin D. Roosevelt definitely had a double. So did Field Marshal Montgomery of Alamein—a former actor and a look-alike named Lieutenant Clifton James. There is some speculation that Napoleon had a double. As to the Third Reich, there is a belief that Rudolf Hess employed a double. I've never heard that Adolf Hitler had one."

"Nevertheless, I'm looking into it."

"What have you found?"

"Nothing yet. I've skimmed all the biographies of Hitler in the State Library in the Cultural Center near the Tiergarten. I drew a blank. But I may find out something yet. This morning I talked to Emily Ashcroft. She suggested I see a very knowledgeable and cooperative reporter at the *Berliner Morgenpost*, a fellow she knows named Peter Nitz. I'm meeting with him in about an hour."

"Good luck."

Tovah studied the director's face for any sign of approval or disapproval. "Chaim, am I being silly?" she asked earnestly. "Am I wasting my time?"

He paid the check and stood up. "Don't stop, Tovah. Keep going, and keep in close touch."

* * *

The glass-and-steel Axel Springer Verlag high-rise building, at Kochstrasse 50, towered over this corner of West Berlin like a Brobdingnagian in the land of the Lilliputians. Here were housed the offices of the *Berliner Morgenpost,* as well as other newspapers, and here Tovah Levine entered at her appointed time for her session with Peter Nitz.

Inside the doors, the walls of the vast lobby were covered by maple paneling. Security guards screened Tovah, and requested her Israeli passport. When the passport was returned to her, it came with a pink slip that allowed her to proceed to the elevators.

In the narrow corridor outside the elevator, on the sixth floor, Peter Nitz was waiting to welcome her. He led Tovah to his office in the *Morgenpost*—six unoccupied work desks, each supplemented by a second desk holding an electric typewriter, shelves of books, a small refrigerator, a television set—and invited her to be seated at the worn desk nearest the door, his own.

Receiving her as a fellow journalist and a friend of Emily Ashcroft, Nitz was immediately cooperative. Listening to Tovah's request for information on a Hitler double, Nitz admitted that he'd never written of one nor even heard of one. Still, he said, it was worth pursuing further, to learn whether anyone else had written about the subject and might provide Tovah with a lead.

"If you'll excuse me for a minute," said Nitz, rising, "I'll go down to our archival section and consult the files of clippings."

After he had gone, Tovah waited beside his desk, then restlessly occupied herself by studying the shelves of reference books on the wall across the way. After a short period, she was aware that Nitz had returned carrying a manila file folder. She hurried back to her place as he sank down in his chair behind the desk, an unhappy expression on his face. He opened the folder. "Not much, I'm afraid. This is a very thin file."

"What's in it?"

"We shall see." He was studiously reviewing the clippings,

slowly shaking his head. "Mostly false alarms. As late as 1950, American MPs zeroed in on a German male nurse in a Frankfurt-am-Main hospital, a man named Heinrich Noll, who very much resembled Hitler. They interrogated him, found out he wasn't Hitler, and released him. In 1951, datelined Vienna, we have this story. Hitler was supposed to have died in 1944 in a bombing attempt on his life, and Martin Bormann replaced Hitler with a double named Strasser. No first name given. No solid source for the story, so you can write that one off. The last flurry in 1969, when a retired German coal miner, Albert Pankla by name, was detained and released for the three-hundredth time because he looked just like Hitler. Apparently, there is not a thing—wait, here's a slip of paper with a notation I almost overlooked."

Nitz read the notation, and wrinkled his brow.

"What does it say?" asked Tovah hopefully.

"I don't understand it. Someone noted here, 'On the matter of Hitler doubles, see the file on Manfred Müller.' "

"Who's he?"

"I haven't the faintest idea. But I intend to find out." He came to his feet. "There's a refrigerator over there with Cokes, Miss Levine. Have one. I'll be right back."

Tovah had no patience for a soft drink. She waited again, a trifle crestfallen, but still curious about what Peter Nitz would return with.

He returned with a single long clipping, scanning it as he reached his desk. "Of more recent vintage. A roundup of some of the older restaurants and nightclubs in West Berlin that have existed since the twenties. Manfred Müller was the most popular entertainer at one of these. Müller bore an uncanny resemblance to Hitler and used to regale audiences in the Führer's time with his stage imitations of Hitler. One day, he did not appear. He was never seen again. No idea what happened. Maybe he retired."

"I wonder if Manfred Müller is still around?"

"The article doesn't say. It does mention the restaurant

nightclub where he used to appear. It used to be called the Lowendorff Club. It is now called Lowendorff's Kneipe. Why don't you look in there and find someone who can tell you about Müller. A longshot, yet worth chasing down. Let me give you the address."

It was really a middle-class beer garden, Tovah saw.

Once inside the outdoor enclosure, a surround and roof of vine-covered trellises that gave it some isolation from the street, she saw a scattering of tables at which young people huddled together over their soft drinks, beers, whiskies. Above the entrance to the indoor part of the club there stood a neon sign, not yet lit for evening, that read in large letters, LOWENDORFF'S, and beneath in smaller letters, FRÜHSTÜCK/KNEIPE.

Tovah intercepted a waiter coming away from a table and introduced herself as a journalist who wanted to interview the proprietor.

"You mean Herr Bree, Fred Bree," said the waiter, impressed. "He's inside. Come along. I'll get him for you."

Tovah followed the waiter out of the sunlight into the darkened beer hall. Here the tables were more formally aligned, none occupied by customers at this midafternoon hour. Beyond that was a waxed floor—Tovah guessed it was for dancing as well as entertainment—and toward the rear there were members of a five-piece orchestra getting ready to rehearse. Talking to them was a wiry young man in shirtsleeves and Bavarian lederhosen held up with red suspenders.

Inside the hall, at the farthest rim of tables, the waiter held out his arm to stop Tovah and said, "Wait." He scurried over to the wiry young man in the lederhosen who had been talking to the musicians, and whispered to him, pointing back toward the entrance. The wiry young man pivoted to locate Tovah, nodded a greeting, and came up the aisle toward her.

"I'm Fred Bree," he said. "You wish to speak to me?"

"My name is Tovah Levine. I'm from the *Jerusalem Post*, and I'm doing a series of articles on the kind of entertainment there used to be in Berlin before the war. We have many readers who emigrated from Berlin, and they are interested in these nostalgic pieces. I was told that a Herr Lowendorff once ran this club."

"Walter Lowendorff—yes, he made this club very popular in the 1930s," said Bree.

"I'm told he had an act here that was a special attraction. A one-man show starring the mimic, Manfred Müller. I was hoping to find out more about this Müller."

"Manfred Müller," mouthed Bree. "Has a familiar ring, but I really don't know anything about him. I wasn't born then. That kind of knowledge would have only been known to Herr Lowendorff or to my father. This neighborhood was severely damaged by the Allied bombings in the last months of the Second World War. After the war, Lowendorff had no heart to rebuild the club. So he sold it to my father, who already owned several *Kneipen*. After my father died in 1975, I inherited the club and have managed it ever since."

"So you would know nothing about Manfred Müller?"

"I repeat, my father might have known, but he is no longer here. Of course, Walter Lowendorff might recall something of his old acts." The young proprieter brightened. "Why don't you ask Lowendorff himself?"

Tovah, whose spirits had been low, felt a surge of hope. "You mean the original Lowendorff is still around?"

"Indestructible," Bree said with a grin. "Really an ancient party, quite creaky in the joints, somewhat short on memory, but he still remembers to drop in on his old club for a daily beer." He took Tovah by the arm. "Let's go out to the garden and see if he's arrived yet."

They emerged into the trellis-covered beer garden, and Bree

ran his eyes over the various customers at the tables. "Not here yet." Bree consulted his wristwatch. "He usually comes by at three. So there's ten minutes or so to go. Why don't you take a table, Fräulein Levine, and wait for him? Let me treat you to a beer. I'll keep a lookout for him and bring him over to you."

"Thank you, Herr Bree."

The proprieter led Tovah to a vacant table, snapped his fingers for a waiter, ordered her a draft beer, and then wandered off to consort with his other patrons.

Tovah, sipping her foaming beer, noted when fifteen minutes had passed, and began to have her doubts that anything would come of this, but then she saw Bree returning with an elderly, doddering man in tow.

Helping the ancient into a chair at Tovah's table, Bree performed the introductions. "Fräulein Levine, this is the renowned Walter Lowendorff. I've already filled him in on your mission. You two get together, while I send over another beer."

Tovah considered the wrinkled old man with some misgivings. His eyes were rheumy, and he looked off at the people at the other tables blankly, an idiot smile pressed into his prune face.

He showed no awareness of Tovah until his beer was set before him. Then at last, after licking at the foam, he focused on Tovah.

"I am writing about some of the more memorable acts and entertainers in Berlin in the 1930s," Tovah began. "I'm told you sponsored some of the best."

"Yes, it is true," said Lowendorff. "The best."

He sucked on his beer, attentive to Tovah over his glass stein.

"I'm particularly interested in one act you had that became famous," said Tovah, struggling uphill. "I understand you had a great success with Manfred Müller, a mimic who did sensational imitations of Hitler."

"Ah, Müller, Müller," said Lowendorff, the foam clinging to his lips as he put down his beer. "The best, the very best."

"I want to know more about him," said Tovah, "I understand he could have doubled for Adolf Hitler."

Either the beer or the recollection of Müller appeared to revive clarity in the old man. "Looked exactly like Hitler," Lowendorff remembered. "Spitting image from the lock of brown hair on his forehead to the fanatical blue eyes to brush mustache. Absolutely Hitler. Also a funny mimic. He could do Hitler to perfection, but satiric, very satiric. Not cruel. Just humorous. The moment he tried out for me, I hired him."

Lowendorff's mind drifted off, and he returned to sucking his beer as he visited the past.

Tovah tried to bring him into the present once more. "You hired Manfred Müller. He did his act here. He was a success."

"Huge success. Every night standing room only. Spectators of every class came from everywhere. Manfred would do little blackouts of Hitler's movements. He would do Hitler in the Munich beer hall giving orders. He would do Hitler in his prison cell dictating *Mein Kampf* to Hess. Hitler ordering the burning of the Reichstag. Outrageous stuff, but to tickle the ribs. Business was never better."

"But then he stopped," Tovah prodded. "I know that he gave up his act when he was still on top. Why did he quit?"

The old man tried to comprehend what Tovah was saying. "Quit, quit? No, no, he did not quit. Manfred Müller was on top of the world, yes. All Berlin was talking about him, until they made him quit."

"Who made him quit?"

"Why, the Hitler gang, of course. One night, after his act, they were waiting for him. Four strongarm men from the Göring Gestapo—or was it Himmler's then?—I forget. They grabbed him, stuffed him into a car, and drove him away. That was in spring, 1936. The last I ever saw of Manfred Müller."

Tovah was at the edge of her chair. "But what happened to him?"

"Never heard of him again. Poof, into thin air. Maybe shot for his audacity. Maybe not. Maybe just shut up."

Or maybe, just maybe, something else, Tovah thought. A man who looked like Hitler, who could imitate Hitler to perfection, might be useful for something else.

"If he lived, could he still be alive?" Tovah wondered.

"Could be, could be. He was a young person, early thirties, maybe a little more, when he was picked up."

Tovah persisted. "Can you think of anyone who might know what happened to him?"

"No, nobody—except . . ." Lowendorff trembled a little at his effort to reach back into some recess of memory.

"Except," Tovah prompted him.

Lowendorff apparently made some discovery in his exploration of the past. "Anneliese Raab. She was Leni Riefenstahl's assistant in the photography of the Berlin Olympics. She knew Hitler himself, Anneliese Raab did, through Riefenstahl. Anneliese was about eighteen years old. She would come to my club often to laugh over the antics of Manfred Müller. Maybe she told Hitler about Müller's imitations. Maybe Hitler told her what he did with Müller. Yes, yes, do see Fräulein Raab."

"You know her address?"

"Everyone will tell you where to find her. She is still famous. Yes, yes, Anneliese Raab is the one who might know what happened to our Hitler mimic."

"Of course I know what happened to Manfred Müller," Anneliese Raab said, as she walked with a springy step through the corridor of the Eden apartment building adjacent to the Palace Hotel at Europa Center. Anneliese admitted proudly that she owned the expensive penthouse they had just left, as well as the apartment that they were about to visit which she had converted into her private projection room. "Müller was an absolutely marvelous performer," she assured Tovah.

Anneliese Raab, a short, compact woman wearing a blond, curly wig and a gray tailored suit, had not been difficult for Tovah to find, since she was well-known in the city, and she had cordially invited Tovah for the interview.

No sooner had Tovah stated the reason for her visit, than Anneliese had telephoned someone in her projection room, and mysteriously asked Tovah to join her in viewing a reel or two of the 1936 Berlin Olympics film that she had assisted Leni Riefenstahl in producing.

"Well, what happened to Manfred Müller after the Gestapo picked him up at the Lowendorff Club that night in 1936?"

Anneliese looked at Tovah with amusement. "Why, he became Adolf Hitler's double, of course. Come, I will show you."

Excited by the unexpected revelation, Tovah Levine followed the German filmmaker into the small, beautifully decorated projection room, with its tiers of maroon leather folding seats.

Anneliese settled herself in a seat next to a control panel and beckoned Tovah to sit down beside her. Anneliese pressed a button beside a microphone and spoke to someone in the projection room above them. "Ready when you are."

"I need five minutes to get the reel on," the disembodied voice from the projection room announced.

Anneliese pulled back and half-turned toward Tovah. "So we have five minutes for explanations. I will tell you what I know."

"About Hitler's double," said Tovah with a catch in her voice. The simple confirmation of this possibility suddenly validated Emily Ashcroft's quest for the truth.

"Yes. Manfred Müller became Hitler's double because of me," Anneliese mused. "Because of what I related to Hitler at a large dinner party that the Führer gave for the American aviator and hero Charles A. Lindbergh. Before the dinner the guests were gathered in groups talking and gossiping. I had met Hitler before at another function through Leni Riefenstahl. Anyway, Goebbels saw me standing alone, drinking, and he drew me into Hitler's circle. I was very young at the time, and really quite pretty. Goebbels knew Hitler liked to be surrounded by pretty girls, so he brought me to join those women who were fawning over the Führer. I don't recall how it happened, but briefly I was standing beside Hitler feeling a little heady. I suppose I'd had too much wine. Anyway, I found myself telling Hitler about the wonderful look-alike, the wonderful mimic named Manfred Müller, who was performing nightly at the Lowendorff Club. Once the words were uttered, I was afraid that Hitler would be offended. Instead, he was fascinated. He put his hand under my elbow and moved me aside until we were almost alone. 'You mean,' said Hitler, 'this actor, Müller, resembles me?' I could see he was really interested, so I said, 'Not resembles you, *mein Führer.* He *is* you, an exact replica of you in height, features, movements. I don't think he even uses any artifices or makeup to look like you. It is one of those accidents of nature, quite incredible.' Then Hitler asked me to repeat where this Manfred Müller was appearing. I told him and knew he would not forget. After that, dinner was served and we all went to our respective places at the tables. The next time I went to the Lowendorff Club, I learned that Manfred Müller was no longer performing. I was told he had retired. Which made no sense, because he was too young to have retired."

"When did you learn Müller had been picked up by the Gestapo?"

"Shortly afterward," said Anneliese. "Months before the Olympic games in August 1936, Leni Riefenstahl had been assigned to make the official film of the events, *Olympia.* To cover the sixteen days, Leni had assembled a crew of one hundred sixty specialists, half of them cameramen and assistant cameramen, and trained them in the Geyer Works. I was Leni's assistant producer. Before that all Olympics films had been dull, flat, one-dimensional reproductions of each competition. Leni was the first to make an Olympics film a work of art, introducing in 1936 the techniques that have become so commonplace today—trenches or pits to keep camera angles low, cameras moving on rails to follow runners, underwater shooting, shots of the activities on the ground from the Graf Zeppelin in the sky. A few days after our preparations had begun, Leni and I were having a snack in the Haus Ruhwals and chatting about the social activities in Berlin. In an offhand way, I told Leni that I had stopped going to the entertainment in the Lowendorff Club because the star attraction, Manfred Müller, was no longer there. Leni nodded. 'I know,' she said. 'Because Müller has gone to work for *unser Führer.*' I was astounded. 'Gone to work for Hitler?' Leni expanded on it. 'Hitler had Müller picked up and brought to his presence, to see if it was true. He saw that Müller was his doppelgänger. So he took Manfred Müller away from Lowendorff. He hired Müller to become his double.' "

"You're sure of that?" Tovah said.

Anneliese pressed the buzzer on the control panel. "You shall see for yourself."

The projection room darkened. "The raw footage of our *Olympia* was one million three hundred thousand feet long. I will show you the first two reels only, from the opening ceremony. Ignore the opening day festivities, the one hundred ten thousand people cheering the ten thousand female performers in midfield, Richard Strauss conducting the orchestra playing 'Deutschland Über Alles,' and keep your eye on Hitler himself on the official stand watching the entrance of competitors of various nationalities."

Tovah watched the screen mesmerized.

"There, there you see Hitler observing the entrance of the

Austrian contingent who gave him the 'Sieg Heil' Nazi salute. Then the French doing almost the same." Anneliese's commentary continued over the muted sound track. "Wait for the Americans, who are last. They will not give the Nazi salute nor dip the Stars and Stripes toward Hitler. You will see Hitler hiding his resentment, but also notice the displeasure in the stadium from spectators. There now, keep your eyes on Hitler. You wonder if it is Hitler or his double. I can tell you, it *is* Hitler that opening day. He appeared in person. Because he felt it could be a propaganda coup. It was the only time Hitler appeared at the Olympics. Yet, you will see him four more times."

As the film flickered on the screen, Tovah concentrated on what she saw.

Anneliese resumed her commentary. "This is the second day of the Berlin Olympics, but the first day of the actual competition. There you see Hitler again. He is congratulating Hans Wöllke, our German shotputter and our first gold medalist. There you see Hitler congratulating the three men from Finland who won all the medals in the ten-thousand-meter event. There you see him congratulating our gold- and silver-medal winners in the women's javelin contest. A most gracious Adolf Hitler." Anneliese paused dramatically and said with emphasis, "Only the Führer who was congratulating the winners on the second day was not Hitler. It was his double doing the job. It was Manfred Müller."

"How can you tell?" asked Tovah.

"I don't have to tell. I know. If I could mark any difference, it would be in studying the ears of the real Hitler and the fake Hitler. The configurations vary ever so slightly."

Later, when the film was done and the lights had gone on in the projection room, Anneliese resumed speaking to Tovah. "While Hitler was proud of the staging of the Olympics, he had no interest whatsoever in actual sports. He had too much else on his mind. He ordered Manfred Müller to appear in his stead. And so perfect was Müller's performance, that not a soul in attendance ever knew the difference. But don't misunderstand me. When it came to an important political event, such as the mammoth Nuremberg Rally which we shot in 1934, and released as *Triumph des Willens,* and other political gatherings after Hitler hired Müller, Hitler always appeared in person. When he was asked to make a showing at some lesser nonpolitical event, he often sent Manfred Müller in his place."

"It's so hard to believe," said Tovah.

"It is true. I'll tell you something that is harder to believe. An American athlete named Carson Thompson wrote a memoir recently claiming that Eva Braun visited the Olympic Village in Berlin to meet the American baseball players."

"How could that have been? I thought Hitler kept Eva Braun in hiding."

"He did, most of the time. But Eva adored everything American. She must have seen *Gone With the Wind* a half dozen times. Also, she adored what she knew about American sports, especially baseball. She expected to do some of the commentary for Leni Riefenstahl's Olympics documentary, so she wanted to learn more details about baseball. She arranged to meet the American baseball Olympians who were in Berlin to put on an exhibition game. At the last minute, Hitler would not let her go in person. Since the arrangements had been made, Hitler sent Hannah Wald, another double, in her place to meet the Americans. Hannah was an attractive young minor actress who posed as Eva Braun."

"Whatever happened to Hannah Wald?"

"I wish I knew," said Anneliese, "but I never could trace her after the 1930s. She evaporated, just disappeared from sight."

"And what finally happened to Manfred Müller? Where did he wind up?"

Anneliese made a helpless gesture. "Here I confess we draw another blank. I know Hitler was using him until 1942. After that, especially with the war going badly for him, Hitler was too beset and too occupied with his generals to bother seeing or talking to Leni or me."

"Could there be anyone around who would know if Manfred Müller is still alive?"

"Well, he had a family . . ." said Anneliese slowly, "at least I know he had a son. I remember what it was. A few years ago I read a feature story somewhere on the children of great German entertainers. There was, to my surprise, a brief mention of Manfred Müller. And there was also a quote from his son, Josef Müller, who worked as an air controller for Lufthansa. Josef said in his quote that he wished he could have seen his father in his heyday. So that gave me a cute sentimental idea. I took the footage you've just seen of Müller playing Hitler in the *Olympia* film and copied it, and I sent the extra print to Josef Müller with a note saying, 'If you want to know what your father looked like in his heyday, here he actually is.' Josef was thrilled to receive the footage and wrote me a thank-you note on his personal stationery. I'd be delighted to find it, contact him, and ask him to call you at the Bristol Kempinski."

"You don't know how much I'd appreciate that," said Tovah.

Later, when they were about to part at the door to Anneliese Raab's penthouse, Tovah paused briefly to speak about something that was on her mind. It was daring, but she decided to do it.

"Fräulein Raab, just one more thing," Tovah said, "something I've been wondering about while we were talking."

"Yes, please?"

"If Hitler had a double, perhaps it was the double who died in the Führerbunker and was cremated—the double, and not Hitler himself."

Anneliese stood stock still. "What an astonishing idea."

"But possible."

"Unlikely," said Anneliese. Then with a shrug, "But, of course, anything is possible." She stared at Tovah. "Only one thing. If Hitler did not die in the bunker—what happened to him?"

7

Chief of Police Wolfgang Schmidt sat across from Evelyn Hoffmann at their usual table waiting until his sausage and beer and her tea had been served and the basket of rolls placed between them.

Gloomily, Schmidt withheld what he had to say until Evelyn had taken a roll, broken and buttered it, and begun to sip her tea.

Schmidt cleared his throat. "Effie, I have some news that is not particularly good, but not entirely bad."

She put down her cup. "Go ahead, Wolfgang."

"I promised you I would stop the British lady, Emily Ashcroft, from nosing around in the past. I'm afraid my initial effort to stop her failed."

"You tried to frighten her off?"

"No, Effie, I tried to terminate her. Somehow the job was interrupted, quite by accident. I'd assigned a good enough man, an experienced one. He penetrated her suite at the Kempinski. Then something unexpected happened. My agent was about to make contact with the Ashcroft woman, when a man, an American named Foster, walked in on them. Foster proved to be very quick and agile, and strong, too. I have since learned that he was trained in the American military for the Vietnam adventure, and has kept in good shape ever since. He interfered. I count it good luck that he didn't knock out my agent and capture him. My man got away."

"Thank the good Lord for that."

"It makes our next move riskier. Because now the Ashcroft woman has been alerted, and is wary. She will not let herself be alone, not for a moment. She even had this Rex Foster give up his own room and settle into her suite."

"Really?"

Schmidt gave a ponderous snort of disapproval. "I gather they are sleeping together even though they are not married. But what else can one expect from English women other than loose morals?"

A crease of amusement touched Evelyn Hoffmann's face. "Wolfgang, not only English women," she said.

"What?" muttered Schmidt, not understanding.

"I was with the *Feldherr* for almost seventeen years before we were married. We were not married when we started sleeping together in Vienna."

Schmidt's cheeks had become red with embarrassment. With force, he tried to defend himself against her mild chastisement. "Effie, my God, how can a comparison be made? You and the *Feldherr* were a special couple. It was as if you were chosen by the Lord to give comfort and succor to a noble leader, the greatest in German history."

Evelyn responded with solemn assent. "That was always my view of it from the time I met him." She rarely spoke of the past in a public place, but now her mind had wandered backward. "How well I remember the first time I saw him. I had just started on the job for the fat one, Heinrich Hoffman, in his photography shop in Munich. Actually, it was in my fourth week on the job. I didn't know my boss was a member of the National Socialist party, and that many of the customers who visited him were his cronies in the party. I was standing on a ladder trying to get a file on a high-up shelf. This friend of Heinrich's came into the shop, a nondescript person, I thought, except for his eyes that glowed and his funny mustache. He was wearing a light trench coat and carrying an oversized felt hat. He sat down opposite the ladder, and I caught him staring up at my legs. I had just shortened my dress that morning. When I came down the ladder, Heinrich introduced us. 'Herr So-and-so,' he said, 'meet our good little Fräulein Eva.' Of course, I learned Herr So-and-so's real name shortly after. Then we met many times. He was always so gentlemanly. He would bow in a courtly way, kiss my hand, and compliment me on my complexion." Evelyn gave a short sigh. "That is where it began, in the photography shop."

"Romantic, a most romantic story," said Schmidt, although she knew that he had heard it before.

Drinking the tea, Evelyn looked over the rim of her cup, her eyes fixed on Chief Schmidt. "Wolfgang, do you remember when you and I met?"

"Wasn't it in 1940?"

"In 1941, at the Berghof, when the *Feldherr* and I were sharing the same bed." She laughed. "One morning his valet burst in on us about some emergency, and found us in each other's arms, in bed, together. It was the only time anyone was ever sure we were having an affair."

"Anyway," Schmidt announced, to recover from his blunder, "you did get married."

"The happiest moment of my life," Evelyn admitted. "But four years before that you and I had met. I remember the day you came on the job in the Berghof, such a stiff young SS trooper assigned to play nursemaid to me."

"To guard you, Effie, when you strolled alone in the woods. The *Feldherr* would not permit you to go anywhere unguarded."

"It was my good fortune to find such a loyal and good friend as you, Wolfgang. I can't imagine what I would do today without someone like you."

"It was my lifetime vow to protect you, Effie."

Evelyn's face clouded. "And now this Ashcroft woman from England is poking into our past."

Schmidt could not deny it, but doggedly he pledged, "I will protect you from her as I promised." Schmidt considered what he would say next. "It will not be so easy now as I thought it would be before. Now, as I told you, she is not alone for even one minute. This Foster is beside her all the time. There are others in her camp, too, I have discovered. A Russian from Leningrad, Nicholas Kirvov, and also an Israeli woman, Tovah Levine, a German Jew who claims to be a journalist. Any and all of them would defend her, if necessary. I must be honest, they enlarge the threat against all that we cherish and hold holy. They have loosely formed a zealous team of amateur investigators. We know, of course, the Ashcroft woman's aim. Rex Foster is a Los Angeles architect trying to reconstruct the architecture of the Third Reich for a picture book. Nicholas Kirvov has acquired, somehow, an early painting executed by the *Feldherr* and is trying to verify its authenticity. Tovah Levine has occupied herself trying to ferret out a 'Hitler double.' By themselves, each of the three appears to be harmless. But when they throw themselves behind the Ashcroft woman's more dangerous quest, they become somewhat more formidable."

"About our main legacy from the *Feldherr,* they know nothing of it?"

"I assure you, Effie, they haven't the slightest idea. It remains our secret."

Fleetingly, Evelyn's countenance reflected some inner regret. "Sometimes I wish it wasn't. All secret, I mean."

"Effie, whatever are you talking about?"

"My critics, stupid historians, who've always pigeonholed me as flighty and dumb." It still rankled, some of the things that had been written about her. "Especially that Nuremberg judge who wrote the book about us in 1950. When writing about me, he wrote that I was 'utterly devoid of political and economic interests' and devoted all my time 'to dress, picnic, and frolic.' "

"*Arschloch!*" Schmidt snorted. The expletive meant "asshole." "Forgive my coarseness," Schmidt said quickly. "It is the only expression that comes to mind. If that idiot, and the others, only knew how the *Feldherr* so often confided his political thoughts to you, and wanted your opinions. How he discussed the Austrian *Anschluss* with you before undertaking it, and how in 1938 he had you accompany him to the political conference with Mussolini in Italy."

"And how his last act was to entrust me with what we are doing now."

"It will remain a safe secret from the Ashcroft team," Schmidt promised her once more. "As long as I continue to know what they are up to, I am not worried and you need not be worried."

"How do you know what they are up to?" Evelyn suddenly asked. "In fact, how do you know so much about them already?"

Schmidt offered a self-satisfied smile. "After the attempt on the Ashcroft woman, Foster came to me as chief of police to report the incident. I guaranteed him full protection for Emily Ashcroft. I told him I'd arrange for the hotel to place guards in the Kempinski keeping an eye on all entrances to the second floor."

"Have you done so?"

"Promptly. As chief, it was the only thing to do."

"Of course."

"I also arranged one more thing," added Schmidt. "On the pretext of having one of our department technicians check the security inside Miss Ashcroft's suite—windows, and so forth—I had phone taps inserted in each of the Ashcroft woman's telephones."

"You have really done this, Wolfgang?" Evelyn said admiringly.

"The very first moment the Ashcroft woman and Foster went out. The listening devices are safely and unobtrusively in place. They will never be detected. They have already begun to show results." Schmidt dipped a hand into his right jacket pocket and pulled out a yellow box and handed it over to Evelyn. "The first day and evening of Emily Ashcroft's telephone calls, going out, coming in, on tape. You can play it when you return home. You won't hear too much that is exciting, not yet at least. She is a bit guarded in whatever she says. But sooner or later something will come through." Schmidt glanced at his watch. "As a matter of fact, right now the Ashcroft woman and Foster have taken the Russian Kirvov on a visit to what used to be Hermann Göring's old Air Ministry."

Evelyn frowned. "Why? I can't imagine why?"

"Neither can I—yet," said Schmidt confidently. "But believe me, and I guarantee this, soon we'll know. We'll know everything. If any danger to us arises, I'll be prepared to prevent it. Effie, I tell you again. You need have no fear."

Evelyn sat back and exhaled her relief. "Wolfgang, I have no fear. Not as long as I have you." She placed the reel of tape in her expensive alligator purse. "I—my husband and I—we both thank you for what you are doing to preserve Germany's future."

* * *

Irwin Plamp, driving his Mercedes sedan through Checkpoint Charlie, had taken them into East Berlin and guided them knowingly to their destination.

He parked near Leipziger Strasse, a block away from the gray rectangular-stone government building, and in pairs his passengers left the sedan and started down the street. Although it was early afternoon, the thoroughfare had only light vehicular and pedestrian traffic.

In the brightness of the warm day, the building they had all sought was the only landmark that seemed gloomy and forbidding.

Nicholas Kirvov, holding the Hitler oil painting in his hand, was the first to cross Leipziger Strasse and study the structure close up. His gaze rose from the inset façade of the ground floor to the four stories rising above it.

Foster came alongside him, followed by Emily and Tovah.

"The onetime Reichsluftfahrtministerium," said Foster. "The Göring Air Ministry of 1945, and the only Third Reich structure to survive the massive Allied air raids."

"Today, it is the Haus der Ministerien," said Emily. "East Berlin's House of Ministries."

Kirvov remained silent as his gaze dropped from the building itself to the building represented in Hitler's oil painting. For at least a minute he compared the two, and finally he turned to the others. "They are both exactly the same," he announced. "The building we see before us and the building Hitler depicted in his painting."

"So now you have seen for yourself," said Foster, "and when you put the oil on exhibit in the Hermitage, you can accurately explain it to all the museum-goers."

"Of course," Emily reminded Kirvov, "thirty-five percent of

the original ministry was damaged in the air raids, so over a third of it has been repaired and restored." She fished into her purse. "Perhaps you'd like to see a better shot of the entrance. I have a photograph that was taken in 1935, which I just received from Oxford, and this closeup shows how the ministry looked before it was damaged and restored."

She found the photograph of the building and gave it to Kirvov.

The Russian was silent again as he stared at the 1935 photograph of the present entrance to the building, then at the actual building, and finally at his Hitler oil.

Watching Kirvov, Emily absently addressed Tovah beside her. "I'm just wondering about that strange expression on Nicholas Kirvov's face."

The expression on the Russian's face was very strange indeed.

He suddenly looked up at the others, bursting out, "How odd! How very odd!"

Kirvov was beckoning all of them to come closer, and they crowded around him.

"Look over there," said Kirvov, pointing at the front of the building façade. "See the ceramic tile mural set into the ministry front at the entrance, almost lost in the shadows behind the twelve pillars? Now look here." He held his Hitler painting aloft and pointed to the same spot on the painting. "Here you see the ceramic mural once again barely visible in the shadows, but visible enough. All right, now . . ." He lowered the painting, propping it against his leg, and held up the early photograph taken of the original ministry in 1935. "Now look closely at the photograph of the ministry as it used to be before it was bombed and restored. What *don't* you see? You don't see any ceramic mural in the photograph. There was no ceramic mural whatsoever when the ministry was first built. The ceramic is on the building only after it was repaired. And it is also in the painting Hitler made of it!"

"Let me see the photo," said Foster, taking it from Kirvov and studying it. "You're right. It's something I missed completely."

"This means that Hitler did not paint the original building!" Emily exclaimed. "He painted it *after* it was repaired!"

"But when was it repaired?" Kirvov asked, puzzled.

Emily could not contain her excitement. "I know exactly how to find out. Let's get to a telephone."

She hastily led the way back to the Mercedes.

"Herr Plamp," she said to the waiting driver, "I need to get to a public telephone at once. Are there any near here?"

The driver considered the request. "There are a few phones in the Café am Palast."

"Take me there," ordered Emily.

After they were all in the car, Plamp put the Mercedes in gear and maneuvered through the streets of East Berlin until they had reached the broad thoroughfare of Unter den Linden. Presently he drew up behind the Palast Hotel. "This is it. The Café am Palast is around the corner. You'll see it. There are public phones in the entry foyer."

The four of them left the car, turned the corner, and entered the café.

Emily gestured at the dining room. "Take a table. I'll be with you in a minute. I'm going to call Professor Blaubach."

Out of the corner of an eye, Emily watched the others being shown to a vacant table, while she rummaged through her purse for the tiny notebook she had prepared with local telephone numbers. She found it, flipped to B, and there was Professor Otto Blaubach's phone number.

She silently prayed that he was in his office.

In less than a minute she had Blaubach on the phone.

"I don't have any news for you on permission to excavate," he said immediately. "But I expect some word by late this afternoon."

"Good, good. I'll be at the Kempinski waiting for your call." She paused. "Professor, that is not why I am phoning you. It is about another matter. I'll explain it all when I see you the next time. What I need right now is some information about one of your government buildings."

"Of what building do you speak?"

"The Haus der Ministerien near the Wall."

"You mean the ministry building, the one that used to be headquarters for Göring's Luftwaffe?"

"That's the one," said Emily.

"What do you wish to know about it?" inquired Blaubach.

"I understand a third of it was damaged in an Allied air raid before 1945. When the East German government took it over, they repaired it."

"Yes, I believe that was done."

"Is it possible to find out when it was repaired?"

"Umm, it is possible," said Blaubach. "I can find out in a few minutes. Where can I reach you?"

"Let me call you back," said Emily.

"Very well, call me back in five minutes."

Emily lingered impatiently by the telephone, watching Foster, Kirvov, and Tovah studying their menus. Foster's profile was strongly etched, and once again she felt the warmth of his face and body. But she would not let the feeling detract from another excitement she felt awaiting Blaubach's return call.

Five minutes had passed. She allowed it to become six minutes, and then she was dialing Blaubach's office once more.

He was on the phone immediately. "I think I have what you want. When the Ministry was repaired and made usable again?"

"Yes, please," said Emily.

"It was rebuilt in 1952."

She had to be sure. "You said 1952. No mistake about that?"

"No mistake whatsoever. It was originally constructed for Göring in 1935. It was damaged, partially, in 1944. It was repaired and reconstructed in 1952. One can see from the lighter-colored stone blocks where the repairs were made."

"Yes, and a few decorations were added, a ceramic tile mural at the entrance for one thing."

"I don't recall. But all the additions and repairs were definitely made in 1952."

Her heart was thumping again. "Thank you so much, Professor."

"Happy to be of service. You can expect to hear from me again later today."

Emily hung up, spun around, and hurried into the café. She could see the three of them waiting for her news as she approached their table.

She did not bother to sit down. Her nerves were taut now, and she remained standing. "Incredible news," she announced. "The old Göring Ministry was not repaired until 1952. That was when the tile mosaic was put on the front. Yet Hitler painted it and included the mosaic." She paused to catch her breath. "That means Hitler could have painted it only after 1952. Seven years after the end of the Second World War. Which means one thing."

Kirvov's head was bobbing, its Slavic countenance flushed by the revelation. "It means Hitler was alive at least seven years after the war, maybe ten, maybe twenty or more. It means Hitler could be alive today."

At eight-thirty in the evening, the four of them were seated at a table in the middle of the Restaurant Kempinski, one of the best restaurants in West Berlin.

"It must be one of the best," said Foster, fingering the menu. "Look at those prices."

"And the place settings," added Tovah.

On the rich white tablecloth, beneath a gold chandelier, the porcelain service platters were shining, and the silverware was gleaming and heavy.

Foster picked up the Scotch that had just been set down before him. "I propose we toast Emily."

They all raised their glasses.

"To your success tomorrow at the Führerbunker."

They all cheerily chimed in, glasses clinking.

Emily felt heady with her good fortune. Three hours earlier, shortly after returning to her suite in the Kempinski with Foster, the telephone in her sitting room had rung. The caller had been Professor Otto Blaubach with good news. His council had just granted Emily permission to excavate, not only the Old Chancellery garden but the mound behind it that for almost forty years had concealed what was left of Hitler's personal Führerbunker. Digging could begin tomorrow for one week. Blaubach had reminded her of her promise to share with him and the East German government anything she found that might be of historical or political interest.

The instant the call was over, Emily had suggested the celebratory dinner, and she and Foster rounded up her guests.

Now that the others with her in the Restaurant Kempinski had toasted the success of her enterprise, Emily sat back, nervously drained. "Yes, I admit it, I'm scared," she said.

"You have nothing to worry about," Foster assured her.

"What if something is there?"

"Emily, I suspect nothing is there, neither Hitler's real dental bridge nor the cameo. I'm positive you're on the right track. What happened this afternoon at the Göring ministry supports that."

Emily eyed Nicholas Kirvov seated at the restaurant table to her left. He was not a demonstrative type, although there had been a perceptible lilt in his tone throughout their drive back from East Berlin. Now, Emily noted, his face was once more impassive. "How do you feel, Nicholas, since your discovery this afternoon? Is your work here finished?"

He seemed to weigh her questions, and considered his answer. "Not quite finished," Kirvov said. "Do you want me to tell you what is on my mind?"

"Please," Emily urged him.

"It is true, we made the discovery that to have painted the oil I own, Hitler would not have killed himself in 1945. He would have had to be alive in 1952 or after. That is an excitement, of course, and of enormous importance. But it all hinges on one thing. That Adolf Hitler himself actually painted the oil with his own hand."

"You examined the oil after you acquired it," said Foster. "You felt certain it had been done by Hitler."

"I still believe that is so," said Kirvov. "Yet, what happened today slightly undermines my faith in the authenticity of the work. Certainly, if Hitler painted it, the anachronism indicates that Hitler was alive in or after 1952, when he was already supposed to have been dead seven years." Kirvov paused. "If what we have learned is true, it means that Hitler went into hiding after his supposed death. It also means that at some point Hitler emerged from his hiding and stood himself before the reconstructed Air Ministry and painted his oil. Somehow, I can't imagine him taking such a risk. It makes me wonder if he really painted the picture."

"Nicholas," said Emily, "suppose he didn't stand there before the building and paint it? Suppose he painted it from a poor photograph that someone, some friend, had taken of the building? You yourself said that in his early days as an artist, Hitler executed most of his sketches and drawings using postcards, merely copied them."

"That is true," Kirvov admitted.

"So maybe he did the same again."

"Maybe," said Kirvov. "But for my own purpose, I've got to be certain that the work was actually done by Hitler. I need indisputable proof of that."

Foster injected himself into the exchange. "Nicholas, surely by now you must know which gallery in Berlin sold the painting to the steward who traded it to you. You can go to the gallery for the provenance."

Kirvov sighed unhappily. "Rex, I am ashamed to admit I do not have the name of the gallery. That is my problem. The steward was to send it to me when he got home. It hasn't arrived." Kirvov fumbled for a Cuban cheroot in his jacket. "Still, I am not through. I have decided to spend another week here. I mean to devote it to verifying the authenticity of the Hitler painting."

"How?" Emily asked him.

"By continuing my search for the art gallery that sold it to the seaman."

"There must be hundreds of art galleries in West Berlin," said Foster.

"There are," agreed Kirvov. "I've already gone through the telephone directory and visited many. But there are columns of them. Luckily, I need not spend time visiting each one. The steward did tell me that he bought the painting from a gallery in the center of West Berlin, not far from the main avenue. I expect he meant not far from the Kurfürstendamm."

"That's what it sounds like," said Foster.

"Which narrows the area I must search," said Kirvov. "Tomorrow morning I will again go in and out of art galleries and show them my painting. Sooner or later I will stumble on the right gallery. If I'm satisfied with their authentication, then it means you too are on the right trail."

"It would mean a lot to me," Emily admitted. "If I can be of any help—"

"No, don't worry," said Kirvov crisply. "You go ahead on

your own path, each of you. I'll manage this detour myself." His eyes came to rest on the blond Israeli girl. "And you, Tovah, what will you be up to?"

"Yes, Tovah," Emily quickly added. "You've been eager to tell me something since last night. I'm sorry we got so involved in other things. Do you want to tell me now, or would you rather . . . ?"

Tovah came on with verve. "It is no secret I have been bursting to tell all of you. It's about Hitler's double." She glanced about her at the other tables and dropped her voice. "If your theory is correct and you can prove Hitler survived, there would have to have been a double that died in his stead. I told you I would look into the whole business of a double. Well, I did." She grinned happily. "Hitler *did* have a double, believe it or not. You *can* believe it. It's true."

Emily blinked at the young Israeli woman. "You can prove it?"

"I have proved it. Listen."

With undisguised relish, Tovah recounted her search for a Hitler double in the person of Manfred Müller, the satiric Hitler imitator, and concluded with her meeting with Anneliese Raab, who had helped shoot the Berlin Olympics film.

"Anneliese told me that Müller has a son in Berlin," Tovah went on. "She's arranging for me to meet the son, Josef Müller. Maybe this can give me the last word on what happened to Hitler's double."

Emily was pleased, but thoughtful. "Wonderful work, Tovah. But"— she considered it—"what if Josef Müller tells you his father is alive and well and leads you to him?"

"Then I'm afraid we've lost," said Tovah. "A Hitler double still alive does not give us a double being cremated next to the Führerbunker in Hitler's place. On the other hand, Josef might tell me that his father died in 1945 under strange and inexplicable circumstances."

Emily turned to Foster beside her, covering his hand with her own. "Rex, tell Nicholas and Tovah about Zeidler."

Without further prompting, Foster addressed Kirvov and Tovah Levine. He gave them the highlights of his interview with Zeidler, and spoke of Zeidler's suggestion that he search out the missing plan for the mysterious seventh bunker at Spandau Prison. Foster intended to see the American director of the prison guards the day after tomorrow.

When he returned his attention to Emily, he said, "Of course, the really crucial undertaking is the one that commences in the morning alongside the Führerbunker. Have you got everything lined up, Emily?"

"Everything, I hope. Professor Blaubach promised me permits would be in order, permits for my driver Plamp and me to take his car into the East German Security Zone, permits for the Oberstadt Construction Company's work truck to follow me, and for Andrew Oberstadt himself with a three-man crew to do the excavating. We start at ten in the morning."

"And then the chips are down." Foster signaled the waiter for refills of their glasses. "Let's drink to that, to the hope that Emily hits the jackpot."

It was midmorning, and they were inside East Berlin.

Tension gripped Emily. She was seated alone in the back of Plamp's Mercedes as they drove cautiously along Niederkirchnerstrasse toward the guardhouse that stood sentinel beside the electronic gate leading into the East German Frontier Security Zone.

Although she had been here once before, with Ernst Vogel, and had met Professor Blaubach at the entrance, this time she felt more insecure, felt alone and vulnerable. Leaning forward, narrowing her eyes as she looked through the car's windshield, she realized that the memory of her previous visit had blurred and everything was now coming into sharper focus.

As the car moved up the street, nearing the gate, slowing, Emily saw that there were a half dozen green-uniformed East German guards in full view. Beyond them was the fence that merged abruptly into the Wall once more. Approaching the gate, she cast about for sight of Andrew Oberstadt, and the truck and equipment he was to bring with three of his best construction workmen. The truck could not be seen, and Emily suffered a stab of apprehension.

They had come to a halt a few yards before the line of waiting soldiers—effectively armed, she could see, with what appeared to be machine guns slung over their shoulders. Plamp hastily left the driver's seat to help Emily out of the rear.

Just as she emerged, she sighted a blue Toyota pickup truck coming toward her. She recognized the muscular, hefty, beetle-browed driver as Andrew Oberstadt, with two members of his excavation crew squeezed into the front of the truck beside him and a third laborer squatting in back.

When Oberstadt's truck had come abreast of the Mercedes, the construction company owner hung out of the cab window to call to Emily. "Sorry to be late. They delayed me at Checkpoint Charlie. Practically dismantled the truck. Anyway, we're here and ready to get going." He nodded toward the soldiers. "I suppose we'll have to go through it all over again here."

"Possibly," said Emily. "Let's see if they've got our entry permits from Professor Blaubach."

Emily started toward the soldiers. To one side of them, near the guardhouse, she became aware of an ominous wooden sign: WARNING! STAY OUT! THIS FRONTIER AREA RESTRICTED!

One of the soldiers, taller than the others, bespectacled, in a dress uniform, stepped forward. Emily saw that he was an officer.

"Fräulein Emily Ashcroft?" he inquired.

"Yes, I'm Miss Ashcroft. Professor Otto Blaubach was to have left permits for me and the others. Do you have them?"

The officer did not give confirmation, but instead held out a hand. "Your passport, Fräulein?"

Emily found her British passport in her shoulder bag and handed it over.

The officer studied her passport photo, then compared it to her face. Without a word he handed the passport back. He peered past her at the Mercedes sedan and then at the Toyota truck. "I count five to accompany you," he said.

"That's right."

"All West German nationals?"

"All from West Berlin. They have their passports. If you wish—"

The officer's hand dismissed the passports. "Before you may enter, we must make a thorough search of your vehicles."

"Please do," said Emily.

"Will you have your friends leave the vehicles, and stand aside until we have finished?"

"Of course," said Emily, turning away. She signaled for Oberstadt and his crew to leave their truck.

Plamp backed away, while Oberstadt leaped down, beckoning to his men.

As this occurred, the East German officer was barking an order to the other guards. Immediately, they hastened into action. One soldier, after retrieving a mirror set on a long handle from the guardhouse, headed for the Mercedes. Meanwhile, the tall officer led two of his other guards to the truck.

Emily joined Oberstadt, who was an inch or two shorter than she and two or three times broader, as he observed the activity around his Toyota. "No nonsense this time," he whispered. "Not doing it only with mirrors. We're getting the full treatment."

Emily saw two of the soldiers on their backs wriggling under the truck.

"What do they expect to find?" Emily wondered.

"Possibly on the lookout for weapons," whispered Oberstadt. He added, "Or for Martin Bormann."

The search of both vehicles took ten minutes. When it was done, and the soldiers had reassembled in front of the guardhouse, the officer strode toward Emily. He gave her six pink cards. "Permission for the six of you to come and go for seven days," he said. "You will enter at ten o'clock each morning. Of course, your vehicles will be searched each time you come and again when you leave. You will leave no later than five o'clock in the afternoon through this gate. You may proceed to your exact destination, as stated, and nowhere else."

"The mound and the area immediately around it," said Emily.

"The Führerbunker area," said the officer more specifically. "You may go through now."

They were inside their vehicles once more, the Mercedes sedan slowly preceding Oberstadt's truck through the gate and into the obstacle course of the East German no-man's-land.

They drove past the watchtower from which two curious East German soldiers followed their progress, and then they swung onto the dirt road and zigzagged their way along the bumpy turf.

When they arrived at the foot of the elongated dirt mound, Emily reaffirmed to herself that it must rise at least twenty feet at its highest point, its summit overlooking the uneven but relatively level surrounding field.

Emily emerged from the Mercedes and stood hands on hips eagerly studying the lay of the mound, which was some distance from the nearest watchtower and quite isolated. Not far to its right was a portion of the five-foot chain-link fence and beyond it in the East Berlin sector the parking lot from which Hitler's Old Reich Chancellery had once risen before it had been thoroughly bombed by American and British planes and shattered by Russian artillery shells.

Andrew Oberstadt had jumped down from the cab of his

truck, and given commands to his crew members, who were gathering together shovels and picks, and sifting screens. Presently Oberstadt reached Emily's side and together they surveyed the scene in the sun.

Oberstadt shook his head. "Looks like a pile of nothing. To think the leader of the German Third Reich lived under all that rubble every day for—what?—two months, three months?"

"The last three and a half months, at least."

"And died there like a cornered rat," said Oberstadt.

"Maybe," said Emily, almost inaudibly. Then more clearly, "You know what we're looking for?"

"Exactly. A cameo bearing the face of Frederick the Great. A jawbone, with teeth and a bridge hopefully intact."

"Yes. Also, anything else you might turn up."

"We won't miss a thing. But first off, you've got to show us where to start. In the former Chancellery garden, I know. Now you'll have to point out the exact place where we're to begin and the dimensions of the dig. Should we get going?"

"This minute," said Emily, rummaging through her purse to find the drawing that she had made with Ernst Vogel's help, a diagram of the Führerbunker and adjacent garden area that Foster had refined for her with his own sketch of the underground structure and photographs taken afterward by the initial Soviet search teams.

Walking slowly toward the left side of the mound, Emily studied the diagram, with Oberstadt in step beside her and peeking over her shoulder.

Abruptly, Emily stopped just past the midpoint of the mound. "Here," she said. "From the lower level fifty-five feet below, they carried Hitler's body up four flights of steps, then Braun's body, to the emergency exit situated right here. There was sort of a blockhouse or vestibule here with a doorway that led into what was left of the garden." Emily took a few steps to her left, with

Oberstadt trailing after her. "About here we will do our first excavation. This is where the Russians found a shallow trench." She pulled loose two photographs that had been clipped to the diagram. "These are pictures of the trench made by a Russian photographer the day after the Soviets overran the area."

Oberstadt examined the photographs, and then studied the excavation site. "It doesn't seem very deep."

"Andrew, don't forget that forty years have passed. In that time, due to Russian bulldozing around here, more earth has been overlaid on the trench. It will not be so shallow or near the surface now. It could be many feet down."

"Don't worry," said Oberstadt. "We'll go way down deep just to be sure."

He looked off and summoned his crew. Crisply, he gave them orders. As he drew the outline of the trench in the turf with a toe of his boot, he told the men to drive stakes around the perimeters, giving an outline of the area they were to excavate.

Emily watched the men go off, then turned back to Oberstadt. "Let me show you the shell crater where the bodies were buried after they were cremated."

She pointed to her diagram. "At this point," said Emily. "Three meters away."

She paced off the distance.

Oberstadt frowned. "This is the next spot?"

"The approximate location of the crater," Emily replied. "The remains of Hitler and Braun were carried to this point in a canvas, lowered about nine feet, and covered with dirt. A short time after, witnesses led the Russians to this crater. The Russians uncovered the corpses, removed them, and eventually identified them as the remains of Hitler and Braun."

"But you are not sure that they found the right bodies?"

"I want either to confirm that the Russians were correct or prove that they were mistaken. Your excavation will give us the answer, I hope." Emily stared down at the grassy plot. "Since we don't have the precise circumference of the crater, you'd better enlarge the area of your excavation."

Oberstadt was again marking the soil with the toe of his boot. "This should cover it," he said, when he finished. "We'll stake it, giving ourselves plenty of leeway."

"Do your men understand what they are looking for?" Emily asked once more.

Oberstadt reassured her with a smile. "They are instructed to filter all dirt through sifting screens. Anything we find, we will call to your attention. You'll be here to look it over and decide on its importance."

"Where and when do we start?" Emily asked.

Oberstadt pivoted, and saw that his crew had finished staking out the dimensions of the trench. One of them was now carrying up shovels and screens.

"We'll start with the old trench, the site of the funeral pyre."

He retraced his steps to the staked-out trench. He looked it over, bent down and picked up a long-handled spade. Stepping to the edge of the trench site, he put his foot on the back of the spade and drove its pointed blade into the earth.

"When do we begin? We begin now." He pushed the shovel deeper into the turf. "The dig is now underway."

Emily swallowed with difficulty and watched.

8

It was an overcast early morning in West Berlin, and Tovah Levine sat at the dining-room table with Josef Müller, waiting until his wife finished serving them breakfast.

Tovah could not help staring at her host as she tried to make out whether Josef Müller had any of the mannerisms of his father, Manfred Müller, Adolf Hitler's double. Tovah could discern no similarities. Josef Müller, who she had figured must be around forty-eight years old, had a beefy, somewhat bloated face, graying pompadour, no mustache, and was otherwise indistinguishable from a million other German white-collar workers.

At first, Tovah had tried to locate him on her own, through

Lufthansa, but learned that he was away on a vacation. His office would give out neither his telephone number nor his home address, and she could not find him listed in the telephone directory. But then, Anneliese Raab had come through as she had promised and given Tovah the younger Müller's home telephone number.

When Tovah had reached him, he was just back from vacationing with his family in the Black Forest region. Tovah had identified herself as an Israeli journalist who was pursuing a story about Manfred Müller's renowned Hitler act. The son had sounded pleased, even cordial, and had invited Tovah to breakfast with him the following morning at his home on Warägerweg not far from Gatow.

With breakfast served, Tovah and Josef Müller were alone with their cold cuts and coffee. A light drizzle had begun outside, and Josef Müller sat contemplating the small raindrops splattering against the windowpanes.

Before breakfast, the son had already answered questions about his father's nightclub career, and spoken of his success in mimicking the Führer. The son had also displayed a scrapbook with yellowing press write-ups of Manfred Müller's performances, as well as ads announcing his long run at the Lowendorff Club. After that, they had discussed the night the Gestapo blackshirts had picked up Manfred Müller after a show.

"Yes, that was always a memorable moment in our family," Josef Müller had admitted, still impressed. "My father was taken to meet with Hitler himself."

"Apparently because Hitler had need of a double. Did you know that at any time before Fräulein Raab confirmed it for you and sent you the Olympics film showing your father as Hitler's double?"

"I had never known for certain. I knew only that my father had met Hitler and had done some errands for him. But I think I vaguely suspected my father's role from hints my mother dropped from time to time. I never knew exactly what my father did for Hitler. My father refused to speak about it. Also, I was very young, maybe seven or eight, at the end of the war. Of course, I understood nothing about politics."

That had been part of their discussion before breakfast, but with breakfast served, Tovah posed her latest question. "So Manfred Müller was Hitler's double during most of the 1936 Olympic games. What I wonder about is—did he continue to act as a double after that?"

Josef Müller concentrated on the trickles of rain on the windows and considered the question. Shifting in his chair, he took up his fork and began to slice and eat the first of his cold cuts. "Yes, as I grew up, I always suspected that my father had continued to work as Hitler's double."

"But you never knew for certain?"

"Not positively. I suppose that Olympics film makes it clear enough."

Tovah resumed her questioning. "Between 1936, the time of the Olympics, and 1939, when the Second World War began, what did your father do? Did he go back to his acting career?"

"Actually, no. My oldest sister has told me that he was around the house a good deal, as if on call. But we lived well. I assume that Hitler had him on a retainer, some kind of regular financial stipend. It must have been a fair salary because, I repeat, we were very comfortable. However, once the war was really underway, perhaps around 1940, my father began to leave the house and go out more frequently. Sometimes he would be gone for days. My sisters were always pestering my mother to know where Daddy was. Our mother would say that he worked for the government, sometimes on special missions for the Führer. She made my father sound like a courier. But, knowing about my father's theatrical career, I eventually guessed that he often served as Hitler's stand-in or double."

"Yet you have no evidence of actual instances when he might have appeared as Hitler's double?"

"No, I don't," Josef Müller said a little unhappily. "I will say this. As the tempo of the war increased, my father was more frequently away and for longer and longer periods of time. In 1944, he was home only a few times, and then he was very close-mouthed. The last time I saw my father—I was just about eight years old—was in the final few months of the war. He came home to arrange for my mother, sisters, and myself to be taken to safety. He decided to move us to the Obersalzberg for the year after the war. I have some recollection that he was to go with us to the Obersalzberg when one afternoon four Gestapo agents arrived to take my father away once more. This was on orders from Hitler. I never saw my father again. He never caught up with us in the Obersalzberg. I have no idea what happened to him."

Controlling her excitement, Tovah asked, "Do you remember the date when your father was taken away the last time?"

"Not the exact date, but I believe it was in the final days of April 1945. The war ended a week or so after that. But my father had vanished and we never heard from him again."

Tovah inclined her head understandingly. The timing was perfect. Everything seemed to fit in sequence.

She studied the troubled Josef Müller. Then she blurted out her next question. "Could your father have been taken to Hitler in the Führerbunker and been with him to the end?"

Josef Müller looked surprised. "My father and Adolf in the bunker? Oh, I don't think so. There would have been no explanation for two Hitlers. Someone would have seen and known. What are you trying to say?"

Tovah drew herself upright. "I think I'm trying to say that maybe your father was made to pose as Hitler and forced to kill himself to allow the real Hitler to live and get away."

The possibility froze the younger Müller's features. "I—I don't think that would have been possible. I can't imagine it."

"There are some people who do imagine it."

Josef Müller tried to recover his composure. "You're saying that my father, made to play Hitler, killed himself—or was killed—and then cremated to deceive the victors? That this was a ruse thought up by Hitler so that he could survive? You think that is a possibility?"

Tovah shrugged. "I don't know. I think that conceivably it could have happened. I haven't been able to prove it yet."

Josef Müller rose to his feet, agitated.

"I doubt if you'll ever prove it," he said. "I've read of Hitler's last period in the bunker. He was there, underground for weeks, never emerging. If Manfred Müller went down and entered the bunker as Hitler, it would have been assumed that Hitler had previously emerged and was now returning. I don't believe that ever happened."

"Are you certain that Hitler did *not* leave the bunker in that last week of his life? Or was *not* seen by someone returning to the bunker?"

Josef Müller's agitation grew. "I'm not certain, of course. The only one who could be certain would be one of the SS or police guards outside the bunker in those last days who could swear that he had seen Hitler—or someone who looked like Hitler—enter the bunker near the very end. If you could find such a person, you might prove what you have imagined—that Manfred Müller went into the bunker while Hitler was still there, and that Manfred Müller died in Hitler's place. If you can find such a person . . ."

"Maybe I can."

"Then you may find out, once and for all, what happened to Adolf Hitler—and—and, yes, what happened to my father. I wish you luck."

* * *

An hour later, returning to the Kempinski hotel, Tovah Levine went directly to the second floor and pushed the buzzer outside Emily's suite. Seconds later, Tovah was admitted.

"I was afraid you'd already be at the dig," said Tovah, catching her breath.

"I was just leaving," said Emily, buttoning her raincoat. Restlessly, she went to the window and gloomily studied the wet street below. "My crew is out there digging away. I think the drizzle is subsiding. Maybe it'll stop altogether." She turned to face Tovah, who was standing in the middle of the sitting room. "You look like you have something on your mind, Tovah. Why are you here?"

"I need your help. I think we can help each other. Can we talk a minute?"

"Of course. Please sit down."

Tovah plopped down on the sofa, waited for Emily to be seated. Hardly able to contain herself, Tovah said, "I just came from seeing Josef Müller."

Emily was completely puzzled. "Who?"

"The son of Hitler's double, Manfred Müller. The one who posed as Hitler during the Olympics."

"Of course! My mind's been in ten different places. So you saw Müller's son? Did it get you any place? What happened to his father?"

Breathlessly, Tovah recited details of her conversation with Josef Müller.

Emily had been listening intently. Suddenly she said, "But the son doesn't know what actually happened to his father?"

"Only that the Gestapo picked him up sometime during what history tells us was the last week of Hitler's life."

"When Hitler was already in the bunker."

"That's the point, Emily. If the real Hitler was down there all the time, without leaving and coming back—and yet Hitler was seen entering the bunker, it would mean another Hitler went down to join the real Hitler. If true, it would make all your conjecturing possible." She paused dramatically. "What we need is someone who saw Hitler enter the bunker—when Hitler was already in the bunker. An SS guard at the bunker entrance might know. You once mentioned meeting such a guard."

"Yes, Ernst Vogel was there on guard duty."

"Can I see him?" Tovah demanded. "Can you call Vogel for me?"

Emily was already moving toward the telephone. "Let me call him right now and find out. Then we'll know."

Emily flipped to the back of her small address book, and immediately she dialed Ernst Vogel.

She had him on the line, and Tovah came off the sofa to edge closer.

After identifying herself, Emily proceeded to the main question. "Herr Vogel, a minor problem has come up for me about how long Hitler was down in the Führerbunker before he killed himself. I thought you might straighten me out."

"I hope I can," said Vogel. "Please speak louder."

Emily raised her voice. "According to the information we have gathered from at least twenty witnesses, Hitler moved from the Old Chancellery into the safer Führerbunker on January 16, 1945."

"Approximately that time," agreed Vogel.

"Now, we know that the last day Hitler was seen in the bunker alive," continued Emily, "was April 30, 1945."

"Correct."

"Very well. The question is—when was the last time Hitler was seen leaving the bunker for—for any reason, a walk, whatever—and seen returning to the bunker for good?"

"Ah, that question. Not difficult to answer. Eva Braun went for her final walk outside the bunker into the Tiergarten on April 19. But it was too dangerous outside, and she quickly returned, never to leave again."

"It is Adolf Hitler I'm asking about, Herr Vogel," said Emily impatiently. "When was the last time he went outside and then came back inside the bunker? According to our best informants, Hitler went outside the bunker at night to give his dog Blondi a stroll, or to watch Eva and two of his secretaries at target practice with their pistols on April 10. Then, on April 20, Hitler went through the tunnel to the Court of Honor of the New Chancellery to show himself at a reception for his fifty-sixth birthday, and newsreel cameras covered his appearance. Following that, he appeared outdoors in the garden beside the Führerbunker to pin decorations for heroism on twenty orphans who were members of the Hitler Youth. After that, he went down into the bunker to stay. That means he remained in the bunker from April 20 on, without ever going out again, for ten days, until his death. Or so say all our informants. Is that correct?"

Emily waited tensely for agreement or contradiction.

She heard Vogel say crankily, "They are all wrong, all of your informants are wrong. You say the last time Hitler went out and returned was April 20? No, that is absolutely wrong. I, myself, saw the Führer return from a walk outside the bunker with a young woman, probably one of his secretaries—I could not see her face—and go inside the bunker very late at night on April 28."

Emily exchanged a flushed glance with Tovah, whose ear was near the receiver. "Wait a minute, Herr Vogel," Emily said. "Although all my other sources say that Hitler was never seen leaving the Führerbunker in the last ten days of his life there, you are saying he left and returned to the bunker just two days before his death."

"Exactly what I am saying. I was standing on guard outside. Hitler himself was returning from somewhere, maybe a short walk, and was going down into the bunker. It was very late, and almost everyone below was asleep. I snapped to attention and gave the Führer a salute. He waved a hand absently at me and went on inside. It was the last time."

"Two days before his death. Did you see him leave to take that walk?"

"No, I wasn't on duty until just before he returned and went inside."

"You did not see him leave, but you saw him return and go inside. Herr Vogel, you are positive it was Adolf Hitler?"

"As positive as I am that I am me when I look into the mirror. It was Adolf Hitler, believe me, Fräulein Ashcroft. I can prove every word I say is true. I kept a duty log of all important arrivals and departures at the Führerbunker, with the exact time of comings and goings. If you have any doubts, I can show you the log. It is in storage with my extra books in the basement. If you will give me—say two hours—I can show it to you."

Emily no longer had any doubts, but she said, "Thank you, Herr Vogel. I'll drop by in two hours."

Emily hung up, a broad smile on her face as she met Tovah's gaze. "You know, Tovah, the person that Vogel saw enter the bunker two days before Hitler's end, don't you?"

"Manfred Müller, no other," said Tovah happily.

Rex Foster had telephoned Spandau Prison and asked to speak to the American director of the month, and his call had been transferred to Major George Elford, who spoke with a flat Midwestern accent.

After identifying himself, Foster had explained his business. "Albert Speer may have left one of his architectural plans behind, one he had borrowed and probably showed to Rudolf Hess before he was released from prison in 1966. I was hoping to find it. I need it for a book."

"Well, we have a lot of the prisoner's leftovers in storage, all right."

"I was authorized to look into this by its rightful owner, the man who loaned the blueprint to Speer," Foster had said. "I'm speaking of Rudi Zeidler, who used to be one of Speer's ten assistants. I can have him call you—"

"He already has," Major Elford had interrupted. "He left a message for me to admit you."

"Also, I'd like to meet you," Foster had added.

"Anything special in mind?"

"Yes. I can tell you better in person."

"Well, okay. How's eleven-thirty today?"

"Fine. I'll be there."

Coming away from the telephone in their bedroom, Foster had mused aloud to Emily, who had been dressing.

"I wish I knew more about Spandau Prison. I know nothing about it except that the seven leading Nazis who escaped the death penalty at the Nuremberg Trials were sentenced to Spandau in West Berlin and checked in to serve their sentences in July of 1947. I hate to go anywhere so uninformed."

"You don't have to be uninformed," Emily had said. "If you want to read up on Spandau, go and see my friend Peter Nitz at the *Morgenpost.*"

And that Foster had done. Nitz had received him at his editorial desk in the Axel Springer Verlag building, had scurried off to the newspaper's archive room behind the main lobby, and had returned with a bulging folder of clippings for Foster.

Foster had read steadily until the time had come for him to set out for his appointment with Major George Elford in Spandau.

Now, reclining in the back of a taxi, Foster was being driven into the British sector at the outskirts of West Berlin where that strangest of all prisons, Spandau, was located.

As they rode along, Foster reviewed what he had absorbed from the clippings he had scanned in the newspaper's Spandau file.

By now, Foster had a slight fix on it and felt more comfortable. Spandau was an old prison, built in 1881. When the Nazis claimed it, after coming to power in 1933, they nicknamed it The Red Castle. Shortly, it became the place where they detained the Reich's political prisoners before sending them off to concentration camps. It had been a prison with 132 cells for 132 prisoners, but at the time the four Allies took it over in 1947 to incarcerate the seven Nazi war criminals, Spandau was jammed with 600 prisoners. The Allies moved them all out, remodeled the dank site to assure supersecurity, and then moved in their seven war criminals.

The control of Spandau had been a four-power operation from the start. A board of four directors—one each from the United States, Great Britain, France, the Soviet Union—ran the prison and met weekly. There were permanent prison guards representing all four powers inside the prison. The outside guards, thirty soldiers from each of the powers, rotated turns in protecting it on a monthly basis.

On July 18, 1947, the seven condemned Nazis entered Spandau. Foster tried to remember their names: Rudolf Hess, Hitler's second deputy; Albert Speer, Hitler's principal architect and also minister of armaments; Erich Raeder, the Nazi admiral; Karl Dönitz, head of the Nazi navy and ruler of fallen Germany in the week following Hitler's death; Walther Funk, who ran the Reichsbank; Baldur von Schirach, leader of the Hitler Youth; Constantin von Neurath, onetime Nazi foreign minister.

Raeder, Funk, and von Neurath had been paroled early because of their advanced years and growing infirmities, Foster recalled. Dönitz had served out his ten-year sentence and been released. Then, Speer and von Schirach, completing their twenty-year sentences, had been freed.

That left one prisoner, Rudolf Hess, serving a lifetime sentence. The entire four-power apparatus was kept up to look after one unrepentant ninety-one-year-old Nazi.

Foster's taxi was rattling over a narrow street, and in moments it had drawn up before Wilhelmstrasse 23, which was Spandau Prison.

Leaving the taxi, paying the driver, Foster turned around slowly to survey the scene of his appointment. The drizzle had ceased, but the red brick prison still glistened from the rain.

The square compound was surrounded by both a wire fence and a high red brick wall. The solid double entrance gate and the brick façade had a medieval look to them. Inside the brick wall were concrete watchtowers manned by armed soldiers equipped with giant spotlights. The wire fence bore a sign in German and English: WARNING—DANGER—DO NOT APPROACH. GUARDS HAVE ORDERS TO SHOOT.

Foster could make out the upper portion of what appeared to be a three-story prison beyond the one-story sentry house.

Mildly intimidated, Foster crossed the sidewalk to the main gate and pressed a buzzer. A grilled wicket opened. Foster gave his name and stated his business. After a few seconds, the gate came slowly open and Foster entered. A warden and two American soldiers, blue-uniformed, machine guns slung over their shoulders, were waiting for him. He was asked to show some identification. He showed his passport. He was quickly searched. He was told to sign in. Finally he was turned over to a soldier who would take him to Major George Elford.

Following the soldier, Foster passed through an enclosed courtyard and entered the administration building of the prison. The soldier spun to the left and pointed. "The prison director's office, sir." Foster rapped, a muffled voice answered, and Foster was shown into the room.

The director's office was plain, undecorated, and Major George Elford was standing beside a golf bag that was propped against the wall. A wiry, leathery-faced man in his forties, Elford dropped his putter into the bag, came forward, pumped Foster's hand and indicated a wooden chair. He pulled another wooden chair opposite Foster and sat down.

Foster pointed toward the window. "I'm astonished by the amount of security you've got out there."

Elford gave an embarrassed shrug. "I'm not sure it's justified anymore. Maybe it was in 1947 when they locked up those seven Nazis. The four powers stuck them in this old prison facility to keep them out of sight of the German population who might have viewed them as martyrs. There were threats at that time that some of the fanatical Nazis still around might try to rescue them, and that went on through the years."

"Actual threats?"

"You bet. Our Allied intelligence uncovered a plot—I think it was back in 1955—that the Nazi Colonel Otto Skorzeny hoped to rescue several of the war criminals. He was good at that sort of thing. He's the one who rescued Mussolini from our troops in Italy. Skorzeny wanted to drop two helicopters into this prison's exercise yard when the inmates were out there. One planeful of Nazi fanatics was to try to fend off the Spandau guards, while the other plane was picking up the inmates and whisking them off. Fortunately, this plot was uncovered and our security was increased. The rescue attempt never came off. But this goes on all the time. As recently as 1981, five incurable Nazis in Karlsruhe were caught building up a cache of explosives to break into Spandau and pull out Hess. All five were arrested."

"It must be easier, in 1985, with only Hess to guard in this huge place."

"Yup, the deputy Führer, a ninety-one-year-old Hess. He's useless now. Except that he might make a good living symbol for neo-Nazi gangs. Anyway, I gather your main interest in Spandau Prison is Rudolf Hess."

"Not Hess himself, as you know," said Foster. "Rather it's the missing bunker plan he may have in his possession that I'm after. I promised to explain the whole thing to you. Now I will, as briefly as possible. And then I hope that you can help me."

Major Elford was biting off the tip of a cigar and lighting it. "Go ahead. I'm listening."

Quickly, Foster told the American officer about himself, his book project, and the one missing plan.

"Then," Foster went on, "Zeidler recalled that he had once loaned the entire batch of seven plans to Speer, while Speer was still here in Spandau serving out his sentence. Apparently, Speer maintained his interest in architecture and hoped to write something about his work."

"True," Major Elford confirmed. "Speer was the only prisoner who kept his full sanity because he spent his free time reading and writing about architecture."

"Well," said Foster, "when Speer finished the last year of his sentence, he must have carried the plans out of prison with the rest of his effects. In fact, he returned all the bunker plans to Zeidler, or thought he had. Actually, he returned only six. We're guessing he may have left the seventh bunker plan behind here in Spandau."

"Why?"

"Zeidler surmised it was an oversight. Zeidler figured that, while trying to identify the location of each bunker, Speer had some trouble placing the seventh one. So while still here, Speer loaned it to Hess hoping that the old deputy Führer might remember Hitler's intentions for that bunker, where he had wanted it built or actually had it built. I suppose Hess was unable to help."

"You suppose correctly. Hess's mind has been shot for a long, long time."

"Anyway, Speer never took the seventh plan back from Hess." Foster paused. "Zeidler expects it may still be among Hess's effects. Zeidler was hoping I could recover it, for my book and his own archives. What do you think?"

Major Elford blew a cloud of smoke, and then stubbed out his cigar butt in a bronze ashtray. "If it's here, you can have it. We don't give a damn about any ancient blueprints."

"Where do we look? In Rudolf Hess's cell?"

"Christ, no, his cell is bare as a stripper's tit. He's got a cot, chair, table, TV set, a few pieces of clothing, little more in there. We cleaned out most unnecessary effects over a decade ago." Major Elford stood up. "If it is anywhere, it's in the prison library. Let's go have a look."

They left the prison director's office, walking past the chief guard's room and the infirmary.

"Straight ahead is the actual cell block," announced Elford, "and also the library."

They strode along the corridor until they reached the converted cell that housed the prisoners' books, and finally entered it.

Elford gestured toward the bookshelves. "The war criminals were each allowed to take out four books at a time—a Bible, a second religious volume, a dictionary, and one nonpolitical novel. Sometimes they were permitted to read history books, but nothing military. Once, by mistake, a history of the Japanese-Russian war of 1901 crept in here. That was the war in which the Japanese whomped the Russians. When the Russians had their month in charge here, they found the book and threw it out. Anyway, under the table, in those three cartons, is where we keep prisoner storage. Hardly anything from the six who got out. Almost all the stuff in there belongs to Rudolf Hess."

Major Elford knelt down and dragged the three cartons from under the table.

There was a sparse number of items in the cartons. Elford began unloading the first one. "Mostly the excess of Hess's outer space collection," said Elford. "That became his hobby after he saw a moon shot on TV. He asked us to write NASA in Texas for reading matter, and all those pamphlets and brochures were mailed from NASA to Hess. They also sent him four color posters of the moon, taken on the moon. They're still on the walls of Hess's double cell. Naw, not a thing in this first carton."

Foster helped the major refill it, and then they turned to the second carton. This seemed to contain wearing apparel. Elford took out a pair of the wooden-soled canvas shoes the prisoners had originally been forced to wear. "Tell you a funny thing," said Elford, examining the scuffed shoes. "Albert Speer designed these for concentration camp inmates when the Nazis were in power. Then, in Spandau, he had to wear them, and one day for exercise he had to run in them. After he had finished running, Speer groaned and said, 'If I had known I'd one day be forced to wear them, I would have put a little leather in them.' "

Foster took a shabby blue cap, a dirty blue jacket, and a pair of trousers out of the box.

"And this?" Foster wondered.

"The prison outfit all the war criminals wore at first. That one was worn by Hess."

Foster was pulling some kind of leather military uniform out of the carton. "What's this?"

"A real historical item," said Elford. "Hess wanted us to hold onto it. It is the Luftwaffe uniform of a lieutenant colonel that Hess wore when he flew from Germany to Scotland in May, 1941. He came down to try to make peace with England. I suppose because he knew that Hitler would be turning against the Soviet Union and attacking it, and he hoped to arrange things so that

Hitler would have to fight on only one front." Elford peered into the carton. "Doesn't look like there's any architectural roll in there."

"That folded paper on the bottom," said Foster.

Major Elford picked it up and carefully unfolded it. When it was partially open, an architectural blueprint could be seen, and it was clearly signed by Rudi Zeidler.

"The seventh bunker," said Elford. "I guess this is what you want."

"Exactly what I want," agreed Foster.

Elford came to his feet with a grunt. "Let's take it to my office and spread it out. Then you can have a good look."

After shoving the cartons back under the library table, they walked quickly back to the prison director's office.

Elford spread the blueprint open on his desk, with Foster standing beside him, and they both examined it.

"Not a bit of identification anywhere," said Foster.

"Not a word," said Elford.

"Strange," said Foster, puzzled. "The other six—their locations were given. On this one nothing."

"You're sure it's an underground bunker?"

"No question about that. You can tell from the location of generators and ventilators for oxygen exchange. It's one of Hitler's underground-headquarters bunkers all right, the missing one. It's damn big, very big. But where did he build it, assuming he built it at all?"

"I suppose it was top secret," said Elford, refolding the plan. He handed it to Foster. "I guess Speer studied it, and couldn't figure it out, and then he turned it over to Hess, hoping Hess would recognize it as you've suggested. I can tell you that at that point Hess remembered very little. When Speer was released, he must have forgotten to take this back from Hess. So now you've got it. I suppose your only hope is to go back to Rudi Zeidler with it. Maybe he'll remember more."

"Maybe," said Foster. "Yes, Zeidler is going to be my next stop. Thanks for everything, Major."

"Thanks for what?" said Elford. "Anyway, here's hoping you get par all the way."

"Meaning?"

"Just don't bogey the seventh, young man," said Elford emphatically. "Don't bogey it!"

As Rudi Zeidler opened the front door to admit him, Foster held up the folded blueprint, waving it triumphantly. "Bunker number seven," he announced. "I found it."

"Good work," said Zeidler cheerfully. Drawing Foster into the house, he asked, "Where? Spandau?"

"Just as you suspected," said Foster. "I was hoping you'd have a look at it now."

"Absolutely," agreed Zeidler, buttoning the gray cardigan he was wearing with fresh white ducks and old tennis shoes. "Let's go to my studio."

Leading the way through the house, Zeidler wondered how Foster had found the missing bunker plan. Foster recounted details of his meeting with Major George Elford in Spandau, and coming across the plan buried among Hess's effects.

Inside the studio, the German architect turned on the fluorescent lights, and together they went to the nearest table. Zeidler took the plan from Foster, unfolded it, and laid it flat on the table. He examined the blueprint carefully, then, frowning, lifted it up and looked on the back to see if there was anything there.

At last, shaking his head, Zeidler refolded the plan and handed it over to Foster. "You're right," the German said. "No site location given anywhere on it."

Foster searched the other's face. "But the drawing itself—does it ring a bell?"

"A tinkle, no more," said Zeidler. "Yes, the plan is mine all right. No question. I drew it and personally signed it. Usually, when I did these designs for Hitler, he would have me print in the site where the bunker was to be built. Obviously, for this one he didn't." As if to reassure himself, Zeidler repeated, "No, he didn't. Not for this one. I wonder why. I can't recall."

"Maybe Hitler hadn't made his mind up where he would have this bunker built," Foster volunteered. "Or maybe he did know, but didn't want you or anyone else to know the location."

Zeidler remained baffled. "Could be. Still, all the other bunkers I did for Hitler were classified secret, yet the location of each was known to me. But not bunker seven. Apparently he forgot to tell me—or didn't want to tell me."

"Well, what I find unusual," said Foster, "is preparing a design for a construction without any idea of where it was to be built."

"Not as unusual as you think," said Zeidler. "For one thing, I knew I was designing something to go underground, like all the others I did. For another, I would often get specific orders from Hitler on dimensions and rooms he desired and so forth. He was fairly good at that. You remember his own experience as an artist. No doubt, for number seven, he specified he wanted an enormous bunker and told me what kind of soil we'd be working with. I would guess he knew from the start what locale in Germany he would use for its construction. If he didn't tell me, you can be sure he told no one. What he had in mind died with him in 1945."

"In fact," said Foster, "you don't know that Hitler actually used your design to construct this bunker at all?"

"No, I don't know that it was ever put together. The only ones who would know whether it had been built might be the slave laborers who actually worked on it."

"You mean all the underground bunkers that you designed and that were eventually constructed were built by slave laborers? By Jews, Czechs, gypsies, captured Poles and Ukrainians?"

Zeidler was hesitant. "Well, maybe not every one of them was built by slave laborers. Certainly we know that the Führerbunker was built by an old Berlin construction company. However, I'd venture to guess that most of the other underground military headquarters—due to the shortage of manpower—were dug out and constructed using enforced slave labor."

"And you're suggesting that one of those laborers might remember digging this bunker, if it was dug at all, and might be able to tell me where it would be found?"

Zeidler was shaking his head vigorously. "No, no, I'm not suggesting that as a serious possibility, Mr. Foster. Simply because there are no slave laborers left anymore. Hitler had them exterminated after they finished a job. He didn't want any of them around to reveal where his various secret bunkers were. When the slave laborers finished a job, they were rewarded with a trip to Dachau or Auschwitz or some other gas chamber. So I'm afraid you'll have to caption bunker seven in your book as 'unknown.' "

"Unless," said Foster slowly, "I could find myself a few slave laborers who survived the war, and who might recognize this plan."

"Why, yes, of course," agreed Zeidler. "You might start your hunt by practicing to find a needle in a haystack."

When Irwin Plamp brought his Mercedes to a halt before the dirty five-story building in Dahlmannstrasse where Ernst Vogel had his apartment and mail-order book business, Tovah Levine came out of the car ahead of Emily.

Eager to get Vogel's final verification of the entrance of a second Hitler into the Führerbunker two days before the end, Tovah hurried toward the bookseller's building.

For the better part of two hours Tovah had impatiently waited in Emily's suite for the time when they could see Vogel.

During that wait, Tovah had been filled in on Vogel's background by Emily. Then she had skimmed the research notes Emily had produced in which all witnesses had agreed that Hitler had not left or returned to the Führerbunker in what was supposed to have been the last twenty days of his life. Yet, all these reports had been contradicted by the one guard who had actually seen Hitler enter just two days before his announced death. Again and again Tovah and Emily had reassured themselves that there had been a Hitler double in the bunker, and he had been the one who committed suicide, while the real Hitler had survived and escaped.

Now, with Emily right behind her, Tovah hastily entered the building, trying to find Vogel's apartment.

Emily pointed to a staircase. "He's up on the floor above, first door to the left of the landing. We should be just on time."

Tovah allowed Emily to lead the way. Reaching the landing, they both turned left into a corridor and halted before the first brown door, somewhat chipped and in need of fresh paint. There was a doorbell to one side and Emily pressed it and waited for the door to open. When it did not open, Emily pushed the doorbell again. Still no response. As if to make sure it was being done properly, Tovah reached over to ring the doorbell herself. She rang it three or four times, but still no luck.

"Maybe the bell's on the blink," said Tovah.

"Maybe," agreed Emily. "All right, let's do it the old-fashioned way."

Emily began to rap on the door, and then as Tovah joined in they both rapped loudly.

The only response came from below the staircase. A rotund elderly lady was waddling up the steps.

"What is it? What is going on here?" she demanded breathlessly when she had arrived at the top. "You are making an awful commotion. I am Frau Lecki, the landlady. Who are you?"

"We are customers of Mr. Vogel," Emily replied calmly. "We

had an appointment to meet with him five minutes ago. He was to show us an important book." She indicated the door. "But he doesn't answer."

Frau Lecki was immediately understanding. "Ach, Vogel, you know Vogel. Half the time he doesn't answer because he can't hear well, and when he takes off his hearing aid, he can't hear at all." The landlady fumbled in her apron pocket for a ring of keys. "If Vogel said he would meet you here, he will be here. I am sure it is only that he is not wearing the hearing aid. Let me find him and tell him he has visitors."

Inserting a pass key into the keyhole, Frau Lecki unlocked the door and pushed it open. She clumped inside, took in the room, and gave a grunt of triumph. "Just as I thought. There he is in his rocker, with the hearing aid off and sound asleep." She beckoned Emily and Tovah. "You come in while I wake him."

The instant Tovah was inside the living room, she sniffed and wrinkled her nose. "What a foul smell," she whispered to Emily. "What can it be?"

But Emily was observing Ernst Vogel, lying back in his rocker, eyes tightly closed. Tovah followed her gaze and held on the slight wizened figure slumped in the rocker, his sunken cheeks almost white, his lips bluish.

"He looks ill," Emily muttered.

Frau Lecki was shaking Vogel by the shoulder. "Get up, Ernst. You have customers here."

Vogel's eyes did not open. Instead his head fell forward, and as the landlady took her hand away, he slid sideways against the arm of the rocker.

"He looks dead to me," Tovah said in an undertone.

Emily dashed forward, and knelt down on one knee in front of Vogel. She grabbed his limp arm and felt for his pulse. After an interval, she shook her head and staggered to her feet.

"How horrible," Emily gasped. She shut her eyes, and shook

her head again. "He's dead, no question. What a terrible thing." Forcing herself to open her eyes, she allowed them to hold on the slumped figure in the rocker. "I think what you smell, Tovah, is potassium cyanide."

"But he was all right a few hours ago," Tovah protested.

"Not anymore," Emily said. "The poor man took the poison or was made to take it. The cyanide killed him instantly."

The landlady was beginning to comprehend, and suddenly she brought her hand to her mouth to stifle a sob. "No, he can't be dead! It is impossible. He was too much alive. He would never kill himself. But he—he has—he has."

"Maybe with some help," Tovah murmured.

But only Emily heard her.

Frau Lecki was already at the telephone. "This is terrible, terrible! I must call the police!" Picking up the phone, she saw the line dangling loosely. "The phone line—it's cut. I'd better call from my room." She turned and ran out the door.

Averting her eyes from Vogel, Emily's attention was diverted by a storage carton on a ledge behind the rocker. "That carton," she said, "it's marked in crayon on the side. It says *Bunker Logs.* He was ready for us."

Tovah hastened to the carton. "The one for April 28, 1945, the one in which he noted the return of Hitler to the Führerbunker." Tovah started going through the logbooks, noting the dates on their covers.

"Make it fast, Tovah," Emily called out. "We don't want the police to find us here." Then she added, "I don't think you'll find it, Tovah."

After another half minute, Tovah turned around. She frowned at Emily. "You're right. It's the only one that's missing."

Emily took Tovah by the arm. "Quick scenario. Someone overheard our phone conversation with Vogel, and learned what he intended to show us—"

"But how?"

Emily was silent for a moment. "I don't know. Possibly a phone tap. Anyway, someone beat us here, and was innocently admitted by Vogel. The caller put a gun to Vogel's head, forced him to bite a cyanide capsule, and then snatched up the logbook and got out of here fast." Tovah allowed Emily to propel her to the doorway. "Now we've got to get out, too," Emily insisted.

"We can't just leave. What about the police? He's been murdered."

"So was my father. I'm almost sure of that. Where were the police then? Let's go. There's nothing we can do here."

"Maybe you're right. We can't afford to get mixed up in this. Nobody knows we've been here."

Emily looked at her. "Except the murderer, of course."

They hurried past the landlady's apartment and ran into the street. Reaching the waiting Mercedes, Tovah asked, "What does this do to our case? Vogel swore he saw Hitler return from a walk, when he had never gone out for a walk. We agreed that the Hitler he saw was a second Hitler, a double, Manfred Müller. Now we don't have Vogel or the logbook."

"We don't need Vogel and his logbook. Two hours ago we had Vogel, and he told us all we wanted to know. We're getting very close, Tovah, very close to the truth. Sick as I feel, I have to get back to my excavation. Where can I drop you off?"

"The Kempinski, please."

When they drew up before the hotel, Tovah opened the back door to leave. She looked at Emily once more. "I hope you're right, Emily, that we are closer to the truth."

"We'll get to it," promised Emily, "as long as someone doesn't get to us first. Now after all this you get yourself some rest. See you later."

Standing at the curb, watching the Mercedes drive off, Tovah knew that she would be too busy to rest. They were very close to the truth. It was time for Tovah to report to her superiors. It was time for her to contact Chaim Golding and the other Israeli intelligence officers in the Berlin branch of Mossad, and bring them up to date. Someone was onto them, and the biggest game of all was still to be tracked down and punished.

They were inside the heavily guarded Frontier Zone of East Berlin, inside the Wall, with Plamp carefully driving the Mercedes over the dirt road carrying them to the mound of the Führerbunker. Emily sat tensely in the back seat, still clutching the pink card that had permitted her entry into the security area.

She tried to distract herself from her anxiety by counting the concrete posts that held the chain-link fence that ran along the road and hemmed them in. But she could not be distracted from what was foremost in her mind. The results of the initial digs. She had been given one week to uncover evidence that Hitler had or had not died as announced, and this was the end of the second day of excavation. By now, she was sure, Andrew Oberstadt and his three workmen would have unearthed the shallow trench and the nearby shell crater. By now, the first phase was over, and she wondered what the dig had turned up.

Looking off to her left, Emily could see the heap that was the grassy and rubble-strewn mound that covered the old Führerbunker. A portion of Oberstadt's Toyota truck was visible from behind the mound. His three men were not in view, but then Emily saw him come around the front of the mound with a spade in hand. He halted, pushed the pointed spade into the earth, and leaned on the handle, watching her approach.

Plamp had swerved the Mercedes off the road and headed bumpily across the uneven field toward the bunker. About fifteen feet from Oberstadt, he brought the car to a halt, turned off the ignition, and left the steering wheel to come around and assist Emily out of the rear.

"Thanks," she said to the driver. She removed her raincoat, adjusted the belt of her blue jumpsuit, planted the heels of her boots in the soggy turf, and strode toward Oberstadt.

"Sorry to be late," she said. "But I didn't think you'd need me around until you'd finished digging up the two sites."

"We didn't need you. Maybe we do now."

"You finished excavating the shallow trench and bomb crater?" Emily asked anxiously.

"We had covered the area with plastic, so we were able to finish both after the drizzle stopped."

"And—?"

"No luck, I'm afraid." Oberstadt confessed unhappily. "Found three minor relics. But nothing you wanted."

"No cameo with a portrait of Frederick the Great? No piece of jawbone with a dental bridge attached to it?"

"Neither," said Oberstadt. "If they were there in 1945, maybe the Russians picked them up. Possibly they were never there where we dug. You want to see what we did find?"

"May as well," said Emily.

Oberstadt left his shovel implanted in the ground and started around to the rear of the mound, with Emily right at his heels, trying to keep her balance on the wet turf.

At the far end of the mound, Emily saw the truck, and the three dirty laborers grouped around the front bumper, having hot coffee from a thermos bottle. They waved to her, and she waved back.

Oberstadt brought Emily to a small yellow towel spread atop a flat rock near the deep ditch of the once shallow trench.

"Here's all we found at both sites," said Oberstadt. From the towel, he held up the first of three objects. "A loose tooth. I think it belonged to a dog."

"That makes sense," said Emily. "Hitler's dogs were destroyed and later buried in this area."

"Then this," said Oberstadt, showing her a moist lump of what could have been wadded paper.

"What is it?" Emily wondered.

"Best I can make out, it must have been a small notebook once with a few pages of writing inside. But it's completely rotted from years of moisture."

Emily nodded. "That also fits. Goebbels's notebooks and papers were thrown into the trench and presumably burned."

"Well, no one will ever know." Oberstadt reached toward the towel and gingerly took up a blackened shred of cloth. "Finally this."

"It doesn't look like anything."

"It's something all right," Oberstadt said. "It's something that was monogrammed that I can read, barely read. See the two initials." He pointed. "Can you make them out? Those initials are E. B."

"Eva Braun," Emily whispered. The reality of the past made her blink. "That must have been a piece of one of her handkerchiefs or else part of what they called in those days step-ins. We're on the right track for sure."

"Wouldn't that tell you that it was Eva Braun, along with Hitler, who was cremated here?"

"Not necessarily. That monogrammed—whatever it was—could have been planted on someone else who was cremated. Now if you'd found that dental bridge or cameo . . ."

"But we didn't, I'm sorry to say."

"No Andrew, don't be mistaken, that's not bad at all. The bridge or cameo might have proved that it was indeed Hitler who was buried here, and less likely an imposter. Since you didn't unearth either item, there's no positive evidence that it was Hitler who was cremated. So far, so good, Andrew." She turned around and considered the huge mound of dirt, grass, and rubble. "There is one more place we must look." She hesitated. "Hitler's last living room and bedroom. To learn whether the cameo or bridge was left there to be used on a double, but was overlooked in the haste of the burial. If neither is there, it would indicate that Hitler got away wearing both of them."

Studying the vast mound, Oberstadt shook his head. "Even if it could prove something, how do we get down there?"

"By digging from the top straight down," said Emily.

"Impossible," said Oberstadt. "Do you know how much we'd have to excavate?" He stared at the summit of the mound. "I'd guess it is twenty feet from the top of the heap to ground level. Then, I think you told me, Hitler's quarters were fifty-five feet beneath ground level, and covered with eleven feet of concrete. That means we'd have to go down seventy-five feet, with countless obstructions, in five days—when your permit runs out. Even if the Russians crushed the concrete, it can't be done easily with a pick and a shovel."

"What about using heavy equipment?"

"I thought of bringing in a tractor and skiploader to speed up the digging of wider areas around the two sites we already handled. I asked the head East German officer about the possibility when we came in this morning. He said absolutely *verboten.* Not allowed."

Emily bit her lip, eyes fixed on the implacable mound. "There must be some way." She snapped her fingers. "I know what. Suppose you dig into the front, at ground level, into the upper level of the Führerbunker. That would save you twenty feet of digging."

"Even then . . ." Oberstadt frowned. "If we tunneled into the top floor, we'd have to shore up all the way so the dirt above doesn't cave in on us. And suppose there is no longer an upper level, suppose the Soviets collapsed it with all their bulldozing? More digging. More time."

"But the lower level, where Hitler lived, it may be intact. It was built to hold up against almost anything. Isn't there some way, using the shortcut I suggested, that you can get to it?"

"I don't know," said Oberstadt studying the mound. "Perhaps if I could double the size of my daytime crew, and then have a second shift continue work into the night, we might figure out how to reach bottom."

"What can I do to make it happen?" Emily persisted.

"First you guarantee me funds to enlarge my daytime crew and take on a nighttime shift."

"I guarantee it."

"Second, you call your man in East Berlin and get permission for us to dig not only in the morning and the afternoon but also at night."

"I'll guarantee permission. I intended to call him anyway, to arrange a pass for Mr. Foster. He could be useful. Don't worry, I'll get you permission to dig overtime."

"Finally, let me see my man in West Berlin."

"Your man in West Berlin?"

Oberstadt smiled. "My father, Leo Oberstadt, who founded our firm. He's incapacitated now, retired, but he's an expert on bunker construction and I'll need his advice."

"What do you mean—he's an expert?"

"He supervised the construction of at least a half dozen Nazi bunkers. My father Leo had a small construction company in Berlin before the outbreak of the war. He was arrested because he was more than half Jewish. In his youth he was as husky as I am, so the Nazis drafted him to be a slave laborer along with other Jews. Then it was learned that Leo had been a civil engineer and builder, and so he was promoted to being a foreman to supervise his fellow slave laborers. He and his slave crews built most of the underground bunkers during the war. All the slave laborers were sent to Dachau, Belsen, Buchenwald before the end of the war, but my father escaped and survived. No one in Germany knows more about bunkers than Leo Oberstadt. So I want to talk to him again tonight, review the design of the Führerbunker, and then I want him to tell me the best way to do it."

"Then you'll go ahead?"

"As soon as you get permission for us to work a second shift. Get me that, and I'll get you into Adolf Hitler's home, sweet home."

That night, in their bed, Emily and Foster tried to make love. Clearly, neither was in the mood for it, and after a few minutes they gave up, and Foster lay beside Emily holding her.

Over dinner they had celebrated Emily's phone calls to and from Professor Blaubach that had finally gained her permission to excavate into the night. They had also intended to celebrate once more their desire for each other. But the passion wasn't there.

Holding her tightly, Foster inquired, "What is it, Emily? What's bothering you?"

"Ernst Vogel," she said almost inaudibly. "His dead body lying there in the rocker. I can't seem to put him out of my mind. I can't help feeling responsible."

Foster caressed her cheek. "You're not responsible. I'm sorry it happened, and that you saw it. Maybe the best thing you can do is to get some sleep."

She yawned. "Yes, sleep. That would be good."

Emily worked the blanket over both of them, turned off the bedside lamp, and fell back on the pillow. In the dark she could make out Foster's profile, and she drew herself close to his body once more.

"Rex," she said drowsily, "tonight you weren't up for it either. Something's bothering you, too."

Sleepily, he summed up his visit to Major Elford in Spandau

Prison. Then he told her briefly of taking the missing bunker plan to Rudi Zeidler.

After that, dead end. Zeidler said there was no one on earth who could possibly identify the seventh bunker—except maybe one of Hitler's slave laborers who might have helped construct it. But presumably all the slave laborers were liquidated before Germany was conquered. If one did survive, Zeidler said, finding him would be like finding a needle in a haystack.

Emily, near slumber, had difficulty speaking. Her mouth was cottony. But she found her voice. "You're looking for someone who worked as a slave laborer?"

"I sure am."

"I've got one for you. Andrew Ober—Oberstadt's father. Slave laborer and still alive. Ask me in the morning. Ask me about Leo Ober—whatever in the morning. Good night, darling."

9

Once he had entered the Weinmeister Höhe district of West Berlin, Rex Foster had no trouble finding his way to his destination. Consulting the map of the city spread on the passenger seat of the rented Audi, he was able to follow the meticulous directions marked for him by the Kempinski concierge. A few turns, and he was on the residential street called Gotenweg where the elder Oberstadt lived.

Foster found the address and the house he sought in the middle of the block, and parked in front of it. It was, he could see, a small white stucco bungalow with a tile roof. It was enclosed by a weathered wooden fence, which protected the modest lawn and two pine trees overhanging the bungalow's porch. This was the residence of Leo Oberstadt, onetime Nazi slave laborer.

The dashboard clock of the Audi told Foster that he was ten minutes early for his appointment, and he sat back in the car to enjoy a pipeful of tobacco and to review the events of the morning.

He had been awakened this morning by the movement and softness of Emily's body against his. Feeling her lips on his cheek and then on his mouth, he had heard her whisper, "Rex, are you awake? I've missed you. I missed having you last night. It seems like a million years."

"It is a million years."

"I love you, Rex."

He had taken her in his arms, caressing her, smothering her with kisses, wanting to consume her. Gradually, her sighing had become a throaty moaning.

They had made love, tenderly, sweetly, slowly, until the fire caught them both and intensity grew, engulfing them, consuming them both.

It had been wonderful, like a long-desired homecoming, and he had known that it was a union he would cherish and remember forever.

When they had finished making love, he had not been surprised that his skin and hers were wet with the perspiration of pleasure. He had then led her from the bed into the bathroom. Turning on the shower, letting the water run warm, he had drawn her under the spray. They had studiously soaped each other's backs and when the froth of soap had been washed away by the water, they had stepped out onto the oval bathmat, and with care they had dried each other.

Leaving her to dress, Foster had gone into the bedroom to order from room service. Presently, they'd had breakfast together. Just as they finished, the phone had begun ringing. Emily had taken it, and the caller proved to be Andrew Oberstadt. Emily had reassured him that she had obtained permission for the nighttime excavation. Then, eyes on Foster, Emily had inquired once more about Oberstadt's father and his role as a foreman of slave laborers. After that had been confirmed, Emily had spoken of Rex's desire to meet with the elder Oberstadt. Fifteen minutes later, Andrew Oberstadt had called back, and Emily cheerfully announced to Foster, "You've got it, Rex, the appointment with Leo Oberstadt. Ten-thirty this morning."

Now the dashboard clock told Foster that it was ten-thirty and time to see Leo Oberstadt. Leaving the car, he unlatched the fence gate, went up the narrow walk to the door, and pressed the bell.

Seconds later a fat woman in a flowered caftan, with a kindly face, faint mustache, and two chins, filled the doorway. Foster identified himself and was immediately admitted.

He heard a querulous, raspy voice call out from an adjacent room, "Hilda, who is it?"

"Your American visitor, Herr Oberstadt," Hilda called back.

"Show him in, show him in!"

Hilda led Foster into an old-fashioned, musty living room. There were doilies everywhere and the television set was blaring. Not until he saw his host shake a cane, and order Hilda to shut off the television and to serve them each a cold beer, was Foster able to locate Leo Oberstadt. His host was propped up in the corner of a sofa, a metal walker beside him. Foster had been told to expect an invalid, and had imagined someone ravaged and withered. Actually, the elder Oberstadt was a large-framed man, probably once muscular, with immobile legs.

"You are the American architect Foster?" Leo Oberstadt's voice scratched out as if it were an accusation.

"I am, sir, and really pleased you could see me."

The elder Oberstadt tapped the other end of the sofa with his cane. "Sit down, young man, sit down." As Foster seated himself, his host went on. "You are a friend of the British lady my son works for?"

"I am."

"You know the foolishness she is engaged in? She wants to dig into the buried Führerbunker and find Adolf."

"Yes, I know, and it may not be foolishness, sir."

The old man took out a handkerchief, hawked into it, and ignored Foster's reply as he went on. "Last night my son brought me the original plan of the Führerbunker. I studied the plan and gave him my advice." His sardonic eyes fixed on Foster. "You are acquainted with the ratpack's last bunker?"

"I think so."

"Of course. You are the American architect wasting your time doing a picture book about the Third Reich buildings and bunkers. All right, let's see what you know." He lifted a rolled-up diagram beside him, pulled off the rubber band, and displayed the plan of the Führerbunker for Foster. "Show me what you would do to get down to Hitler's suite without taking forever."

Foster bent over to examine the plan, although by now he felt that he knew it by heart. After a few moments, he spoke up. "First, let's remember this bunker was built of reinforced concrete. It had to be to protect its occupants from artillery shells and bombs. Therefore, no matter what the Soviets did—bulldozed it, maybe even blew up parts of it—I suspect the lower level of the bunker is still largely intact. With this in mind, I think the easiest and fastest way to get into it would be to start digging on the side where the one upper emergency exit existed. This should lead to four flights of concrete steps that go down to the central corridor. I'd guess those steps are still there. If they are, it might require no more than a few days of digging and shoring up to get below to Hitler's rooms." He raised his head. "That's how I'd go about it, sir."

Leo Oberstadt's eyes held on Foster with a glint of approval. "You're a smart young fellow," he said. "Exactly what I advised my son last night, although he had the same idea. That's how he is going to go about the excavation. It should work, if anything will." He pulled back the Führerbunker plan and rolled it up. "All right, young man. Now we can talk. My son told me this morning you want to meet a former slave laborer."

"Yes, sir. I have a few questions I need answered."

"Maybe you've come to the right party," said Leo Oberstadt. "There are not many of us around. We're a small club. I am one of the few surviving veterans responsible for building most of Hitler's ratholes. You want to know how I became a slave laborer under the efficient Third Reich?"

In a relentless, rasping monotone, Leo Oberstadt recounted his story. Foster listened, fascinated at how Oberstadt's reliving of the past made it come alive in the present.

Leo Oberstadt's father had been part Jewish, part Lutheran, and his mother had been Jewish. He himself was in his twenties, a civil engineer and a partner in the family's modest construction business, when the Second World War broke out. Hitler's conquest of Europe was well underway when Leo's parents' religious origin was discovered. His mother, father, and he were arrested and thrown into a concentration camp. Within a month, his parents were sent off to the gas chambers in Auschwitz. "I never saw them again. I also was slated for extermination in Auschwitz, and had already been ordered into the death chamber, when a Nazi officer—an SS doctor—noticed my powerful shoulders, and chest, and biceps, and yanked me out of line. A directive had just come through from Albert Speer. Hitler wanted able-bodied young men from the *KZ Häftlinge—Konzentrationslagers Häftlinge*—concentration camp prisoners—Jews, Poles, Czechs, Ukrainians, gypsies—to serve as slave laborers who could construct a series of underground bunkers throughout Germany."

Leo Oberstadt toiled as a slave laborer on two subterranean bunkers outside Berlin—backbreaking, sweaty, inhuman work with hundreds of other prisoners—when it was learned that he was actually a civil engineer with experience in his father's business. After that he was elevated to serving as a construction foreman, forced to take orders from Nazi guards and give orders to his fellow prisoners.

When their last job was almost complete, perhaps two months before the war ended, all of Leo's fellow slave laborers were led away to be liquidated. Leo alone, as their foreman, was allowed to stay alive the final two months to supervise the construction of rooms, offices, technical facilities in this last bunker. All the actual labor was done by young and fanatical members of the Hitler Youth. At no time before this construction began, or during his two-month imprisonment in the partially completed bunker, did Leo have the faintest notion as to where in Germany it was located. He had been brought to the job in the beginning blindfolded, and each night he was led away from the bunker site blindfolded until that last two months.

Then one morning he was blindfolded again and thrown into the back of an army truck by SS troopers. He could hear heavy cannonading all about him. He was being driven off somewhere, and he sensed he was to be executed, but his eyes were covered and his wrists were bound and he was helpless.

After a slow roundabout drive—a drive that took what he guessed to be at least twenty minutes—Leo heard one of the guards shout, "Get rid of him here! Let's beat it before we're ambushed!"

Roughly lifted to his feet, Leo felt himself being shoved and pushed, until he was heaved off the truck to the pavement below. As he landed in the street, momentarily stunned, his blindfold fell off. He could see the German truck starting to wheel away as three of the SS troopers in the rear aimed their rifles at him.

Frantically, Leo flung himself on his face, trying to avoid execution. But as the shots rang out, and he fell, one bullet caught him low in the back. He flattened out, was about to lose consciousness, when he saw before him a Soviet company of Red Army soldiers and three tanks break out of a onetime wooded area—now rubble-strewn, filled with stumps—and begin firing over him at the fleeing German truck. He thought that he heard the truck blow up, and then he sank into darkness.

"I woke up in a Russian field hospital," Leo Oberstadt recalled painfully. "Surgery saved me, although I lost most of the use of my left leg. Eventually, when my background became known, I was released. I revived my father's old construction company. I married. I had a son. I worked hard. My business prospered during the rebuilding of Berlin. About five years ago, I lost the use of my other leg and had to retire." He fell silent, and picked up the stein of beer that had been served. He drank, licked his lips, and said, "Now, Mr. Foster, what can I do for you?"

"I'll tell you exactly," said Foster. He spoke of his architectural book once more, and of the seven missing pieces, all underground headquarters bunkers inside West Germany. He told of the six he had found through Zeidler, each of their locations identified, and of the seventh bunker he had recovered from Spandau Prison. "I've located six bunkers. It's the seventh one, the only one Zeidler did for Hitler that bears no site identification, that I must know about. It is the largest of the bunkers, by far, and Zeidler thought that a laborer who worked on it might recognize it by its dimensions."

"Let me see," said the elder Oberstadt.

Foster tugged the folded plan of the seventh bunker from his jacket pocket, opened it, and handed it across the sofa to his host.

Leo Oberstadt sipped his beer and examined the plan. "You are right," he rasped, "a big one, a very big one. And—very familiar."

"You recognize it?" Foster asked eagerly.

The elder Oberstadt nodded.

"What we have here is the last bunker I worked on before

they took me out to shoot me." He handed back the plan. "In fact, I'm certain this is the one."

"But where was it built?"

Leo Oberstadt looked at Foster with surprise. "Where was it built?" he repeated. "Why, I already told you. In Berlin, of course."

"How can you be sure? You were underground most of the time, and then you were blindfolded."

The old man shook his head slowly. "No, not all of the time, and not always blindfolded. I told you that they took me out of the bunker with my eyes covered to shoot me. They drove me what seemed to be twenty minutes away—it could have been only ten minutes away as the crow flies, but they had to go around the rubble—before they realized that they were about to be attacked by the Russians coming out of the devastated woods area. So they dumped me and tried to run and failed."

Foster seized on the last. "The Russians coming out of the woods area? What woods?"

"Why out of the Tiergarten, of course. Today, it once again is one of the loveliest sites we have in Berlin. A short walk from what was then Hitler's Chancellery—and the Führerbunker. Somewhere near there, I am sure, this seventh bunker was built."

It surprised Nicholas Kirvov that, although it was still morning, he was so weary. He sat lumpily at the metal outdoor terrace table of something called Delphi's Taverna, and nursed his cup of dark tea. He stared across the terrace into the thoroughfare named Kantstrasse, and thought what a high-flown name it was for a street that was so low-down and second-rate. From the Esso gasoline station at the corner to the sex shop without windows but with provocative posters mounted beside it there were only cheap, nondescript stores. He could not imagine what kind of art gallery would be located in this block, but his list promised him there was one, the Tisher Gallery, probably no more than another half block away, and he had vowed to overlook no art gallery in central Berlin.

What had made him stop for this brief respite was not weariness but discouragement. Despite his heavy frame, he had always been proud of his strong legs and his ability to bound up endless steep staircases. At home, he had always been propelled by enthusiasm. Here, in Berlin, he had become cramped in the legs and footsore because of frustration.

He had been on his feet, and hiking about, for hours yesterday and since early this morning, trying to cover every art gallery in the Kurfürstendamm area. After all, that ship's steward, Giorgio Ricci, if sure of nothing else, had insisted that he had purchased his Hitler oil not far from the Ku'damm. So Kirvov's goal had to be somewhere in this section. Yet each of the galleries he had already visited had rejected his Hitler painting without interest as a work they did not recognize and had never handled.

Kirvov realized that the sun was finally peeking out from between gray clouds, and automatically he shifted his chair from under the partial shade of a tree to catch some warmth. Momentarily, he wondered if he should not quit his tiresome search and return to Leningrad, and then go on to join his wife and son on their vacation in Sochi. After all, he told himself, he had already managed to identify the subject of the Hitler painting. It was certainly Göring's Air Ministry building. Identification enough to satisfy any viewer of his Hitler exhibit. Still, he had gone on, and knew that he would continue to go on, for another reason. Presumably Hitler had died in 1945. Yet his painting of the Göring Air Ministry had been painted in 1952 or later. In some respects, Kirvov had a literal mind. It did not entertain artistic discrepancies. Until this anachronism was explained, Kirvov knew that he would not leave Berlin.

The sun had warmed and somehow revived him. He quickly downed the last of his tea, paid up, and descended into Kantstrasse.

In five minutes, Kirvov saw the sign beside the door of the large modern shop on the ground floor of the six-story office building. It read:

GALERIE TISHER BERLIN
ANKAUF-VERKAUF

Kirvov moved over to the display window. There were three large paintings, naturalistic, of Berlin scenes.

Promising, Kirvov thought, and he walked back to the main entrance and went inside. The beige carpeting and blond paneled walls gave the room a lightness that only slightly offset the gloomy darkness of most of the hanging oils all around. There was a small desk, and a bespectacled young man at work behind it. A curving stairway led up to a small mezzanine which also displayed framed paintings for sale.

Kirvov proceeded under the crystal chandelier to the young man writing at the desk. Aware that a customer was approaching, the young man came hastily to his feet, brushing his straw-colored hair away from his glasses.

"Mr. Tisher?" Kirvov inquired.

"Yes, I am Tisher. If I can be of help . . ." His eyes fell on the painting, wrapped in felt, that Kirvov was carrying under his arm. "You perhaps have something to sell? We are always—"

"Something to inquire about," said Kirvov. He laid his package on the desk, uncovered it, and held up the painting. "I hoped you might recognize this."

Tisher took up the painting and squinted at it, wrinkling his nose. "A Berlin scene, I would presume. Probably from the Third Reich period. Not very good." He looked up. "Yes, we get—and get rid of—some of these from time to time."

"I was hoping this was one of those you got rid of. A gallery around here, possibly your own, sold it to someone I know. I acquired it. I'd like to know more about the provenance of the painting. I'd like to know if you handled the sale."

"Offhand, I don't recognize this one. However, I'm not the person to consult. Our manager, who also makes most of our minor acquisitions, may be able to tell you with more certainty." Tisher put down the painting, cupped a hand to his mouth, and called up to the mezzanine. "Fräulein Dagmar! Can you please come down for a moment?"

Nervously, Kirvov waited, watching the staircase. Soon a pair of legs materialized, and then a long formidable-appearing lady, possibly in her thirties, with severe features, horn-rimmed spectacles, black hair cut short.

Tisher turned toward her. "This gentleman has a question. Perhaps you can help him." He peered past Kirvov toward two customers, a youngish couple, who had just entered. "If you will excuse me," he said to Kirvov, and was off to attend to business.

"Yes?" Fräulein Dagmar was saying to Kirvov.

"I'm here about this," said Kirvov, taking up his painting and handing it to her. "Do you recognize this work?"

She merely glanced at the oil and looked at Kirvov. "Of course," she said. "I had this piece in the gallery for almost a year before I sold it. It is one of those Nazi pieces a few nostalgic collectors like, something very much in the style of Hitler's own art, although I could not definitely authenticate it. To me, a piece of junk I kept around in storage for a collector, and when none came, I finally had a whim to exhibit it. Two or three weeks later there was a buyer, a foreigner, an Italian as I recall. He knew little about art, but he was intrigued that it might have been done by Hitler himself. He bought it."

Kirvov felt a sense of excitement. "I know who bought it," he said. "What I want to know is who sold it. I mean, sold it to you." He pressed harder. "You must have a receipt of purchase."

Fräulein Dagmar stiffened. "I do. But I am afraid I can't reveal this to anyone. Our transactions with clients who dispose of their art must necessarily remain privileged information. I am sorry, but I simply cannot tell just anyone who comes in off the street."

In desperation, Kirvov sought his wallet. He fumbled inside it, and drew out his card, passing it to the lady, "I am not just anyone off the street, Fräulein, as you will see."

She looked down at the business card with disinterest, and then her head jerked up, her eyes widening behind their thick lenses. "You—you are Mr. Kirvov, curator of the Hermitage museum in Leningrad?"

"I am."

Fräulein Dagmar was immediately respectful, even awed. "Forgive me, I apologize. This is an honor. What can I do for you?"

"Simply tell me how you got the painting, who sold it to you. In the Hermitage we have a large collection of early paintings and drawings by Hitler. They are historic curiosities. When I acquired this one I determined to show it as part of an exhibit that will be widely attended. As curator, I feel it is my duty to establish the provenance of this work. I hope you will help me."

"I certainly shall try!" said Fräulein Dagmar enthusiastically. "You deserve our cooperation. Let me find my copy of the purchase slip."

She hurried off on her long legs, disappearing behind an office door. Smiling for the first time this day, Kirvov slowly and lovingly wrapped his treasure in its felt cover once more.

He had hardly finished when Fräulein Dagmar was striding toward him again, carrying a slip of paper. "The person who sold it to us was a German woman in her early thirties, my guess. Her name is Mrs. Klara Fiebig. I remember that she told me she had got the painting as a gift from a friend or relative. She did not like it, but kept it out of sentiment. Her husband did not like it either, because it was a Nazi work. Finally, he insisted that she get rid of it. So she came to us here at Tisher. I did not see much of a market for it, but I checked in the office and realized that it just might be a Hitler or an excellent imitation of a Hitler, so I decided to buy it as an unusual minor item." She handed Kirvov the slip of paper. "This is the address Mrs. Fiebig gave me on Knesebeck-strasse. It is off the Ku'damm, an apartment district, a short taxi ride from here but not too far to walk either."

"I thank you very much."

"I bought it for a pittance." Then she added regretfully, "I wish I had sold it for more. I did not know it was quite so valuable."

"It is not, as art. Only as history."

Kirvov walked swiftly out of the gallery, his legs springy and once more strong.

Waiting patiently outside the door to the Fiebigs' third-story apartment after ringing the doorbell, Kirvov realized that his tension was mounting. He held the covered painting more possessively under his arm, and continued to debate within himself what excuse he might use to gain admittance for this interview.

Not until he heard footsteps behind the door did the excuse come to him.

The door was opening, and Kirvov girded himself.

In the doorway stood a rather tall young brunette, dark eyes, tilted nose, wearing a light pink maternity gown. Since she was slender, showing no sign of pregnancy, Kirvov guessed the gown was a premature celebration. She appeared to be in her thirties. She was gazing at Kirvov with curiosity.

"Mrs. Klara Fiebig?" Kirvov inquired.

"Yes," she replied tentatively.

"My name is Nicholas Kirvov. I've been given your name. I wanted to have a brief word with you."

"About what?"

"About a work of art," said Kirvov.

Klara's expression was puzzled. "Art? I know nothing about art. I don't understand."

This was it, Kirvov knew, and he must not give her time to think. "Let me explain," he said, digging into his inside jacket pocket for his wallet. He pulled out his embossed calling card, put his wallet back, and handed her the card. He spoke quickly. "I'm the head of the Hermitage art museum in Leningrad. It is quite well known—"

"Of course, I've heard of it," she said, still concentrating on the card.

"I've come to Berlin to interview some collectors about German art."

"But I'm not a collector," Klara said.

"I am aware of that. I merely want your opinion, your thoughts, on something I hope to write about and exhibit. Please, may I have a word with you? It won't take up much of your time."

He took a decisive step, putting a foot across her threshold, as if expecting to be invited inside.

Klara Fiebig seem flustered. "I don't know. I'm not—"

"Thank you for your kindness," said Kirvov. He was inside her entry hall. "I won't be a minute."

"Well, all right, but I'm sure you are wasting your time." Her good manners got the best of her. "You may sit down. But I'm really very busy today."

"A minute, no more," said Kirvov. He was already in the parlor, automatically noting the tasteful prints on the wall. He glanced at a wheelchair in the corner, then sat down in one of the armchairs that flanked the coffee table.

He began to unwrap his Hitler painting, as Klara Fiebig

lowered herself onto the sofa near him. He was aware that she was watching him guardedly.

He had the painting out, and held it up for her to see. "I am told that you once owned this painting," he said. "I am told that you sold it to the Tisher Gallery."

She eyed the oil briefly, but showed no reaction or recognition. "This painting," she said. "What is so important about it that you must know?"

"It is a rarity of the Third Reich," said Kirvov, "and as such is of interest to me as a museum curator and a collector of German art. I want to authenticate it." He stared at her. "I must learn where you got it."

Klara squinted, studying the oil closely. At last, she shook her head. "No," she said, "I never saw this one before. I did once own an old painting of a Berlin street scene that my husband considered ugly. So finally—I do not remember when—I disposed of the piece."

Kirvov tried to determine her sincerity. Her expression gave no evidence of familiarity. Kirvov repressed his disappointment. "Mrs. Fiebig, the lady at the Tisher Gallery, a Fräulein Dagmar, when I showed her this painting, she remembered it and remembered having bought it from you. It was she who gave me your name and address. Does that jog your memory?"

But Klara was adamant in her denial. "Your lady at Tisher is confused completely. She is mistaken. I never saw this before."

Kirvov searched for a crack in her composure, but there was none. He suspected that she had seen the painting before, and even had owned it, yet there was no way to prove it. Slowly, he began to wrap the painting once more. "Very well," he said. "It must be a mistake."

"It certainly is," said Klara, standing. "I am sorry you wasted your time."

Kirvov was on his feet, and she showed him the door.

"I appreciate your help," he said. "Too bad I couldn't learn more about the oil. It would have been useful."

As she opened the door for him, she could not resist one last question. "This oil of yours, what is so interesting about it?"

Stepping into the corridor, Kirvov replied offhandedly, "Oh, simply that Adolf Hitler painted this work in 1952 or after."

"How ridiculous," Klara snapped. "Everyone knows that Hitler died in 1945."

"Exactly," said Kirvov. "That's what makes this painting so interesting. Good day."

Throughout the rest of the afternoon Klara remained shaken, as she awaited the arrival of her aunt Evelyn Hoffmann.

The moment she had observed that the menacing stranger, the Russian curator, had left the apartment building, she had rushed to the bedroom to awaken her mother, who was napping.

Once her mother was fully aroused, and sitting up, Klara was apologetic. "Mama, I hate to bother you like this, but I had to. There is something I must tell you."

"What is it, Klara? You look frightened."

"I am frightened, Mama. Remember the painting of the government building that Aunt Evelyn gave Franz and me on our first wedding anniversary? The one Franz hated so much, until I had to get rid of it?"

"Yes, of course."

"Well, a man was just here, an art expert, who said the painting was done by Adolf Hitler."

"Ridiculous!"

"That's what I told him. And even crazier, he insisted that Hitler painted it seven years after the war—"

"This crazy man, who was he?"

"I'll tell you . . ."

She rapidly recounted everything of Nicholas Kirvov's visit.

When she concluded, Klara added helplessly, "Mama, I don't know what this is all about. But this Kirvov is going to write about it. I'm afraid Aunt Evelyn will find out that I sold her present. I —I'd better see her and explain before she hears of it. I'll call her right up."

"Klara, you know Aunt Evelyn doesn't have a telephone. But I know how to get hold of her. Just leave it to me."

"I want to see her today."

"If it can be done. Now help me out of bed. Then leave me alone in here. I'll take care of everything."

That had been two hours ago.

Klara knew from her mother that Aunt Evelyn had been informed and would be over soon. She waited expectantly in the parlor for her aunt, eager to see her, but dreading the confession she would have to make about selling the picture.

Ten minutes more passed, as Klara's nervousness increased, and then there was the doorbell and there was her Aunt Evelyn, attractive and composed, and now seated across from her.

"I'm sorry I had to drag you out like this, Auntie."

"No matter, no problem at all. My only concern was that something might be wrong with you. Are you all right? Your pregnancy?"

"I'm fine, Auntie," Klara said. "But there is something wrong, and I thought I had better tell you about it as soon as possible. I—I have a confession to make, and I only hope it won't upset you."

"Klara, dear, nothing you say can upset me," said Evelyn. "I love you dearly. Tell me what you have to confess."

Klara swallowed. "Auntie, it's about the painting."

"Painting?"

"The one you gave to me and Franz on our first wedding anniversary. The one of the Berlin government building that was in your husband's collection of German art. You remember?"

Evelyn nodded. "Yes, now I remember."

"Well—" Klara gulped, then blurted, "Auntie, a year ago I sold it—sold it to a gallery."

Evelyn seemed bewildered. "Sold it?"

"I had to," Klara pleaded, and rushed on. "I'll be honest with you. Franz never liked it, but because it was a generous gift from you I kept it. Then, one evening, maybe a year ago, Franz had some of his friends, his fellow teachers, over here for a card game. He showed one of his friends, the art instructor at his school, the painting. This friend asked Franz what he was doing with such a terrible painting around. Franz asked what he meant. His friend said the painting was clearly a picture of one of the Nazi government buildings, and obviously had been done by a Nazi artist who painted in the style that Hitler favored, even possibly painted by Hitler himself. At any rate, Franz's friend was positive it was a work of Nazi art." Klara swallowed. "Well, you know how Franz feels about the Nazis. Anyway, when his friends went home, Franz came to me and asked me to get rid of the piece. I told him I couldn't, that it was a gift from you. 'Nevertheless, get it out of here,' he insisted. 'Your Aunt Evelyn will never know. Just get it out of here.' So, much as I didn't want to, I—I went to some gallery in the neighborhood and sold it to them, and just forgot about it." She swallowed guiltily. "I hope you'll forgive me, Aunt Evelyn."

Evelyn Hoffmann remained composed. "Is that what you wanted to see me about, Klara? I completely understand. After all, your first duty is to get along with your husband. I'm sorry he was displeased by the painting, and you had to sell it, but if that's all there is to it—"

"That's not all, Auntie," Klara interrupted. "There is something else that happened."

For the first time, Evelyn Hoffmann's face betrayed an indication of concern. "Something else?"

"Early this afternoon," Klara hurried on. "A man came by

here, an art curator from Leningrad, a man named Nicholas Kirvov, and he had the painting with him. The painting you gave us. Apparently he had seen it at the Tisher Gallery and acquired it from them. He wants to show the painting in an exhibition of German art he is mounting at the Hermitage in Leningrad. He wanted to know more about the painting, for his catalogue or maybe an art book, I'm not sure."

"What did you tell him?" Evelyn asked slowly.

"Not a thing. I told him I'd never owned the painting nor even seen it before. I didn't want to get involved in this."

Evelyn showed her approval. "You behaved correctly, Klara. There's nothing to worry your head about. If all that is worrying you is that I might learn you sold it, and be upset—well, don't give it another thought—"

"There's something else, Auntie. Something really strange and spooky."

"What's that?"

"When Mr. Kirvov was leaving, I asked him what was so interesting about his painting. He said that the painting was done by Adolf Hitler, and it was done in 1952. I told him that was absurd, that Hitler couldn't have done it because he died in 1945. Mr. Kirvov said yes, that was what made the painting interesting."

Evelyn Hoffmann straightened herself. "That *is* absurd. Mr. Kirvov must be a lunatic."

"That's what I thought, Auntie. It couldn't have been painted by Hitler, could it? I mean, where would you have got such a thing?"

"It was not painted by Hitler," said Evelyn Hoffmann firmly. "That would have been impossible. My husband, your uncle, would not have permitted anything by a Nazi to be in his collection. Your uncle was an old-fashioned Social Democrat. This man who visited you, he was talking utter nonsense. I can't imagine his motive. Anyway, we know this city is filled with crackpots and provocateurs. You can forget the whole thing, dear Klara. As for selling off the painting, I do understand, and you can put your mind at ease." She rose, leaned over, and pecked a kiss at Klara. "I will always love you, dearly. Now I must hurry off to an appointment."

Evelyn found Wolfgang Schmidt at their isolated restaurant table, so absorbed in his lunch that he did not see her at first. She noticed that he was busy slicing and swallowing a grilled *Leberwurst,* and chomping on a piece of Westphalian pumpernickel, which he was washing down with a strong beer.

She smiled at his appetite and was about to sit down when he became aware of her presence, came ponderously to his feet, still chewing, and made a motion of kissing the back of her hand. "How good to see you, Evelyn," he said as they both sat down. He gestured at his plate. "Forgive my not waiting. I was too busy to eat earlier, and my stomach was rumbling."

"And I am late," she said.

"Will you join me? The sausage is excellent."

"Not today, Wolfgang. I have no stomach for food. I think I'll have a glass of white wine . . ." She saw a waitress approaching and called out, "A glass of Kallstadter Sammagen, please." She turned back to him. "I was hoping that you could see me."

"Your message was enough, Evelyn. Liesl said it was urgent. Is that so?"

"I'm afraid it is. At first I had no idea how important, but a message from Klara is unusual, so I lost no time seeing her." Evelyn nodded gravely. "Yes, Wolfgang, it is important."

He wiped his mouth with his napkin and eyed her. "You will tell me about it?"

"It concerned the painting I once gave Klara."

Schmidt was momentarily confused. "Painting?"

"It was long ago, so you may have forgotten." She tried to explain the painting. "Many years before, in a time when the *Feldherr* was bored and restless, I had an idea to keep him occupied. I took a hasty photograph one late day of the Reichsluftfahrtministerium—Göring's old place—and gave it to the *Feldherr* so he could busy himself rendering it as a small painting."

"Of course I remember. Then you gave this painting to Klara as an anniversary present."

Evelyn waited for her wine to be served, and for a while stared at it gloomily. "It was a mistake, that gift. I should never have done it."

"Why not?"

"Because Klara sold it. Of course, she had no idea of its value. Her husband did not like it, so she sold it to a local gallery. A Russian obtained it—a Russian who is the curator of the Hermitage in Leningrad—"

"Nicholas Kirvov," Schmidt said promptly. "One of Miss Ashcroft's new friends."

"I was afraid of that. Yes, Kirvov. He recognized that it had been painted by the *Feldherr*. Kirvov is an expert in such matters. He wanted to know more about it, and traced it to Klara. He called on her."

"But she could tell him nothing," said Schmidt. "She knows nothing."

Evelyn took a sip of her wine. "That is not the point, Wolfgang. Of course she could tell him nothing. But he was able to tell her something."

"Tell her what?"

"Before leaving, Kirvov told her that the painting was interesting because it had been done in 1952 or after, although the artist was supposed to have died in 1945."

"How could he have known that?"

"I have no idea, Wolfgang. I really don't know what put Kirvov onto this." She took another sip of wine. "I only know that now Kirvov is suspicious that the events of 1945 may not be as they have been reported."

Schmidt grunted, and automatically cleaned his plate as he tried to think. "You believe it is serious?"

"Very serious."

"Possibly."

Evelyn sighed. "We must be wary, Wolfgang." She shook her head. "I am sorry I let that painting out of my hands. It could be damning."

"You need not worry," Schmidt assured her. "I can take care of the painting. It will soon not exist as evidence."

"You are sure?"

"I promise you. Meanwhile, I must give this whole matter more thought, try to anticipate Kirvov's next step, try to think of precautions." He reached out for Evelyn's hand. "Do not worry, Effie. Meet me here again tomorrow. I will have a defense. Our intelligence is excellent. We will be ready for any threatening act. We will move faster." He began to rise. "Tomorrow, Effie. Right here."

"I will be here, Wolfgang, you can be sure."

The handsome old woman had walked the distance on foot, vigorously for her age, and Nicholas Kirvov in his rented Opel had followed her slowly until he had seen her turn off the Ku'damm and disappear inside a restaurant that bore the name Mampes Gute Stube.

Fortunately, Kirvov was able to find a parking place less than a block away. Hurriedly, he left the car and strode back to the restaurant. Approaching, he could see that the Mampes Gute Stube was a combination enclosed sidewalk café and restaurant.

The café area was glassed in and had a sloping roof. Since Kirvov thought that he had seen her go through the café into the restaurant beyond, he felt it safe to enter the café area.

Inside, he found the café quite elegant, round tables set on green carpeting with chairs upholstered in green velveteen. He looked around and saw one unoccupied table, near the central aisle. Going toward it, he noted through the door of the restaurant that a bar and dining room were visible. The older woman was not visible.

Seated, Kirvov accepted the menu from a waiter. He was not hungry, but he knew that he had to order something. Glancing at the list of desserts, he settled on sour cherries and cream, and placed his order.

Smoking, he reflected on what had taken place earlier in the afternoon. The meeting with Klara Fiebig had been fruitless. Yet, leaving her apartment, he had been suspicious. He wondered whether she had been lying. There was no way to find out unless, in a panic about his visit, she left the apartment to meet someone else. He had decided to sit and wait in his Opel, parked on Knesebeckstrasse, and keep an eye on Klara's building.

After two hours or more, his vigil had seemed useless. Three people had entered the apartment building—an elderly man carrying a shopping bag, a good-looking older woman, a boy with some schoolbooks in hand. No one had emerged from the building. Obviously, Klara Fiebig had found no reason to panic and leave. Finally, Kirvov had made up his mind that his suspicions about her had been senseless. He had reached a blind alley.

About to start his car and drive away, he had paused when he had seen the entrance door of the apartment building open and two women emerge. One was Klara Fiebig holding the arm of the handsome older woman he had seen enter the building earlier. Klara spoke to the older woman, and the older woman nodded, and then they kissed. Klara had gone back inside the building, and the older woman proceeded down the street. In his rearview mirror, Kirvov considered the receding figure of the older woman. She had come here to visit Klara. Perhaps she had been summoned by Klara. A tenuous lead, but still a lead.

Kirvov had made a U-turn and, at a distance, had followed her to the Kurfürstendamm, and then crept along, honked at by other drivers for his slowness, until he had seen her go inside the restaurant.

Now, spooning his cherries and fresh cream, he was waiting for her to emerge from inside. To what end he did not know, but still he had nowhere else to go. So he ate and he waited, and finally he smoked.

At least forty more minutes had passed, and Kirvov had just paid his bill, when his patience was rewarded. There she was, the handsome older woman, starting down the café aisle, followed by a big erect grizzly bear of a man, a healthy specimen for one in his sixties or seventies. Watching them come near, then pass him, Kirvov saw someone in a purple dress, a middle-aged female, rise from another table and reach out to get the big man's attention.

"Wolfgang," the female greeted him. "How are you?"

The big man named Wolfgang stopped and shook her hand. "Ursula. It's been a long time." The handsome older woman, who had preceded him, halted and turned, distracted. For an instant the big man hesitated, and then he introduced the two women. "My dear, this is Ursula Schleiter. Ursula, please meet Evelyn Hoffmann." A waiter intervened, noisily setting down some plates, and Kirvov lost the rest of the conversation.

Then he saw the big man named Wolfgang leading Evelyn Hoffmann out of the café. On the sidewalk of the Ku'damm, they exchanged a few words and parted, going in different directions.

Quickly Kirvov rose and decided to follow Evelyn Hoffmann once more. Probably an exercise in futility. Still, she was the one tie to Klara Fiebig.

On the Ku'damm, well behind her, he did not have far to go. Evelyn Hoffmann's immediate destination was the corner bus stop across the street. She queued up with the others waiting for a bus, and in a few minutes a yellow double-decker bus, with the number 29 above its windshield, rolled to a halt. Kirvov watched until he saw the Hoffmann woman step into the bus, and then he whirled around and hastily made for his parked car.

Driving on the Ku'damm once more, Kirvov kept the bus in view all the way along the busy boulevard to Breitscheidplatz, watching to observe whether Evelyn Hoffmann left the bus, and saw that she didn't. Falling directly behind the bus, he slowed his car at every stop to confirm that Evelyn Hoffmann was still aboard, and remained satisfied that she was.

Staying close to the bus, he marked a whole series of new signs blur past—Tauentzienstrasse, Kleiststrasse, Lützowplatz, Landwehrkanal. Going through this unfamiliar territory, he noted they were fifteen minutes away from their start, and there was no doubt that she was still on the bus.

Since the bus was slowing down, Kirvov put his foot lightly on his own brakes and also slowed. The bus came to a halt on Schöneberger Strasse, and Kirvov came to a halt behind it. Automatically, he bent to see if anyone was leaving the bus. Two people were exiting. One of them was Evelyn Hoffmann.

As the bus pulled away, Kirvov watched Evelyn Hoffmann walk to a curb, glance to her left, then cross a broad street, and with familiarity cross another. She stood momentarily before a modest café one shop from the corner, and then she opened the front door and went inside. Kirvov, who had been idling his car on Schöneberger Strasse, cruised toward the café. He turned left at the corner and drove past it slowly. The name above read CAFÉ WOLF. It was near the corner of Stresemann Strasse and Anhalter Strasse.

Kirvov sought a place to park on Stresemann Strasse, and

observed several empty spaces. He slipped into one, parking diagonally against the curbing, shut off his motor, and left the car.

Momentarily, standing on the sidewalk under a tree, Kirvov tried to get his bearings. The north end of Stresemann Strasse was blocked by a wall, obviously the Berlin Wall that enclosed the Frontier Zone. Kirvov started to stroll toward the end of the street, constantly glancing over his shoulder to see whether Evelyn Hoffmann had departed from her café yet.

At the Hervis Hotel, Kirvov crossed over to the opposite side of the street near an empty lot, actually a deep depression where the basement of a building had once stood, a building that had long ago been destroyed in the war. The lot was now weed-covered and unkempt. Kirvov began to walk back to the café Evelyn Hoffmann had entered.

There was a series of what seemed to be small shops. There was the Modellbau, a store that sold model kits of autos and airplanes, then Küchler, an auto-radio specialist, then the Gesamtdeutsches Institut, a historical archive that resembled a library inside, then Pizzera Selva, a neighborhood pizza parlor, next a hairdresser, then Café Wolf, with a tobacco shop and used bookstore on the corner.

There were windows on either side of the café's front entrance, and two rows of planter boxes before the windows. Kirvov glanced inside, could make out a bar and bar stools, some circular tables, a jukebox. He could see a waitress in a sweatshirt and blue jeans serving a couple at one table. He could see another couple toward the back. He did not see Evelyn Hoffmann.

Even though she could not know who he was, Kirvov determined not to continue searching inside and risk becoming obvious. Nor did he wish to linger in front of the café. Directly across the street there was the concrete island with the bus stop, Askanischer Platz. To the right of the island was a street called Bernberger Strasse.

Leaving the café, Kirvov recrossed the street and stationed himself on Askanischer Platz, keeping an eye on the Café Wolf as he waited for Evelyn Hoffmann to emerge for her ultimate destination. Once on the island, Kirvov felt too conspicuous, and strode to the corner of Bernberger Strasse. There he smoked and casually watched for any movement out of the Café Wolf.

For a half hour or more there was no activity. The day was beginning to wane, and soon it would be nightfall. Kirvov continued to keep the café entrance under surveillance. At last one of the couples he had observed inside left. Soon after, another couple left.

Kirvov waited restlessly for the appearance of Evelyn Hoffmann.

A young man left the Café Wolf. Possibly the bartender. Maybe not. Then the waitress, a sweater over her sweatshirt, still in her jeans, stepped outside to water the plants, then went back inside. Soon she emerged and departed.

But no Evelyn Hoffmann.

Kirvov began to feel foolish. There was not a shred of evidence that the Hoffmann woman would lead him to anything useful, except that she had apparently had some connection with Klara Fiebig, who had not recognized the Hitler painting anyway.

It was early evening now, and Kirvov became alert when he saw the lights inside the café go out.

Definitely the Café Wolf was closed. Yet Evelyn Hoffmann, whom he had seen go into it, had never come out of it.

Surprising and inexplicable.

Kirvov tried to explain this unusual happening to himself. Perhaps Evelyn Hoffmann had left by another door in the rear. Perhaps she owned the café or was married to the proprietor and lived upstairs.

All likely, yet somehow unlikely. That was Kirvov's gut feeling. She would have had no reason to leave by some unobserved door. Somehow, from her dress, her manner, she was too well-off and sophisticated to own a café like this or dwell on its premises.

But still she had gone in and not come out.

That was a mystery that deserved explanation.

Tired of standing alone in the darkness with nothing to see, Kirvov started back to his car. One more sidelong glance at the café. Absolutely closed, shut down, darkened. And Evelyn Hoffmann inexplicably inside.

Kirvov had to report this to someone, and puzzle it out. Emily Ashcroft and Rex Foster, who were as involved as he was, for their own reasons, were the obvious choices to consult. Kirvov knew that he must go to the Bristol Kempinski at once and find them.

"There is something I must talk over with you," Kirvov said.

He had intercepted Emily Ashcroft, Foster, and Tovah as they were leaving the Kempinski.

"Then join us right now," Emily had replied. "It's an early dinner tonight. I have to get out to the Führerbunker again in the morning. Oberstadt has a night shift coming in tonight and I want to see how well they did."

Tired as he was, Kirvov had gone along, and now he sat with the others at a table that gave them privacy because it was set off by wood dividers from tables occupied by other dinner guests. They were in the second-floor restaurant of the Café Kranzler on the corner of the Kurfürstendamm and Joachimstaler Strasse.

A waitress had appeared, and they all consulted their menus and ordered hurriedly.

Once the waitress went off, Foster turned to Kirvov. "Nicholas, what's on your mind?"

"Well . . ." Kirvov was briefly reticent. "This may not be serious or useful to any of you. It is just a strange incident that I felt you should hear about."

They were attentive as Kirvov began to recount his multiple adventures during the day. There had been his pursuit of the art galleries, and his coming across the one that had acquired and sold the Hitler painting. There had been his call on Klara Fiebig, and her insistence that she had never seen the painting.

"Do you think she was lying?" Emily asked.

"I think so," said Kirvov. "At least I thought so when I left her, because I hung around outside to see whether she might leave to contact someone to report I had called on her."

"Did she leave?" Emily inquired.

"No. But someone called on *her*, because later she saw that person out."

Kirvov described that person, a rather stately, well-groomed woman in her sixties or seventies named Evelyn Hoffmann. Anyway, she had some connection with Klara Fiebig. So Kirvov had followed her to Mampes Gute Stube, a restaurant on the Ku'-damm. After an interval she had emerged with a big man called Wolfgang. The pair had separated, and the Hoffmann lady had taken a bus to an area near the Wall, with Kirvov shadowing her. She had gone into a place called Café Wolf on Stresemann Strasse.

"I hung around for hours, waiting for her to leave to see where she went next," concluded Kirvov. "But she never left. The place closed down and she never came out. That's the mystery."

"Could she have a room there?" Tovah asked.

"I doubt if she would live in a place like that," said Kirvov. "She's too grand for it."

"Have you any explanation?" Emily asked.

"None. I hoped one of you might have one."

Emily gave a helpless shrug. "I certainly don't. The whole thing is like Alice going down the rabbit hole."

Foster addressed himself to Kirvov. "You said this Café Wolf is somewhere in the area of the Wall?"

"Stresemann Strasse. It runs right into the Wall about a block away."

"With the mound of the Führerbunker just on the other side," said Foster.

"Maybe it's all my own foolishness. Do you think Evelyn Hoffmann is worth pursuing further?"

"It may be a waste of time," Foster said. "Time is what we don't have much of. Let's sleep on it."

Emily nodded her agreement.

Emily and Foster were in their suite after dinner, and both were readying for bed, when the telephone rang.

Emily picked up the receiver. The caller was Kirvov and he sounded agitated.

"I'm very upset," he was saying. "I'm back in my room at the Palace. I had to call you."

"What's wrong, Nicholas?" Emily wanted to know.

"My Hitler painting. It's missing. I'm afraid it's been stolen."

"What do you mean?" said Emily. "Where was the painting?"

"I left it in the trunk of my car when I joined you at the Kempinski. I had a rented Opel, and I put the painting inside the trunk. I locked the trunk and I also locked the car doors."

"Where did you park the car?" Emily asked.

"There was a place, so I parked in the street. When we were through with dinner and I left you, I went to my car. The doors were still locked. After I drove back to the Palace, I opened the trunk to take out the painting, to take it up to my room, but it was gone. Someone had stolen it."

"But who else would know about the painting besides ourselves, the art dealer, and the young lady you saw, Klara Fiebig?" Emily said. "That's all, isn't it?"

"Nobody else, I believe—"

"Somebody else," Emily interrupted. "I left out one name. Evelyn Hoffmann. She could have known."

"Yes," Kirvov admitted. "She could have."

"You were wondering earlier about pursuing Evelyn Hoffmann," said Emily. "We thought it might be a waste of time. I've changed my mind. I think she's well worth looking into." She was lost in thought a few seconds. "Nicholas, in the light of this new development—well, you've come this far. Now go all the way. Why don't you station yourself near the Café Wolf early in the morning and see if the Hoffmann lady materializes again?" She hesitated a moment more, then added, "In fact, Nicholas, since Rex has permission to join in on my dig . . ." She addressed herself to Foster. "Rex, can you replace me at the Führerbunker tomorrow?"

"Glad to," said Foster. "But where are you going to be?"

"I'm going to keep Nicholas company on Stresemann Strasse. I want to have a look at this Evelyn Hoffmann. Presuming she reappears. I think she will. Then we may finally be on to something."

10

The day started at Stresemann Strasse with three of them, and it ended there with only one of them.

It started at nine o'clock on a sunny morning, after they had learned that the Café Wolf opened for business then. They had arrived just before that, Nicholas Kirvov at the wheel of the rented Opel, Emily beside him, and Tovah in the rear seat. They parked on Stresemann Strasse, less than a half block from the Café Wolf, on the opposite side of the street.

Momentarily, they were alerted by the arrival of two persons at the café door. Kirvov immediately recognized them as the young waitress and the bartender. The waitress unlocked the front door to let them in. Kirvov shook his head. "Employees," he said.

For a brief time, Emily continued to watch the café entrance. "You're the only one who has seen Evelyn Hoffmann," she reminded Kirvov. "Neither Tovah nor I have any idea of what she really looks like. So we're depending on you, Nicholas."

"Trust me," Kirvov said. "I will be on the alert. This is an important matter to me, too."

After turning on the car radio, at low volume, to a music station to divert Emily and Tovah, Kirvov devoted his entire attention to gazing through the car window at the entrance of the Café Wolf.

An hour and a half passed, and Kirvov saw no one resembling their quarry leaving the Café Wolf, although four patrons were seen to enter. At the two-hour mark, all four customers had departed separately and been accounted for.

Emily began fretting about how Rex Foster was doing at the excavation site, where the digging into the mound was to have begun, yet she refused to leave to join Foster.

"I want to *see* this Evelyn Hoffmann," Emily stated with determination.

Restlessly she picked through her purse, intending to apply fresh lipstick. Suddenly, Kirvov spoke up. "You want to see Evelyn Hoffmann? You can see her now. Look."

Emily bolted upright, and leaned against Kirvov to stare out the window. In the rear, Tovah was also staring out her window.

They could all make out the impressive brown-haired woman, perhaps five feet six, slender, posture erect, moving with a healthy stride, neatly attired in a powder-blue suit, crossing the street to the concrete island that was Askanischer Platz.

"Evelyn Hoffmann," Kirvov whispered. "I guess she's going to the bus stop on Schöneberger Strasse." She had disappeared from sight now, and Kirvov quickly opened the car door and stepped out. "Let me make sure," he called back.

He strolled up the street to Askanischer Platz, casually looked off to his right, and then busied himself lighting a cigarette. A yellow double-decker appeared and headed for the bus stop. Kirvov dropped his cigarette, ground it out with his shoe, and took a few steps toward Schöneberger Strasse.

Briefly out of view of the women in the car, he almost instantly reappeared and came swiftly back to them. He jumped into the driver's seat, turning on the ignition. "She's on the bus, all right," he announced, backing up. "We're going to tag along behind her."

Kirvov began reversing the general route he had taken in pursuit of bus 29 yesterday. He stayed behind it, braking when it stopped to release passengers, and resuming his pursuit each time the bus moved again. When they attained the Kurfürstendamm, Kirvov fell back slightly, allowing two other autos to slide in between him and the bus.

After a short ride up the crowded thoroughfare, Kirvov spoke once more. "She'll get off at the next corner, if she's going where I think she is going."

He slowed, double-parking, and narrowed his eyes as the bus stopped once more. A half dozen persons came out of the bus. One of them was Evelyn Hoffmann.

Emily and Tovah watched, quietly fascinated.

Kirvov put the car in gear. "She'll walk up Knesebeckstrasse," Kirvov predicted. "She'll go to the third floor of an apartment building in the middle of the block to see our Klara Fiebig. Let's park and find out whether I'm right."

Hastily parking near Steinplatz, Kirvov stepped out onto the sidewalk and raced back to the corner, peering up Knesebeckstrasse intently. When Emily and Tovah caught up with him, he gestured off. "I was right. I just saw her go into an apartment building. Let me check it out, just to be positive it is the same building. Wait for me here."

Kirvov was gone only a few minutes. When he returned, he nodded with satisfaction.

"The same building," he stated. "She's visiting Klara Fiebig."

"I wonder what's going on there," said Emily.

"We'll find out yet," replied Kirvov. "Let's just hang around here. If it goes as before, she should leave there shortly. Soon as she does, we'll disperse, do some window shopping. Once she's on the Ku'damm, we'll follow her at a safe distance."

"Do you know where she'll be going?" Tovah asked.

"I have an idea," said Kirvov. "I can't be sure, but let's wait and see."

The tiresome wait, heightened only by their expectations, lasted almost forty minutes.

"I can see her again," Kirvov stated abruptly. "Let's separate. Let's give her a quarter of a block start on us, and then follow her."

The two women hastily distanced themselves from Kirvov, as the Russian moved sideways a few yards to plant himself before the display window of a camera shop. Emily and Tovah moved farther away to become absorbed in another window featuring the latest French ready-to-wear fashions.

Kirvov kept the corner in view, and when Evelyn Hoffmann appeared, he saw her hurrying toward the Kurfürstendamm without bothering to so much as glance at the shop windows. Obviously she had some exact destination in mind. Once she was caught up in the flow of pedestrian traffic, Kirvov signaled to Emily and Tovah. Breathlessly, they reached him.

"I can still see her," said Kirvov. "Let's go."

Stringing out, with Kirvov in the lead, they pushed through the crowds of shoppers, tagging after Evelyn Hoffmann, always keeping her in sight.

At the stoplight on the Ku'damm she halted, waited for the light to change to red, and with others crossed the avenue.

Kirvov held up a hand as Emily and Tovah drew up alongside him.

"I think I know where she's going," he said. He pointed down the street to a sign that said MAMPES GUTE STUBE. "The same restaurant I followed her to yesterday. Let's see if she goes in."

They watched.

Evelyn Hoffmann left the sidewalk and entered Mampes Gute Stube.

"What do we do next?" Tovah wanted to know.

"We post ourselves near the restaurant," Kirvov said. "She's probably gone inside to meet with the big fellow I saw her with yesterday, the one called Wolfgang. I wonder who he is."

"Let me find out," Tovah volunteered. "If they separate when they come out, you two can stick with her while I follow him."

"Good idea," said Kirvov.

"How long do we wait here?" Emily wanted to know.

"Based on yesterday, I'd say they should come out in a half hour to an hour."

"Then let's get off our feet," said Emily, nodding toward a small sidewalk café with a half dozen metal tables. "I'm hungry. We can have something to eat while we watch for them."

They found a table at the small café, and ordered *Käsetorte* and *Kaffee.* By the time they had been served, and had eaten their snacks, a half hour had passed.

Thirty-five minutes passed, and Kirvov was paying the bill, when Emily gripped him arm.

"Nicholas, there she is, with a man, probably the same big one you mentioned. Can you see?"

Kirvov peered across the vehicle traffic. He nodded. "Yes. The same as yesterday. Evelyn Hoffmann and her friend Wolfgang." He came to his feet. "My guess is they'll part company now. Tovah, you follow him. We'll catch up with you later at the Kempinski. Emily, she'll probably cross the Ku'damm and walk to the bus stop at the next corner. Anyway, I hope so. You follow her. That'll give me time to get to the car. I'll catch up with you, and then you can tell me if she's already on the bus."

They watched Evelyn Hoffmann and Wolfgang engage in a short conversation on the sidewalk before Mampes Gute Stube. Then the Hoffmann woman and the man shook hands and parted company, starting away in opposite directions.

"All right," said Kirvov urgently. "You know what to do."

He hurried off for his car.

A few minutes later he was in the car, and cruising along the Ku'damm, trying to find Emily, when he saw her at a curb signaling him. He pulled up and pushed open the passenger door. Emily fell in beside him, her forefinger pointing straight ahead.

"The bus," Emily gasped. "You're right. She just took the bus, that one a block ahead of us."

"Perfect," said Kirvov, swinging his car away from the curb and accelerating.

Closing in on the bus, he stayed behind it and he could see it was traveling the same route he had covered yesterday.

Fifteen minutes later they observed Evelyn Hoffmann descend from the bus, cross Stresemann Strasse, and enter the Café Wolf.

"Full circle," said Emily, as Kirvov parked the car in a slot that again gave them an unobstructed view of the Café Wolf entrance. Emily knit her brow. "And what do we do now?"

"We wait, Emily," Kirvov said. "We just sit here and wait and see whether she comes out this time."

"What if she doesn't come out again? What do we do then?"

"I don't know."

"I know," said Emily enigmatically. "But let's wait and see."

One hour passed.

Eventually another two hours had gone by.

Emily was becoming more and more restless. "When does the damn place close?"

"In less than an hour."

"This is a waste of time," said Emily impatiently. She took hold of the door handle. "She's not coming out. But I'm going in."

Emily started to open the car door, when Kirvov grabbed her arm. "Wait. You can't go in there."

"Why not?" Emily demanded. "It's a public eating place. I'm the public and I want to eat. I also want to see if Evelyn Hoffmann is in there."

"Don't do it, Emily. It could be dangerous."

"Nonsense." She was already out of the car.

"Emily, what happened to your father wasn't nonsense. She may be a neo-Nazi. Please remember your father—"

Mention of her father made Emily turn around in the street. She leaned down toward Kirvov and considered his worried countenance. "I am remembering my father," she said quietly. "That's why I must know what's going on in there."

"Then I'm going with you."

"No, Nicholas. You stay here. Probably nothing is going on, and there's some innocent explanation, and we can bring this futile chasing around to an end. But if something *is* going on—all right—I'll be out of there and back before closing time. If I'm not, then you know what to do. Let Rex Foster know, and he can go to the police."

"I wish you wouldn't do this," Kirvov implored her.

"I must," Emily said. She shut the car door and started for the Café Wolf.

As if hypnotized, Kirvov watched her, and finally he saw Emily enter the Café Wolf.

* * *

Inside the Café Wolf, Emily tried to get her bearings. Quickly she scanned the interior. Another middle-class neighborhood restaurant, but immaculate. To her left a bar with a row of brown stools, a circular staircase, a phone booth, a potted plant. To her right a number of round tables, one of them occupied by two women deep in conversation. At the bar, a young woman in a sweatshirt and leather pants, a towel over her arm—apparently the waitress—was laughing at something the young bartender told her.

The waitress saw Emily and started toward her. "Fräulein, would you like to be seated?"

The waitress pulled a wooden chair away from a table and Emily sat down.

"I just wanted to get a bite," Emily said.

The waitress looked sorrowful. "I am afraid the kitchen is closing, and in a half hour the café will be closed. Maybe I can still get you a bowl of hot *Bohnensuppe.* I can see if—"

"Not that," said Emily, who had no stomach for bean soup.

"Maybe you would like a beer or coffee?"

"A beer will be fine. Any kind."

As the waitress tripped off to the bar, Emily surveyed the room more carefully. The two women occupying a nearby table were rising to go. Both were overweight and poorly dressed. Neither one even slightly resembled Evelyn Hoffmann.

As the pair departed, Emily resumed her study of the premises. There were only two places that Evelyn Hoffmann could have gone. One was up the circular staircase, which might lead to an apartment or offices; the other was into the kitchen nearby. There was a swinging door that led into the kitchen and beside it an open pass-through window for the chef to put out food orders.

The waitress was back with a beer and the check.

Emily tasted the foam, and observed the waitress collecting the salt and pepper shakers for refills. As the waitress went into the kitchen, and the bartender went out the door, Emily was alone to figure out what to do next. She decided to explore where the staircase led.

Coming to her feet, she went quickly to the stairs. As she put her foot on the first step, she noticed two plastic signs nailed to the wall to her left. The first read: ACHTUNG STUFEN! (Watch your step!) The other was more disheartening. It read: TOILETTEN. To make sure, Emily continued ascending the steep steps on tiptoe. The landing revealed two doors. One was marked with the silhouette of a woman, the other with the silhouette of a man. The toilets, all right, and nothing more on the landing. Nevertheless, she opened the door to the women's toilet. There was a tiny anteroom with a sink in it and two water closets, both visible and empty. After a moment's hesitation, she tried the door to the men's loo. Expecting anything, she found only an unoccupied urinal and toilet, and a sink.

Unhappily, Emily went back down the steps into the restaurant. The waitress was still out of sight. Emily returned to her table and her beer, and contemplated her next move.

She saw the waitress reenter the room, eye her, and then approach once more. The waitress said, "I am sorry. We are closing in five minutes. If you will please settle the bill."

"Of course," said Emily. She unclasped her purse, found two deutsche marks, and gave them to the waitress. For an instant, she considered questioning the waitress, describing Evelyn Hoffmann and inquiring where she had gone. Before she could make up her mind, she realized that the waitress was heading for the kitchen.

With a sigh, Emily stood up to go.

At the swinging door, the waitress looked back to call out, "*Auf Wiedersehen.*"

She disappeared into the kitchen.

At the front door, Emily hesitated. She glanced over her shoulder. The kitchen remained the one possibility that she had not explored.

Why not? She could see whether there was another exit at the rear that the Hoffmann lady might have taken. Or at least she could invent some question to ask of the waitress. Indeed, why not?

Emily wheeled about and resolutely she headed for the kitchen. Without further hesitancy, she pushed through the swinging door. It was the usual white tile kitchen. A steel sink, counters, wood chopping block, commercial range, refrigerator, cupboards.

Emily looked about. The waitress was nowhere in sight. There was some kind of corridor, though, straight ahead. Emily started for the corridor.

Suddenly, out of the dimly lit recess of the corridor, a tall, muscular, blond German youth loomed, obviously the cook since he was wearing a white chef's cap and a white apron.

Startled, Emily stopped in her tracks, blinking up at him.

"Fräulein," he said softly, "your identity card, please."

"My what?"

"Identity card. I must see it."

"I—I'm not sure I know—" she stammered.

But the tall young man interrupted her, an edge to his voice. "Who are you?"

"I—why I'm a customer—I just wanted to—but, no, I'd better go now."

"I think not." The young man had reached under his apron and brought out a businesslike Mauser 7.65 automatic. "You come with me." He waved the gun menacingly. "Come walk ahead of me. *Schnell!*"

Heart pounding, legs leaden, Emily forced herself past him, and into the frightening corridor.

Café Wolf had closed down.

And no Emily Ashcroft.

First no Evelyn Hoffmann. Then no Emily Ashcroft.

Kirvov stood in the growing darkness of Askanischer Platz, staring at the locked door of the blacked-out restaurant across the street. He tried to imagine what could have happened, but he had not the slightest clue. He only knew that it was serious and sinister, and that something must be done.

His first instinct had been to rush the front door, break into the quicksand of Café Wolf, find Emily if possible, and uncover the mystery once and for all.

Common sense restrained him. If he went inside, and also disappeared, no one on the outside would have any idea of what had happened to Emily and himself. Still safe in the street, he remained Emily's only contact with the outside world, the lone witness able to summon rescue. He reminded himself of Emily's last directive to him: *I'll be out of there and back before closing time. If I'm not, let Rex Foster know, and he can go to the police.*

Emily had been right. There was no other sensible choice.

Kirvov stumbled back to his car, started it, and was off to seek help.

Arriving at the brighter, more normal world of the Bristol Kempinski hotel, he left his car with the doorman and hurried into the lobby.

As he strode to the reception desk to call Foster, he saw a young blond woman leaving the counter, starting toward the bar. Then he recognized that she was Tovah Levine.

"Tovah!" Kirvov called out, hurrying to intercept her.

She stopped and lifted her hand with a greeting. "Hi there, Nicholas."

"Tovah, something terrible has happened. I've got to find Rex immediately. We must get to the police."

She studied his agonized expression briefly, then, looking concerned herself, she took his arm. "I was about to meet someone who—who knows the police. Come, you can tell us what's going on."

Kirvov held back. "Tovah, this is urgent. I can't waste a minute."

"Please, Nicholas," she insisted, "come with me."

Reluctantly he gave in, going in step with her the length of the long lobby. The luxurious bar area, except for a bearded man playing the brown Steinway piano, appeared empty. Then Kirvov noticed a man rising from one of the chairs grouped around a table in a darkened corner of the room.

Tovah brought Kirvov forward to the man who was waiting, a man taller than Kirvov, with the tanned regular features of a cinema star or an athlete.

Tovah said, "Nicholas, I want you to meet Chaim Golding, a Berlin friend." She said to Golding, "This is Nicholas Kirvov from Leningrad. I've told you about him. Another Hitler hunter."

Golding reached out to shake hands, but Kirvov took his hand only briefly, then swung toward Tovah. "Listen, Tovah, I have no time to socialize now. Another time maybe. At the moment, there is trouble. Emily has disappeared. I don't know what happened. I must get Rex and go to the police. I'll tell you all about it when we're alone." He cast Golding a look at once nervous and apologetic. "This—this is a private matter. I must go."

Tovah gripped his arm once more. "To get the police? No. Sit down. Mr. Golding knows about the police."

"But—"

"Sit down," Tovah demanded with an authority in her voice that Kirvov had not heard before. "You can speak in front of Chaim Golding." She shot Golding a questioning glance, and Golding nodded. Tovah went on to Kirvov, "If we have trouble, Mr. Golding will be more useful to us than the Berlin police." Then she added in an undertone, "Nicholas, Chaim Golding is Mossad, and so am I."

For an instant, Kirvov showed his bewilderment. "Mossad?"

"Israeli intelligence department," said Tovah. "I am a journalist, that is true, but it is also my cover for being a Mossad agent. Chaim Golding is my immediate boss, head of the important Berlin section."

Kirvov displayed a glimmer of recognition. "Mossad. You mean, the Entebbe operation and all that. Yes, I have read about you." He lowered himself to the edge of a chair. "But still, the police—"

"Never mind the police," said Tovah, sitting, pausing while Chaim Golding dropped into his chair across from them. "Mr. Golding's local Mossad is more powerful—and more trustworthy—than the Berlin police. Now tell us what happened to Emily."

Kirvov began to resist once more. "I'm not sure there is time for this—"

"There has to be time," Tovah insisted. "We must talk before acting. We have no choice. Tell us when you last saw Emily."

Quickly, Kirvov described what had happened since he and Emily had parted from Tovah on the Ku'damm. "I came right here to inform Rex, and to get the police to break in there, to break in and investigate."

"The police will not break in and investigate," said Tovah flatly. "They are the last ones to be notified."

Kirvov was totally at a loss. "What do you mean?"

Tovah's countenance was intent. "When you and Emily went off to follow Evelyn Hoffmann, I flagged a taxi and I followed her friend Wolfgang."

"Yes?"

"I followed him, all right, straight to a four-story building at Platz der Luftbrücke 6," said Tovah. "Over the building entrance there was a sign. It read: *'Der Polizeipräsident in Berlin.'* You understand that, Nicholas?"

"The headquarters of the Berlin police chief."

"Yes. I soon discovered that the man I was following was Wolfgang Schmidt, the chief of police. Do you understand what I am saying? The head of the Berlin police is associating with the

Hoffmann woman. The same woman who has been calling on Klara Fiebig, the one who owned your Hitler painting. Very suspicious. As an accredited journalist, I had no trouble going from the information desk, where I learned Schmidt's identity, to the publicity department. I came away with a very lovely portrait of Chief Wolfgang Schmidt. Of course, I turned it over to Chaim Golding."

Golding stirred, came forward in his chair, addressing Kirvov in a low voice. "Schmidt was able to join the Berlin police, and rise in rank after the war because his credentials were so excellent. He had proof that he had been an enemy of Hitler, and was one of the leaders in Count von Stauffenberg's attempt to assassinate Hitler in 1944. You know of the von Stauffenberg conspiracy against Hitler, do you not?"

"I read about it, when I was younger, in Soviet history books on the war," said Kirvov.

"To refresh your memory," said Golding, "Klaus von Stauffenberg was an aristocrat and a poet who became an officer under Hitler. Von Stauffenberg had always secretly opposed the Führer because of his misuse of power. Von Stauffenberg and others, who were higher placed, were determined to get rid of Hitler. Six efforts were undertaken which were either aborted or were failures. Finally, after the invasion of Russia proved to be a fiasco, von Stauffenberg determined to bring an end to Hitler. When he was summoned to East Prussia to meet with Hitler and two dozen of the Nazi high command at a wooden building at Wolf's Lair, in Rastenberg, East Prussia, von Stauffenberg stuffed a pair of two-pound time bombs in his briefcase. He joined the meeting around the conference table and propped the briefcase against an upright slab that held the table. With the bomb due to explode in seven minutes, von Stauffenberg excused himself to make a telephone call. Meanwhile, Colonel Heinz Brandt found that the briefcase was in his way, and he moved it aside, farther away from Hitler. Then the bombs exploded, ripping apart the room. Four persons were killed, but not Hitler. He suffered only superficial wounds and burns. Meanwhile, von Stauffenberg returned to Berlin, assuming that Hitler was dead. He and other conspirators began to pass out orders for the takeover of the government. Of course, Hitler caught up with him and the others. Over seven thousand arrests were made, and two thousand suspects executed. Von Stauffenberg was shot to death. He was lucky. Others were garroted with piano wire in the Plotzensee barracks, and then hung from meat hooks. According to government records, a few conspirators got away, and one was Wolfgang Schmidt. He had credentials signed by von Stauffenberg himself thanking him for his role against Hitler. With these credentials, Schmidt was welcomed into the Berlin police department and is now the chief of police. All well and good—"

"It sounds impressive," admitted Kirvov.

"—except for one thing," said Golding. "Schmidt's credentials were a lie, a sham."

"A lie?" echoed Kirvov.

"Wolfgang Schmidt was a tried-and-true Nazi from the very beginning and remains one today. Schmidt was one of Hitler's staunchest and most favored SS police guards at the Berghof, Hitler's residence above Berchtesgaden. Hitler even entrusted Eva Braun's protection to him. When the end was near, Hitler took some of the documents confiscated from von Stauffenberg, had them doctored, and gave them to Schmidt as a farewell gift. With his new persona, Schmidt eventually joined the postwar Berlin police force. This secret Nazi, he is the chief of police here today."

"But if you know all this—"

"Why didn't we expose him? Because, my friend, we never knew all this until Tovah checked on Schmidt and led us to investigate him. So you see, Mr. Kirvov, why we cannot depend on the Berlin police. Any effort to rescue Miss Ashcroft, from wherever she is in the Café Wolf, would have to go through Chief Schmidt. I assure you, Chief Schmidt would find some pretext not to be cooperative. Indeed he would endanger all of you further. You understand now, Mr. Kirvov?"

Kirvov was shaken. "I—yes, I do. But . . . ?"

"Something must be done for Miss Ashcroft, of course. We must find her as soon as possible. But her disappearance will have to be traced by you, by all of you, and by the agents of Mossad as well. We are undercover here, yet very strong and well equipped. For our part, we will immediately surround the Café Wolf and keep it under observation."

"But what can we possibly do?" asked Kirvov.

"You and Tovah must consult with Mr. Foster at once. Tovah saw him a short while ago. From what I've heard, he may have something to say. If he does, Tovah will notify us. If he doesn't, we will try to instigate some kind of action on our own. It will not be easy. Remember, whoever the enemy is, they have the chief of police of Berlin on their side. Now go on up and talk to Mr. Foster. I hope we can act in time to—to save Miss Ashcroft from harm."

As Kirvov and Tovah came quickly to their feet, Golding also rose.

"Just one more thing, Mr. Kirvov," Golding said, "an amusing and possibly illuminating sidelight. About this Café Wolf. Do you know that when Eva Braun was first introduced to Adolf Hitler in that camera shop, Hitler gave his name as Mr. Wolf? Yes, Mr. Wolf. Now, both of you, Godspeed."

After supervising the ongoing digging at the Führerbunker site—Andrew Oberstadt had expected his night crew to break into the emergency exit early this evening—Rex Foster had returned to the Kempinski to wait for Emily. Hunched over the blueprint of the Führerbunker, which was spread on the sitting-room desk, he had been puzzling over certain aspects of the drawings and slowly coming to certain conclusions. Foster had even telephoned the architect Zeidler to ask him a question about the blueprint of the Führerbunker.

When the doorbell rang, Foster responded eagerly. He wanted to tell Emily what was on his mind, and then together they would return to the East German Frontier Zone.

Opening the door, he did not hide his disappointment. Standing before him were Tovah and Kirvov. "Oh, hello," Foster said. "I was expecting Emily—"

"We want to speak to you about Emily," Kirvov said.

Foster drew them into the room. They both sat down, and he drifted back to the desk, keeping his eyes on them. Their expressions were grim, and Foster was at once concerned.

"What is it?" he said. "Is Emily all right?"

"We're not sure," Kirvov replied, "Let me explain . . ."

When Kirvov finished, Foster was pale but controlled. "Why didn't you try to go in there after her, Nicholas?"

"I considered it, even after the place was closed," Kirvov answered. "But I didn't know whether I'd be able to come out of there again, and if I couldn't, no one would know what had happened to either of us. Before she went in—"

"That was damn foolish of her," Foster interrupted, agitated. "I'm sorry. Go on."

"She was determined to go in alone," Kirvov tried to explain. "Before going in, she told me that if she did not come out, she wanted me to find you and you were to get the police—"

"The police should be alerted at once."

Foster was about to reach for the telephone, when Tovah shook her head. "No use, Rex. Now it's my turn. Let *me* explain."

Hurriedly, she told him about herself and Mossad, and then what she could of Wolfgang Schmidt's background.

"I'll be goddamned!" Foster exploded. "And I actually went

to Schmidt to ask his help after Emily was almost murdered. The Nazi son of a bitch." He exhaled. "Okay, so much for the police. Where does that leave us?"

"With Mossad as our backup, Rex," Tovah told him.

"You mean Golding can really help us?"

"He can and will. It's a risky business, but Mossad has the capability to act inside Berlin. Beside the organization's trained agents—I don't know how many are undercover in the city—there are hundreds of other reserves in the Berlin community, anti-Nazis of every type and their offspring, experts at everything from armament to machines, who can be called upon to do whatever is necessary for the cause. Obliteration of the last vestige of the Third Reich is all they care about. Anyway, Chaim Golding wants to know what you think can be done, before he risks taking more obvious action."

"He mustn't do anything obvious," Foster said. "No direct action yet. The police might interfere and stop it all." He swung back to his desk and rapidly reviewed the bunker plans spread before him. "The fact is, I do have one thought."

Still studying the diagram of the Führerbunker, Foster said, "There's something definitely strange in this plan of the Führerbunker. It would be clear to any architect. Actually, I called Zeidler about this design of his. He knew it wasn't exactly right. He said that Hitler himself ordered his bunker laid out this way, and Zeidler could only follow orders. But there certainly is something missing, and if it is what I think it is, it will tell me the location of the seventh bunker."

Kirvov was confused. "What seventh bunker?"

"This one." Foster pulled his second blueprint out from beneath the one of the Führerbunker. "The one underground bunker Hitler ordered that has never been identified. Now I have an idea where it could be. It all depends on what I find when our dig gets into the Führerbunker."

"You expect to go into the Führerbunker?" Tovah asked with surprise.

Foster was putting on his jacket. "Tonight. By the time I return to the frontier area, the side of the mound should be excavated and there should be access into the Führerbunker."

"You think it still exists?" said Kirvov.

"Why not? It was originally built deep underground and reinforced by steel and concrete. Not even the Russians' bulldozing later could have made a dent in it, at least not in the deepest area Hitler used down below."

"You can't go alone," protested Tovah. "Maybe I can—"

"I have a permit to get in," said Foster. "You don't. You and Nicholas stay right here, and let Golding know what I'm up to. If I need you, I'll be in touch, somehow, you can be sure."

Within the East German Frontier Zone, most of the great mound that covered the Führerbunker was lost in the darkness of the night. Only one side of the mound, the west side, was brightly illuminated by three gigantic spotlights.

At the rim of the circle of light, Andrew Oberstadt, in soiled overalls and muddy boots, stood observing his night shift as the men cleared away a wider passage that led into a gaping hole in the side of the mound. They were shoveling up more dirt and debris, dumping it on two heaps, when Foster arrived.

Oberstadt acknowledged Foster's reappearance with good cheer. "Well, Rex, I think we've just about done it. Be ready for you any second. It worked, going through the old emergency exit at ground level. I looked in myself a little while ago. Couldn't resist seeing what shape it is in. Not bad, considering forty years and the Russian bulldozing. The concrete roof appears to have protected the Hitler area below. The stairwell seems mostly intact. A few steps near the top broken, but as far as my flashlight could show me, the rest of the stairs seem to be in usable shape. You want to wait until morning to go down there?"

"I want to go down there right now, Andrew."

Oberstadt's reaction was a dubious one. "It's going to be pretty difficult looking for that cameo and the dental bridges in that hole. Even with portable lighting, it'll be difficult to find anything so small."

"That's not what I'm looking for tonight, Andrew. I'm after something bigger."

Oberstadt shrugged. "Well, you know what you're doing. I guess daylight wouldn't make it any easier down there. When do you want to start?"

"This minute."

"Mind if I join you?" said Oberstadt.

"I could use you in the first part of the operation. It would be helpful. If I find what I want, it would be better if I stayed down there alone."

"We'll need some fluorescent hand lanterns," said Oberstadt. "One for each of us."

"I'd like you to bring something else, also," Foster said. "Something that could cut into concrete."

"I have a battery-operated saw."

Foster thought about it. "Bring the saw, and also a chisel and hammer."

As Oberstadt hastened off, summoning a workman to give him a hand, Foster stared mesmerized at the gaping hole in the mound. Since it was partially illuminated by the standing spotlights, he approached it to see the condition of the old emergency exit.

Stepping between the panting laborers, he reached the hole and bent to enter it. There had been a vestibule, he remembered hearing, that led to the outdoors from the four flights of steps. Most of it had been crushed, and now cleaned out, and the opening had since been shored up with timbers by Oberstadt's crew. Vaguely Foster could make out the concrete steps, heavily layered with dirt, several of the top ones misshapen, the rest plunging steeply downward into the darkness.

Suddenly there were powerful beams of light from behind him. Oberstadt was at his heels, handing him a large fluorescent lantern, retaining the other, then reaching back to one of his men to take a canvas sack of hand tools and the saw.

"Ready when you are," said Oberstadt.

"Let's go," said Foster.

"Watch your step," Oberstadt cautioned him.

Foster led the way, as he perched precariously on the first smashed step, one hand on the wall, then eased downward to the next one, and the next, each one partially broken, but after that he could see that the caked treads were in good condition. With his lamp in front of him, Foster descended, and he could hear Oberstadt right behind him.

Down and down they went, the full four flights. Forty-four steps, Foster remembered, and when he had counted the forty-fourth, he knew it was right, that he was at the bottommost level of the original Führerbunker.

Here, in this lower labyrinth, fifty-five feet beneath the point he had entered, it was stifling. It was difficult to breathe. He took a step, and the dust eddied up, making him cough.

"You all right?" Oberstadt's voice sounded and resounded.

"Okay. Let me make sure where we are."

He knew the design of this lower command bunker. There would be eighteen cramped rooms stretching forty-five feet ahead, and this nine-foot-wide central corridor with its low ceiling led to all of them. But now, his mind on Emily, Foster was interested in only six of the rooms, Hitler's and Eva Braun's private suite, but mainly he was interested in two of the rooms, Hitler's living room and personal bedroom.

Foster held out his lamp and tried to take in the condition of this lower bunker. It was a mess, intact but a mess. The once clean rust-brown ceiling and corridor walls were black with dirt and age, and spider webs hung everywhere. Here and there, before him, there were pools of stagnant water, and areas of crusted mud.

Walking a few tentative yards farther, Foster called back, "The door should be right around here, on the right. Let me see."

Then he saw it, through the shell of what had once been a waiting room, the thick fireproof steel door that he had read about, the one that led into Hitler's bunker living room.

The handle of the door was there, badly rusted, and Foster hoped that it was still workable and that the door could be pushed open.

Balancing his lantern, he found the door handle. It was cold. He clamped his hand on it, and turned it. With a groan of protest, the lock gave way. Foster leaned against the door to shove it open with his weight, but the pressure was not necessary. Creaking, the door slowly moved aside.

For long seconds Foster remained immobile, as if unable to bring himself to leave the present and enter the past. Then he stepped forward into history. As he swung his lamp around, the black pit mushroomed to life in its bright gleam, and seconds later it was doubly illuminated by the reinforced brightness of Oberstadt's light beside him.

The image so long in his mind had furnished the ten-by-fifteen-foot living room and prepared him for what to expect. There would be a desk or writing table to one side holding a framed photograph of Hitler's mother. On the carpet there would be three old chairs and directly ahead a small round table and the blood-stained blue sofa upon which the Führer and his bride Eva Braun had slumped in death.

But the image was dissipated by reality, and Foster realized that this was forty years later and that he stood in the present.

Although the Führerbunker had been quarantined by the Russians to keep out Red Army troops and the curious public, some souvenir-hunting Soviet medical personnel and soldiers had gone down below the first two or three days. They had been scavengers, seeking either mementos or furnishings for their devastated homes in Russia.

Foster squinted about, wherever the lantern beam gave him light. The carpeting had been ripped up and carted away. Two of the three chairs were missing, and the third broken in parts so that it resembled kindling wood. The round table was gone. All that remained of the past were Hitler's desk on one wall and the moldy, filthy sofa on another.

But Foster was searching for something.

"Hold your light on the desk," he ordered Oberstadt.

He moved ahead, and with one hand pulled the desk away from the concrete wall. He peered behind it, at the wall, then dropped to his knees and felt along the wall. It was smooth, dirty but smooth.

Standing, he said enigmatically, "Not here. Let's go into the next room. That should be Hitler's private bedroom."

The wooden bedroom door was stuck. Foster yanked at it a couple of times, and at once it flew open, fanning up a curtain of dust. Foster covered his nose and mouth, waiting for the dust to settle. Then he stepped inside the bedroom, with Oberstadt close behind him.

This room was smaller than the living room. There was a single bed, narrow as an army cot, and it was stripped down to the frame. Even the mattress had been removed. Foster guessed that there had been a nightstand and lamp beside it once. Now they were missing. All the other furniture, whatever pieces there had been, had long ago been confiscated. But across the room a four-drawer bureau, too bulky to be taken away, still stood sturdily against the wall.

Foster examined the bedroom walls and ceiling. They were concrete, and there were cracks everywhere.

"Odd," said Foster. "Cracks here but not in the living room. Yet the same concrete."

Oberstadt was playing his fluorescent lamp against a wall, studying a crack. "I don't understand. None of this should have cracked." He had found a screwdriver and was prying into a crack. "You know, somehow I don't think these fissures happened naturally. They might have been man-made."

Foster agreed. "Simulated," he said quietly. "A form of camouflage."

"A what?" asked Oberstadt, puzzled.

"To make everyone ignore the real thing. You'll see. Here, help me move aside the bureau."

They both set down their lanterns, took the sides of the bureau, and pulled it away from the wall.

"Let's bring it nearer the center of the room," Foster said. "Okay, now take your lantern and shine it on the wall behind the bureau."

Oberstadt did as he was told, and Foster was on his knees closely studying the wall that had been hidden behind the bureau. He ran his forefinger along four parts of the wall. "Yup, just what I suspected. Hand me your screwdriver, Andrew."

Oberstadt gave him the screwdriver, and Foster pried away at the slits he had detected. Soon an outline in the wall took form. It resembled a rectangular panel four feet wide and three feet high.

Foster got to his feet. "Just what I was looking for," said Foster.

"What was that?"

"Andrew, I've been an architect for a long time. I can't imagine anyone building a windowless room like this without some kind of interior escape hatch to supplement the door."

"But there is an emergency exit. We just came down through it."

"No, I'm speaking of a private exit. There was none on the plan of the Führerbunker. I couldn't believe it. Therefore, I reasoned, one must have been added afterward. By Hitler himself. A secret exit."

Oberstadt's ruddy features showed disbelief. "That's a secret exit?"

"I think it is."

"But why? You mean in case of a gas attack?"

"In this case, something more. A means of getting out of here undetected."

"You mean he . . . ?"

"We'll know soon enough. You have your saw?"

"I sure do."

"Okay." Foster pointed at the four lines on the wall. "Let's go at it. I'm expecting it to be a slab that will come out. Let's see if it does."

"You bet!" said Oberstadt enthusiastically. He set down his lantern and bag of hand tools, and picked up his saw.

As Oberstadt went to the wall, and lowered himself to his knees, his saw poised, Foster said, "I hope it's not noisy."

"It's noisy but it will be quick. If this is only a slab, then it has been cut to fit the opening and I won't be going through solid concrete. That looks like mortar that you've dug out. It should be easy as putty, and no louder than humming." He paused. "What's the difference anyway? I thought this was an escape exit."

"Still could be. Depends—where to, and what's on the other side."

"What is on the other side?"

"I won't be sure until you finish."

"All right, here goes."

Oberstadt triggered the saw, and it gave out a low, steady

hum. He set the blade against one of the lines on the wall, and immediately the noise became a metallic whine.

Holding his own lantern up higher so that Oberstadt could see better, Foster was surprised at the progress the saw was making. It was going through the lines as if they'd been drawn on a piece of cake.

Oberstadt paused only once. "You're right. It's a slab—wire mesh covered by mortar inside—and it should come out soon."

Ten minutes later he shut off his saw and laid it down. His fingers dug into a side of the slab and rocked it slightly.

"It was freestanding to begin with," Oberstadt said. "It's been lightly mortared in place, but now it is completely loose. Want to give me a hand?"

They each took one side of the slab, and began to tug at it, gradually pulling it out of the wall.

"Not too heavy," grunted Oberstadt, "because it's not solid concrete. Feels like no more than a hundred pounds." They slipped it to one side, and leaned it against the solid wall of the bedroom.

Quickly, Foster, on his knees, moved toward the hole in the wall, raised his lantern, and looked inside.

He backed away. "Just what I expected."

"What did you expect?"

"A tunnel like the ninety-foot one Speer constructed earlier, running from the Old Chancellery underground to the New Chancellery. Only Speer didn't build this one. I'm positive this one was built by Hitler's slave laborers."

"Now what?" Oberstadt asked.

Foster smiled. "Now we part company. I have to go in there to see if I can find someone."

"Someone? You'd better let me come along."

"No, Andrew. In this case two's a crowd. One person can do it more quietly. This had better be done as quietly as possible."

Oberstadt was doubtful. "You're sure you want to go alone?"

"I think I better do it my way." He stuck out his hand. "Thanks, my friend. You'd better get back up top. If I need you, I'll call you."

"You're the boss," Oberstadt said, rising.

"I'll keep this one lantern," Foster said. "And—well, you might leave me a chisel and hammer."

"Chisel and hammer. You've got them." Oberstadt passed them along, took hold of his own lantern and tool bag. Leaving Hitler's bedroom, he turned once. "Good luck, wherever you're going."

Foster stuck the tools in his trouser pockets. He considered the rectangular hole in the wall. There was no question now. Hitler and Eva had gone out of the Führerbunker this way, had managed to have the slab replaced with the help of confederates, who also moved the bureau back against the slab in the wall.

And then Hitler had fled through the catacomb, under the city, to where? Foster suspected he knew where, and he suspected that Emily might be there now and certainly not alone.

With care, Foster, gripping the lantern tightly but pushing it ahead of him, crawled through the hole.

Emerging from the hole into the tunnel, he took the lantern by its handle and then stood upright. There was room enough. The tunnel rose to an arched ceiling four inches above his head. Beyond the range of the light beam, there was darkness.

He checked the luminous dial of his wristwatch. Then, holding the lamp out before him, he began to walk slowly. He placed one foot in front of the other cautiously, and on his rubber-soled boots noiselessly.

It was a long, clean tunnel, no cobwebs, no dirt. Just concrete on all sides, his beam of light shooting ahead, and darkness beyond its reach.

On and on he walked.

He checked his watch. Twenty-five minutes on the move. At least a thousand yards covered. To what end?

And then he saw. His whitish beam of light had hit a dead end. A solid wall of concrete blocked the end of the tunnel. But then, with knowledge of his destination, he felt sure that the obstruction could not be solid concrete. It, too, had to have an opening, an exit point. Unless it had been cemented solid.

Quietly but swiftly, he reached the wall that barred the tunnel. He was up against it, inspecting it minutely, hunting for signs of exit marks, and soon, low in the center, he found the telltale signs.

He set down his lantern, knelt, looked closely, dug his fingers into the top of the square slab, smaller than the one at the entrance to the tunnel, and felt a wave of relief as he realized it was loosely set in, not cemented into place, just shoved into its hole.

He reached for his chisel and as quietly as possible began to pry at the square slab.

It was easily moved, and not thick, and it almost fell into his eager hands. He had it free, and quietly set it behind him onto the floor of the tunnel. There was a square hole at ground level that could comfortably accommodate his body. Through the hole, he realized, dim illumination was shining. He snapped off his lantern and put it to one side at the edge of the tunnel.

Flattening himself on the ground, he squirmed through the hole. Coming through it, he could see a wooden partition a few yards ahead, with a wooden door built into it, but the door was not flush with the concrete floor, and a sliver of light, subdued, shone through it.

Quietly, quietly, Foster pushed himself off the floor and to his feet.

His heart was going faster now, adrenaline flowing.

On tiptoe, on rubber soles, he approached the door. No lock. He turned the handle, and drew the door back a few inches.

The first thing he realized was that he was perched on some sort of mezzanine—with a staircase leading down to . . .

And then his jaw fell open. Stretching out before him, well below, dimly lighted for the sleeping hours, was another Führerbunker, but enlarged, more than twice as wide, more than twice as long as the original. A neat warren of closed cubbyholes, probably offices, certainly sleeping quarters.

And he knew at once what he had found.

Hitler's secret seventh bunker.

With astonished eyes, he took it in. Hitler's refuge beneath the city of Berlin, hidden away and populated for forty years. An undetected city beneath the city.

His eyes scanned the incredible sight below, and almost instantly he realized that he was not alone here above the secret bunker.

He was not alone. He had company.

11

What Foster saw, what his gaze was riveted upon now, was the back of a guard, a young Nazi soldier in a gray uniform, a swastika band around one slack arm, the other arm propping up a submachine gun. Circling his waist was a belt with a holster that held what might be a Luger .08.

To Foster, it was evident that the soldier's head had dropped forward, chin resting on his chest.

He was breathing heavily, and he emitted a series of snores.

He had dozed off during his boring night duty. He was seated on the landing of a staircase that appeared to run down to the bottom of the vast bunker and he was certainly asleep.

Foster's next move was clear. He did not give it a second

thought. He pulled the hammer out of his trouser pocket, gripped the handle, slowly pushed aside the door a few inches more, and slipped through.

Crouching low, Foster advanced lightly on his rubber soles toward the back of the slumbering guard. Foster's peripheral vision caught sight of no one in the bunker stretching below.

A few feet behind the slouched guard, Foster tried to hold his breath and gradually rose to give himself more leverage.

Foster was above the young Nazi now, staring at the other's mat of sandy hair. Foster lifted the hammer up over his shoulder. He took aim.

The hammer flashed downward, the impact hard and sure, striking the Nazi a solid blow at the base of his skull.

The victim uttered no sound. He began to fall sideways, unconscious, and his submachine gun, jarred free of his leg, was beginning to fall, too.

Desperate to prevent the sound of a falling body or a clatter from the submachine gun, Foster darted out his free arm, hooking it around the youth's body, holding it, even as his hand reached forward to keep the submachine gun upright, and his fingers just managed to clutch it.

One more glance at the area below.

No one had been alerted. No one in sight.

Still, Foster knew that he dare not lose a precious second. He was in the subterranean land of the enemy, heirs to the most ruthless killers of modern times, and he must be ready. Returning the hammer to his trouser pocket, he took a firm hold of the submachine gun with his right hand and lifted the inert guard off the landing with his left arm. Inching backward, he eased himself and his burden through the door.

Lowering the body to the floor, Foster studied his victim. A young snub-nosed man, maybe early thirties, his eyes closed. The blow had broken the skin, probably fractured the skull, and there was a light trickle of blood on the Nazi youth's neck. Foster could not tell if the inert guard was still breathing or if there was any pulse. Whatever his condition, the guard would be unconscious a long, long time, maybe forever. Studying the body, Foster could see that the young man was slightly shorter than himself, but with similar measurements. Foster was satisfied that the change would work.

What came next was familiar to Foster. He had done it once on a Viet Cong corpse before an infiltration in Vietnam. He had seen it duplicated in movies. Yes, it was a familiar act, and he hoped that it would be enough. Kneeling, he hastily started to strip the outer garments off the unconscious soldier, removing his gun belt and holster, his high-buttoned tunic, his trousers, his shoes.

Foster cast around for a spot to hide the limp body. Noticing what appeared to be a built-in storage cabinet against a wall, he stood up, went to it, and tugged the pair of doors open. It was indeed a cabinet with three mattresses stacked on the floor. Foster hurried back, dragging the soldier's deadweight, and with difficulty lifted him onto the top mattress, stretching him out there. One more examination. Not a sign of consciousness. There'd be no danger from this guard.

Quickly, Foster stripped off his own clothing. Throwing his garments into the storage cabinet, he closed the doors. Then he returned to the Nazi's uniform and began to get into it. Finished, he found the gray uniform a bit baggy, the trousers a few inches short, but not a serious misfit. He fixed on the gun belt, drew the Luger from the holster, studied it, and confirmed that there was a bullet clip in the grip.

Now he was ready. Wearing the Nazi uniform was repugnant to him, but the disguise was worth any cost since it offered him the one hope of reaching Emily. He prayed that she was still alive, and, if alive, unharmed.

With more confidence, he went through the door to the landing where he had first seen his victim dozing during sentry duty. Briefly he crouched surveying the scene below. In his architect's mind's eye, he tried to overlay upon it the seventh bunker design he had gone over so many times and committed to memory.

The bunker below fitted its blueprint perfectly. It had been designed, Foster knew, after the general pattern of the smaller Führerbunker, but on a much larger scale. He could see all the lesser rooms on either side of the wide central corridor. From what he had seen of the plan, the large suite would be at the far end of the corridor. It was the kind of suite that would accommodate someone in command, someone like Adolf Hitler.

No question that Hitler had prepared the suite—and this bunker—for himself and Eva Braun.

The possibility that Hitler himself might be there struck him more forcibly. Hitler. If not Hitler, certainly Evelyn Hoffmann, because now he was convinced that Evelyn Hoffmann was none other than Eva Braun.

And if Eva Braun controlled the suite, it was likely that Emily might be there, too.

That would be his destination, that large suite, and he would go straight to it.

He expected that there might be other night sentries, at least one or two, along the corridor, and he was ready for any challenge.

He started down the staircase, clumping sure-footed in his too-tight Wehrmacht short leather boots, descending to the near end of the dark green carpeted passage.

Confidently, he undertook his tense march between the two rows of closed doors toward the command post.

No one in sight.

And then someone.

Lolling at one side of what appeared to be an office door,

another night sentry, another young one, a lanky blond busily cleaning his fingernails, his Heckler and Koch set against the wall beside him.

Foster advanced toward him without a break in stride. When almost abreast of the sentry, Foster reconsidered whom he should ask for. Frau Evelyn Hoffmann or Frau Eva Braun. Instinct made him revert back to what he had originally planned to say.

Out of the corner of his mouth, Foster spoke to the second sentry in perfect German. "Have an urgent message for the Number One." No gender. No name. The neuter Number One. Safe. He hoped.

The sentry hardly bothered to look up. "She's probably asleep by now—but if it is something special, you better go ahead."

Foster saluted, and, with his best military bearing, like a soldier carrying a vital message to his leader, continued to march straight ahead. He waited for the sentry to reconsider, summon him back, but the summons did not come.

Arriving before the suite at the far end of the corridor—no openings, all wood, complete privacy—he remembered the design on the drawing of the seventh bunker. Turning left he hurried down the hall, and there was the door to the suite.

Uncertain of what might be awaiting him inside, Foster put a hand on the brass knob and twisted it as quietly as possible.

The entrance door gave, and he was standing inside a small reception room furnished with a modest desk, a swivel chair, and two pull-up chairs. No one was in the room. Then another door.

Easing off the heavy military boots, he moved stealthily to the next door. No lock. He opened it. He peered inside. Two floor lamps were all that lit the windowless room. What he saw was a combination living room and office, an oversized oak desk to the right, and across from it a couch and two overstuffed easy chairs facing a wood shelf resembling a mantel, with filled bookshelves under the mantel instead of a fireplace.

As far as he could see, the long room was unoccupied.

But he was wrong.

"Rex—" a hushed female voice called out.

He knew that sound had come from Emily, who was struggling to lift herself above the back of the couch and be seen.

In his stocking-feet, Foster rushed to the couch. Emily, bound hand and foot, had sunk down on the couch once more, was lying on her back, waiting for him. Kneeling, working swiftly to undo the thin knotted rope that held her, he managed to smile at the disbelief showing in her pale face. Her auburn hair was in disarray, and her tweed skirt had hiked up above her knees—obviously from her efforts to free herself—but she seemed uninjured.

"Are you all right?" he whispered, loosening the knots.

She nodded.

"Anyone else here?" he whispered again.

"Ssh," she said. "Yes, in the bedrooom. Be careful." Then, as her arms came free, "How did you get in here?"

"Never mind. You'll see."

He was untying the strands at her ankles, and he helped her to a sitting position. "God, I was praying you'd be all right." He was up on the sofa beside her, embracing and kissing her.

She clung to him, then moved her mouth to his ear. "I wouldn't have been all right in the morning. They're holding me for questioning. A horrible man named Schmidt was here a few hours ago—"

"Chief of police, Berlin, and a closet Nazi."

"—to use Sodium Pentothal on me, to find how much we know, so we can be found and eliminated. But just as he was coming here, he was notified he must appear immediately at a hearing tonight concerning Ernst Vogel's death. To prove it was suicide not murder. Apparently important, because he had to rush back for that. He promised he'd return in the morning to administer the Sodium Pentothal and question me. I'm supposed to be the first of our group. Once I talked, I was to be killed and cremated. When he left, Schmidt told her he'd work on me early before going to Munich."

"Her? Told her?" repeated Foster. "Who do you mean? Who is she?"

"Eva Braun. The real thing. Calls herself Evelyn Hoffmann. But she boasted to me that she's Eva Braun."

"And Hitler?"

"Gone. Dead. Long ago. He and Eva were down here under the city a long time, eighteen years before Hitler died of Parkinson's. She's been running the show ever since."

"Incredible," he said with astonishment. "What do they want?"

"To survive. Not just themselves, but the Third Reich. Look up there."

She came weakly to her feet and led Foster to the mantel.

"Next to the Grecian urn that she worships, that holds Hitler's ashes. Between the urn and Kirvov's Hitler painting. The printed words in the frame are Hitler's."

Foster moved closer. The hand lettering of the framed quotation hung on the wall was in German, but simple. It read:

> THE CONFLICT BETWEEN RUSSIA AND THE UNITED STATES IS INEVITABLE. IT WILL COME. WHEN IT COMES, I MUST BE ALIVE—OR MY SUCCESSOR WITH THE SAME IDEALS—TO LEAD THE GERMAN PEOPLE, TO HELP THEM ARISE FROM DEFEAT, TO LEAD THEM TO FINAL VICTORY.
>
> —ADOLF HITLER

"Je-sus," Foster muttered.

"His actual words once to an SS officer."

"That's what he lived for?"

"And she, too, what she lives for today."

"But how, Emily?" He paused, thinking. "I wonder what they're planning?"

"I don't know. I never heard."

"Then let's find out right now." He drew the Luger from his holster. "Let's pay her a visit. She's in the bedroom?"

"The one adjoining the bedroom Hitler used to occupy. She won't talk, Rex. She'll never tell."

He considered this, then whispered, "The Sodium Pentothal. They intended to use it on you. Do you know where it is?"

Emily nodded. "Schmidt left it in the upper right-hand desk drawer. I heard him say it was good for twenty-four hours."

"Find it, Emily. And take this rope from the couch. We'll need it."

At the desk, Emily held up a plastic bag. "Hypodermic needle, something to use for a tourniquet I guess, and a yellowish solution." She called to him softly, "Sodium Pentothal. Here it is."

"Truth serum." He studied the Luger in his hand. "Show me the bedroom. It's time for the truth."

Fifteen minutes had passed, and now Eva Braun lay stretched on her back on the bed, roped at wrists and ankles to the brass bedposts, and gagged. Her eyes were open, but no longer terrified. They were unfocused.

Sodium Pentothal. Perfect, Foster thought, standing over her.

To this point, it had been easy, actually, Foster told himself. Their sudden appearance and the lights had startled her into an instant awakening. The gun at her head had assured her submission, and then, her silence.

"Okay, Emily, now find her some clothes and have her dress," he said.

When Emily had found the clothes, he had handed her the gun and stepped outside the bedroom door.

Returning to the bedroom, he had found Eva, fully clothed, lying down once more, Emily pointing the Luger at her.

"Step two," he had told Emily. "Give me the gun. Get the rope."

After they had tied her to the bed, he had asked Emily for the Sodium Pentothal.

For the first time, Eva Braun had protested with agitation. "No, no, no," she had begged, but Foster had been able to think only of the six million victims of the holocaust who had used the same words, begged for life and been denied. The monster's wife, herself a monster now, had also to be denied. Foster stuffed the gag in her mouth, and then with deliberation he had prepared to administer the truth serum.

Working from his memory of what he had witnessed in Vietnam, Foster had filled the hypodermic needle with the solution. Then, using the tourniquet, he had sought a good vein in her wrist. With care, he had inserted the needle into the vein, injecting her intravenously.

Removing the needle, he had watched Eva. "Should take effect in less than a minute," he had said to Emily.

Staring down at Eva now, he could see that her eyes were glazed and that she was groggy.

"Okay, that should last anywhere from an hour to two or three," he said. "I'll give her a booster shot later." He took Emily by the arm. "We can leave her for a few minutes." He holstered the Luger. "We have something else to do."

He hurried Emily out of the bedroom, through the short hall into the sitting room.

Momentarily, Foster was lost in thought. Then he asked, "Emily, any idea how many Nazis are hidden down here?"

"Eva told me, 'There are over fifty of us.' "

"Any idea who they are?"

"She talked about that, too, rather proudly. A handful of Hitler's old circle who were declared missing. Many of the Hitler

Youth sent down here before Hitler moved in. Most of them now grown men with families of their own. No children here, no one under sixteen. Pregnant wives are always sent out to Argentina, to bear their children. The wives return alone. The children are raised, taught, and trained by Germans in Argentina. Only after the youngsters become sixteen are they sent back to Berlin to take their places in the bunker."

"But all hardened Nazis."

"More than that. Hardened Nazis, yes, but all of them murderers, trained to kill."

"To kill whom, Emily?"

"To assassinate anyone above ground who might threaten them. She spoke of the necessity to liquidate—her word—anti-Nazis, prominent Jews, Nazi hunters, and dangerous foreigners like my father." Emily blinked. "She admitted my father's 'accident' had been prearranged. She also admitted that her followers had been responsible for at least two hundred murders in the last twenty years. They'd snuff you out in an instant, if they knew you were here. They're ruthless, Rex, absolutely vicious."

"All right," said Foster. "I have an errand for you. I'm going to get you out of here now. I'm going to show you the way I came in, because that's the way you're going out."

"On an errand?"

"Yes. You'll leave from under the mound, from the Führerbunker and through the old emergency exit. You'll wind up in the East German Frontier Zone. Oberstadt's up there. He'll have no trouble taking you through the gate. Get to a phone as quickly as possible. Get hold of Tovah Levine at the Bristol Kempinski. She and Kirvov are standing by. Tell her we've found them all, and tell her to inform Chaim Golding immediately."

"Chaim Golding?"

"Head of Mossad in Berlin. Tovah is one of his agents. He has the personnel and facilities to do what I want him to do. Tell him

I want the rats down here exterminated, all of them, at once, tonight."

Emily's eyes had widened. "How, Rex?"

"The way the Hitler gang did it to the Jews at Auschwitz. But more exactly, the way Albert Speer once planned to get rid of Hitler."

"He was going to send gas through the ventilator of the Führerbunker."

"That's right."

"And throw in a grenade of nerve gas called Tabun. Absolutely lethal."

"Only this time the Mossad fighters will probably use a far more sophisticated gas, but one equally lethal. Tovah is waiting in our suite. The plan of this bunker is on our sitting-room desk. Golding will know how to go about it. But this bunker must be airtight. You came through the other entrance beneath the Café Wolf?"

"Yes. The guard forced me down some stairs to a steel vault-type door. He unlocked it and pushed me through."

"Okay. See that the Mossad agents take out the guard in the Café Wolf, and go down and lock that metal door. Then let them pump in the gas. In minutes every last Nazi should be wiped out. Do you have your watch?"

"Yes."

"Let's coordinate the time, Emily. Okay, I have one-twenty in the morning."

"One-twenty in the morning," she said. "Got it."

"Tell Tovah that the Mossad agents are to start pouring the gas in at precisely three in the morning. Precisely three. Now let's get moving. I want to see you out of here, and then I'm going back to give our Eva Braun the third degree. Let me get those klutzy shoes back on . . ."

"Hey, Rex, wait a minute. What do you mean, you'll get me

out of here, and then stay on to question Eva? What'll happen to you when that gas pours in?"

"I'll be out of this bunker before then, and out of the old Führerbunker, too. I'll meet you at the top. When you've finished with Tovah and Golding, come back to the Führerbunker. With your credentials, the East Germans will let you in again."

"I'll be waiting for you."

He took her by the arm. "You'll be waiting for us," he said. "I'll be coming out with Eva."

Emily looked startled. "Why Eva?"

Foster grinned. "We need one survivor to prove that Hitler did not die in 1945, that he got away. We need someone to support the sensational new ending to your biography."

She kissed him. "Crazy man, I love you."

At first, with Emily in tow, he had been worried, but then it had proved easier than the first time.

There had been two Nazi guards in the corridor this time, absorbed in chatting. Plainly one was about to relieve the other on duty, and, in his own swastika-adorned uniform, Foster had been more military in bearing and more intent on business than when he had entered.

He had hustled Emily to the mezzanine door, and helped her through the square hole into the tunnel, telling her where to locate the lantern and instructing her exactly how to exit and what to expect.

And then, alone, he had returned to Eva Braun's bedroom.

After removing her gag, Foster settled on the edge of the bed. Her eyes were open, a bit foggy, fixed on the ceiling. Foster wasn't sure how the truth serum worked, or exactly where to begin his questioning, but back in Saigon he had seen Sodium

Pentothal used as a truth serum on Viet Cong prisoners and he felt it would operate in the same way now. He had heard a captain mention that it was like getting someone to talk in his sleep. It removed his inhibitions, swept away any coating of lies, made him speak freely from his subconscious. The thing was to be simple and direct, and if the drug began to wear off too soon, to administer a booster shot to keep her drowsy yet not let her fall asleep or go into shock.

He decided that he would begin with a few easy questions, to get the feel, and then he would plunge right into the heart of the matter and leave before the Mossad agents flooded the bunker with their deadly poison.

"Your name is Eva Braun, is it not?" he began.

Her gaze left the ceiling to try to hold on the person speaking to her. "Evelyn—Evelyn," she started to say, then said, "Eva. I am Eva Braun Hitler."

There was an incredibility about this, an awesomeness, that the notorious woman of so long ago was on the bed identifying herself.

"Eva, do you remember the date April 30, 1945?"

"Yes. It is the date everyone believed we died. But we fooled—deceived them all. We escaped."

"How did you fool—deceive everyone?"

"Using the actor and actress who were our—our doubles. I forget her name—no, I remember—Hannah Wald—and his was Müller, I think, yes, Müller. The two of them were brought to the Führerbunker the night before. They were so frightened. I'm sure they suspected. We kept them in our quarters—that day, no, night, they were dressed in our clothes, then Bormann shot Müller and forced Hannah—poor thing—to take cyanide. The bodies were put in the room where the dogs had been, and . . . the next day . . ."

She faltered and drifted off.

"The next day," he prompted her. "What happened the next day, Eva?"

"The next day we, my husband and I, we arranged them on the sofa. Then . . ."

Again, she faltered.

"Then what, Eva?"

"Then from the bedroom we crawled into the tunnel to the new bunker and Bormann—when the others carried the bodies outside—Bormann returned to the bedroom alone, replaced the panel, the slab, and pushed the dresser against it. Then I suppose he left the room."

"Where did Bormann go?"

"He was to meet us and stay with us in the other bunker after."

"Did he?"

Momentarily, Eva seemed bewildered. "No. Bormann was to meet us at the other entrance—"

"The Café Wolf?"

"It had a different name then. It was a bar in the same place. But—I—I don't know—Bormann never came. Later, some said he was killed leaving the Führerbunker—by maybe a Russian artillery explosion. I don't know."

Foster saw that her attention was drifting, and he hoped that her memory was not impaired.

"Eva, this bunker to which you and Hitler escaped, when was it built?"

"After Stalingrad. The Führer had the plan."

"Wasn't Hitler afraid the laborers would give away the secret location?"

For a while she was silent. "I don't know—I never thought about it."

"So you lived down in this bunker, and no one ever found out about it?"

"No one."

"Did Hitler ever leave the bunker to go up into the city?"

"No, never, of course not."

"And you—did you ever leave here while Hitler was alive?"

"I wanted to, of course, but the Führer would not permit it. Not until we had the baby . . ."

Had the baby? Foster could not believe his ears. He searched her bland face for some indication of fantasy. He said slowly, "You and Hitler had a child?"

"Everyone knows that." Her tone was impatient.

"Yes of course. So you had the baby—"

"Before my husband became seriously ill. Once we had Klara, my husband wanted her raised normally inside Berlin but never to be known as our daughter. So after all those years in the bunker, I was allowed to go out and take Klara with me. The Café Wolf was there by then and I went out—"

"Who did you give Klara to?"

"My former maid—the first Liesl. Wolfgang Schmidt knew that Liesl had settled in Berlin. He felt it was safe to tell her about our escape, especially after giving her a large sum of money. Schmidt arranged for Liesl to take Klara as her own child."

"That was your first time outside. When was the next?"

"A few years later." There was a pained expression on Eva's face when she resumed. "After my husband died."

"He was very ill?"

"Only toward the end. Before that he was getting well. He kept busy planning the future, sometimes reading, listening to music, even painting. I made him paint to distract him." She seemed confused once more. "No, it was before he died—some years after Klara's birth—that I went out the second time. I wanted to take photographs of some of his favorite old buildings for him to copy—to paint—but I could find only one—Hermann's building—the Reichsluftfahrtministerium on Leipzigerstrasse. A number of years later, I saw the Wall for the first time—an architectural atrocity inflicted on a wonderful city—"

"And your husband died. When?"

"When the American president died, was killed, Kennedy, in Texas. It was on the radio. My husband died of Parkinson's disease on that day." Her eyes teared up. "We had a ceremony. Then we cremated him."

"After that you came out of the bunker?"

"Once a month, maybe, to see Klara and Liesl and sometimes Schmidt. No one could recognize me anymore, so there was no problem. Gradually, I began to leave the bunker more often, soon every week, to see Klara, as her aunt Evelyn. Lovely Klara, something to cling to. Also, of course, there always was the work—"

"What work?"

"You know, to carry on what my husband had been doing."

"You mean to encourage an armed conflict between the United States and the Soviet Union?"

"Oh, that was going to happen anyway, my husband was always sure." She smiled faintly. "It will be a wonderful day, to see them annihilate each other. We dislike the Soviet Union and the United States equally, although America has had one leader we've come to respect. I mean the cowboy president who honored our forty-nine Waffen SS dead in the Bitburg cemetery last spring. My husband would have appreciated his thoughtfulness. But all other Americans and Russians remain our enemies. It will be good to know they have destroyed each other."

"This American and Russian conflict—when was it to happen? Did you know when?"

"Someday, someday in the future." Her voice became almost inaudible. "But first—first there was something more important. To be ready when the time comes. Germany must be ready. Germany was all that mattered. To make Germany strong again. To be ready for its reemergence."

"How?"

"By eliminating our enemies. Schmidt will get rid of the foreigners tomorrow, just as he has dealt with so many of our enemies over the years. Then he goes to Munich to begin a tour of Germany. He will meet the persons who have contacts with the one hundred fifty-eight organizations of Nazi sympathizers like the Brown Action Front in Rosenheim and the Belsen Scene in Düsseldorf. But more useful will be his meetings with respectable and trustworthy German backers, industrialists, politicians, war veterans, others who are friends, to set up the new party."

"The new party," Foster repeated quietly. "What kind of party?"

"Maybe one of the old ones, to take it over, or start a new one. National Socialism again. With another name. Schmidt will decide."

"And Schmidt will be in charge?"

"Yes, Wolfgang Schmidt. It has to be someone with the best anti-Nazi credentials for the public. When it is formed, the party, when it is in place, and after America and Russia have destroyed each other, we will resurface as the nucleus to take over the party, to assume control."

Foster stared at her. "This is what you've been planning?"

"For many years." Eva shook her head. "There was so much—so much to do and I always worried my husband would overwork, in his condition—but he sent them millions of American dollars in Argentina—and Dr. Dieter Falkenheim prepared the nuclear materials, brought them here to the bunker—he is here with them. To be feared, every country must have a nuclear capability."

The words *nuclear capability* sounded unnatural, coming from Eva. It was as if she was parroting others, perhaps even her departed husband. "That is true, Eva," Foster agreed. "But still, you must start by taking control of Germany. I'm not sure this is clear to me. Can you tell me again—how would you do it?"

There was more impatience. "The normal way. It is obvious. The political party will be in readiness. There will be plenty of money. There are many wealthy ones throughout Germany and in South America who remember the old days, the good days, and want them back. They want power again. They will help us become the majority party. They will welcome us when we resurface and lead it. We were getting prepared when my husband died."

"And he left you to carry on, Eva?"

For the first time, no answer. He asked again, still no answer. Eva's eyes were beginning to focus on him.

Time for a second shot, he decided. Quickly he applied the tourniquet, located a vein, injected the hypodermic needle. Then he gave her another minute, praying he had not put her to sleep.

Eva's eyes remained open, but became unfocused once again.

Bending closer to her, Foster resumed. "Eva, we were discussing your role. You were left to carry on—to carry out the political plan."

"To be in charge of our faithful ones down here. But on the outside it is Wolfgang Schmidt who works with us. He knows everyone. He has the right connections. He will be our—our—"

"Your front man. Your leader."

She nodded.

Foster began to question Eva more closely about the details of the takeover, and she rambled on with the answers.

As she continued to speak, mouthing Hitler's expectations of the nuclear holocaust he foresaw, and the revival of another holocaust inside Germany, Foster's mind went to the perpetrators of Hitler's first holocaust and their heirs. With a shiver, he glanced at his watch. *If* everything went right above ground—if Mossad's agents had not been thwarted—the means to end this madness should be near happening. And if it was about to happen, there was barely time enough to get out of the bunker before Mossad's lethal gas began pouring in.

Yes, it was time to get out, and to take Eva Braun with him.

"Eva," he said, "do you have a flashlight?"

"A strong one. In my bedside-table drawer. I keep it handy for when we have a power failure."

Rising, he opened the drawer and withdrew the flashlight.

"Okay, Eva. I'm about to untie you. We're going for a walk."

He had laid down the flashlight and bent to undo the knots at her ankles.

Suddenly a huge black shadow fell upon the wall in front of him.

Startled, Foster whirled around.

There, in the bedroom doorway, filling the entire doorway, was the mammoth figure of Wolfgang Schmidt.

For a frozen instant, face to face, Schmidt was equally surprised and immobilized. Then, like a savage animal, he came to life. "You, Foster, you sonofabitching bastard!" he roared. "What in hell do you think you're doing here? What are you doing to her?"

Implacably, like a vengeful giant, his beefy red face crossed with fury, he began to advance into the room.

As Schmidt reached beneath his jacket for his holster, Foster shouted at him, "Don't make another move, Schmidt, or you're dead!"

But Foster knew that he could not fire his own Luger. The shot would certainly bring a half dozen underground Nazi guards on the run. Instead, Foster snatched the flashlight from the bed as Schmidt jerked free his Walther P-38.

Flinging himself at the giant, Foster slammed the flashlight down on Schmidt's gun hand. Schmidt gasped with pain as his automatic flew free, plummeting to the floor.

Desperately, Foster kicked at the gun as hard as he could.

The force of his foot sent the gun skidding out of the bedroom, ricocheting off the hallway wall, and bouncing away out of sight toward the sitting room.

Infuriated, Schmidt hammered a pawlike fist against the side of Foster's head, driving him against the foot of the bed, where he crumpled to his knees.

Spinning away, Schmidt rushed out of the bedroom to retrieve his weapon.

Foster sprang to his feet, stumbled, and went swiftly in pursuit of Schmidt.

In the sitting room, he could see Schmidt eyeing him as he reached down to recapture his gun. Schmidt's meaty hand had touched the automatic when Foster made a leaping dive toward his body.

Schmidt crashed to the floor, the gun once more eluding his grip. With another roar, Schmidt pushed himself to his feet as Foster also staggered upright. In a frenzy, Schmidt lashed out at Foster, missing, missing again, but with his third blow he caught Foster flush on the jaw and sent him reeling hard against the mantelpiece.

As his shoulders hit the mantelpiece, Foster raised his arms and grabbed at the mantel to maintain his balance. Striking Eva's precious Grecian urn, he dislodged it and sent it tumbling to the floor with a loud thud.

Schmidt, murder in his eyes, massive arms extended, a wild Neanderthal man, was coming at Foster for the kill.

Foster thought he was done for.

Propelling himself forward, almost into his adversary's clutches, Foster raised himself upward, letting loose a powerful judo kick. Bewildered, Schmidt tried to grab the flailing leg, deflect the kick, but he was too slow. Foster's flashing foot caught him hard and full in the groin. The German doubled up in agony, trying to stifle his cry of pain as his hands dropped to his crotch.

Sucking for breath, Schmidt sank to a knee, and immediately Foster was upon him, driving his foot against the German's temple.

Schmidt toppled sideways to the floor, momentarily stupefied. But he was strong as an ox, and trying to rise once more. In those seconds, Foster knew that if Schmidt recovered, got up again, he himself might not survive the other's brute strength.

Frantically, in mortal terror, Foster sought some weapon, anything that could be a weapon. There was none, and then his fingertips touched the bronze of the overturned Grecian urn on the floor. Grabbing it in his two hands, Foster swung around toward Schmidt, who was shaking his head, trying to rise. Foster lifted the urn high and, with all his strength, brought it down hard, smashing it against the German's skull. Schmidt's head fell back, seemed to fall sideways against a shoulder, and Foster struck him again and again with the urn, until the German's groan became silence, and his eyes closed, and he keeled over on the floor unconscious. Foster stood breathless over him, aware that the urn had become uncapped in his attack and that the gray ashes it had contained now covered Schmidt's still countenance and his chest.

Putting down the urn, Foster, panting, kneeled beside Schmidt's limp body to make sure he was out. Plainly, the German was totally unconscious and might remain so for a half hour or more. Foster peered at the shattered crystal of his wristwatch. If everything had gone on schedule, soon, very soon, this room and the entire underground bunker itself would be filled with deadly gas. Schmidt would die, with all the others, long before he could ever recover consciousness. And, Foster reminded himself, he would die, too, unless he made haste.

To be certain that Schmidt's body would not be discovered before the lethal vapors came through the ventilator, Foster sought a means of hiding the police chief's body. Then he remembered that he had passed Hitler's bedroom in the hallway. Gripping his fingers under Schmidt's armpits, and with great effort, he dragged the inert body through the room and into the hall to Hitler's bedroom. Opening the door, Foster pushed Schmidt inside, and pulled the door shut.

Leaning against the door, Foster gave himself a few moments' breathing spell. Then, realizing that time was running out, and that he might be trapped with the others, he shook himself into action. With effort, he moved to the adjoining doorway and entered Eva's bedroom.

He was not sure what he would find. Had the brawling so nearby aroused her, brought her back to normality?

Incredibly, Eva was lying there as peacefully as he had left her. She was still glassy-eyed, in a netherworld, blissfully unaware of what had taken place outside the room.

Foster picked up the flashlight, shoved it into a pocket, and approached Eva one more time.

Standing above her, he repeated what he had said before. "Eva, I'm going to untie you, and then you and I, we're going for a walk."

She blinked at him uncomprehendingly.

Fast as possible, Foster began to free her from the bed.

She was dazed and compliant, and no trouble at all.

Foster had held her arm as they went through the secret bunker. The one guard on duty whom they passed snapped to respectful attention when he recognized Eva Braun, but ignored Foster, still clad in the Nazi sentry's uniform.

After Foster had attained the mezzanine with Eva, he took one backward glance. He was able to make out what he had overlooked before—other soldiers on duty at the far end, none of whose paths he had crossed earlier with Emily, or just now with Eva.

Eva had remained uncomprehending but obedient when he had told her to crawl from the bunker that had been her home since the end of the war into the darkened tunnel. With his own clothes in one hand, his flashlight in the other, he had squirmed in after her. He had switched on her flashlight, enabling himself to close the hole into the bunker and ease the slab back into place.

Then, with gentle urging, the flashlight glowing on the concrete in front of them, he had moved her along the now familiar route underground to the opening that led into Hitler's old bedroom inside the smaller Führerbunker.

She had gone through it on her knees, with Foster on his own knees behind her.

Setting down the flashlight so that its beam encompassed part of the hole, he had lifted up the second slab and edged it toward the opening. Alone, using every ounce of his strength, he had managed to get the slab into place, kneeing it here and there to make it fit solidly. Then, taking up the flashlight, he had pulled her away from the bureau and, summoning what reserves of strength he had left, had pushed the bureau against the wall. Now the seventh bunker was truly sealed up.

To orient both of them, he had aimed the beam of the flashlight in an arc around the dusty, cobwebbed bedroom. When the light fell on the frame of Hitler's bed, he thought he heard her gasp.

Now he was guiding her through the doorway into what had been the Führer's sitting room in the last months of the war.

This time he ran the flashlight beam slowly around the room, holding the beam on the sofa, the broken chair, the walls, the desk, the place above it that had once held Frederick the Great's picture and, finally, on Eva's face itself.

Her face was ashen, a study in shock, and he heard her gasp a second time, more audibly. Her hands crept up to her mouth, and at last her words came through her fingers. "The Führerbunker," she said. "The sitting room, our room."

He wondered if the forty years had fallen away, and she was reliving what she had lived then, her happier moments with Hitler, her long-desired marriage to him, the wedding reception with his staff and toadies.

"Oh, my God," she whispered, "what have they done to it?"

"The Russians came," Foster said matter-of-factly.

"The animals," she said with a tremor.

And now he knew that she was back into the present, with the drug fully worn off and her senses returned.

She blinked into the flashlight. "Who are you? How did you get me here? I want to go back—"

"You can't go back," he said curtly. "That's the past." Then he added, "The past is dead, or the last of it will be in minutes. I have other plans for you." He held the Luger in his free hand, so that she could see it, and he aimed the flashlight beam in front of her. "Now we're going up to the top, up the staircase to the old emergency exit."

"Why?"

"I want the truth, Eva. All of it."

"I won't tell you anything, not a thing. And my name—my name is Evelyn Hoffmann," she reminded him haughtily.

"Move!" he barked and prodded her with the gun.

She moved, and he followed her through the reception room to the stairwell, and then up the concrete steps to the top.

At the last opening, the one leading out of the mound, she held back.

"Out you go," he ordered, pressing the muzzle of the Luger into her back.

Stumbling, she stepped into the cool night air, and stood very still in the immediate area along the mound of earth inside the East German Frontier Zone. It was dark, but not completely. A few slivers of light shone down on parts of the field from the East German watchtowers.

"Emily!" Foster called out, passing his flashlight in a semicircle to catch sight of Emily, who had promised him she would be back and waiting.

But no one was visible anywhere.

His heart fell, and he wondered what had happened to Emily, and whether she had got out of East Berlin and contacted Tovah and Golding and the Mossad agents.

He wanted Emily here, to reassure himself that she was safe and to know that finally the epilogue to the Hitler story was being played out.

He held the Luger in one hand, put his flashlight on the ground, and with his free hand awkwardly divested himself of his Nazi uniform and got into his own work clothes. When he was done, there was still no sign of Emily. Minutes were slipping away and he was in despair.

And then he saw, at some distance across the field, a light that seemed to be approaching. It was approaching, bobbing as it drew nearer, a lantern being carried by someone, and as it came closer he was able to make out that it was being carried by a woman.

He knew that it was Emily at last.

Suddenly, there was a loud report from behind him, and twenty yards away the distant light abruptly dropped down and the figure carrying the light went down with it.

In a burst of fear, Foster tightened his hold on his Luger, and dashed toward the light on the ground, certain that Emily had been shot.

But she was rising to her feet when he reached her, groping for the lantern.

"Are you all right?" he wanted to know, helping her upright, holding her.

"I tripped on something, that's all. Hurt my knee a little, nothing more. Thank God you got out with no trouble."

He took the lantern from Emily and was hastening her back to the gaping excavation in the mound.

"I have most of what we wanted to know from her. We can get the rest later. The main thing is that they have a plan to revive National Socialism in Germany. They want to be ready to take over again. Hitler dreamed of an inevitable nuclear war between Russia and the United States, as you know. They want to be in place for that. She gave me all the details."

"Nazism again in Germany?" said Emily with disbelief. "That can't be. They must be mad."

"Obsessed. It was the last of Hitler's great hopes. Tell me, did you get hold of Tovah and her Mossad people?"

"I did. Tovah said she'd get hold of Golding, have him round up the Mossad agents and the supply of gas and head for the Café Wolf and the bunker ventilation system. If it went well—"

"Meaning if they weren't discovered by Schmidt's police."

"Schmidt. What will we do with Schmidt?"

"He's been taken care of. He turned up in the bunker. It was a little hairy for a few moments, but I was lucky to have age and speed on my side. I left him unconscious down below. If Golding comes through with the gas, that should take care of Schmidt, too."

"Well, let's pray they're releasing the gas into the bunker right now. Unless there's a slip-up, every one of those Nazis should be dead in a few minutes."

Foster was satisfied. "Afterward, the German military can remove the bodies, and ventilate the place. Then you'll have all their papers and you'll have Eva Braun—"

"Eva!" Emily exlaimed. "Where is she?"

"Why, right here with me," Foster said uncertainly. "I brought her here . . . she was right here . . ."

He waved his lantern looking for her.

But Eva Braun was no longer there.

"She's gone," Emily gasped. "When you turned your back on her, she must have taken off."

"She's not going to get very far in this Security Zone."

"We can't just stand here. Let's try to find her," Emily insisted.

Foster briefly considered this. "Not now, Emily," he finally decided. "Not by ourselves. We can't go wandering around here searching for Eva." He peered into the semidarkness. "Never mind about Eva. She's not going very far. She's trapped. Let the East Germans catch up with her."

"But we want her."

"We'll get to Eva, once they pick her up." He had Emily by the arm and was hurrying her across the field toward the East German guardhouse. "First, let's be sure Golding got the message and delivered the goods. That's what we must know."

Once past the guardhouse, Foster had a change of mind. "Emily, you go ahead alone. Take my car, along with your papers, and get over to the Café Wolf. Find out whether there's going to be a happy ending. I'll grab a ride and be right behind you. Right now I want to hang around here for a little while. I am beginning to miss Eva. Maybe I'll get another chance to look for her. Please go, Emily. I'll catch up with you—and be on your guard, just in case."

12

For several minutes after Emily had left for the Café Wolf, Foster remained outside the East German Frontier Zone, peering through the wire fence near the gate where three guards and their commanding officer stood. Foster watched for any movement in the semidarkness of the field that would give some sign of the reappearance of Eva Braun.

There was no one, no sign of Eva anywhere visible. In those minutes, Foster knew that Hitler's wife would not be showing herself. Yet she would never get away, Foster was certain. The woman was bottled up, and with the coming of daylight she would be spotted and caught and would fall into the hands of the East Germans. Still, Foster knew, no matter what happened, Eva

Braun would not be lost to them. Later in the day, he or Emily would notify Professor Blaubach of the arrested woman's real identity. Foster could imagine Blaubach's stunned surprise.

But for now, Foster felt it was hopeless—and pointless—to continue to stand there and wait. A more immediate matter was on his mind. He had to know whether the underground Nazis had been executed. He wished he had not given his car to Emily, or at least had accompanied her on her trip to the Café Wolf. He needed a car now.

Foster started walking briskly toward the officer in charge of the gate, one Major Janz, a decent enough person who had treated him with courtesy so far. When Major Janz saw him approaching, he secured the Soviet SKS carbine hanging from his shoulder, and met Foster halfway.

"I've been waiting here for one of my colleagues to finish up and come out, but I'm afraid I can't stay any longer," Foster explained. "Would it be possible for you to call a taxi for me? I know this is a bad hour, but there must be taxis around somewhere."

"Absolutely," said the major. "I'll have one of my men call the Palast Hotel. Taxis should be there looking for a return fare to West Berlin."

Major Janz called back to a guard, instructing him to phone for a taxi for Herr Foster.

Foster thanked the major and resumed his vigil at the wire fence. Again the forbidding darkness gave him no clue to Eva Braun's whereabouts.

Suddenly he was aware of Major Janz at his elbow. "No problem," the major was saying. "A taxi will be here in ten or fifteen minutes."

"I certainly appreciate this," Foster said.

The major lingered a moment, eyes on Foster. "Now everything is all right?"

"Quite all right, thank you."

But turning away from the fence, Foster wasn't sure everything was all right—for himself or for any of them, yet. It depended on what was happening far below ground in the secret bunker. Because if Schmidt and his fanatics had escaped extermination, it meant that they would be rising soon to hunt down Emily and himself, and Tovah and Kirvov as well, to extract vengeance and to kill.

Behind the wheel of Foster's Audi, Emily headed for West Berlin. Once more, there was the delay at Checkpoint Charlie, longer than usual because of the hour of her appearance, but soon she was cleared and she stepped on the gas pedal, speeding the compact through the empty streets toward her destination.

By the time she reached Askanischer Platz, and sought a parking place beyond it, her mind was on only one thing. Fervently she prayed that Tovah had been able to contact Golding, that Golding had been able to summon up help from Mossad's fighters, and that they had been successful in liquidating the insanity hidden beneath the city.

Was it over, she kept asking herself, *was it done?*

In the stillness of the bunker suite beneath Berlin, there was a movement.

Slowly, slowly, the door from Hitler's bedroom was opening.

A meaty hand pulled the door further. Wolfgang Schmidt, shaking his blood-encrusted head, was crawling out.

Upon recovering consciousness, he had tried to reconstruct what had happened. He had returned to the bunker to be sure that the Ashcroft woman was still prisoner, and to learn whether Eva was all right. He had not found the Ashcroft woman where he had left her, and had gone to Eva's bedroom to check. There he had come upon that son of a bitch Foster, and Eva tied to the bed.

There had been a fight, Foster and himself, and somehow he had been knocked out. His head was splitting with pain, and he was sure he had been hit on the head by something heavy and suffered a concussion. Only his superb physical condition, his natural strength, had enabled him to survive.

Bracing himself against the hallway wall opposite, weakened though he was, Schmidt managed to lift himself to his feet.

Reeling, he made his way to Eva's bedroom. She was not there. The bed was empty. And Foster, he was gone too. On rubbery legs, Schmidt turned toward the sitting room. He entered it. Also empty.

On the floor he saw his Walther P-38. He picked it up.

He tried to imagine what had happened.

Foster had probably taken Eva hostage, and somehow got away by whatever means he had used to get in. All of them down here had been discovered, and they would be exposed and destroyed forever.

Wavering, Schmidt tried to reason. Foster could not have gone to the police after seeing their chief in the hideout. To whom, then, would Foster have turned for help? Possibly the commanders of the four powers occupying Berlin. Possibly to reveal the secret of the bunker and to seek their military help.

Somehow, this gave Schmidt a glimmer of hope. He knew the leaders of the four powers, knew them personally, and he knew how impossible it would be to make them move swiftly on anything, no matter how critical. They were always entangled in red tape, and hearing what sounded like a fantastic cock-and-bull story would not impel them to mobilize for action quickly.

Before anything could happen, there still might be hope, real hope.

Even though his head throbbed ceaselessly, despite the pain

in his skull, Schmidt tried to reason further. Surely, while Foster sought help, he had left his allies above ground to keep an eye on the Café Wolf exit. But there could not be many of these. They could easily be overcome.

There was still a chance to escape, Schmidt decided. He need only alert the trusted guards and other occupants of the bunker down here. Heavily armed with their latest weaponry—their machine guns and portable rocket launchers—they could easily make their way out of the bunker, through the Café Wolf, cutting down any feeble resistance with a hail of bullets.

Their breakout could succeed. They could escape, and be free, and scatter to hide away for another day.

Alert the guards, alert the rest of the Nazis in the bunker, get them on the move, and fast.

There was time, there was time. They could overcome and win.

Schmidt staggered through the sitting room, through the reception room, and stumbled out of the suite.

He made for the corner, turned it, and a short distance off he saw one of the Hitler Youth on duty.

He opened his mouth to call to him, to alert him and everyone, and as he opened his mouth he gagged.

His hands went to his throat. There was a foul acrid stench, and he was suffocating. His hoarse voice was trapped in his throat. A vise was closing on his throat, strangling him, and uncontrollably he was beginning to tremble.

He tried to shout to the young sentry, but there was no sentry.

Through his blurred vision, he saw that the sentry had fallen to the ground, and was writhing there, and then was lifeless.

Choking, Schmidt became dimly aware that something terrible was happening.

There were amethyst-blue crystals filtering through the ventilator shaft, covering the floor.

Then Schmidt knew. He had been to Auschwitz. He had seen the crystals before. And he knew what they did.

He felt himself sinking, felt himself gasping for air as he lay outstretched on the floor. He tried to inhale air. But there were only these fumes.

And then he closed his eyes in death.

Parking the Audi, hastily leaving it, Emily saw Tovah running from the Café Wolf toward her.

"Emily, Emily!" Tovah called and came alongside her, breathless. "We were so relieved when we heard from you. What an experience! And to have really found their hideout!" She looked about. "Where's Rex?"

"He'll be along in a little while. I'll tell you about the whole thing later. What I want to know is—did Golding and his people actually deliver?"

Tovah was nodding her head enthusiastically. "They did it, they certainly did. But not with Speer's Tabun nerve gas. No, something more poetically appropriate. They found the camouflaged ventilator shaft on Rex's blueprint of the secret bunker. They dropped in an endless quantity of Zyklon B crystals—prussic acid—the same substance the Nazis used in the death chambers at Auschwitz to kill eight thousand Jews a day. Our agents just dropped enough of those deadly crystals into the underground hideout to exterminate a thousand Nazis in minutes. How many did you say were down there? Fifty or more?"

"Something like that."

"Well, they're all dead now, Emily, every single one of them. I had word from Chaim Golding. His men are finished by now and packing up their equipment. In a day or two, the city can clear out the gas fumes, then the army will go in and remove the corpses. Too bad there isn't a survivor to tell us what it was all about."

"Rex did save one," Emily said.

"He did?"

"He brought Eva Braun up with him."

"Eva Braun! I can't believe it! He has her?"

Emily hesitated. "He does and he doesn't. While we're waiting for Rex, let me explain. Let's take a walk and I'll tell you what happened."

As she put her arm in Tovah's and they started off, Emily wondered once more what had happened to Hitler's wife and what she was doing this very moment . . .

From the moment that the American man called Rex had rushed off in the darkness to give help to his fellow conspirator, the girl called Emily, Eva Braun had acted upon instinct. A lapse by her captor had given her an opportunity to be free, and she had taken it.

Snatching the flashlight that he had left on the grass, Eva had ducked inside the black hole that had once been the Führerbunker's emergency exit. She had stumbled past the timbers that shored up the dug-out passage until she touched its deepest recess near the top of the stairwell. There she had tried to hide in the darkness, wondering whether she was really free and if so how she might escape this East German no-man's-land.

Then she had heard them returning, the conspirators Emily and Rex, and she had realized that they had halted short of the exit. They had been speaking to one another excitedly, especially the man, in English, which Eva understood fairly well from her language classes in school and her long acquaintance with the sound tracks of Hollywood films that her loved one had always permitted her to enjoy in the Berghof.

The one named Rex had spoken clearly with knowledge about their secret political plans, their timetable to revive and reconstruct the Germany that the *Feldherr* had given his life to establish and that she and Schmidt had sought to preserve. In her hiding place, Eva had puzzled at how Rex could know so much. Certainly she had not revealed this to him at any time, unless she had been drugged. Yet, she had no memory of drugs. Perhaps he had seen some notes on this in her desk, or even learned of it elsewhere.

But the most frightening news had been what she had overheard Rex tell the woman Emily. *Schmidt has been taken care of. I left him unconscious down below.*

Then, continuing to listen, Eva had overheard something that was immediately more shocking. Someone—"Mossad," she had heard Rex and Emily say—the terrible Jews themselves—were releasing deadly gas in her underground home of so many years. They were in the barbaric process of exterminating all the loyal ones, the good ones, Schmidt and all the others, the ones who had worshiped her husband and cared about her. An impossible savage act, but there was no doubt it was being done.

Abruptly, she had heard her name spoken outside, and Eva had listened and overheard that the two of them had just realized she was missing. They had become aware that she had slipped away. She had trembled in the darkness, fearful that they would guess where she had gone, and come with their lantern in search of her and find her. She had shuddered at the thought of being captured and put on public display, mocked and reviled and tortured, the one thing her beloved husband had always feared and swore he would never permit to happen.

And then she had heard the voices again from outside, and had understood that they were leaving, both hastening to get to the Café Wolf to reveal Eva's disappearance and to learn whether the effort to massacre all her followers with gas had been concluded.

Soon, she had become aware of the fact that the voices of the two were receding, and after that there had been silence, and she had finally determined that they were gone.

Huddled there in the dark, Eva had still been afraid to move. She had to be sure that she was safe, and she needed time to think.

She had remained huddled there in the blackness of the excavation, and realized that only one obsessive concern clung to her, dominated her mind. It was no longer the party's future. Nor was it Schmidt, her husband's perfect heir, the ultimate Aryan, faithful to their ideals and devoted to their cause. Like the party, he too was lost.

It was something else that obsessed her.

It was the atrocity that was being committed by the foreign conspirators and their Jewish gangster collaborators on her comrades and followers in their underground home. Poison gas was infiltrating their sealed catacomb, and in minutes they would all be dead, and there would be no one to inherit the earth after the Soviets and the United States destroyed each other one day.

Eva's first thought had been to try to save them, warn them down below and rescue them. She could use the flashlight, might be able to remove the cement block, find her way back alone to the tunnel that led to the secret bunker, and sound the warning.

But then she knew it was too late, far too late. Time had passed since she had overheard that the poison gas was being poured in, and by now the mass execution had taken place and her subterranean home had become a mass grave.

She stood chilled, as realization of her own loss engulfed her. At once, she knew what must be done, should be done, and she remembered how it could be done.

Remembering, she straightened her shoulders, stood erect in the darkness.

Her husband had always insisted that he would not be trapped alive by his barbaric conquerors and paraded about as an exhibit. "*Tschapperl* . . . little thing," he had told her once, "if we're captured, we will be put in cages and hung up in the Moscow zoo." Indeed, through his foresight and cleverness, he had eluded his avengers. Afterward, in their hideout, reading of the Nuremberg trials, he had always deplored those weaklings who had cooperated with the spectacle. Strangely, the one of the group that he had hated as a betrayer near the end had been the one he had come to admire, Hermann Göring. The fat man had shown bravery, and true loyalty, by escaping the noose and by having the courage to take his own life at Nuremberg.

Now Eva was applying her husband's belief to what would undoubtedly soon happen below.

In a day or two, the killers would go down there. They would clear out the lethal gas, and find dozens of pitiful corpses and remove them. Then they would have everything else as their trophies of the unending war. They would have her husband's precious remains resting in the urn. They would have his mementos of a great life lived. They would have her long-kept journals, her secrets, and the truth that would lead them to Klara.

They would have their history to revise.

They would have their spectacle.

Now it came to her, the steps that her husband had taken to prevent such a demeaning occurrence.

Yes, in their last week in the old Führerbunker he had told her about the two secret levers. They were twin levers and each had heavy-duty wiring that led inside the hidden bunker. One lever could be activated from the lower level of the Führerbunker, the other from a spot in what had become the Café Wolf. Either one, activated, could release a detonation charge inside their underground home and blow it to bits.

But now, Eva realized, with all that gas filling their hidden bunker, an explosion and fire would be devastating beyond belief. The explosion would obliterate everything below.

Her husband's logic in laying out this destructive device had been simple. If the Russians came to the Führerbunker too soon, there would be time enough to destroy their underground haven so that the world would never know that he had intended to escape capture. With the escape bunker demolished, he and Eva could heroically take their own lives before falling into the grasp of the enemy. As to the twin back-up lever inside the Café Wolf, it would serve a similar purpose if their escape succeeded. For if their hideout was ever discovered in the years after the escape, he could still have their haven obliterated, and themselves as well.

He would never allow a spectacle.

Nor would she, she told herself now. That was all that mattered. To obey his wishes.

The lever in the Café Wolf was out of reach.

But the lever in the Führerbunker, far below, had never been discovered, she knew, so it could still be workable.

Her husband had shown it to her once near the very end of the war. He'd had an army electrician install it, and then had the electrician liquidated. Where had she seen this emergency lever forty years ago? She concentrated hard while reviving her memory of that day, those moments.

Yes, it had been down in the lower bunker, in Johannes Hentschel's cubbyhole, the engineer's room with its diesel motor that had provided them with air, water, electricity. When Hentschel had been asleep, her husband had taken her into the engineer's room, across the corridor from her bedroom.

"There are two important things for you to see, Effie," her husband had told her. "Here, above this counter, is the *Notbremse* —the emergency brake. If there is an assassination attempt on me, you pull this up. It will black out this bunker and seal every door. But there is something even more important for you to know. Under the floor." He had tugged a concrete block out of the floor and pointed to a red switch. "That is the special lever that can activate a charge of cyclonite that will blow up and destroy our secret bunker, if ever it must be done. Remember, Effie, remember this." Then, petulantly, he had added, "I must always think of everything."

Over the bridge of years, she remembered it exactly, as if she had just been shown it.

At once she sought and found the concrete stairs leading down to the lower Führerbunker. She did not really need the light. She could have managed the descent in the darkness or blindfolded, since she had made it so many times in those last weeks here, still so vivid in her memory.

As quickly as possible she picked her way down to the bottom. Flashlight in hand, she proceeded up the rotting and moist middle corridor, ignoring her suite, their suite, going straight ahead. Then she slowed, recalling once more the location of Hentschel's cubbyhole.

Her flashlight glared into the cramped small room, and she knew that this must be it. She went down on her knees, holding the flashlight in one hand, as her fingers clawed at the chipped and dirty concrete block. She broke one fingernail, then two, tugging at it, and at last the block gave and came upward.

She pointed her flashlight inside the hole, and there, dry, uncorroded, was the red switch, the special lever.

Without hesitation, she bent over, gripped the lever and yanked hard at it. It moved, and she pulled harder. There was a click, and she knew the system was alive and was now activated.

In two minutes it should take effect.

Holding her flashlight, she jumped to her feet, spun back into the corridor, and headed for the stairs. She went as fast as she could flight by flight up to the top.

She had just arrived inside the emergency exit when she heard the rumbling of the earth outside. She had stumbled to the exit opening when the explosion detonated the gas far below. The earth many meters before her and off toward the Wall and beyond it erupted as if a mammoth volcano had blown its top. A sheet of fire, a curtain of red, appearing a thousand feet high, reached for the sky. The roar of the explosion echoed and re-echoed, a hundred times greater than the blast of the Russian artillery and Allied aerial bombardments she had listened to in the last weeks of the war.

In the Frontier Zone and in West Berlin far away there was a wild inferno.

The air before her was black with clouds of smoke and showers of dirt and debris, and she turned her head aside to protect her eyes.

For a long time she shielded her sight and waited. But her heart was beating joyously.

Don't worry, my darling, she told him, no spectacle, not now or ever.

Only when she heard the distant sirens did she venture into the open. The heaven was a fiery red blanket above. The debris and dust were gradually settling, and she discarded the flashlight and tried to see through the gray mass. Then she saw what she wanted to see and headed toward it.

When she neared the shattered section of the Berlin Wall, there was an opening in it wide enough to go through with a tank battalion.

Eva stood there triumphantly examining the breach.

Once more, she realized, she was the Merry Widow. All her friends and the remains of her beloved one wiped out and only rubble beneath in the endless rent in the earth. The Merry Widow, yes, widow, yes, but she knew that she was not alone.

She walked straight ahead, out of the East German Security Zone, toward the break in what had once been the fearsome Wall, and she walked into West Berlin.

The sirens were louder.

Eva Braun kept walking.

* * *

When the door to the apartment on Knesebeckstrasse opened, Eva was relieved to see that it had been opened by Liesl from her wheelchair.

As Eva staggered inside, Liesl stared at her with bewilderment. "Eva," Liesl gasped, "what are you doing here at this hour? My God, look at you . . ."

Eva had forgotten how begrimed she was, and she ignored it now. Bending over Liesl, she whispered fiercely, "They found us out, they destroyed our place—"

"They—they—?"

"The foreigners who were searching for us."

"But how?"

"Never mind. Everyone else is lost. I managed to escape. Now we must all leave before they find us."

"Leave?"

"Not lose a minute. I have a taxi downstairs waiting. I had a few marks in my pocket. The taxi will take us to the Bahnhof. Can you make it to your feet?"

"With my cane, I'll be all right." Liesl hesitated. "Eva, are you sure?"

"They'll come for us, I'm certain. We must not be here."

"But Schmidt? Where is he?"

"He's dead. They went after him. Now it's us." Eva surveyed the living room. "Klara, where's Klara? And Franz, is he here?"

"He left for the school early. Klara is in the kitchen preparing breakfast for me." Liesl trembled. "Klara, what can we do with her?"

Without hesitation, Eva said, "She must come with us. Immediately."

"She'll refuse. She won't understand."

"She'll be made to understand. We'll tell her the truth."

"Eva, how can we?"

"We must. There's no choice. We must tell her and all of us must leave."

Liesl seemed to pull herself together. "All right. But—but it would be better if I am the one to tell her. Let me go into the kitchen. I can't imagine what the shock will do to her—"

"It must be done, Liesl."

"I was always afraid of this. But yes, it must be done."

Eva looked off toward the kitchen. "I can do it."

"Please let me, let me do it first," insisted Liesl, maneuvering her wheelchair around. "You go to my bedroom. Start packing for us."

"There will be no packing," said Eva. "Only a small bag for the money. You still have the money?"

"All of it, yes. In my bottom drawer with the passports."

"That's what we need. We can buy anything else when we get to where we're going. You're sure you can manage Klara?"

"I—I don't know."

Eva watched the old woman roll her wheelchair toward the kitchen. Then, purposefully, Eva left the living room and strode into the hall, past the Fiebigs' bedroom, into Liesl's bedroom.

Glancing at the bedside clock, she made for the closet. There she found a small overnight bag on the upper shelf, brought it down, tossed it on the unmade bed. She unlatched it, lifted the lid. With that done, she went to the dresser and drew out the bottom drawer. Beneath the sweaters were the boxes of currency. She began to transfer them to the bag. When the bag was filled, she closed and locked it.

Doing so, she heard a shrill cry, then a keening sound from a distant room, the kitchen.

Eva's eyes sought the clock. Only a few minutes had passed. As she took the bag off the bed she heard footsteps, and quickly wheeled to see a wild-eyed, distraught Klara in the doorway.

For a moment Eva felt compassion and pity. "Klara, I'm sorry, very sorry—"

Klara's voice was strained. "This is a joke, isn't it, a cruel and sick joke?"

"It's the truth, darling . . ." Eva started for her daughter, wanting to embrace her, but Klara backed away.

"You're not my mother. You can't be. I don't believe it."

"I *am* your mother," Eva said steadily. "And he *was* your father."

"No, never! You're a crazy person! None of this is true!"

"It's true, Klara, darling. I am your mother, and he was your father."

"Never in a million years!" Klara screamed. "Not that monster—!"

Eva was across the room in an instant, hand upraised. She slapped Klara hard. "Don't you dare!" she shouted. "I won't have you speak of him that way! Not now or ever!"

Klara burst into tears, convulsed, shoulders heaving.

There was no time to straighten out the child now, or to console her over the shock. There was only time for strength. He would have wanted it.

"Klara," she said firmly. "We must go now. We must not be found."

"No," Klara whimpered. "I won't go. Franz—our life—our child—"

"You can't stay," said Eva. "All of us, we must leave."

"No."

"Klara, we can't let them find you. Now will you do as I tell you?" She tried to make herself heard over Klara's hysterical sobbing. "Do as I tell you! You will, won't you?"

As he was driven toward Stresemann Strasse, Foster felt weariness to the marrow of his bones. He had been on the move, constantly, for an exhausting day, a hectic night, a savage morning, without rest, and for the first time he was beginning to feel sapped of all his strength.

Furthermore, the overcast, the low hanging clouds above, added to the grayness of his mood.

Then, nearing his destination, he began to discern that the overcast was not caused by clouds, but by a steady pall of smoke. At once his curiosity was piqued, and he became alert.

The source of the smoke might be from the explosions he'd heard and the fire he had seen a half mile from Checkpoint Charlie. As the driver slowed the car, Foster could make out above and beyond the buildings to his left the peak of a steady mountain of flame that extended into the distance. It was not the kind of blaze that came from the incineration of buildings alone. It was the kind of fire that he had seen before, resulting from a gas explosion.

Going past Askanischer Platz, he saw a large gathering of spectators. Fire engines, firemen, endless lines of hoses spouting foam, filled Stresemann Strasse, and all of the buildings were thorough wreckage, every timber still aflame.

At once he understood and knew what was happening. Leaving the driver and taxi at the corner, Foster raced to Askanischer Platz. Approaching, he knew what had taken place.

The gas-filled secret underground bunker had somehow been destroyed. The result was evident—

Götterdämmerung.

The hiding place of Hitler's mad pack had been incinerated. There would be nothing left of the underground bunker but a hole in the ground.

Shoving his way through the curious mob, Foster saw Kirvov, then Tovah, and at last Emily among the spectators. He elbowed his way toward them, grabbed Emily, hugged her tight, and returned her kisses.

Emily was clinging to Foster again. "It's over," she breathed. "Thank God, it's over."

Foster gave his attention to the sputtering and simmering fires in front of them. "When did this happen, Emily?"

"About an hour after the Mossad agents filled the bunker with gas. No one down there escaped. Golding told me about it. Then, just before dawn, there was that thunderous explosion. Everything blew sky high, and it's been aflame ever since. Maybe the gas was ignited by accident."

"Maybe," said Foster. "Maybe not."

"Somebody down there could have ignited this by lighting a cigarette," Emily speculated.

Tovah shook her head vigorously. "Impossible. You forget, they were all dead down there well before the explosion."

"Of course." Emily shrugged her shoulders helplessly. "I can't imagine what happened."

Foster was peering beyond the row of fire trucks down the length of Stresemann Strasse. Destruction of everything from the Café Wolf to the Berlin Wall itself had been complete. Even a portion of the wall had been torn asunder and crumbled. Through the gaping hole, at least forty or fifty yards wide, could be seen the vast crater which extended into the Security Zone.

Foster touched Emily, and pointed to the huge breach in the wall. "If anyone was inside there, and wanted to walk out, they could have just strolled through it."

"You mean anyone like—say—Eva Braun."

"Yes, Eva Braun." Foster reached for Kirvov's arm. "Nicholas, where does Klara Fiebig live?"

"Knesebeckstrasse, right off the Ku'damm."

"Then what are we waiting for? That should be our last stop. We may still get our hands on Klara—and Eva."

* * *

They gathered with Nicholas Kirvov as he insistently pressed the doorbell, and kept knocking on the apartment door.

There was no response for a long time, but finally they heard someone inside, and the door was slowly pulled wide open.

A round-shouldered youngish man, maybe tall on another day, with tangled black hair, thick spectacles perched on a hooked nose, gaunt features, was staring out at them uncomprehendingly. Foster could see that the youngish man was in a daze, his magnified eyes red-rimmed and swollen, his sunken cheeks tear-streaked.

Kirvov hesitated. "You—you are Franz, Klara Fiebig's husband?"

The youngish man facing them moved his head up and down slowly, dumbly.

"Where is she?" Kirvov said. "We must speak with her."

Franz Fiebig continued to stare at them, actually through them, and fresh tears began to form. "You are too late," he said, and he turned away.

Foster stepped forward. He went into the living room after Fiebig, and the others trailed him inside.

Fiebig stood disconsolately in the middle of the room, back to them, and then he shuffled almost directionless toward the corner, and fell into an overstuffed chair. He was weeping again, and trying to find a handkerchief. Foster took out his own, slowly went to him, and handed him the handkerchief.

"Too late?" Foster prompted him.

"She's dead," Fiebig said, moving his head from side to side with disbelief. "I came home from school to have lunch with Klara. I found her dead in our bedroom. She committed suicide."

"Suicide? Why? Do you know why?"

Fiebig did not reply.

Foster lowered himself to one knee next to Fiebig's chair.

"Perhaps I know why, Franz. I think we all know why." He paused. "Her mother was here to see her. Her mother—Eva Braun."

Through his thick lenses, Fiebig focused on Foster, and wiped his cheeks. "Yes," he murmured, "her mother—Eva Braun. That's what happened."

"How did you find out, Franz?"

"The note. Klara left a note on the dresser."

"Do you have it?"

"I tore it up. I flushed it down the toilet after the doctor came."

"Can you—can you remember what Klara wrote you?"

Fiebig dropped his chin to his chest and stared at the carpet. Foster leaned forward to catch his words. Fiebig was speaking in a hushed monotone.

"Evelyn—Eva—Eva Braun came here in a great hurry. She told Klara the truth. That she was Klara's mother. And her father . . ." He could not bring himself to utter the name. "She learned about her father. Liesl confirmed it all. Eva and Liesl told her they were leaving, must leave, and Eva insisted that Klara accompany them. Poor Klara, my poor dear Klara."

"What else did she write?"

"Eva and Liesl wanted her to go with them, but then they were afraid her hysteria could give them away. They said she needed to pull herself together first. When she did, she was to meet them at a certain place. Klara did not say where. If she would not come to them, they told her, she must disappear, that life would be impossible for her here. Under no circumstances could she stay here. Klara wrote, 'Eva said my father would have demanded it. He would never have allowed me to become a spectacle. I must never be found by our enemies.' Then—then—Klara wrote, Eva and Liesl left and she was alone, and she had nowhere to go, yet she knew that she had to leave somehow. 'I'm sorry, so sorry, Franz,' she wrote, 'but they are right. Someday, someone will find out. I cannot hurt you or mark our child for life. So I am leaving. I will love you forever.' " He began shaking his head. "Oh, no, no, no, she didn't have to leave me. I loved her so. I didn't care. There was no blame. She was a victim. I would have loved her until eternity."

He covered his face, and broke into sobs.

Foster struggled to his feet, shaken and deeply moved. "The doctor—is the doctor here, Franz?"

Fiebig gestured toward the other rooms.

Foster trudged through the dining room, into a hall, and found the first bedroom. Entering, he was assailed by a bitter almond smell, a telltale smell.

The doctor, a graying heavyset German, a handkerchief at his nose, was seated beside the double bed, a pad on his knee, writing his report. On the bed was a figure covered from head to toe by a sheet.

"Doctor—" Foster called out.

The elderly physician raised his head.

"—I'm a friend of the Fiebigs, and I think Franz needs some help. He's in pretty bad shape."

The doctor nodded. "Who can blame him? How else can he be? Never mind, I'll be giving him something, and seeing after him." His eyes strayed to the covered body. "Too bad, too bad, a terrible tragedy."

"She did kill herself?"

"Yes, certainly."

"How?"

"Cyanide capsule. I can't imagine where she got it."

But Foster could.

He left the room, and returned to the others. He signaled Emily, Tovah, and Kirvov.

They followed him out of the apartment.

* * *

It was the morning after.

A balmy, clear day, and the sun bathed the city in its warmth. Arms linked, Emily and Foster stood on the roof of the Europa Center office building for one last look at the beautiful and disturbing city of Berlin. Near the Wall, a trail of smoke still rose to the sky, but beyond Budapester Strasse below, they could make out the bright green expanse of the Zoological Gardens, and the Tiergarten beside it, with glimpses of the Bellevue Palace and the Reichstag, and farther on the snaking blueness of the River Spree.

It was a gorgeous city, this Berlin, Foster thought, a beautiful city that had been visited by endless horrors. Yesterday, another nightmare had been averted, but he suspected that Berlin's nightmares would never cease. Danger and doom were part of the city's character.

"At least now," said Foster, "you have the real ending of the Hitler story. You can tell the world the truth."

"The truth?" Emily reflected. "I doubt if it will ever be known. I'm a historian. I must have proof of everything I write. What proof do I have now? Can I prove that you and I talked to Eva Braun? Can I prove she wasn't an imposter?"

"But the hidden bunker," said Foster. "What about the bunker?"

Emily shook her head sadly. "To the wide world there is no bunker, never was such a bunker, only a huge hole in the ground where it is unlikely that anyone could have lived. The bodies, all evidence, crushed, incinerated, eliminated. There is only one person on earth who can prove the true ending. She was our only proof of the truth, and now she's gone," Emily reflected. She took Foster's hand. "We'll never find her, will we, Rex?"

"She's out there somewhere all right." Then he shook his head. "But no one will ever find her."

Once more Emily gazed in silence at the city beneath them, and then off beyond its boundaries. "The Merry Widow," she said, "that's what her family and friends called her when Hitler first took her into his life. The Merry Widow, because she was almost always alone." Emily continued to stare into the distance. "Well, she is still alone, with her mystery, and maybe she will be to the very end."